Critical acclaim for *The Undrowned Child*

'Sumptuous Venetian adventure ... a great romp for more literary readers'   Fiona Noble, *The Bookseller*

'What an amazing sense of place the writer establishes – Venice is really the central character! The cast of characters too is fresh and quite extraordinary – how I loved those mermaids and their way of life. I didn't put it down as the story sweeps on with such speed and wonder that there's no place to stop.'
                    Wendy Cooling, children's book consultant

'a stunning debut novel ... Part fairy-tale, part historical fiction, this is writing that is alight and alive ... A beautifully told allegory that captures the power of language, this has definite crossover appeal.'
                                        Jake Hope, *The Bookseller*

'Atmospheric, beautifully written and about Venice ... a superb volume of adventure encompassing all that makes a good solid read. Includes ghosts, retribution, death, mermaids, seahorses, bravery ... Absolutely brilliant. Read it in Venice if you can, if not, then read it and visit as soon as you can ...'
  Sue Chambers, Waterstone's Harrods (waterstones.com)

'A wonderful alternate world historical fantasy, pitting myth and legend against science. Underlying environmental themes and well-drawn characters, including curry-loving mermaids, add depth to a satisfying literary adventure.'   www.thebookbag.com

THE
UNDROWNED CHILD

CHILD

Michelle Lovric

The American School in London
Middle School

The Christine Siegfried Award
is given to

Natalie Vann

June 2014

Orion
Children's Books

Also by Michelle Lovric

The Mourning Emporium
Talina in the Tower
The Fate in the Box

First published in Great Britain in 2009
by Orion Children's Books
a division of the Orion Publishing Group Ltd
Orion House
5 Upper St Martin's Lane,
London WC2H 9EA
An Hachette UK company

5 7 9 10 8 6

Text copyright © Michelle Lovric 2009
Map copyright © Ian P. Benfold Haywood 2009

A CIP catalogue record for this book
is available from the British Library.

ISBN 978 1 4440 0094 7

Printed in Great Britain by Clays Ltd, St Ives plc

The Orion Publishing Group's policy is to use papers
that are natural, renewable and recyclable products and
made from wood grown in sustainable forests. The logging
and manufacturing processes are expected to conform to
the environmental regulations of the country of origin.

www.undrownedchild.com

THE
UNDROWNED
CHILD

Contents

Venice in 1899

The numbers follow the sequence of the story.
The most important sites in the city are marked on the
map itself.

VENICE

SAN MICHELE

MURANO

CASA DELLA MISERICORDIA

FONDAMENTE NUOVE

LAGUNA

ARSENALE

SAN ZACCARIA

S. MARCO

PALAZZO DUCALE

RIVA DEGLI SCHIAVONI

SAN PIETRO DI CASTELLO

SANT' ELENA

LAGUNA

SAN GIORGIO MAGGIORE

ECCA

LAGUNA

A case of baddened magic

The fog that fell upon Venice that evening was like a bandage wrapped round the town. First the spires of the churches disappeared. Then the palaces on the Grand Canal were pulled into the soft web of white. Soon it was impossible to see anything at all. People held their hands out in front of them and fumbled their way over bridges like blind men. Every sound was muffled, including the sighs of the steam ferries nosing through the black waters. It would be an exceedingly bad night to fall in the water, for no one would hear a cry for help.

On the dark side of twilight, at the Fondamente Nuove, nine members of one family, dressed in their Sunday best, stood in the dim halo of a gas-lamp. They were arguing with an old gondolier standing in his boat below.

'We simply have to get across to Murano. Our daughter's to be baptized at San Donato during Vespers,' explained a studious-looking young man cradling an infant in a pink bonnet. Proudly, he held out the baby over the ledge for the gondolier to inspect. Being a Venetian child, she gurgled with delight at the waves crinkling beneath her.

'Not in this fog.'

I

'It'll lift as soon as we pull away from shore,' insisted the young man's brother. The whole family nodded vigorously.

'No one is going anywhere in Venice tonight, *Signori*.'

'But the priest is waiting for us . . .' pleaded a grey-haired woman, evidently the mother of the young men.

'I'll eat my oar if he is, *Signora*. He'll know that only a fool and his dog would set out in *this*.' The gondolier gestured into the whiteness.

Then the baby's mother spoke out in a low sweet voice. 'But are you not Giorgio Molin, *Signore*? I believe my second cousin is married to your uncle's brother?'

The gondolier peered under her bonnet. 'Why, Marta! The prettiest girl in Venice and you went off and buried yourself in the Archives,' he clucked. 'Imagine, a vision like you working there! Enough to give the librarian palpitations.'

At the word 'Archives', a look of anxiety crossed Marta's face. She quickly glanced around, murmuring 'Pray, do not mention that place here. Especially on this day.'

In the mist, the water stirred uneasily.

Suddenly the baby chuckled, stretching her tiny hands out towards the gondolier.

'Look, the little one knows her kin!' he grunted.

'I'm forgetting my manners, dear Giorgio,' said Marta, and she introduced her mother, her father, her cousin, her uncle, her brother-in-law and parents-in-law. 'And this,' she smiled adoringly at the studious young man, 'is my husband Daniele – that librarian you mentioned.'

The usual pleasantries were exchanged.

'So won't you take us, Cousin Giorgio?' asked Marta Gasperin, finally. 'It would mean such a great deal to me.'

'Family is family,' sighed the gondolier.

'Family is everything,' declared Marta Gasperin, bending to kiss the old man on the cheek, at which he flushed. She added, mischievously, 'Family and *books*, of course.'

2

'You've still got that teasing tongue, I see,' Giorgio Molin grumbled, handing her down into the gondola. 'You be careful or that baby of yours will grow up *clever*. And *that*'s no good in a girl.'

Thank you, thank you kindly,' whispered each uncle, aunt and cousin as they climbed into the boat. Ten was a heavy burden for a gondola. But the Gasperins were a tribe of low height and delicate build. They arranged their party clothes carefully as they sat down.

The fog did not lift as Giorgio Molin kicked off from the sea wall. He set his face grimly in the direction of Murano. It would be kinder, he supposed, not to share his misgivings with the family who were now chattering about the supper that would be served after the baptism.

The thick, white air churned around them. The waves swallowed up their words and laughter. The words and laughter sank all the way down to the sea bed where a certain skeleton had lain twisted in chains for nearly six hundred years.

A tremor rattled through the bleached limbs. A red glow lit up the empty ribcage. Bony fingers twitched, and an emerald ring sent a green light searching through the waves and shifting seaweed. Soon a dark, sinewy tentacle, long enough to encircle a house, came creeping over the floor of the lagoon.

Picture those gentle people in the gondola, warming up the mist with their laughter, handing the little baby from arm to loving arm, kissing her toes and fingers, whispering her name like a prayer.

They had but a few seconds more to live.

No one saw the seagulls approach. They cruised in silently from the lagoon islands, looking for trouble and carrion. If they could not find something dead to feast on, then they were not too squeamish to kill. These were the birds known as *magòghe* to the Venetians, ferocious grey-backed gulls of terrifying size.

The birds crested the rooftops of Murano and swept in over the cemetery island of San Michele. Their beaks twitched as they smelt the bodies freshly buried there. For a moment they hovered overhead, bruising the water with their shadows.

Then a voice stole inside their heads. It howled, 'Minions! We have new corpses to make tonight!'

Foam flecked the yellow beaks of the *magòghe*. Their cold blank eyes rolled up in their heads.

'O Master,' they thought. 'Tell us what to do.'

Now, from the soul of the bones beneath the water, came orders that soaked the gulls' brains with hunger and fury. They wheeled above the waves, shrieking with every breath.

But out in that fog-swaddled lagoon, the harsh screams of the birds were swallowed up in an instant. No one on Steam Ferry Number 13 heard a thing.

The ferry had left the Fondamente Nuove just one minute after the gondola bearing the family Gasperin. It should not have set forth in the fog. But the captain himself was from Murano, and eager to get home that night. He had made this trip a thousand times. He knew that if he set course north-east across the lagoon and kept a steady speed, he would skim the jetty at the Murano side in just six minutes. There would be no other craft in his way, not in wicked weather like this.

If the captain had held up his lamp at exactly the right moment, then he might have seen the slender black gondola weaving across the water just in front of him. But exactly at that right moment the lamp was knocked out of his hand by the first gull. Then a dozen others swept into his cabin, ripping at his eyes and his hair. He fell against the tiller and

4

slumped on the floor. The *magòghe* swarmed over his body until they covered it entirely. Mercifully, he was unconscious when they started to feed.

Back in the passenger cabin everyone felt the lurch as the captain lost control of the tiller. Perhaps somebody heard the faint crunch of wood as the prow of the *vaporetto* sliced through Signor Molin's gondola like a sword. The passengers' own shrieks drowned out the pitiful sounds of the Gasperin family crying out for one another as the ferry passed over them and a vast green tentacle threw itself around the ruined prow of the gondola and dragged it deep down below the waves.

The last person to drown was Marta, and her last words, floating out over the heedless water, were 'Save my baby! Please save my baby . . .'

At this, a disembodied laugh rattled out across the lagoon, a sound even bitterer and uglier than the shrieks of the *magòghe*. That noise alone rose above the fog, and echoed around the shores of Venice like the snarl of an approaching thunderstorm.

The ferry ploughed blindly into the jetty on Murano, splintering its rickety poles to matchwood. The passengers scrambling ashore soon discovered their dead captain. For the first few hours everyone was occupied with spreading the news of his unspeakable death and blessing their stars that they had all survived what might have been a dreadful accident.

No one was waiting for the gondola on Murano. Giorgio Molin had been right about one thing: the priest had long since given up on the baptism and the festive supper he had hoped to join. He assumed that the fog had changed all the plans. The gondolier's wife thought nothing of her husband's absence: he often slept on his boat during those hot June nights.

It was only when the fog finally lifted, a whole day later, that questions began to be asked as to the whereabouts of the Gasperin family. And almost at the same time the first body was washed ashore at Murano. It was Daniele, still clutching the bonnet of his beloved Marta. She was found a few hours later, her skirts billowing like a beautiful jellyfish, in the bay of Torcello. Her father-in-law floated face-down close by.

They found all the bodies in the end, except that of the baby.

Stories flew about. 'Such a tiny little mite, the fish ate her,' people whispered.

Some fragments of an antique Venetian prophecy

…When Rats flee town on frightened paws…

…Come-to-life are Black Death's ancient spores

…Who shall save us from a Traitor's tortures?

That secret's hidden in the old Bone Orchard.

1. A startling afternoon

June 1st, 1899

The blow came without warning and from nowhere. Just one second before, Teodora had been happily browsing in an old-fashioned Venetian bookshop, a dim, crumbling building that spilled out onto a square with a canal at one side. This was no ordinary bookshop. For a start, it was lit only by whispering gas-lamps and yellowy candle-stumps. A large brass mortar-and-pestle stood on the dusty counter instead of a till. There were no piles of famous poets, or detective stories or fat novels for ladies. In fact, there was just one battered copy each of all manner of interesting books like *Mermaids I Have Known* by Professor Marìn. And *The Best Ways With Wayward Ghosts*, by 'One Who Consorts with Them'.

And the bookshop was empty of other customers apart from one fair-haired boy no older than Teo herself. He was elegantly dressed with a linen waistcoat, spotless boots and a cap at a rakish angle. He stood at a lectern, reading *The Rise and Fall of the Venetian Empire*, which was as big as a safe and had no pictures at all. Occasionally he looked up to give Teo a princely, disapproving stare.

9

For Teodora was not just gazing but sniffing at the tall shelves. Those shelves were like coral reefs, looming far above her head, full of deep, mysterious crevices. The shelves went so high up into the painted ceiling that Teo (being the kind of girl who liked to imagine things) could imagine fronds of seaweed waving up there. But down at her level – and Teo was embarrassingly small for eleven – somewhere between the books, and even over the tang of mould and the sweetish whiff of dust, she could *definitely* smell fish.

Indeed, she'd been smelling fish since she arrived in Venice three days before. She would not eat fish, because she believed it was cruel to kill them (Teo was a vegetarian), but *this* fish smell was so delicious, so fresh and alive, like perfumed salt – that she suddenly thought to herself: 'This is what pearls would smell of, if they had a smell!'

The fair-haired boy harrumphed and looked down at his book. In Venice, he seemed to be implying, one *reads* books, not sniffs at them.

Teo lived in Naples, hundreds of miles to the south. Her parents – that is, the people who'd adopted her – had brought her to Venice for the first time, and with the utmost reluctance, as it happened. Teo had been told that she was adopted as soon as she was old enough to understand it. But she'd never known any other family or any other home but Naples, and she'd always been perfectly happy with both. At least, until she was six years old. That was when she had found a book called *My Venice* at the library. Leafing through pages illustrated with oriental-looking palaces floating on jade-green water, Teo had felt a lurch just like hunger inside.

To get to Venice had taken Teo five years of skilful and dedicated nagging, with postcards of Venetian scenes left on the top of the piano, a Venetian glass ring for her mother's birthday and other hints that were far from subtle. Her parents, who normally loved to think up treats for Teo, had always seemed oddly unwilling to bring her here, offering one unconvincing excuse after another.

There had been moments when Teo daydreamed of doing something outrageous, such as running away from home, and making her own way to Venice. She might even have done it, if only she'd had a friend to share the adventure with. But bookworms like Teodora are not generally known for their wide circle of adventurous friends. So they tend to have their adventures in their minds' eyes only.

At last Fate intervened. (Or so Teo whispered to herself when her parents couldn't hear. They were scientists, and prided themselves on being thoroughly modern and rational. In other words, they weren't great believers in Fate.) In the last few months Venice had been engulfed in a wave of strange and sinister events. Teo's ticket here came in the form of an emergency meeting of 'the world's greatest scientists' summoned to save the threatened city. An invitation to her parents had fluttered into the letterbox.

To think they had *still* tried to keep Teo at home! At first, they had insisted that she should not miss any school. Although it was nearly summer, it was still term-time, and the examinations were looming. But her teacher had given permission instantly, saying in front of everyone, 'Teodora's excused the exams. She's going to write me a lovely story about Venice instead.' No one likes a teacher's pet: naturally the other children had glared. Teo was mortified.

Then her parents declared that the situation in Venice was so very dangerous at the moment. As if that would keep her away!

'No one has actually died yet,' she had told them.

They'd had to admit that was true.

II

So finally she was here, and the real Venice, despite or perhaps precisely because of its tragic situation, seemed at least twice as precious as she'd imagined.

Almost more than anything else she had seen, Teo loved this old Venetian bookshop. She liked the stone mermaids carved above the doorway, the reflections of water playing on the walls. She liked the old bookseller too, with his creased-up face, velvet breeches and waistcoat, and his scent of talcum powder and candle-grease. He sometimes peered at her with a curious expression, as if he knew her from somewhere but could not quite place her. He never told her not to touch. And even warned her to keep a grip on *Smooth as a Weasel and Twice as Slippery* by Arnon Rodent.

'It has a tendency to fly out of people's hands,' he mentioned kindly.

She looked at him closely – or rather, just above his head as he spoke. For Teo had a very unusual gift. When people spoke, she saw their words actually written in the air above them. Also the manner of their speaking: some with the curt efficiency of typewriting machines, some like laborious handwriting, others with flourishes and heavy under-linings. The old bookseller spoke like a scroll of parchment unrolling, each word beautifully distinct and old-fashioned.

Teo didn't really know what she was looking for on those bookshelves, but she had the strongest feeling that there was something marvellous here, if she could only just find it.

'Teodora! It really is time to leave, sweetheart,' her father called from outside. Tommaso and Aurelia Naccaro, friends and fellow scientists from Naples, were waiting for them back at the hotel. With their daughter Maria. At the thought of Maria, Teo's face knitted into a rather unbecoming frown.

Teo's parents were heartily fed up with this decrepit, dusty old bookshop. Being scientists, they liked things that were shiny and new, like the laboratory where they worked, and their home in Naples, which was a masterpiece of modernity.

'Just a minute,' Teo called to them. 'Just give me one more minute, please . . .'

And that was when it happened.

Teo was standing on tiptoe to reach for *Lagoon Creatures – Nice or Nasty?*, yet another volume by the busy Professor Marìn. Suddenly she felt a rush of air, and a sharp blow to the head, an intense pain and the feeling of warm blood falling down her face.

Then nothing at all.

'Is this what it's like to die?' was her last thought before she fainted away completely. Teo was not a melodramatic sort of child, but nothing like this had ever happened to her before.

That is, as far as she knew.

When she woke up, her parents were kneeling beside her, desperate worry written all over their faces. Her mother was wiping blood off Teo's face with the hem of her pinafore. The bookseller hovered with a silk handkerchief so worn that it looked like the wing of a white butterfly against the sun. But Teo herself was still remembering what she had seen while she was unconscious – vast beautiful fish-tails thrashing around, a sinister white hand, something dark and oily swimming right over her head, the creaking of wood. The face of that princely, fair-haired boy frowning at her. And a . . . dwarf ? Yes, most certainly it was a dwarf, but a familiar-looking dwarf, as if she might know some dwarves in her real life!

What had happened was simply this: a book, a solid little book, had fallen from the top shelf directly onto Teo's head and knocked her unconscious. When she came to, she was clutching that book in her hand, and her father was trying to

13

pry her fingers off it. The fair-haired boy had vanished.

Once Teo was on her feet again, her parents started to fuss. In an effort to calm them, the old man handed Teo the book that had hurt her. 'Here, a gift. It is,' he told them humbly, 'extremely valuable. Indeed I never saw one like this before. I can see your daughter truly loves books,' he added, pleadingly, to her parents. 'A true young scholar, you know, in the old-fashioned way, like the scholars I used to know. They all came here . . .'

The bookseller was lost in his memories for a moment. To call Teo 'a true young scholar, in the old-fashioned way' was quite blatantly the biggest compliment that he could offer.

The book was positively the oldest she had ever seen, the leather all discoloured and the binding soft as velvet with age. The pearly, fishy smell hovered around it like a halo. Strangely, there was no title, just a vivid little coloured picture inset on the front cover. It showed the face of a lovely girl or very young woman, just her head and the tips of her pale, bare shoulders. Her hair was brilliantly shiny, almost as if wet. She seemed so sad that it hurt to look at her.

But, as Teo gazed at her face, the girl in the picture *winked at her*.

Teo's skin suddenly felt fragile and powdery, as if it could break up at any second, as if she was made of meringue. The girl had resumed her still, sad pose on the book's cover, but her cheeks were definitely flushed now. Teo quickly glanced around. No one else was watching. Her parents were still talking severely to the unfortunate bookseller.

'I'm perfectly well, Mamma,' she interrupted. 'Really! My head doesn't hurt at all,' which was not exactly true. It ached horribly, like a vast bell tolling in her brain, and her vision was more than a little cloudy. Nevertheless, she looked at her mother in her most determined manner (usually reserved for people who wanted to copy her homework). 'This book is

14

wonderful. *Please* mayn't I just take it?'

She held it up to her mother's nose. 'What do you think of this smell? Isn't it amazing? Like fish, only lovely.'

But her mother could not smell a thing. 'It must be the blow to your head, my love. Only *you* could get knocked unconscious in a bookshop,' she chided gently. 'Let me have a look.'

Teo flinched away in pain. It hurt far too much to put her straw hat back on. Her parents hustled her outside before she could even open the book. Her mother's arm was around her, protectively, but Teo turned and gave the bookseller a little wave, keeping her fingers discreetly by her waist. He was standing in the doorway, gazing back at her with an uneasy, slightly guilty look. His hand was on his heart, as if he was trying to calm its beating.

'Where did the boy go?' Teo asked, as her mother opened a parasol over her head. 'That very serious boy?'

'What boy?' Her parents exchanged worried glances. 'We didn't see anyone.'

They walked slowly through the clammy streets to San Marcuola to catch the steam ferry to their hotel which was just opposite the Rialto fish and fruit markets. A simple building set back from the Canal, it went by the strange name Hotel degli Assassini, which means 'Hotel of the Murderers'.

As they passed a toyshop at Santa Fosca, Teo heard music behind her. It sounded like a choir of rollicking schoolgirls singing lustily at the tops of their voices, but at a little distance, as if behind a pane of glass. The jaunty melody was familiar but Teo could not quite make out the words. She felt as if she *should* know them; she felt sure that she did, but they evaded her, like the threads of a dream that you struggle to grasp after a heavy sleep. She twisted out from under her mother's arm and spun around. The music stopped dead. The street was deserted. The toyshop was closed. Nothing

15

stirred, not even a rat, for which she was rather grateful, as the Venetian rats famously grew as big as cats.

'What is it now, Teodora, pet?' her father asked.

'Didn't you hear that singing?'

Her parents looked at her with deepening distress. Her father growled, 'What singing? It must be this infernal heat, Leonora, on top of that blow.'

'Figure of a pig! Utter bilge and old tripes too!'

The rough, girlish voice came from behind Teo's parents. It was obvious that they had heard nothing. Teo peered over their shoulders into the toyshop window. Inside, a wax mermaid doll rudely mouthed, 'Slow as slime on the uptake! Ain't got a noggin' idea, 'ave they?'

Teo thought the better of mentioning the bad-mannered doll to her parents, who were now tut-tutting at the salt-eaten bricks falling out of walls and the blistered paintwork dropping off in pieces from the beautiful palaces they walked past.

On the ferry, Teo placed the book carefully on her knees. The pearly smell was really quite powerful now. Her parents sat beside her, absorbed in the programme for the gathering of scientists. Teo glanced around. Not one single passenger was sniffing or looking in her direction. It was safe to have a good look without drawing attention to herself.

The beautiful girl on the cover kept her eyes downcast. For the second time Teo wondered why the book had no title printed on the front. 'What kind of book,' she wondered, 'doesn't tell you its name?'

But the strangest thing was this: when she opened it up Teo saw that *her own name* was written inside the cover in an antique hand script that had already gone brown with age.

Welcome to Venice, Teodora-of-Sad-Memory, said the book. *We have been waiting for you a very long time.'*

2. A puzzling evening

at the Hotel degli Assassini, June 1st, 1899

Arriving back at the hotel, Teodora endured Maria's mocking look stoically. At supper, Teo pushed her food around her plate. Bedtime had never seemed so long in coming. She'd not had one moment to be truly alone with her new book since they left the bookshop, and she was literally feverish with impatience.

It was towards the end of that interminable supper that Teo began to feel seriously unwell. Green and purple spots swam in front of her eyes. She kept shaking her head to clear the roaring in her ears. It sounded like the sea – no, an ocean! – in a shell. When the waiter brought the cheese-board, there was a large carrot carved in the shape of a mermaid sitting between the Dolcelatte and the Pecorino. Teo could have sworn that the carrot-mermaid flexed her tail and plunged her little hand inside a smelly Gorgonzola.

'Tyromancy, ye know,' remarked the mermaid. 'The Ancient Art of Divination by Cheese.'

Then she pulled her hand out and inspected the green cheese-mould on her tiny fingers.

17

'Lackaday!' she moaned. 'Stinking! It goes poorly for Venice and Teodora, it do!'

Teo rubbed her eyes. When she opened them again, the carrot-mermaid lay still and silent on the board.

'How *is* your poor head, Teodora?' asked her mother as they left the dining room.

At that moment a violent and strangely prolonged clap of thunder made everyone jump. The lamps dimmed. The needle of the gramophone slid awry with a screech, and the silver coffee service shivered on its tray. There was a general chorus among the guests of 'Oh my, the heat has broken!' and 'At last!'

The lamps were still flickering as Teo's mother lifted her daughter's fringe with a gentle hand.

'My goodness!' Teo's mother turned her around to face the mirror in the hotel lobby. A ragged purple bruise had bloomed all around Teo's forehead.

'How revolting,' remarked Maria, looking at her own dainty reflection with satisfaction.

Teo muttered, 'Not everyone wants to look like a pink rabbit in ruffles.'

Her words were swallowed up in the rain that now hurled itself against the windows as if it meant to shatter them. A glass ornament in the shape of a mermaid juddered towards the edge of a sideboard. Teo gently nudged it back to safety. As she straightened it on its lace doily, the glass mermaid opened her lips and tinkled, 'Not much chop, your friend, aye! Nary a brain to rub together.'

Teo squeaked loudly and turned a shade paler, if possible. Everyone in the room twisted their necks around to stare at her.

'This won't do at all. We must get someone to look at you,' worried Teo's father, above the din of the rain. 'I'd never forgive myself . . . Go and lie down, child. Maria,' he added, 'you're peaky too. Are you quite well?'

It was true: Maria's peach-like complexion had turned a little greenish.

Outside her bedroom, her parents argued in whispers that were perfectly audible from Teo's position at the keyhole.

'I told you we shouldn't have brought her. Something was bound to happen.'

'But she has no idea . . .'

'No idea about *what*?' Teo wondered. Then the handle started to turn and she had to run back to bed. Her mother's anxious face appeared around the door. In her hand was a familiar bottle of an English patent medicine, Velno's Vegetable Syrup. She groaned.

It was agony waiting for the hotel to find a doctor who would come out on a wild night like this. Teo sat propped up on fat pillows, the book safely hidden under the lowest one. She could feel it, temptingly thick, in the small of her back.

The doctor was an elderly man on stilty legs, his sparse hair flattened by the rain. He made her look into the light of a candle, and gently swivelled her head around. His words appeared to Teo in a fussy, careful script when he murmured, 'Strange, such green eyes in a girl from Naples . . . Any history of medical problems in the family?'

'I'm adop—' Teo started to say, but her mother shook her head slightly. 'Why doesn't she want the doctor to know?' pondered Teo.

He pushed an icy thermometer under her tongue, and listened to her heart, which was sometimes thudding like a steam train and then suddenly not beating at all for whole seconds at a time. He seemed to be far away, down the other end of a telescope, when he started to ask her questions. What with the roaring in her ears, and the pain in her head, it was impossible for Teo to concentrate. Odd, vague answers stumbled out of her mouth. 'I see with my ears in Venice.' And 'The bluest of fins!'

Teo felt freezing and burning at the same time; her skin was a cold crust over boiling lava. Her forehead hurt as if it was about to split open.

'That's quite a fever. It would be prudent to take her to the hospital.' The doctor's tone was grim. 'I suspect a concussion. And I don't like to see that colour in a little girl's skin. I'm seeing too many children like this at the moment, and . . .'

Teo's mother motioned him away from the bed.

'Is our daughter in danger?' she whispered, searching the doctor's face. Teo took the opportunity to drag the book from under her pillow and slip it into the breast-pocket of her pinafore.

His answer was sombre. 'Madam, in Venice, at this moment, we are all in danger.'

'But the *Mayor* says it's safe here. We read it in the paper.'

At the mention of the Mayor, the doctor's kind face creased into a cantankerous expression. He said sternly, 'I repeat. By bringing your daughter to Venice, you have juggled with Fate.'

'But they're scientists. They don't believe in Fate,' whispered Teo, as she slipped slowly from consciousness.

The last thing she heard were sweet, rough voices in her ear, singing like the choir she had heard in the street. This time she could hear the words clearly, as well as the accents, which were not exactly refined. None of those girls had been near a finishing school. Maria would have called them 'common'.

To the tune of 'The Jolly Roger' they now sang,

"Twas Fate what brung ye here, Teo-do-ra
"Twas Fate what called yer name
"Twas Fate what dropped that book on-yer-head
"Twas Fate what pulled the train . . .'

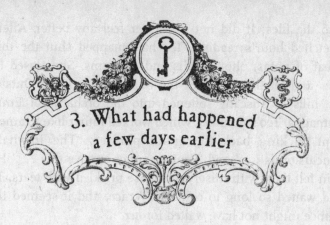

3. What had happened a few days earlier

May 27th, 1899

On the long train trip from Naples, both pairs of parents had dozed, worn out from nights in the laboratory preparing for the great gathering of scientists. When her father settled into an even rhythm of soft snores, Teo had gently lifted the slab of papers from his knee and delved inside.

Maria threatened, 'I could wake 'em up and tell 'em what you're doin', if I had a mind to!'

'Absolutely right, all that you're lacking is a mind.'

Maria opened her mouth and shut it again. In a moment, Teo had forgotten Maria's sulky little face in the seat opposite. She read as fast as she could. Who knew when her parents might wake up and take the papers away from her? Some of it had been too technical to understand, but the main message was clear as cut glass. Venice was dying. And dying fast, like a patient in a hospital where the doctors know no cure, like Teo's poor Nanny Giulia, who had wasted away from consumption.

Teo's eyes welled up at the memory. The last thing she wanted was for Maria to catch her crying, so she dived back

21

into the files. It did not make her feel any better. After a wretched hour's reading, Teo had snapped shut the thick sheaf of notes, photographs and diagrams. She closed her eyes and let the clatter of the train fill her head. Outside, the hills of Tuscany softened into the orchards of Emilia Romagna. Teo's memory, which worked rather like a camera, kept clicking back to certain phrases. 'The inevitable conclusion is . . .' and 'Venice cannot survive this . . .' Her skin felt tight with misery; her nose prickled with tears. Teo had waited so long to come to Venice, and it seemed that Venice might not have waited for *her*.

Now everyone knew that Venice was sinking into the sea, a little more each year. But what Teo had just learnt was this: what held the city up was in fact . . . *water*. When the first Venetians built their town, they had rammed millions of poles into the mud to form the foundations for their houses. Beneath that mud was an *aquifer*, a cushion of water that pushed up against the mud, the poles and the buildings, and kept Venice afloat. Teo pictured a sky-blue cushion, softly bulging with water, with Venice resting on top of it like a comfortable cat in a basket.

But Venice's *aquifer*, she had just read, was now mysteriously disappearing. As its cushion of water deflated, the city was capsizing into the lagoon. No one could work out where the water was going or why the lagoon had suddenly grown so very salty that many marine animals were dying.

Meanwhile the water temperature was also rising. It was as if there was something underneath the city, heating it up like a warming-pan in a bed. Diving parties had been sent below, but soon came racing back – the warm, soupy water had attracted a school of large sharks, some four yards long. Lately, their grey fins had been seen slicing down the Grand Canal. No one knew what those monsters were eating. But

22

several tourists had disappeared without a trace, and the rumours were running wild.

So now famous scientists were on their way to Venice from all over the world, to see what could be done. The train from Naples bristled with bearded men wearing monocles, each squinting over the same thick folder of notes that was now weighing so heavily on Teo's spirits.

As the train rolled into the plains of the Veneto, Teo had opened the file again. However disagreeable the truth, it was better to know, surely? Maria rolled her eyes. She rearranged her pink silk skirt disdainfully on the train's worn seat and retied the ribbon on her green travel cape into an even more ostentatious pussycat bow.

A moment later she whimpered, 'Ouch! A horrid Venetian mosquito bit me!'

'Shame, how is the mosquito?' asked Teo, without looking up.

The first mystery the scientists would tackle was what had happened to Venice's ancient marble wells. In the last few weeks the wells had started to burst their iron covers, and to send out great fountains of *hot* water. It all began in Campo San Maurizio, quite a surprise for some American students who were enjoying a late-night picnic of ham rolls on the steps around the well. For *them* a warm shower was rather welcome. But the well water was growing hotter by the day. When the well in front of the church of San Zaccaria sent up a steaming geyser, a whole wedding party was painfully scalded. And the water jet that shot out of the well in San Giacomo dell'Orio knocked the spire off the belltower. Then the scientists had tested the water and discovered that it was not only at boiling temperature, but poisonous to drink.

'Dear me!' thought Teo.

But as she scanned more documents, she had been horrified to see that the Venetian authorities were stubbornly intent on pretending that *nothing was wrong*. The Mayor of Venice had contributed a letter to the notes, in which he gaily insisted that it was a great deal of fuss over nothing.

'A temporary fault,' he smiled patronizingly from the handsome photograph he had somewhat unnecessarily included with his letter. 'Our friends at the Water Company have the situation under control. All the tourists can still take a nice warm bath in the evenings in their hotels. No one should cancel their visit to Venice.'

Teo had impatiently turned the page on the luxuriant moustache of the Mayor. She stared at sepia photographs of *acqua alta*. Now this 'High Water', as everyone knew, was perfectly normal in Venice. Many times each year the lowest points of the city, like the great square at San Marco, filled up with water that came gushing from under the stone paving. But in the last few weeks, the pictures showed San Marco dry as the Kalahari Desert. Instead, the highest parts of the town, the ones that *never* flooded, were suddenly filling with water for hours on end. People were left standing on chairs in their kitchens, or clinging to the branches of trees.

The firemen and the officers of the Water Magistrate rushed around, taking the wooden flood pontoons to places where they had never been needed before. But when the tide surged up, it arrived with such remarkable force that the pontoons just sprang up and floated off, sometimes with terrified people on board.

And the water that carried them away was always warm and dark as blood.

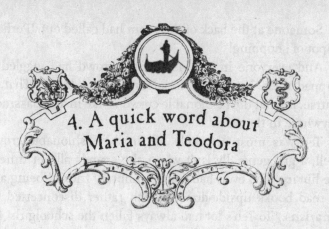

4. A quick word about Maria and Teodora

Maria was supposed to be Teo's best friend; for this trip anyway.

But the truth was that Teo was as fond of Maria as she was of cod-liver oil.

Naturally Maria, with her perfect glossy hair and her chronically bored expression, had always been one of the 'fashionable crowd' at school, the ones who cunningly adapted their hats and school pinafores to the latest style. The kind of girls who, even at eleven, could cause a carriage accident just by gazing at the coachman with their heads on one side.

The fashionable crowd took pride in being far too modern to show much interest in schoolwork. They affected drawls and babylike lisps.

Like Teo's teacher, but for different reasons, Maria's form-mistress had been quite content to let her pupil out of school to go to Venice.

'Perhaps it will put an idea in her head,' Maria's teacher had sighed. 'Perhaps a museum . . . a spot of art, some culture, you never know.'

Someone at the back of the room had called out, 'Perhaps a spot of shopping!'

And everyone in the fashionable crowd had giggled or clapped then, betraying Maria for a cheap laugh. That, of course, is what the fashionable crowd is like in any classroom anywhere in the world.

Teo was most definitely not in the fashionable crowd. Well, a girl generally isn't when she spends all her time in the library. (Teo even had a special library trick of being able to read books upside-down, which rather disconcerted the librarians.) To Teo's lot had always fallen the schoolgirls' full repertoire of nasty little tricks: the tea-party invitations ostentatiously handed out to everyone else but her, the mocking compliments on her clothes, and the sudden silences or sniggering when she entered a room.

The parents, of course, did not have much idea of the undercurrents of schoolgirl life. The adults innocently assumed that their daughters would amuse themselves together in Venice while the scientific gathering was in progress. No suitable replacement had yet been found for Teo's poor Nanny Giulia. Maria's always gave in their notice soon after arrival: Maria's tantrums were legendary among the nannies of Naples.

In a whispered conference in the corridor, as their train approached Venice, Teo had convinced Maria that it would be far better if they were to secretly spend the days ahead separately: 'You can do what you want. I can do what I want. We only need to meet up in the evenings when our parents come home from their meetings.'

'You'd *really, really* like that, then, Dora?' drawled Maria.

Teo nodded fervently.

'Then it's goin' to cost you something, ain't it?'

'But *you* want it too . . .'

'Or I could stick to you like glue, Te-Odore.'

26

And so Teo was forced to bribe Maria with a great deal of her allowance. Maria seemed to spend all their joint pocket-money on scarves, belts, beads and Venetian slippers. It was the height of fashion that summer to wear crests: on scarves, printed all over skirts and even leather shoes. By the·end of the second day in Venice, Maria was already covered head-to-toe in crests.

'How exceedingly subtle,' Teo had observed sarcastically.

Maria, with characteristic brilliance, riposted: 'Go and boil your head, Dora.'

Astonishingly, Maria's parents didn't notice the profusion of crests at all. It crossed Teo's mind that Maria might be trying to attract their attention. That, as usual, failed miserably. Maria's parents prided themselves on being far more interested in the next professorship than in what their foolish daughter wore. Maria's father was highly competitive, and talked out of the corner of his mouth like a robber, and wore shiny suits like one too. Aurelia Naccaro barely spoke to her daughter. If Maria wanted their attention she would need to come home with an essay marked 'A'.

And that – given that Maria's head seemed to Teo like an empty church where dust streamed in the sunlight – was not likely to happen in the conceivable future.

5. Too many children are sick in Venice

'**W** *arm as blood*,' Teo murmured.

She was awake, she thought, but she could not open her eyes. She smelt carbolic soap, heard the brisk tap of shoes on a polished stone floor. Distant voices echoed down long corridors. Teo felt oddly separate from her own body, as if she herself hovered a few inches above it.

The last thing she remembered was tucking the old book into her pinafore before the doctor picked her up from the hotel bed and carried her down to his boat. Later, much later, she would recall shreds of the journey, the long black boat rocking under the stars, the moonlit windows above as they passed through the looming canyons of floating palaces, her mother's frightened eyes gazing down on her, the rain falling quietly and persistently, a tall grey fin following them all the way down one canal, the back of a shop hung with sinister white masks like skulls, each with a single black spot by the nose.

Then a gondola stacked with ivory tusks and black wood had sidled past them, followed by another, draped in black crêpe, bearing a tiny coffin covered in white flowers. Her mother had clutched her father's arm and pointed at the coffin.

'The Mayor promised this city was safe for children, Alberto,' she had whispered. 'Is it really? Is it?'

Teo came slowly back to consciousness in a brightly-lit room with a high ceiling, a porcelain stove and a grated window down which the rain continued to cascade. She was lying fully dressed up on a simple iron bed. When she finally opened her eyes, an ugly nurse in a blue cap was looking down on her with ferocious disapproval.

The doctor was trying to persuade Teo's parents that they should go back to their hotel. 'She's in the best possible hands,' he added firmly.

'And that's a fact,' added the nurse, thin-lipped, as if to say, 'there shall be no mollycoddling of little girls *here*.'

To hurry everyone out, Teo obediently swallowed the hot *tisana* that the nurse held up to her lips. It left a bitter, chalky rime on her tongue.

'Now I'm so sleepy,' she yawned hugely at her mother, who finally seemed to be on the point of leaving, though with many anxious looks back.

'Do turn off the gas-lamp as you leave, Mamma.' Teo forced out another yawn.

The moment her parents' footsteps had faded, Teo leant over and relit the lamp beside her bed.

She climbed down from her bed and walked unsteadily to the door. Peering around it, Teo had a glimpse of endless corridors, nurses passing with lamps from room to room, from which came the faint sounds of children moaning. A little girl cried out, 'Leave my hair alone, you brute!'

All the nurses had their backs to Teo. She closed the door and wedged the handle with fire-tongs from the porcelain stove.

Returning to the iron bed, Teo stumbled. She was still a little dizzy. And how long before the *tisana* started working? Quickly, she pulled the book from her pinafore.

The beautiful sad girl on the cover had changed her position. She was now gazing down intently with her head a little on one side, as if encouraging Teo to open the book and read its contents.

The thick paper inside was a dark cream colour, like milky breakfast coffee, but with a pearly sheen. The inscription to *Teodora-of-Sad-Memory* was still there. She told herself, 'But of course, it could be another Teodora. There must be thousands of Teodoras. And I'm from Naples. No one in Venice remembers me, do they?'

How could they?

She turned the page. There was an illustration, of another young girl operating a small hand-cranked printing machine. She was drawn only from the waist up. Above the engraving were some words about the book. The thing was, the book didn't seem to think that it exactly *was* a book. Instead, it introduced itself as:

The Key to the Secret City
for the children of Venice

Below that was printed what must be the publishers' name: the Seldom Seen Press.

Teo cast a knowing eye over the engraving of the printing press. She liked everything to do with books. The best lessons at school this past term had been about Johannes Gutenberg, who invented the printing press four hundred years before. The teacher had brought in a working model of Gutenberg's machine. Then she had shown the children how to slot individual letters into wooden forms to 'compose' a page, to brush ink over a metal plate, then run them through a heavy mangle . . . all this to produce a single shaky but real printed page.

'Like magic!' Teo had marvelled at the time.

And there had been the added joy to it that when Maria had taken her turn at the press, her new *mousseline de soie* dress had been splattered by a slick of ink that had coursed off the roller while Teo turned it. Teo didn't mean to do it. It just happened.

Grinning at the memory, Teo turned to the next page of *The Key to the Secret City*. This was set in large type with many curly decorations. It was hard to understand, and Teo realized that the words were written not in Italian but in old Venetian dialect, which was more like Latin or French. This was a word game. Teo loved word games. And indeed, when she put half of her brain into Latin mode, and a quarter into French, leaving the rest for Italian, and squinted with one eye, reading aloud and hearing the sounds of the words – then she discovered that she could understand the Venetian dialect quite easily. Well, almost easily.

The page said; *We will show you our city, we will show you our heart.*

'Oh yes, please!' whispered Teo, feeling warm with pleasure.

A strong smell of wet varnish filled the room. Teo glanced up as the window rattled violently. The storm was gathering force. Then she looked again, and a scream tore out of her throat. *The Key to the Secret City* slid to the floor as Teo leapt up and clutched her pillow in front of her.

A dark figure stood hunched by the window. He had twice the bulk of an ordinary man. His bare arms were grooved with muscle and sinew. He was like some kind of monstrous joke, a crude sketch of a Blackamoor from a Penny Dreadful magazine: his skin was blacker than coal and his eyes bulged white in his broad, furious face. Broken chains dangled from his neck and legs.

A groaning creak came from his joints and a thin stream of blood fell from his lips as he began to move towards her.

6. An hysterical conniption?

around midnight, June 1st, 1899

'I t's a *statue*, you foolish child!' The nurse was shaking Teo harder than was really necessary. What harsh breath the woman had!

The nurse had hurt her wrist wrenching the handle of the door that Teo had wedged with the tongs. And now the other children on the wards, woken by Teo's screams, were wailing in a dismal chorus down every corridor.

'But it moved! There was blood in its mouth! And I *know* it wasn't here before.'

'You know precisely nothing, young lady. You are indulging in an hysterical conniption.'

Having supplied her own excuse, the nurse slapped Teo's face for good measure.

The doctor hurried in and gasped at the sight of the vast statue, 'Dear God, not here too!'

Teo, one hand on her smarting cheek, bellowed, '*What* not here too?'

The nurse threw her a threatening look as the doctor sank into a chair, 'Child, I hardly know. Someone is playing a very silly and sinister joke on Venice, just at a time when laughter is quite uncalled for. These statues have started appearing in people's homes, in bakeries, and now in the hospital. The strange thing is, they're very like Brustolons.'

'Brusto . . .?'

'Andrea Brustolon. Venetian sculptor. Two hundred years ago he carved these Blackamoors with ebony skin and ivory eyes . . . once upon a time these people were . . . well, no, never mind what they were, child.'

'Why not?'

'Well, it's a . . . long story, and not a very nice one.' The doctor wouldn't meet her eyes. 'Anyway, you used to see the Brustolons only in museums or the grandest palaces. Suddenly they're appearing all over the place.'

'If they are antiques, why do they smell of fresh varnish?' queried Teo.

The doctor did not seem to hear her. He lowered his voice and grumbled to himself, 'The Mayor has insisted on keeping it out of the papers, but that only means that it's more of a shock when it happens to someone.'

He rose and placed his hand on Teo's forehead. 'And indeed this shock has not done your fever any favours.'

Quickly, he felt her neck and under her arms, whispering, 'Nothing, thank God!'

Teo persisted, 'But there was *blood* in its mouth!'

'I know, I know. Our practical joker has a truly twisted sense of humour. Look.' The doctor pulled a scalpel from his pocket and poked about inside the mouth of the statue. Out came a fat sliver of wriggling red slime. The doctor opened the window and flung it out into the rain.

'Our prankster puts medical leeches full of blood inside the statues' lips. They drip . . . Anyone would think someone was trying to *frighten* Venice to death, or at least out of her wits.'

Teo had a hundred more questions to ask. Where did the

blood for the leeches come from? Who would want to frighten a city . . . *to death*? And the doctor had a hundred reasons why Teo should lie back in her bed and rest quietly.

He picked up *The Key to the Secret City*, which had fallen on the floor.

'I believe you like to read, child? Read yourself back to sleep then.'

The doctor seemed not to notice the girl on the cover giving him a smile and then nodding to Teo. But Teo did, and her hands tingled as she took the book.

The nurse harrumphed and stalked out of the room. Permission to read in bed was apparently her definition of spoiling a child rotten.

'But the . . . Brustolon?' pleaded Teo, pointing a shaking finger at the statue. 'I can't sleep with him looking at me like that, as if he wants to kill me.'

'Don't tell Nursie.' The doctor smiled. He opened a drawer and pulled out two crisp white sheets. In a moment the Brustolon looked like nothing more frightening than a lump of rock under a picnic blanket.

A pale little boy in a nightshirt suddenly hurtled into the room. Teo glimpsed a nasty blackened swelling on his neck. His head had been cruelly shaved. The child looked wildly from Teo to the doctor and then fled back into the corridor.

'Aha!' the nurse's voice rapped nearby. 'Got you!' From the corridor came the sound of fearful snivelling, a thwack and then loud crying.

The doctor made for the door, 'Now I have to go and stop Nursie from killing them with "kindness". They're only children. And they're frightened. She forgets that. We are overstretched, you see – so many children here with high fevers just now.'

The doctor's face darkened and he mumbled to himself, 'I have a mortuary full of dead children, and still the Mayor insists on funerals only by night. All so that his precious tourists don't see!'

When he saw Teo staring at him in horror, he patted her hand, 'Don't listen to me, child! How I ramble on! Anyway, you've not got whatever it is that ails the others. You've just had a blow to the head. Speaking of that, enjoy your book, dear. I'll be off now.'

After a few wary glances at the shrouded Brustolon, Teo opened the book again at the place where she had left off. What she read next made her frown.

Venice is so much invaded by foreigners that we Venetians need to keep another city for ourselves, one that fits between-the-Linings, one that nobody else can see. This book is a key to that Secret City, a Venice that is private for Venetians alone. This book must never fall into the hands of foreign children or adults.

Teo was crushed. The book seemed to be saying 'Keep Out'. Nevertheless, she turned back to it, and made a translation of the old Venetian dialect on the next page for herself, writing it down slowly on a piece of paper (naturally, in Teo's pinafore there were *always* pencils and paper):

In Venetian we say 'andar per le Fodere', literally to 'go between-the-Linings' – which means to follow secret paths. In these pages are ways for children to andar per le Fodere to places and stories in Venice, in and along ways that are not known to adults or foreigners, and which Venice herself has forgotten in the mists of time.

It is important that the children of Venice remember these special stories, for if not them, then who? And it is this secret knowledge of the city that will one day help save Venice from her greatest enemy and her most terrible danger.

Teo's chest clenched tight. It was partly pleasure, the lovely shivery feeling of being on the inside of a huge secret, but there was a stab of fear too. The words 'terrible danger' rang in her head.

There was a little guilt mixed in, too.

Underneath her delight, Teo was miserably aware that she wasn't a Venetian child. And that therefore she should *not* have this book. She was one of the very outsiders from whom Venice needed privacy. Venice was crowded, it was true. The strange happenings lately seemed to draw even more tourists, just out of morbid curiosity. Teo reflected bleakly: 'Everyone's cramming in to make sure they get a look before she goes under. Like people looking at an accident in the street. It's hideous!'

In fact, Teo supposed sadly, she was an outsider everywhere. Her parents were not her parents. She was an only child, who, with no gift for friendship, felt at home only in the library or a bookshop. She was not just in the wrong place all the time, but she sometimes felt as if she had been born in the wrong century.

But this book had literally dropped on her head and into her hands.

'I didn't ask for this to happen,' Teo pointed out to herself. 'The book chose *me*.'

It had been quite a day. Teo was numb with exhaustion. The pain in her head was beating again like a drum in a procession. Outside, the wind howled against the window. She lay back against the pillows, and the book subsided into the blanket. The ringing in her ears had changed pitch, and now sounded like singing or chanting; like that schoolgirl choir again. Her eyes drifted over to the porcelain stove. Was that the shape of a mermaid picked out in the ironwork of the grate?

She closed her eyes to listen better.

Yes, she had heard that music before. Once again came the sensation of water all around her, as if she was floating out to the blue heart of an unknown sea.

A draught of cold air made her open her eyes. The Brustolon's white sheets were rustling.

'It's a *statue*,' she told herself aloud, in a firm voice. 'And it's the *wind*.'

The sound of the singing filled her head like honey, making all her thoughts sweet and slow.

'*Andar per le Fodere*,' she whispered drowsily, 'go between-the-Linings . . . Goodbye.'

Her final conscious thought was not of Venice, or herself, but of Maria, and the last time she had seen her. Teo was suddenly shot through with a piercing anxiety. 'Maria,' she mumbled, 'I really, *really don't* think you should . . .'

The music stopped. The mermaid in the grate was rattling the stove with her tail. She opened her mouth. Teo saw a little pink tongue and pearly teeth. A rough but sweet voice urged, 'Yoiks! Ye should not trust that perfidious lass, O Teodora-of-Sad-Memory! She lies like a hairy egg!'

'Are you talking to me?'

'Gorblimey! Who else? How about a civil how-do? That dafty girlie Maria, I tell ye – have an eye to her. Last time I saw a mouth like that, it had a hook in it. *He*'s taken her to him. Now she's hornswaggling ye too, Lord love yer 'eart.'

'Maria? Who's taken her . . .?'

Teo never finished that sentence, because at that moment the Brustolon's vast arm thrust itself out of the sheet, and wrenched off the fabric.

The last thing she heard was the mermaid shouting, 'Ye scurvy dog! Ye'll niver . . .'

When a young nurse bustled into Teo's hospital room the next morning, she screamed at what she saw, and dropped the glass of hot milk on the floor where it shattered into a thousand sharp fragments.

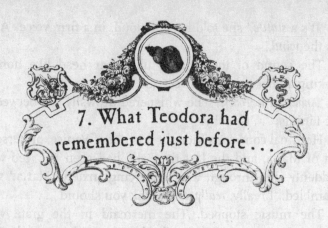

7. What Teodora had remembered just before . . .

just before lunchtime, May 30th, 1899

Unfortunately, the girls' agreement to avoid each other had not worked as well as they had planned. Venice was so very small. Teo kept bumping into Maria. They would give each other sickly smiles and pass on by, but every time it gave Teo a nasty jolt to remember that she was in effect lying to her parents by pretending to be with Maria.

So Teo's conscience had hit her quite hard, when, across the small square of Sant'Aponal, she caught sight of Maria twirling a new parasol covered with crests. Bending down towards her was a handsome youth of about sixteen years.

He turned to point something out to Maria, and Teo noticed a big green glass ring on the middle finger of his left hand.

Maria was all smiles, as if he was an old friend. A friend in Venice? Maria wasn't at all impressed with the city. 'Stupid place,' she scoffed every chance she could, especially when she saw how it infuriated Teo. And one time, when the parents weren't listening, she had added with quite remarkable venom, 'Personally *I* won't be fussed if – I mean *when* – it sinks into the lagoon.'

Teo thought, 'Of course Maria looks more enthusiastic about Venice now she's found a Venetian boy to flirt with.'

Teo hadn't called out a greeting, but sneaked up quietly, hiding herself behind a bulky American lady until she was right beside Maria and the boy. The air felt oddly cold around them, as if they were standing in a deep shadow, even though the sun blazed hotter than ever.

'Why Maria, how exceedingly nice to see you!' Teo had announced loudly, making Maria jump six inches in the air, her hair swishing like a horse's tail. As the curtain of hair fell back onto Maria's shoulders, Teo turned to the young man, only to discover that he had melted away. But his disembodied voice floated through the air, urging, 'Don't forget, little Mariella, never forget . . .'

That voice had a peculiar accent. Something about it made Teo squirm. It was rather like that feeling when you've cut your fingernails too short: painful and somehow shaming. Teo's mouth filled up with a bitter taste.

Teo was an extremely observant girl. And she had a remarkable memory that stored pictures, and even whole pages of books, just like a camera. To fix the young man's image in her mind, she quickly ran through what she'd discerned when she was spying on them from across the little square. He might indeed be described as handsome, but it was in the repulsively flawless way of a shop mannequin. What ordinary boy carried a cane and wore an emerald ring? His eyes had glittered coldly, she remembered – and perhaps they were also just a little too close together?

And the mole by his nose had been so very black, and so perfectly oval . . .

Then there was his voice. 'Don't forget, little Mariella, never forget . . .'

The young man's words had written themselves in front of Teo's eyes in a sinister Gothic script. They looked as if they had been put down with a goose-quill pen. And they lingered, even after he had disappeared.

A picture of words – words *without* their owners underneath them – now *that* had never appeared to Teo before. The sight of that Gothic script was just as disturbing as the tone of the young man's voice, especially because of the contrast: such a young man, and such antique writing. It simply didn't make sense.

'What's this "little Mariella" business?' was Teo's first question to Maria. Then her attention was caught by something glinting on Maria's ear.

Teo whistled. Maria was wearing a single earring with a little emerald hanging from it like a spinach-green teardrop. The hoop of gold was driven right through a hole in her pretty little ear lobe. Around the hole the skin was angry and red. For years Maria had wheedled to have her ears pierced, and her parents had always refused.

'Little girls don't mutilate themselves,' Teo had heard Maria's father shout more than once. 'Get that idea out of your empty head.'

Maria's silly clothes and crests were one thing, but a hole in her ear and an emerald earring?

'You'd better get rid of that frightful thing before your father sees it!' Even to Teo, her voice sounded priggish.

'Anyway,' she added more sympathetically, 'that hole looks infected. Does it hurt?'

Maria answered back with a shrill torrent of abuse – the words 'boring bookworm' and 'frump' were involved – as were some detailed comments on Teo's own fashion sense. Which, if the truth were to be told, was not Teo's strong point.

'Beg pardon,' replied Teo stiffly. 'Keep the wretched earring by all means! Hope your ear gets gas-gangrene and drops off.'

Standing right next to her, Teo had realized that Maria

also reeked of musky perfume. She had now recovered from her surprise enough to give Teo a maddening smug and secretive smile. It was obvious that the smile and the perfume had something to do with the young man with the perfectly oval mole.

Teo had absolutely known in that moment that she should tell her parents, or Maria's, about the young man. But then she would have to confess to her splendid days roaming around the city on her own. And that would be the end of them.

'Maria can look after herself!' Teo thought defensively. 'Anyway, her parents don't exactly fuss after her, do they? Not like mine! Sometimes I wonder if they even remember her name.'

But inside Teo had felt uncomfortable, and a little concerned. For all her dressing like a miniature adult, Maria was young for her age, and, Teo suspected, also rather unhappy. If that boy was up to no good, then Maria would be vulnerable to flattery. Perhaps he was after Maria's pocket money, which was, of course, swelled with Teo's own.

Just as Teo was softening, Maria had spoiled it all, drawling, 'So tell me 'bout your romantic adventures in Venice, Dora. Ain't *you* met any nice Venetian boys yet?'

'Boys!' Teo had scoffed, thinking of the half-witted specimens she knew in Naples.

'Remind me, what is the point of boys? Personally, I'd rather have Bubonic Plague!'

The urgent tinkle of mechanical music interrupted their quarrel. In a toy emporium behind them, a music box was slowly opening its lid. The strange thing was that there was no one to do that, or to wind it up. It was lunchtime and the shop was closed, with its door bolted.

Inside the music box, instead of the usual ballerina, a tiny tin mermaid swam around her wire carousel. Now music box

41

ballerinas usually have empty, pretty smiles. But this mermaid wore an expression of utter terror. As the carousel turned, Teo saw why. Just an inch away from the mermaid was a white serpent with a vicious expression painted on its tin face. The music increased its tempo; the mermaid and her pursuer went faster and faster, as did Teo's heart.

Maria laughed out loud, 'Divine! Shame your pocket money's gone, Te-Odore.' She clinked a bracelet made of linked metal crests.

The face of Maria's young man had swum into Teo's mind then, and she had shivered violently, as if someone had placed a cold hand on her chest.

And that cold feeling was exactly what Teo was remembering that night in the hospital when the iron mermaid told her to 'have an eye' to the 'dafty girlie Maria'. And she was still shivering when the smell of varnish washed into the air, and the Brustolon began to emerge from under his shroud of sheets.

8. A surprising awakening

an hour before dawn, June 3rd, 1899

Teo stretched out on the mossy tomb. *The Key to the Secret City* lay heavily on top of her chest. She lifted it up. By the light of the gas-lamp, she could see that the girl on the cover appeared to be asleep.

Teo was in a vine-covered graveyard. The moon was waning and the sun beginning to warm the deep blue above her. The storm was over. She could not remember why or how she had got to this place. Shouldn't she be in a hospital bed in Venice? The last thing she could recall was the Brustolon moving and the iron mermaid shouting in the grate . . . Then – absolutely nothing. Had he . . .?

She tried to drown that question with less terrifying ones. Where was she? Was she even in Venice? Where were her parents? Her clothes were uncomfortably wet with dew, as if she had been out all night in the open. Every bit of her body was sore and stiff. Her head ached violently and her mouth was dry as feathers.

Her eyes focused on a tattered poster nailed to the lamp-post. Extraordinarily enough, the poster showed a girl who looked rather like Teo herself.

43

REWARD, it said, **LOST GIRL**.

Teo shot up straight. That picture *was* her. That was her school portrait, a photograph taken just six months ago: a rather prim picture of a good little girl.

Rising stiffly from the tomb, she pulled the poster off the lamp-post and read:

GONE MISSING
FROM THE OSPEDALE CIVILE
DURING TUESDAY'S STORM

**Teodora Stampara, 11 years old, from Naples,
with curling dark hair, green eyes, slight build,
a large bruise on her forehead. When last seen,
the girl was wearing a blue skirt, green bodice and
a white pinafore. She appears to have walked out
of her hospital room during the night of June 1st,
after sustaining a severe blow to the head.
She is in urgent need of medical attention.**

The print became smaller: **Desperately sought by her parents . . . anyone with information leading to . . .**

She felt guilty, thinking of her parents and all their worst fears made real by her disappearance. She must find them instantly!

That was easier said than done. She still had not the least idea of where she was. Nor had she any idea how long she had been missing. It had been sufficient time for someone to print some posters and put them up. How many days did that take?

'Well, it's no use staying here,' she decided, picking up the book.

That book! It was only since she'd been given *The Key to the Secret City* that her life had taken this strange turn. Given all that had happened, it did not seem excessively odd to Teo

44

to speak to the book itself, 'Tell me! What is happening to me?'

The girl on the front cover stirred and yawned, and went back to sleep.

'I suppose you'll answer when you're ready,' Teo sighed, and tucked the volume into her pinafore.

She walked a little unsteadily through the beautiful park of the graveyard, pausing at a Ladies' Convenience that was as stately as a mausoleum. She washed her face with cold water and tried unsuccessfully to rearrange her curls into some kind of discipline. She stared at her face in the mirror: strained, frightened, and a little wild in the gaslight.

'You look as if you've seen a ghost!' she said to herself.

As she walked, Teo passed more posters fixed to trees. A forest of Teodoras, all staring hard, reproached her for wandering away from the hospital.

The gardens thinned out and she found herself on the outskirts of a town. She shouted for joy to see it must be Venice – it could be no other place, not with such palaces, canals and gondolas. She had been afraid that she was somewhere else entirely. Soon she would get her bearings, and find her parents. And something to eat. Her belly was hollow with hunger.

The town was stirring, like the dawn. At every step she expected some passer-by to look at her, and recognize her as the LOST GIRL, and exclaim aloud. But none of the early-rising Venetians took the least bit of notice of her. She plucked up courage to talk to a kindly-looking lady, but the woman just pushed passed her, as if she was a beggar.

'Well, you can't blame them,' Teo conceded. The girl in the poster had her hair nicely done in plaits and sat calmly with her hands folded in her lap. Teo's hair was loose and disordered, her pinafore was filthy and she was far paler than she had looked in the photograph.

She walked deeper into town, desperately searching for a landmark she knew or a street name with which she was acquainted. The winding narrow streets remained stubbornly unfamiliar. She stopped at a mask shop that looked curiously bleached: instead of the usual colourful merchandise, the windows were stacked with plain white masks that looked faintly like skulls, apart from a single black spot, like a mole to the side of the nose.

'Why all white?' she wondered. 'So creepy!'

'You ain't niver e'en seen the half of it, child! There's bliddy doings afoot now.'

The rough female voice came from an antique shop next door. Teo peered into the gloomy window. An unusual chalice rocked on top of an old sideboard in there. It was in the shape of a porcelain mermaid holding up a scrimshawed nautilus shell. As Teo watched, the chalice filled up with a dark red liquid that brimmed and then cascaded down the edges of the nautilus. Teo backed away.

At last she came upon a narrow triangular square sign-posted 'Campo dei Mori', the square of the Moors.

'I *know* the Campo dei Mori!' Teo clapped her hands with relief. 'That's where Signor Rioba lives!'

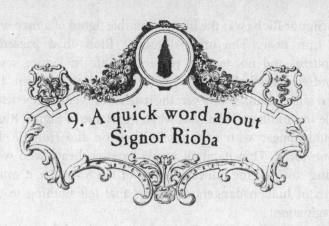

9. A quick word about Signor Rioba

Not everyone agreed with the Mayor that Venice was perfectly safe.

In the days after Teo's arrival in Venice, single pages had begun to appear all over the city, printed in an old-fashioned typeface on thick antique-looking paper that had a beautiful pearly sheen to it and a slight smell of fish, too. Teo had picked them up whenever she saw them on the tables of cafés, in gondolas, on the steam ferries – because they always made her laugh even though the contents also upset her.

The handbills warned: **'People of Venice, the bursting wells are just the beginning. Your city is in danger. Don't listen to that yellow-waimed scut of a Mayor. If he weren't so spineless I'd make soup out of his bones! You shall see more honest faces than his upon a pirate flag.'**

The handbills were signed **'Signor Rioba'**. The newspapers were full of speculations about what this could mean.

'Why,' demanded the newspapers, **'should "Signor Rioba" come to life again right now? Signor Rioba would not appear for nothing. What is going on???'**

For Signor Rioba was at once a mystery and no mystery at

47

all. Signor Rioba was the life-size marble figure of a man with an iron nose. The original Signor Rioba had passed a colourful and not terribly respectable life in Venice seven hundred years before, as a soldier and spice merchant. But ever since then, whenever the rulers of Venice needed a little reminding of what was what, the statue of Signor Rioba would appear with a handbill stuck on the front of his stone tunic. This handbill would expose cheats who were trying to trick the honest citizens of the town. Or it would warn of hidden dangers, in terms that left nothing to the imagination.

Now here he was again, louder and ruder than ever. And instead of a single sheet, his handbills were these days fluttering all over the city, literally tripping her citizens up.

Some people insisted it was none other than Signor Rioba who had caused ghostly bells to ring out from the empty towers of abandoned churches.

'No doubt about it,' declared one fisherman. 'A bell chiming without a human bell-ringer to tug on the rope – that's an absolutely cast-iron sign of evil luck! I reckon that Signor Rioba knows what he's talking about.'

'Listen to the bells!' Signor Rioba had urged, on the very day that Teo was taken ill. **'Take heed, Venetians! Lest your enemy torment the living hearts out of ye! Starting with the children. Are you all blind? Methinks the whole of Venice has fewer eyes than my esteemed rear end.'**

And now there he was! Teo had seen his picture in the papers: the stone figure was unmistakable. Teo walked across the Campo dei Mori and stood in front of Signor Rioba. For a long time she gazed at his glaring face and the great iron nose that protruded from it. Triangular in shape, it would have been formidable even if not made of iron, the kind of nose that would keep you at a distance, and cast a long shadow at lunchtime.

The stone man clearly had no very noble opinion of the world. His motionless body seemed to trap centuries of anger inside it, like a prehistoric fly caught forever in a drop of amber. Teo leant forward and daringly ran her finger down the sleeve of his short stone tunic. There was a musty smell to it. Then she put her hand on his chest.

Under her fingers she felt a distant thumping, like a stout heart beating far away. Then a drop of moisture, like a tear, trickled down his nose and onto Teo's own cheek.

'Why, Signor Rioba!' she smiled courteously. 'I am so pleased to meet you!'

And she was. His looks were tough, but something about that strapping heartbeat gave her a warm feeling towards him, as if he was an old friend.

As Teo turned to leave, the sky suddenly darkened and the air filled with an unbearable din. A dense flock of seagulls had come wheeling in from the lagoon, screaming and flapping their wings like windmills in a storm. In the clashing flurry of feathers and beaks, Teo thought she glimpsed something exceedingly strange happening in the Campo dei Mori. She could have sworn that she saw Signor Rioba shake his stone fist at the gulls. And that over their shrieks she had heard a voice of gravel and honey utter a hideous curse.

'Death and smothering upon ye, *magòghe*! May the Devil tear ye sideways, ye vile ones, servants of a viler master!'

And then the swearing *really* poured out of his stone mouth. Teo had never heard the like. But instead of words, she saw squiggles and curves dancing in the air. *Arabic?* She guessed, 'Moors are from Morocco and speak Arabic and that is what this is? Or is he from Morea, as I've read? So is that ancient Greek?' Whatever the language there was no mistaking the furious intent.

She called to Signor Rioba, 'If I had a swearing tongue as nasty as yours I'd take a soothing syrup for it, Sir!'

49

Signor Rioba's mouth snapped shut. The next moment the seagulls had gone and the little square was once more quiet as a grave.

10. A gruesome theft

break of dawn, June 3rd, 1899

Teo had been walking for what seemed like hours. Her feet burned with blisters.

The spire of a vast brick church soared above narrow streets strung across with washing lines. High over Teo's head, chemises and long-johns waved their empty sleeves and legs like a troupe of dancing ghosts in the ambiguous pre-dawn light.

Even though it was so early, the side door to the church gaped open as Teo approached it. Sounds came from inside, of stone scraping, and, oddly, some most ungodly cursing.

Wearily, Teo walked up to the door. 'I'll just sit down in there a while,' she told herself. 'Maybe the workmen can tell me how to get back to the hotel.'

Whoever was working in the church was doing so without the aid of gas-lamps or candles. The dark air smelt of mould and drains. Stumbling over the threshold, Teo held her ears against the painfully loud screech of stone-cutting. When her eyes adjusted to the gloom, she made out a scene so bizarre that she supposed she must still be in the grip of a *tisana*-flavoured dream. Instinctively, she flattened herself against the door, veiled by its shadow.

Stone gargoyles crouched in a circle around an ornate tomb like a temple embedded in the wall. Just below the pediment stood a black casket topped by a man's head in marble. Above him were grim paintings of a torture scene; below an inscription picked out in gold on slate. The gargoyles – lynxes, wolverines and lizards – were leaping up at the casket, trying to pull its heavy stone lid away. But their grainy grey bodies were far softer than the black marble, and they were all severely chipped. Sharp snouts were blunted; fragile ears were falling off all over the place.

Teo saw an old Gothic script hovering in the air. There was something familiar to it, something she must have seen in a library book perhaps?

The voice purred venomously, 'You'll pay dearly for your feebleness.'

Teo started violently then, for inside her pinafore *The Key to the Secret City* began to wriggle as if trying to get out. 'What, you can *move* too?' Teo whispered to it.

A sharp corner dug into her ribs. She suppressed a cry of pain and clamped her hand down the bib of her pinafore, hissing 'Shhhh'.

Meanwhile, the gargoyles scrabbled at the marble in a blur of paws and snouts, only to lose more of their toes and noses. Panting, they leant back against the tomb, staring fearfully into the dark recesses from which the terrible voice had come.

'Must I perform every task myself?' the voice howled with fury. 'Begone to your posts, before dawn comes and the foolish Venetians see you!'

They did not need to be told twice. Those that still had enough limbs to do so slunk away from the tomb, scampering up into the rafters of the church. They pushed themselves out through holes to their perches above the street. Those that were too mutilated lay on the ground, their little stone ribcages juddering in and out with fear.

Teo cowered in the shadow of the door. She ached with pity for the poor creatures, but she dared not rush to their aid.

The voice taunted the wounded gargoyles, 'Missing our tiny legs, are we? Shall I tend to you myself? Or shall I send my Butcher to lend you a hand?'

The gargoyles shook their heads violently, making begging motions with their poor shattered paws. One of them looked over towards Teo, and its round stone eyes widened. It opened its mouth as if to say something. Teo froze. At that moment the book in her pinafore suddenly grew unbearably heavy, like a huge stone on her chest.

'Wha-a-t . . .?' she whispered, as *The Key to the Secret City* dragged her all the way down to the floor behind a pew just as something yellowy-white and indistinct came swooping out of the back of the church. To Teo, crouching on the cold stone, it seemed like a giant albino bat, big as a man. Its head and body were furred in a dirty white pelt. It shied sharply away from the altar with a hiss, then settled on a confessional box and folded up its tent-like wings. Something green glittered on one of its talons. Teo could not see its face; just its pointed ears and head in silhouette.

At the same time another figure came stumbling out of the sacristy. It was a man in a bloodied butcher's apron. Teo covered her mouth when she realized that he was carrying his head under one arm. Both his arms ended in bleeding stumps: his hands dangled from his neck on a chain. From his torn neck came a bubbling, grunting noise, but no words. Somehow worse was the fact that his feet were attached to his body from the backs of his legs, though his thick arms swung from the front of his body. The gargoyles mewed and squeaked piteously at the sight of him.

'Thank you,' Teo whispered to the book. 'I guess you were

saving me from *that*. What if those two had seen me?'

The bat-creature growled an instruction to the headless man. He shuffled on his back-to-front feet towards the tomb. The gargoyles arranged themselves in tiers so that he could step over their backs up to the black sarcophagus. With a single blow of his handless arm, he smote the marble lid off the sarcophagus so that it dropped on the gargoyles and crushed them instantly to fragments and powder. He tumbled to the ground on top of them, landing heavily. His head rolled away into the aisle.

'Is he dead?' Teo asked herself, and the book. 'Or he was already dead?'

Then the bat-creature swooped up and dragged something fragile and leathery from the opened tomb, something that was definitely not a skeleton. It flew straight out of the church door with its prize flapping from its jaw. Outside, a flock of gulls saluted its appearance with a cacophony of shrieks.

As the creature passed over Teo she felt a violent rush of freezing air that knocked her flat in its wake. She glimpsed its face, briefly – it was almost human, with a large nose, eyes and mouth like a man's but not quite settled in their shapes. A black spot floated near the nose. The features seemed carved out of a milky jelly that had not set. The eyes were lividly rimmed with red, but smooth and blank as pure white marbles.

Teo lay trembling on the stone flags. The bat-creature did not come back. The headless man stirred, rose to his knees and crawled with unerring instinct towards his head. Soon he was busy greedily gathering the remains of the gargoyles and pushing pieces of stone into the mouth of the head he had tucked again under one arm.

Teo had never wanted her parents so badly.

11. A poor welcome

mid-morning, June 3rd, 1899

Teo could have wept with relief when she finally glimpsed the marble curve of the Rialto Bridge. The hotel was close by, and her parents, and a warm bath and food and safety, and normal life.

She half staggered, half ran the last hundred yards down the narrow alley that led to the hotel, and pounded up the steps to Reception.

The manager did not look up as Teo approached his desk. Instead, he hunched over his newspaper, and hugged himself, as if he had suddenly felt a chilly draught. Teo caught sight of her own picture on the front page. With her habitual skill at reading upside-down, she made out a headline, **'NO SIGN OF MISSING GIRL.'**

'Oh yes there is!' Teo sang out cheerfully. 'Are my parents in?'

The manager ignored her, and pulled a jacket over his shoulders.

'Are my parents not here?' Teo asked, and, 'Aren't you exceedingly warm, *Signor*?'

The man acted as if she wasn't there at all.

'I suppose not everyone likes children,' Teo said pointedly, 'but it *is* polite to answer questions. Even from children.'

The manager pulled the newspaper rudely up in front of his face, so he could not see Teo any more. **June 3rd**, it was written, at the top.

'That means,' thought Teo, 'that I've lost a whole day. Where was I?'

Teo ran up the stairs and knocked on the door of her parents' room. Her heart thrashed painfully when she heard her mother sobbing inside. Her father spoke low, comforting words.

They did not seem to hear her knock, so Teo let herself in.

'Don't worry, I'm back!' she trilled joyfully. 'Everything's fine!'

Her parents gave not the slightest sign of having heard or seen her. Teo shuddered to see that a Brustolon had appeared in their room. It glowered in a corner next to her parents' travel trunk, giving off a strong smell of varnish.

'Do close the door, Alberto,' implored her mother. 'It must have blown open in that cold draught. Where did *that* come from, in this heat?' She dabbed her face with a handkerchief.

Teo ran over to her mother and sank to her knees in front of her. She put her head in her mother's lap and wrapped her arms around her mother's knees. She rested her cheek on the warm silk of her mother's skirt. It smelt of soap, and perfume, a trace of laboratory formaldehyde and, well – *home*.

'It's all right!' Teo cried out, her voice choked up with emotion. 'You can stop crying now.'

But her mother stared blankly over Teo's head, and a new tear trickled down her face.

Teo jumped up and tugged at her father's waistcoat, 'But I'm *here*!'

His voice was stony, 'I've said it before – we should never have come. There is something not right at all about this city, and not just the water . . .' He turned on the Brustolon and gave it a heartfelt kick. The statue's expression of livid hate was already adapted for such treatment. Teo trembled, remembering the Brustolon in the hospital. But this one remained motionless. A ray of sunshine blazed over its ivory eyes for a moment, but then the sun passed behind a cloud and the Brustolon's face went blank again.

Teo's mother sobbed, 'It's the not knowing that's the worst. Whether she's dead or alive.'

'*Dead or alive?* But I'm here right in front of you!' Teo expostulated.

'And Maria's quite sure she hasn't seen our Teodora?'

'She swears she knows nothing, Alberto. Why would she lie to us?'

'Maria would lie to you as soon as look at you,' protested Teo. 'What about *me*? Look at me, Mamma!'

'If only we'd never gone into that bookshop,' Teo's father groaned.

'If only!' wept Teo, clinging to his hand, unseen.

Teo backed out of the room.

The manager had not been snubbing her. He had simply not seen her.

Teo was invisible.

How had this happened? The newspaper! Perhaps that would fill in the part of her story that she had clearly missed? She ran down to Reception. The manager had his head bent over his ledger. Behind him lay a stack of newspapers with a red banner: **'SPECIAL AFTERNOON EDITION!'**

Teo quietly lifted the top copy and made her way to

the hotel kitchen. No one shouted at her, although it was supposed to be out of bounds to children. When the chef's back was turned, she helped herself to some bread rolls and an apple. Then she ran up to her bedroom. It was untouched, all her things still on the bureau, her clothes in the armoire, her books by the bed.

She drained the stale water in her ewer, saving just a few drops to wash her hands in the basin. Then she gnawed hungrily on the rolls and bit into the apple. She threw herself on the bed and scanned the front page for news about her disappearance.

She instantly recognized the picture of the tall brick church under the headline.

'BRAGADIN'S SKIN STOLEN FROM TOMB!'

Someone, Teo read, had done something unspeakable with the tomb of the Venetian hero Marcantonio Bragadin. The great Bragadin, the paper explained, had been murdered in a particularly cruel way by the Turks after the Battle of Famagosta in 1571. They had cut off his nose and ears, and skinned him alive. Bragadin had withstood all his tortures in noble, uncomplaining silence. When he finally died, the Turks stuffed his skin with straw and paraded it through their streets. In the end, the Venetians had managed to steal their hero's body from the enemy and had laid it to rest in their Church of Santi Giovanni e Paolo. But now – such an outrage! – during the previous night, some intruder of superhuman strength had prised open Bragadin's casket and taken out the skin. As if the poor hero had not suffered enough!

The newspaper printed a copy of Signor Rioba's newest handbill:

'Venetians! Are ye all bone from the knees up like his Swineship your Mayor? What are ye thinking of? Find ye the skin of Marcantonio Bragadin if ye want to save your own! There are worse enemies than the Great Turk afoot! Remember the Butcher Biasio! The cannibal who slaughtered children and sold 'em in stew at Campo San Zan Degolà? Had his hands cut off and got beheaded between the columns of the Piazzetta, you say? But take a care for your children, Venetians – he's still got a taste for them.'

The apple fell out of Teo's hand. She shuddered – the headless man who came out of the sacristy!

The newspaper concluded, **'For all our Signor Rioba rants about Turks and Butchers – there were no witnesses to the theft of the hero's skin. The police are mystified.'**

'Yes, there was a witness!' thought Teo. 'But no one will be able to hear me tell them what happened.'

The next item was about Teo herself . . . .

'Teodora Stampara, who was suffering from suspected concussion, was last seen on the night of June 1st. A nurse found her bed empty, and signs of a struggle. Strangely, no one saw the girl leave the hospital. Posters of her have been put up around the city. Her parents and police have expressed grave fears for her safety. She may be suffering from loss of memory . . .'

Teo was indignant. 'But I'm not! I remember everything, almost. The mean nurse, the Brustolon, the doctor. And the book.'

What was it that the book had said, that it would take her, where was it? Oh yes, between-the-Linings of the city? Had she somehow got trapped between-the-Linings? And that was why no one could see her? The pain, the fever – was that what happened when you moved from one side of the Linings to another?

Yet it sounded quite comforting, 'between-the-Linings'. Teo imagined something silky and soft, herself safely tucked up inside, like a chrysalis in a cocoon. Also, if this was true, then *The Key to the Secret City* should be able to show her a way *out* of the Linings and back to the real world.

Teo pulled the book from inside her pinafore. The girl on the cover looked concerned. Teo nodded to her and opened it to the place she had been reading that night at the hospital. She addressed the page reproachfully, 'Now help me! You got me into this mess!'

Even as she spoke, the words disappeared and luminous pictures filled the creamy paper, lively as a tableau inside a shaken snow-globe.

Faces smiled and screamed from those pages. Stories unfolded like plays. The sun rose and set inside the book. Perfumed senators strutted in their red robes in San Marco. The vicious flaying of Marcantonio Bragadin happened in front of her horrified eyes. The Doges' Palace burnt and was rebuilt. Masked dancers romped at balls. The original Brustolons appeared in elegant drawing rooms. Napoleon arrived to conquer Venice; the city grew dark and subdued. The Austrians marched in. San Marco was silent. The city was under siege, with cannon balls pounding the buildings. Cholera raged through the population and the stench of death hung in the air. Funeral dirges were sung. Then the Austrians slunk out, and the city gave itself up to joy . . .

Hours later, Teo shook herself. Her neck was stiff, her leg had gone to sleep, and the sun had gone down. For a while, she had almost been able to forget her predicament.

It was immediately brought back to her.

The door handle turned and her mother's sorrowful face appeared, lit up with a faint ray of hope.

Her father's voice urged, 'No, Leonora, don't torture yourself so.'

'You're right, Alberto,' replied Teo's mother in a pathetically small voice. 'She's not here. But I could not resist checking. Don't blame me for that. Look, a maid has dropped an apple-core on the floor!' She tutted.

Teo closed the book and lay back on her bed with the warm weight resting comfortingly on her chest. She fought back the tears.

How could she make contact with her parents, and explain that she was perfectly safe, only inconveniently invisible, hopefully just for a little while?

'But am I truly perfectly safe?' Teo finally forced herself to face the hideous possibility that had haunted her all day.

The possibility that she had died.

'I died in the hospital,' she whispered aloud. 'That's why no one can see me. That's why I woke up on a tomb in a graveyard. I never thought to read what it said! Was it my name on the headstone?'

Teo remembered the funeral gondolas bearing children's coffins down the Grand Canal. The doctor had spoken of too many children sick, too many cases of fever. The little boy with the shaved head and the black swelling on his neck – what was that? Had she too fallen victim to whatever was killing the children of Venice? Or was it the Brustolon . . . he could have . . .? Had the Mayor ordered her to be buried secretly? So even her adoptive parents would not find out?

Could the Mayor of Venice be so devious? So cruel? Teo pondered the smooth face, that lustrous black croissant of a moustache. He could certainly be that *smooth*.

At the thought that her life was over, before it had really begun, Teo was overcome with grief. She let the tears roll down her cheeks and onto the pillow. Then she sat bolt upright with a scream. 'If it wasn't the Brustolon, was I killed by the Butcher Biasio? He has a taste for children! Signor Rioba said so. But how can I be dead?'

She rallied her spirits. It was better to be bewildered than dead. 'I am all in one piece, not cut up for a stew! But if I'm not dead, what am I? A kind of a living ghost?'

One of the big, ferocious seagulls cawed suddenly outside her window, in a note of triumph. No doubt it had caught itself something vulnerable.

The Key to the Secret City stirred in her hands, as if trembling. The girl on the cover put her hands together beseechingly.

12. Life as a ghost

June 4th, 1899

Teo began her new life as a living ghost.

From that first night she still slept in her hotel room. But it was simply too painful to follow her parents as they searched for her through the streets and markets, showing her photograph to everyone, earnestly asking questions, shaking hands, looking hopefully into people's eyes.

Back at the hotel, she scribbled a letter to tell them what had happened. Yet as soon as she finished the page, the writing disappeared. She carried her dresses into her parents' room and spread them on the bed. But when she returned to her own room, they were still hanging up in her armoire. She used her father's shaving brush to write a soapy message on the mirror. Her words 'Mamma! Papà! I am . . .' faded away before they had even dried.

Even as she sobbed, Teo realized that, bad as they were, things seemed much worse because her belly was hollowed out with hunger. She helped herself to a rather eccentric meal of semi-baked piecrust, raw peas and stewed pear from the hotel kitchen while the chef was busy for a moment in the meat-safe.

'My bed and board were paid in advance,' she told herself defiantly, as the chef set up a great howl about the big hole in his piecrust.

Once she had eaten, Teo went up to her bedroom and tried to think through her situation. 'There are always rules,' she reasoned. 'I just have to understand how this works.'

This much she had already understood: no one she knew could see her, or hear her. She cast no shadow. And anything she picked up, whether it was an apple or a cup of water, immediately disappeared from everyone else's sight, though Teo herself could see those things perfectly well.

After a few painful experiments, she learnt that she could *not* pass through doors or walls. Nor could she fly like an angel; she couldn't even jump down five steps at once, as a badly skinned knee proved. She could not see through other people's clothes, which was perhaps fortunate. But she still saw what they said written out in words above their heads. Using *The Key to the Secret City*, she tested all her old skills. She could still read upside-down and she could still remember whole pages of what she read, as if she had taken a photograph of the page.

'Just like when I was alive,' she thought.

And just as if she was alive, Teo still got hungry, thirsty, sleepy, hot, bothered and cross.

'It's just that I don't exist for anyone else,' she whispered to herself sadly. 'Except to make them feel a little cold. And why am I whispering? No one can hear me!'

That afternoon she set out to lose herself in Venice, to try to forget what had happened to her. And, indeed, it helped. The constant panorama of new sights soothed the pain, for whole minutes on end.

She had a guide, of course. *The Key to the Secret City* was now teaching Teo to *andar per le Fodere*, to go between-the-Linings like a real Venetian child.

Turn left here, the book told her. *Now look up ... This is the place where the pirates came ashore to steal our women ... This is the palace where the devil in the shape of a monkey made a hole in the wall ...*

There were maps that came to life when she turned the page, with all the streets glowing in sequence to show her how to get to her destination. *The Key to the Secret City* had torn pieces of paper stuck inside it too, and fingerprints from small hands. There were old faded sweet wrappings and yellowed advertisements carefully cut out of newspapers.

'At least one Venetian child's already made good use of this book,' Teo supposed. The girl on the cover smiled before lowering her eyes discreetly.

The Key to the Secret City seemed to be able to read Teo's mind. She had only to think, 'I wonder where Marco Polo lived?' and a quick secret route to the Corte del Milion would be illustrated on the page. If she felt hungry *The Key to the Secret City* showed her the way to the nearest *pasticceria*, and helpfully puffed out the delicious smell of its special cake, with a picture and a caption, so she knew what to grab and pocket.

'Not stealing,' Teo told herself when the baker scratched his head at a sudden vacancy in his oven dish, 'More like *learning.*'

But in the bakery at San Barnaba, the baker's young apprentice shouted at Teo when she lifted a hot sugared bun from his tray, 'Oi, you! Drop it!'

'You can see me!' Teo gasped.

'I see a thief,' the boy grumbled.

'Are you ... a ghost too?' asked Teo.

'And are you mad?' he retorted, reaching out to grab her arm.

The baker loomed up behind his apprentice. 'Talking to yourself again, scamp?' he boxed the boy's ears.

Teo had run away with a lesson learnt. *Children* could see

her. And they didn't seem to see any difference between her and themselves.

Another thought crossed Teo's mind. Perhaps it was only *Venetian* children who could see her? Now *that* was something she could test on Maria. And if Maria could see her, well, then Teo could ask her to explain to her parents what had happened, insofar as she *could* explain it.

Then it struck Teo that in all the time since her . . . 'accident' . . . she had never once laid eyes on Maria. What was Maria up to? Was she with the young man with the too-perfect face?

Teo sighed. Would Maria be any use, anyway? She might as well ask a pig to do algebra. 'Can't' and 'shan't' were Maria's favourite words, unless it was some little thing she could do to ingratiate herself with the fashionable crowd. Teo turned back to the book, and its comforting distractions.

All day she'd been soaking up dialect as fast as she could. She eavesdropped shamelessly. Having no one else to talk to, she spoke to herself in dialect all the time. Her trick with Latin and French was working well, and soon she found that it was relatively easy to talk and think in Venetian.

But when she helped herself to a little dictionary in a bookshop, she was put back in her place with a shock. The same fair-haired boy whom she had seen in the old bookshop at Miracoli suddenly materialized beside her. So she had not imagined him after all! He looked hard at the bulge in her pocket that marked the stolen dictionary, and muttered, 'What can you expect from a *foreigner*?'

He was as smartly dressed as before, with a different linen waistcoat, shining boots and a crisp white shirt. At least the Venetian boy did not denounce her to the storekeeper. And his reaction proved her theory – children did not see her as a ghost, but as one of them, an inferior specimen, to be sure, but nothing to remark upon.

66

Outside the bookshop she winced at the sight of another of the **LOST GIRL** posters on a lamp-post beside the canal. Her eyes slid to her reflection in the bookshop window. She was by now quite unrecognizable as the tidy little person in the posters. She looked more like an urchin that had been dragged up by wolves in a forest.

'Don't ye fret, young Teodora, yer a credit to yesself,' said a hoarse voice comfortingly. Teo turned but all there was to see was a ripple spreading in the still water of the canal.

A hot wind blew a piece of paper around her ankle. It was the latest of Signor Rioba's handbills.

Teo brought the handbill back to her room and studied it alongside the discarded newspapers she had rifled from the manager's waste basket.

Apart from the gushing wells, the ghost bells, the floods and the sharks, there was a new problem, this time with Venice's lighting. Each night, without fail, all the gas lamps in the city flickered and then slowly spluttered out. Every expert in the Veneto region had been called in, but, night after night, just after ten, the lights died and the city was plunged into blackness.

Even hand-held lanterns appeared to be affected by whatever mysterious force had extinguished the gas lamps . . . they never lasted long, and tended to fail just as people were making their way over bridges or walking near the edges of canals. From the black water came the ominous sound of loud splashing every time someone lost their footing.

The newspapers were full of it – **'CITY ON ITS KNEES!'** – without its faithful gas lamps. Even more sensational was the appearance of a ghostly light in the palace known as Ca' Dario, which enjoyed the reputation of being the most haunted house in Venice.

Ca' Dario was a gigantic hunchback of a building, lurching sharply to the right, its foundations clawing into the bank of the Grand Canal. Funnel-shaped chimneys were clustered like toadstools on the top. No one had lived there since the most recent owner had committed suicide, the last in a long string of suspicious deaths inside. No Venetian wanted to enter its grim gates, not even the city rat catcher. Not even the city rats. *The Key* had taught Teo that these vast and fearless creatures were known to the Venetians as *pantegane*.

Signor Rioba had plenty to say on the subject. **'Beware Ca' Dario! Only evil flows out of that palace. Evil. And Sickness. And Death. Oh, ye could not be counting the number of lies they're telling ye. More than the hairs on the poor flayed skin of Marcantonio Bragadin. More than the hairs up the nose of your great left-legged baboon of a Mayor.'**

The police were ordered to break down the doors and find out what was causing the strange light inside Ca' Dario. Even *they* dragged their feet, making excuses about paperwork and protocols, until the newspapers jeered at them as cowards. Eventually a squad of no less than thirty nervous policemen forced the door down. They found nothing inside, except shifting moonlight, a pile of ebony wood, a huge vat of varnish and a heap of elephant tusks.

Meanwhile the Mayor, who fancied himself as something of an old-fashioned intellectual and a poet, sent a letter to the papers.

Teo scanned the swollen paragraphs: **'The collective imagination of the town has created this phenomenon of** light in Ca' Dario . . . architectural genius . . . Each of those funnel-shaped chimneys is an oculus to draw the light of the full moon straight down inside . . .'

'What *is* he going on about?' thought Teo irritably. She'd been to see Ca' Dario glittering in the dark. 'If that's natural moonlight in Ca' Dario, then I'm a polar bear!'

The Minister for Tourism and Decorum took up the cause too: **'. . . time to bury all these ancient superstitions about Ca' Dario . . . not a place of evil . . . the city's lighthouse in our present little difficulty. Brava Ca' Dario! . . . encourage more tourists to come to Venice, just to see our splendid Ca' Dario by moonlight. And by the way, whoever's pretending to be Signor Rioba is a mischief-maker and a clown. And we're on his trail, too.'**

'*Oh really?*' Teo barked. There was something about the Mayor that made her gnash her teeth.

Another fish-scented handbill from Signor Rioba fumed: **'Take care, Venetians! Have ye all been beaten with the stupid stick, like your Mayor, who has the immortal gall to tell ye everything goes well? Which is pure, distilled Fool's Talk. Your ancient enemy is here again. And your Mayor is going messages for him. Ca' Dario is a sign. Take notice, while ye still can. Time is running out.'**

Ancient enemy? That was new.

Squinting at the lettering, Teo grew dizzy. She felt queasy and her head ached. It was hard to steal nutritious things like poached eggs or potted shrimps, which slid between her fingers and splattered on the floor, making the hotel cook swear horribly. A diet of cakes and fruit left her body as weak and disconsolate as her thoughts.

'What would my parents do to make me feel better?' It was a desolate notion. As was the answer: Teo dosed herself with Dottore Dimora's Nerve Pabulum Pills, washed down with a swig of sour spirit of Scurvy Grass from the Morelli

Pharmacy at Rialto. The only effect was to make her rather queasier than before.

By now her spirits had sagged so low that she was almost ready to welcome the sight of Maria. And in that forlorn state she made her way to Maria's room. Her knock went unheeded. She opened the door and gasped. Even though it was late at night, Maria's bed lay empty and untouched. A brown insect scurried across the floor on a hundred tiny legs.

Teo returned to her own bedroom. She stood by the window, gazing out at the black water lit only by a few wretched stars. A procession of funeral gondolas quietly slipped down the Grand Canal, each with one pathetically small coffin aboard.

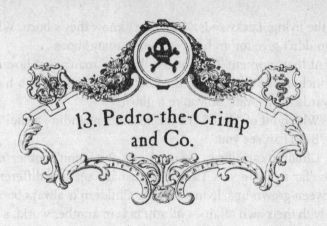

13. Pedro-the-Crimp and Co.

the morning of June 5th, 1899

It was then, as if sensing that Teo had reached her lowest point, that *The Key to the Secret City* began to introduce her to its own circle of acquaintances.

Those acquaintances were ghosts.

It started on the *traghetto*. Teo made her way unseen into the gondola that ferried people between San Samuele and Ca' Rezzonico. The sun beat down on passengers crowded together like stalks of asparagus tied in a bunch. Venetians, the book had explained to Teo, always stood up in the *traghetto*. Only tourists and foreigners lacked the sea-legs to balance as the boat crossed the Grand Canal.

'Move over!' The voice was gruff, and the nudging elbow cold as ice. Teo flinched away.

'I'm talking to yer, girlie! When Pedro-the-Crimp talks, yer listens, right?'

Teo turned to face a snaggle-toothed man in moth-eaten breeches and a velvet jacket that looked a hundred years old. His face was deeply etched with misery.

'You can see me?' she asked eagerly.

'And why not? I's dead. I's got the pleasure of watching

71

all the living. Lucky sods. They don't know they's born. What I wouldn't give for an hour in their sweaty shoes . . .'

At that moment Teo noticed that the man's feet hovered an inch above the floor of the boat. She reached out a hand towards him, 'Wait! So you're a ghost?'

'Which bit of "dead" are yer not understandin', girlie?'

'But I can see you.'

'Children can always see us ghosts. But it don't bother 'em, not s'far as I can see. They don't usually see any difference between grown-ups, living or dead. Children is always bound up with their own affairs – *all* adults is in another world, s'far as they's concerned.'

'But you can see *me*. Adults . . . just . . . can't at the moment. How is it that you can see me? Does that prove that I am a ghost?'

'Whoa there, girlie. Pedro-the-Crimp don't know what yer is. There's something missing about yer, s'true. Yer cold, but yer isn't cold *enough* . . . how did yer die?'

'I didn't die! At least I don't remember dying.'

'Doesn't even know if she died, does she?' jeered Pedro-the-Crimp. 'Is it mad yer are? Well, I can tell yer that yer's not prop'ly alive, girlie, else the grown-ups would see yer. Yer don't look much like an angel to me. Tell me what yer did, and I'll tell yer if yer is a ghost.'

'What I did?'

'What bad thing?'

'You mean to be a ghost you have to do a bad thing?'

The thin man looked shifty. 'Well, some people, the lucky ones, the simple ones, they goes straight to their reward when they dies. But some of us has a bit more . . . homework to do on earth before we can be at rest. A bit of straightening out, yer know. Now, I don't suppose yer'd like to help an old man . . .'

Teo felt uneasy. 'What bad thing did *you* do? What's a crimp?'

The man was suddenly furious. He flapped his hands, snarling, 'He killed my horse! What could Pedro-the-Crimp do? I loved that mare! Let me show you her daguerreotype . . . It's in me back pocket.'

Instead of reaching around to the seat of his trousers, Pedro-the-Crimp thrust his hand right through his body. It came back outside with a 'plop' and a faded picture of a soft-eyed dappled mare was in his fingers. She stood beside a much younger version of Pedro-the-Crimp with the Church of the Mendicanti in the background.

Pedro-the-Crimp stroked the picture with a grimy finger. 'That mare was my life,' he moaned. 'She would of brung me a cup of hot chocolate in bed if she could. My neighbour poisoned her on account of his own nag losin' a race to her on the mainland. Should that spiteful tick be allowed to live after that? Yet I's sorry for what I did. I wishes I had not. I's sorry as all-get-out, I am. I wishes I could get out of this cold . . . So now yer know, girlie . . .'

Suddenly his face contorted. He took a step towards her, his hands outstretched.

She could smell his rotten breath as she teetered on the edge of the boat and the shark-haunted water beneath.

Over the ghost's shoulder, Teo saw the other side of the canal approaching fast. When it touched the poles at Ca' Rezzonico, she leapt out ahead of all the other passengers and pounded down the narrow alley to San Barnaba, with Pedro-the-Crimp's cries ringing out behind her.

'I's sorry, girlie, I wunt hurt yer for the world, I wunt. I jest wants to get out of the cold . . .'

What a sorrowful collection of faces came to inhabit Teo's photographic memory in the next few days! She learnt to recognize that sudden chill at the back of her neck that meant a ghost was walking nearby. Like Pedro-the-Crimp, the other ghosts of Venice were sunk in their own miseries. Some, however, were curious about Teo.

'What are you? And why are *you* so sad-forlorn, girlie?' an old-lady ghost asked Teo. 'That's a bone-deep grief you're carrying.'

Some ghosts patted her hand consolingly with their chilly fingers – or paws. Teo had a feeling that they were also checking to see how cold she was. When they found her skin still faintly warm, they always jerked their hands back, confused.

Then, if they noticed the old book under her arm, they nodded at her, and gazed beseechingly, as if *she* might be able to solve whatever bitter mysteries enfolded them. Teo wished with all her heart that she could do something for these unhappy creatures, but *The Key to the Secret City* did not offer any explanation. No matter how often she asked why the ghosts were sad, or what could be done for them, the book always wrote the same reply, *This and many other things shall be revealed one day.*

It was only on the third afternoon of her ghostly existence that Teo remembered that there was someone in Venice who might know what had happened to her. She mentally kicked herself very hard indeed for not thinking of him before. The old bookseller at Miracoli – he had given her the book! He must know something about it.

She ran directly to the bookshop. By now Teo knew the streets so well that she hardly needed to consult *The Key to the Secret City* for directions. Her heart was in her mouth all the way. At last she would have answers. She would insist on them!

As she galloped through Santi Apostoli, it crossed Teo's mind that the old bookseller might not be able to see or hear her. He was an adult, after all, and alive. No, she argued with herself, he lived among magical books, and handed them out to children! But what truly sent Teo hurtling in his direction was the memory of his face. He had looked at her as if she was family, or somehow dear to him. She was in sore need of a look like that right now.

She was out of breath when she rounded the corner of Campo Santa Maria Nova. The bookshop was boarded up. Glass from its smashed windows lay glittering on the ground. Tattered books flapped feebly in the breeze. Teo picked one up. The cover was familiar – it was one of the books she had seen on the day that *The Key to the Secret City* fell on her head: *The Best Ways with Wayward Ghosts* by 'One Who Consorts with Them'. Then she scooped up *Mermaids I Have Known* by Professor Marìn.

Raising her eyes, Teo cried out with shock: there was a poster nailed up to the boarding of the ransacked shop:

FATAL INCIDENT ON THE NIGHT OF JUNE 1st.

ANYONE WHO WITNESSED THE ROBBERY AND MURDER IN THIS BOOKSHOP PLEASE CONTACT THE POLICE IMMEDIATELY. YOUR HELP COULD BE VITAL IN SOLVING THIS BRUTAL CRIME.

14. Campo San Zan Degolà

the afternoon of June 5th, 1899

June 1st: that was the very day that the kind bookseller had given Teo the book! So it was also the same night that she had disappeared from her hospital bed. Was it a coincidence that both of them should have been snatched out of the world at exactly the same moment?

Teo peered into the shop through a gap in the boards. There were red streaks – of blood? – on the floor. She could not bear to think of the frail old man being hurt. And yet he was more than hurt. He was dead.

She was suddenly aware of *The Key to the Secret City*, hard against her chest. Tucking the other books under her arm, she wrenched *The Key* out of her pinafore and flung it to the ground.

'Murderer!' she shouted at it. 'What have you done to us? Shame on you! That nice old man! And me just a child!'

And for a moment she had a childish desire to stamp on *The Key* and to rip out its pages and scatter them all over Campo Santa Maria Nova. Perhaps then she would break its spell, and come back to life, and be visible to her parents.

The book landed face-upwards on the hot stone of the

square. The girl on the cover looked surprised and hurt. She folded her arms and lowered her eyes. The book opened itself to a spread of blank white paper. New words wrote themselves across the page: *We are sorry, Teodora-of-Sad-Memory. Your burden is great.*

'But *why*?' Teo moaned. 'Why me?'

To find that out, we must hasten to Campo San Zan Degolà.

The page flicked itself over, and a map appeared, with Teo's own boots in miniature on the page. The boots started walking through the map. She was to cross the Rialto Bridge and head towards the station.

Why should she follow those little black footsteps? The bookseller was dead. She was possibly dead. *The Key to the Secret City* had something to do with both those facts. There was something else too: the name Campo San Zan Degolà rang a disturbing bell in Teo's head.

But she picked up *The Key* and began to trudge towards Rialto, first tucking *Wayward Ghosts* and *Mermaids I Have Known* into the side-pocket of her pinafore. As she passed over the Rialto Bridge, a black boat passed beneath her, stacked high with hundreds more of those sinister blank white masks with black spots by the nose.

Teo grumbled all the way to Campo San Zan Degolà.

She paused at the corner of the entrance to the desolate little square. And there was *Maria*. Maria, whom Teo had not seen in all the days since she had woken up in the graveyard, Maria whose bed lay mysteriously empty at night.

And Maria was again talking to the young man with the mole by his nose. Her teardrop earring sparkled in the sun, though her ear was red and swollen. Her fingers were busy as usual, making little touches to her perfect hair. Even so,

Teo's first instinct was to rush to the girl and throw her arms around her.

But a powerful feeling of fear swept over Teo as she looked at the young man. Like last time, there was something about him that made her feel dreadfully uneasy. Her stomach churned and a nasty taste washed into her mouth. Purple and green spots floated before her eyes. She feared that she might faint. His profile and the back of his neck were visible to her. Teo suddenly saw that the collar of his shirt did not quite hide a thick growth of white hair, a furry, dirty matting like the hide of a wild animal. Even as she watched, the fur was growing, creeping up towards his ears.

Teo panted, holding herself upright by leaning against a newspaper stand. She was concealed from view, but close enough to hear Maria chattering. At that moment *The Key to the Secret City* pushed itself open in Teo's hands. Instead of its usual white, the page was black as night. White, spidery writing crawled over it, showing in diagrams a whole new language for Teo: the language of facial moles.

In the old days, the book explained, *Venetians would buy little fake moles made of gummed velvet to stick on their faces. They were considered beauty marks. For the blackness of the mole made the Venetians' white faces look more luminous. Positioning these moles in different places was a way to send messages. Some moles were signals of love, or showed that the person was blessed with good luck. Other moles were not so fortunate. They meant 'false friend' or 'liar'.*

The last mole was one Teo recognized with a shock. *The Key to the Secret City* showed that a perfectly oval mole by the side of the nose meant – *a murderer.*

So those white masks Teo kept seeing, with the black spots, were murderers' masks! Teo flicked the page, impatient to learn more about the murderous moles and people who had them. But the paper turned white again, and a strange kind of poem started to write itself out line by line.

When flows the tide against all reason
And swells the flood all out of season
When the wells gush fountains hot and sour
And ghost bells ring in bell-less towers

When streets turn black as the armpit of Hell
And unnatural beasts in the canals do dwell
When the House of Darkness fills with light
And Signor Rioba begins to write

When someone steals a second skin
And the Butcher Biasio prowls again
From its ruins the razed palace rises
And sweet cake a bitter taste disguises

When Rats flee town on frightened paws
When the books close under Lions' claws
Come-to-life are Black Death's ancient spores
Our old Foe's once more abroad.

Where's our Studious Son? Who's our Lost Daughter,
Our Undrowned Child plucked from the water,
Who shall save us from a Traitor's tortures?
That secret's hidden in the old Bone Orchard.

The wells gushing fountains! And bells ringing in bell-less towers! That was exactly what was happening now. Signor Rioba was certainly busy writing again. The High Water was doing the opposite of what it should – flowing 'against all reason'. And the town was dark as death by night! Teo wouldn't have thought to describe it as 'the armpit of hell' – but old poems were always rather melodramatic. What could be more unnatural than the sharks in Venice? There was no doubting whose skin had been stolen. So who was 'our old Foe'? And who exactly was the Lost Daughter, the 'Undrowned Child'? Or the 'Studious Son' for that matter?

By the time Teo looked up from the poem, both Maria and the young man had vanished. She barely registered that fact.

Teo's hands prickled with pins and needles. For it was in that moment that she remembered just why she had flinched when she saw the name of this square, Campo San Zan Degolà – this was where the Butcher Biasio had kept his shop and slaughtered children for his famous stews!

'Would serve you right if I left you here,' Teo remarked to *The Key to the Secret City*, but she tucked it back in her rather crowded pinafore before running away as fast as she could.

15. The past is catching up

dawn, June 6th, 1899

Ghosts, it seemed, did not need much sleep.

On Teo's fourth morning as a living ghost she woke before dawn.

She had hidden *The Best Ways with Wayward Ghosts* and *Mermaids I have Known* in her wardrobe, but *The Key to the Secret City*, on her bureau, had opened itself in the night. Throbbing footsteps showed her that she should hurry straight down to San Marco.

By now, she'd been there many times. But this time something was different. As she approached, she saw Venetians stopping dead as they entered the square. Then they shouted in horror.

Teo stole to the front of the outraged crowd. All San Marco was decorated with a dreadful display of antique instruments of torture swinging gently from the lamp-posts, like the bodies of hanged men.

Automatically, Teo sat down on the stairs at the edge of the square and opened *The Key to the Secret City*.

These appalling tools are shameful objects from the darkest days of human history, explained the book. Then an illustrated key explained what each of the tools could do, even the horribly obvious ones like Maiming Storks, Knee Splitters, Tongue Rippers and Eye Pincers. There were Garrottes for slowly strangling people to death, Inquisitional Chairs with nails and leather straps, and Iron Maidens – grim coffins spiked on the inside to impale living people for a lingering death.

'How *disgusting*!' thought Teo. 'And surely not in *Venice*!'

The book was mute on that point.

The town had also awoken to fresh handbills festooned everywhere: jammed into letterboxes, pushed into railings, tucked into pots of red geraniums, littering the bottoms of boats. No one could avoid Signor Rioba's new messages, illustrated with crude woodcuts of a huge shark, its jaws clamped over the Rialto Bridge, which was shown in flames. Underneath were ominous sentences, **'Remember your past, Venetians, and learn from it! Do not ye listen to that hyena of a Mayor. He's not honourable enough to spit on.'**

'So when in the past did the Rialto Bridge burn?' wondered Teo. The handbill's image of the Rialto market tweaked her empty stomach. She hurried across on the Santa Sofia *traghetto*, keeping a wary eye out for Pedro-the-Crimp. She grazed at the fruit stalls, helping herself to a sunset-coloured apricot and a fistful of fat red cherries. None of the grown stall-keepers could see her, though when Teo passed, their dogs strained at their leashes, sniffing and mumbling into their little beards. And all the stallholders' children glanced at her with a single dismissive expression. It said simply, 'Thieving foreigner'.

The white hump of the Rialto Bridge drew Teo's eyes. How could a stone bridge burn? *The Key to the Secret City* stirred restlessly inside her pinafore. The girl on the cover looked like someone who was about to go to the dentist. When Teo opened up the book it showed her a date, *1310*, and the words, *the past is catching up*. A line of ink slid down the page like a long blood-red tear. Teo felt cold, in spite of the fierce June heat. A grey fin sped past her down the Grand Canal.

'Don't ye be thinking on those dogs-of-fish, but of him what summoned 'em,' squeaked a young female voice.

Teo's eyes lit on a miniature mermaid lying on her side, with her head propped up on her hand, among the *branzini*. She was no bigger than a doll.

Teo looked left and right. The fishmonger was busy with customers, his back to her. No one else had noticed the mermaid. Teo bent down to peer at her. The mermaid's hair was blonde and her eyes green. She was exquisitely beautiful. Her voice, though, was not exactly refined.

'And have ye a care to those pretty poles, girlie! Proper 'orrible, they is. Yew knows what I is talkin' about here, dontcha, Teodora? Da past is catching up! Wot a rigor-mole!' the mermaid added warningly. Then she burrowed among the fish on the stall and disappeared.

'Pretty poles'? All along the Grand Canal colourful, striped poles stood at the edge of the water. In olden days, the noblemen had kept their fleets of gondolas tied up to them. The Venetians still used the painted poles to moor their little boats. Teo glanced across at the red and white poles of Santa Sofia's *traghetto*. Then she started. She could have sworn that two of those poles twisted around in front of her eyes, as if they were completely flexible – alive, even. In the sunlight they seemed to glisten. They looked just like huge tentacles.

16. That boy again

The **LOST GIRL** posters were curling up on their lamp-posts. Teo's disappearance had been relegated to the bottom of page one, and now to inside the newspaper. Fresher horrors had claimed the headlines.

Teo sat down to read the papers at an old-fashioned café in San Giacomo dell'Orio where no one seemed to clear the tables before lunchtime. A surprisingly large number of people forgot to finish their brioches or drink half their hot chocolate. Or perhaps it was not so surprising, given what they were reading as they ate their breakfasts.

Now fishermen from Burano and Pellestrina had claimed that their boats were jostled by sea serpents in the water during their nights' trawling. The men had rushed back to shore and positively refused to go out to sea again, not until the matter had been properly investigated by the authorities.

The Mayor had been interviewed, too. A fresh photograph had been issued to the press; a new top hat had evidently been bought for the occasion.

He scoffed, **'It's not news that the fishermen saw visions – there was a regatta yesterday afternoon, and a great deal of**

84

wine was drunk. Sea serpents! More likely terrible headaches. Visitors in Venice should not worry. But they should take a lesson from our fishermen and avoid heavy drinking in the hot sunshine.'

A shadow fell across Teo's newspaper. A boy was standing behind her, impertinently reading over her shoulder. With a prickly flush, she realized that this was the fair-haired boy with the linen waistcoat, the one who had witnessed her sniffing the bookshelves at Miracoli and stealing the Venetian dictionary.

She wondered if he knew what had happened to the poor bookseller.

This time, the boy condescended to speak to her. 'Of course the Mayor's just babbling,' he remarked in a superior tone and in pure Venetian dialect. 'All he wants is to keep the tourist dollars, francs and pounds in Venice. As if we wanted any more foreigners here! The place is already groaning with the ignorant rabble. They don't know the difference between Venice Beach in California, and Venice, Italy. They turn up here just the same. Unfortunately.'

'Unff . . . fortunately?' stammered Teo. She had almost forgotten how to speak to someone who wasn't a ghost.

When he heard her accent, the boy deliberately moved backwards one step. Then he looked her up and down, taking in her lamentably scuffed shoes, her birds'-nest hair and the pinafore on which she had, as it happened, just spilt a new dribble of hot chocolate to join several older ones.

'You're from *Naples*,' he pronounced finally. 'How is it you understand our dialect?'

There was an excluding sort of emphasis on the 'our' and a disparaging one on the 'Naples'.

Teo was about to try to explain her appearance, and her reasons for needing the dictionary he'd seen her pocket. But then she understood that none of this would change the boy's disdainful attitude towards her. In fact, it was nothing personal. From her reading of *The Key to the Secret City*, Teo knew exactly why this boy felt so superior. Only that morning, *The Key* had written out a famous Venetian proverb for her: *Every time a Venetian mother gives birth, a great lord is born in this world.*

In other words, the Venetians thought themselves great lords compared with everyone else in Italy, and perhaps the world. Teo was manifestly from the South, so this boy must assume that her ragamuffin appearance and her apparent criminal tendencies were just part of the misfortune of not being born a Venetian.

But the boy was no longer looking at Teo. He had already noticed the old book in her lap. His eyes softened and gleamed.

'Renzo,' he introduced himself curtly. He did not say, 'Pleased to meet you.'

In Teo's head the boy's words were written out in a tidy script, as in a handwriting manual, with everything carefully perfect. This Renzo's writing would get ten out of ten in his school report if it had not been just a little too crammed up. Teo's mind worked rapidly. Perhaps she could make friends with this Renzo and he could talk to her parents for her? He looked a credible kind of boy, well-dressed and well-spoken.

Renzo was looking at her expectantly, so she responded. 'I'm Teodora. Well, Teo to my friends.'

'May I join you, *Teodora*?' he asked formally and pointedly. He certainly had the cold manners of a lord. Teo felt a flash of annoyance, but, on the other hand, it was interesting to meet a real Venetian, rather like having a butterfly land on your hand. She'd so longed for living human company and conversation that she could put up with a great deal more absurd snobbery than this.

He sat down opposite her, and ordered himself a hot chocolate. He didn't offer her one, which was probably a good thing, as it would have confused the waiter if Renzo had ordered a drink for an apparently empty chair.

Meanwhile, without so much as a 'please', the boy reached out and lifted the book off her lap. He took it as if it belonged to him, indeed as if all the books in the world belonged to him.

But as soon as he touched the soft leather, Renzo lost his cool demeanour, stroking it with a reverent hand. Jealousy darted through Teo like an arrow when the girl on the cover flashed a satisfied smile up at him. That smile was wasted on Renzo; he already had his nose buried deep inside the book.

'Remarkable!' he exclaimed in undisguised delight. The pictures showed themselves moving and changing just as they did for Teo.

Meanwhile it was clear that he had forgotten her existence, pawing greedily through *The Key to the Secret City*. He murmured certain dates under his breath, whispering authoritatively, 'Oh, of course! Marin Falier!' and 'So *that's* how the church looked before Napoleon knocked it down!' and 'Well, of course, 1571! Poor Marcantonio Bragadin.'

This Renzo was clearly a library-rat like herself. He was taking far too long with the book. She itched to demand it back, but she didn't want to seem too unfriendly.

Abruptly Teo said, 'You must be wondering about this hideous bruise on my head.' She blushed.

Renzo tore his eyes from the book with obvious reluctance. 'I hadn't noticed it at all. Your eyes are so green. I thought all you people from Naples had brown eyes.' It was Renzo's turn to be embarrassed and he buried his eyes back in the book, carefully raising his elbows like a fortress around it.

It wasn't nice to feel excluded from *The Key to the Secret City*. Leaning over the table, Teo used her library trick of reading upside-down, this time aloud. She read out the history of the courtyard where they were sitting.

'How did you do that?' Renzo was impressed, in spite of himself.

'That's how we read in Naples, didn't you know?' teased Teo, and she was gratified to see that Renzo took her point. He had the grace to blush. Perhaps he'd think twice about insulting her origins again.

Renzo edged *The Key* a little closer to himself.

'As if he deserved it more than me,' Teo sensed resentfully, 'young *Lord* Renzo, or whoever he thinks he is.'

'You can't take it away,' she insisted, tugging the book back out of his hands. 'You can look at it *with* me, if you want.'

Renzo's eyes travelled over Teo's dilapidated appearance once more with loud but silent disapproval.

17. Insiders and Outsiders

a fiery-hot morning, June 6th, 1899

The clock struck ten.

'Don't you have to go to school?' Teo asked the boy.

Renzo waved his hand in an airy fashion. 'I have an understanding with my teacher,' he said loftily. 'When the other children catch up with me, that's when I'll need to make an appearance.'

'I'm sure the other children love *you*,' thought Teo.

'Anyway,' continued Renzo, 'I've told him I am working on a special history project.' He glanced at *The Key to the Secret City* with a greedy eye. 'And I suppose I am now.'

Once Teo started to share the book with Renzo, things began to move in a new direction. *The Key* seemed to be working twice as hard, perhaps because Renzo was such a mine of history and so could ask much more interesting questions. And real objects appeared between its pages or dropped out of somewhere in the binding. By the end of the first day, Teo had in her pocket an ivory token dated 1785 for leaving her coat in the cloakroom at the Fenice opera house, a tiny golden mosaic tile from the Basilica of San Marco, and a long, white whisker from a Syrian cat. These ferocious striped cats, Renzo told her, had been imported into Venice centuries ago to help destroy a plague of rats.

'Where are they now?' she asked longingly. Teo adored cats but her protective parents had never allowed her one on the grounds that they were 'unhygienic' and 'uncontrollable'.

'Over the centuries the Syrian cats interbred with the local cats and became domesticated; that is, spoiled, lazy and overfed. These days, if a Venetian cat passed a *pantegana* in the street it'd just flick up its tail.'

An image of a fierce Venetian rat scuttled across the page of the book.

Everywhere they went, people waved and chatted to Renzo. Everyone had a kind word for him, a message for his mother or a warm cake to put into his hand. Renzo did not condescend to introduce her.

The adults, of course, could not see Teo. But the Venetian children saw her only too well. What they saw was a *Napoletana*. They looked at Teo out of the corners of their eyes, barely acknowledging her.

Renzo could have said to the children, 'This is Teo, my friend,' or even, 'I know she's not from round here, but she has more about her than you would suppose.' It clearly didn't occur to him. That hurt a little every time it happened. But Teo had been sneered at and snubbed by experts, that is, schoolgirls, back in Naples. She could deal with that. What hurt Teo more now was discovering something she had been missing all her life.

Until she met Renzo, Teo hadn't even known what it was to belong to a *place*. But Renzo, in contrast, clearly felt as if this city was his mother, or something very like her. He was somehow related in spirit to every other Venetian. They were a *tribe*, not merely a group of people who happened to live in the same place. For the first time in her life, Teo started to seriously wonder about where she had come from. She had never truly hungered to know about it before. Her adoptive father had offered to tell her, 'It is your right, Teodora, and intellectual curiosity is nothing to be ashamed of.' But Teo knew he was being noble, and that it would hurt him and her mother deeply if she asked about her past. '*You* are my parents,' she'd declared. 'I don't need anyone else.'

Anyway, she loved them, and was proud of them. And Naples was the only town she'd ever known.

But knowing isn't the same as belonging. Renzo *belonged*, not just to his parents, but to his city. It made him a different kind of person to herself.

'Quite apart from the fact that's he's clearly alive,' Teo pointed out to herself, 'and I may well be dead. At least he doesn't seem to feel cold around me, though.'

She knew it was ridiculous, but she felt the prickling of tears at the back of her nose after she had said goodbye to Renzo and was picking her way back to the hotel at the end of the day. Nothing could be cosier than Venice in the evenings, the deep blue sky arching over the enclosed island, with the lights of the shops all aglow, and the endless affectionate greetings of one Venetian to another, people lingering on doorsteps to exchange one last word, rocking comfortably back and forwards on the long vowels of their dialect, raising their hands above their heads in a special salute they made to one another.

Teo prowled around the town like a love-starved stray cat, pressing her nose against windows, as if looking for someone to take her in and make her their own.

All over Venice Teo roamed, hour by hour. For supper, she helped herself to strings of spaghetti and fingerfuls of ice-cream from people's dishes. She gnawed on scraps in hotel kitchens. There was only one place she gave a wide berth: Campo San Zan Degolà, home of the Butcher Biasio.

18. An appointment

an awkward breakfast, June 7th, 1899

'Same time tomorrow?' Renzo had suggested.

Teo took her place at the café with mixed feelings. Part of her looked forward to seeing Renzo again. Yesterday had whetted her appetite for company and conversation. The other part dreaded his sneers about Naples. But what she feared most of all was that Renzo had decided that putting up with a shabby *Napoletana* was too high a price to pay for spending time with *The Key to the Secret City*. And if he did not turn up, then she'd have no chance to ask him to talk to her parents for her.

Renzo strolled in ten minutes later, and sat down at the table without greeting her. He pulled the book towards him. Teo fought a desire to grab it back.

When he opened the book, all the pages stayed obstinately blank.

'Strange,' stammered Teo. 'It's never done that before.'

Renzo regarded her cynically, as if she had made the whole thing about the book up, even though he'd been a part of it for hours on end the day before. His expression said, very clearly, 'Well, what can you expect from a *Napoletana*?'

He rose gracefully from his seat and turned to leave.

From the open book on the table there came a soft, scratchy noise. Renzo leant back over the table eagerly.

Words appeared on the blank page: *From now on, your journeys shall be by night.*

'When?' asked Renzo.

'*Why?*' asked Teo.

And together, if you please.

With that last emphatic comment, the book flipped itself shut.

'I daresay it's not up to us to ask.' Renzo adopted an ironic tone. He waggled his head at Teo, in a movement that she now understood as a Venetian way of saying goodbye. He scribbled down something on the napkin. When he handed it to her, Teo saw that it was his address.

'Bring candles,' he ordered. She realized that he was anxious not to be left out, and that he did not want to have to ask her where she lived.

'See you later, I suppose,' murmured Teo uncertainly. She was not at all sure how she was going to manage night-time excursions with a boy who despised her in a shark-infested city where the wells gushed poisoned water and the lights didn't work.

As if that wasn't bad enough, Signor Rioba's latest missive, nailed to a tree, now caught her eye. She pointed, and Renzo's smile disappeared into a tightly-folded mouth. For Signor Rioba's warning seemed specifically and personally directed at them.

Teo read it aloud: **'Venetians, keep your children in by night if ye love them. The Butcher is abroad and he would find them most delicate eating.'**

All afternoon and evening, Teo dozed fitfully in the sweltering air, trying to save up energy. She left her hotel room only once, to help herself to some cheap candles and a box of matches from the manager's storeroom.

As soon as it grew dark, which took, agonizingly, until ten p.m., Teo quietly let herself out of her room and down the stairs. She paused in an archway and opened *The Key to the Secret City*. The full moon illuminated the page that swiftly showed her the way to Renzo's house, a small, neat place in the back streets of San Stae.

Renzo was waiting at his window. He climbed out onto the sill and deftly slid down a thick old wisteria vine in the courtyard. It was clearly not the first time he'd used that vine instead of the stairs.

'Ciao, *Napoletana*,' he murmured casually, as if late-night rambling was something he did all the time. He carried a pair of small lanterns, into which the children slotted the candles that Teo had pocketed.

They swung their lanterns as they walked down the empty streets, making swollen shadows on the crumbling walls. They tried to laugh, pretending to see bears and wolves in those shadows. The one thing they never mentioned was the Butcher Biasio, though their darting eyes made it obvious that they were thinking about him.

Renzo lamented, 'Look at this place – deserted! Everyone's afraid and shut up in their houses. Venice is dying.'

Teo wanted to cheer him up. 'But Renzo, Venice is still famous. Everyone loves her.'

Renzo had bristled up like an angry cat. 'Forget it,' he snapped rudely. 'You wouldn't understand, *Napoletana*. What *this* city once was – your Naples didn't even have it to lose.'

Then he turned on her, pointing with a shaking finger. '*You* should not have that book. You don't have a drop of

94

Venetian blood inside you. What makes you think you're entitled to it?'

'So *that's* what is bothering you, is it?' Teo's own voice was suddenly sharp. Renzo dropped his eyes, embarrassed at last.

Teo was too stung to tell him the truth, that she had been adopted, and that she could be from anywhere, not necessarily the Naples he despised. He probably assumed she lived on pizza! (Naples was the birthplace and headquarters of pizza. Yet Teo was that rarity – a girl from Naples who hated pizza.) Having seen her steal the dictionary, Renzo probably assumed that she was just some Naples guttersnipe who had pilfered *The Key to the Secret City* too.

Now the book itself rustled and fell open in her hands. Teo directed the light of her lantern onto the page that was offered, which showed a sepia photograph of a pair of children standing solemnly side by side for the camera. The boy had his arm around the girl's shoulder in a comradely, protective sort of way.

'How extraordinary!' she exclaimed. The children's faces were just like hers and Renzo's, even though the photograph was old and grainy, and the fashions were from fifty years before, from the very dawn of photography. Behind the sepia children were the Campanile and the Basilica of San Marco.

'The book's trying to tell us to be kind to one another . . .' She hardly dared say the words aloud.

'How peculiar,' declared Renzo. 'The book makes it look as if you were in Venice before,' he laughed uncertainly. 'Not very likely, is it?'

He did not, of course, deign to apologize. But he gave her a lordly smile, and Teo had to make do with that.

95

They walked gingerly, feeling their way along the railings of bridges. After a while, it became clear, to their relief, that they could trust *The Key* to steer them safely away from the dangerous gushing wells. But there was no way of avoiding the canals, except by extreme caution.

They paused from time to time to relight the candles in their own lanterns. Like the town's gas-lamps, the candles guttered frequently for no apparent reason. Outside their uncertain circles of light, the blackness was solid, except when they passed Ca' Dario. The haunted palace was as ever bathed in a harsh white luminosity, which made it appear as a vast frame of stone with a cage of cold glass hanging inside it. As they watched, a gondola arrived stacked with elephant tusks. Silent black figures opened the water gates and dragged the tusks indoors.

'Look at that!' breathed Renzo. 'It's supposed to be uninhabited.'

Yet white steam poured out of Ca' Dario's chimneys into the black sky. When the children stood in the Campiello Barbaro, gazing up at the palace's tall windows, they heard a rhythmic thumping and intermittent sawing. There was a strong scent of something that definitely resembled furniture varnish, overlaid by a smell of sawdust.

On the Grand Canal outside, a whole flotilla of gondolas passed, each bearing yet another little coffin. Teo gasped – at least twenty dead children tonight.

'What is it?' Renzo asked impatiently. She pointed to the grim procession.

'Worst-kept secret in Venice,' barked Renzo. 'At school there are empty places in every classroom. Let's get away from here.'

A heavy dew had fallen and the streets were slippery. Teo walked only on the grey stones, avoiding the stripes of white marble that decorated every pavement in elegant patterns, even in the humblest quarters of Venice.

'How do you know to do that?' asked Renzo suspiciously.

'To do what?'

'Avoid the Istrian marble?'

'You mean the white stone? My feet just do it automatically. Why?'

'It's one of our private Venetian things, to know that the Istrian marble is more slippery than the granite when it's humid.'

Teo shrugged. 'Had you considered the possibility that there might also be the odd fragment of marble in Naples? The city has *some* history, you know.'

Renzo was adamant, 'Not *Istrian* marble.'

Teo gave up. It was true, she had been bluffing. She didn't actually understand how she knew to avoid the slippery stones.

The book was leading them towards one of the quietest parts of the city, on the northern fringes, a long way from San Marco and Rialto. They crossed the Fondamenta della Misericordia, turned right into the Campiello Treviani, then passed over the bridge to the Calle Vechia and under a crumbling archway made of bricks and holes – mostly holes.

Teo exclaimed with surprise. Through the archway, the labyrinth of Venetian streets suddenly opened up into a breathtaking panorama of a high sky, islands, stars and sea. On their right a basin of water bobbed with little boats. Beyond it lay the lagoon. On their left, a tall, achingly lonely building jutted out into the waves. To its rear loomed a line of five black cypress trees, stretching up like huge goose feathers into the midnight blue sky. The vast garden was entirely walled in. Teo had not seen a garden of that size anywhere in Venice before.

'This is the Sacca della Misericordia,' Renzo whispered in an awed voice. 'I believe the book is taking us to the House of the Spirits!'

As if in agreement, the great bell of the Church of Madonna dell' Orto suddenly and very emphatically struck midnight.

19. The House of the Spirits

midnight, June 7th, 1899

'House of the Spirits, what's that?'

As she uttered the words, Teo's tongue stretched out along them and she wanted to repeat them over and over again. She was quite sure she'd never seen it before. Yet she felt that odd sense of familiarity again, an emptiness in her stomach and a fullness near her heart.

Renzo drew himself up for another of his history lessons. 'It was originally part of a noble palace, the Contarini del Zaffo. Sixteenth century. The House of the Spirits was a kind of Pleasure Pavilion. Built at the end of the garden. It was supposed to be for parties and entertainments, and other more secret things.'

'Secret things?'

'People met there to discuss unconventional or magical ideas. Especially during the Inquisition, when the laws on free speech were terribly tight. A band of intellectuals called the Academy of the *Incogniti*, the Unknowns, held their illicit meetings there. Even our famous artist Titian and his poet friend Aretino . . .'

Renzo paused to explain these two geniuses but Teo

98

interrupted, 'I know perfectly well who they are. And *Pietro Aretino*, by the way, fled here from Rome *in 1527*. He wasn't *born* Venetian.'

She resisted the temptation to say 'So there!' and stamp her foot. It was time Renzo understood that she also knew what the inside of a library looked like.

Renzo whistled under his breath and continued, 'Now it's a place for old nuns who've spent their lives looking after the poor, handicapped, and deformed. They pass their last days here, in the House of the Spirits, on the edge of the lagoon.'

'A lovely reward for them,' reflected Teo. 'The place is so beautiful.'

'But other people say it is haunted. Because there's a wind that whistles through the house like a banshee at certain times. It's also said that the garden of the House of the Spirits has a strange echo, and that people talking or singing in there can be heard all over Venice. Listen!'

When Renzo stopped speaking, Teo heard something that made her want to run away. It was a great chorus of whispering – hundreds of distinct voices, all pleading and calling at once. Most of them were men, many were gruff, and others tearful; still more, threatening. To Teo, the voices appeared in a jumble of antique scripts, some from the fifteenth century, some from the eighteenth and everything in between.

'That doesn't sound much like nuns,' she observed dubiously. It didn't sound like anyone she'd be pleased to meet on a dark night.

'If it's not the nuns . . .?' Renzo's voice rose uncertainly.

As they moved a few steps in the direction of the noise, a sudden drop in the temperature confirmed it for Teo – the garden of the House of the Spirits was indeed full of ghosts. The book flew out of Teo's hands and landed on the parapet of a bridge, where it spread itself open in a shaft of moonlight. The children ran up, half eager, half afraid.

The Key to the Secret City immediately began to tell the stories of those voices crying out from the garden. There were murderers and misers; a wretch who'd set fire to an enemy's house, only to burn down his whole street. It gave Teo a terrible pang to see among them children who'd wilfully caused their parents unbearable grief by running away from home. Each face appeared briefly and confessed its sins, begging for forgiveness. Then it faded away and another pitiful face formed on the page.

'We have to go in *there*?' asked Teo. 'With *them*? Is the Butcher in there?'

No! wrote *The Key to the Secret City*, *Biasio is presently with his Master*.

Now it had got them thoroughly terrified, *The Key to the Secret City* traced a little map. The footprints of two children, unmistakably Teo's and Renzo's, being marked 'T' and 'R', marched alongside the tall, narrow sea-wall of the House of the Spirits. On the other side lay the lagoon – the home of large and hungry sharks.

'How can we do that?' exclaimed Teo.

Renzo studied the wall. 'There's some kind of ledge near the bottom, like a skirting-board.'

'Never in a hundred years!' protested Teo. 'It's narrower than our feet!'

The voices in the garden rose up in a mighty yowl.

'Well, if you're too frightened . . .' challenged Renzo, 'I'll go by myself.'

He set the ring of his lantern between his teeth and started to climb from the street to the corner where the ledge began. He immediately lost his footing, and had to swing for the mast of a nearby boat. He slid down into the boat, tumbling onto his back, his face as white as a pillowcase. He mumbled, 'Not going to work.'

'But that's *exactly* the way to do it,' cried Teo. 'Climb from boat to boat, until we get to the water gate. Unless, of course, you're afraid of tearing your smart clothes.'

She tucked the book into her bodice, hitched up her skirt, hung her lantern over her elbow and set about scrambling down into the first boat.

Six boats along they reached a tall gate fashioned from great loops of black iron. Grabbing a convenient drainpipe, it was possible to lever themselves from the last boat to the wall, and then it was easy to gain a foothold in the ornate ironwork of the gate. In moments the children had scaled the gate and dropped down below into the garden of the House of the Spirits. Where they straightaway tripped over the low inner wall and fell flat on their faces, all tangled up in each other, and in what seemed to be a rosemary bush – from the medicinal smell that arose from its needling crushed leaves. Their lanterns were extinguished in the fall. They had landed on the edge of a path paved with tiny chips of pale gravel, pieces of which had stuck to their faces, that, in the moonlight, looked as if they were covered in carbuncles.

Teo and Renzo scrambled to their feet and cautiously stepped out onto the path. They shivered. The air in the garden was freezing, as if it was midwinter inside those walls, while outside them the summer night held Venice in thick, hot blackness.

The ghosts did not appear, nor did they utter a single moan. Yet both children felt distinctly that they were under the minutest observation.

A terracotta-coloured palace stood on their left. On their right, projecting out into the lagoon, stood the creamy House of the Spirits, looking more like a dream of a building than a real one, its arched windows reflecting the moon and clouds scudding across the sky. The path leading to it was bordered by the sea wall which, strangely, had windows through which they could see the boats, the houses and rooftops of Venice and real life, ordinary life, insofar as life in Venice could be called ordinary at the moment. On the other side of the path stretched the garden, shimmering with ghostly outlines of clipped trees, statues and vines.

The candles in their lanterns flickered back into life. The children raised them to look around. It was so beautifully neat, more of a giant, living chess set than a garden where children might play. And such a scent rose from it in the dark – of herbs and cut grass and . . . and on top of all these things Teo breathed in a powerful whiff of salty-sweet perfume like that of *The Key to the Secret City*.

It took a good pair of ears to hear it, but suddenly there was a slight noise of snapping stalks of grass. Teo, her skin prickling, saw that Renzo's face had grown taut with fear. The imprints of dozens of feet appeared on the immaculate lawn. All those empty footprints were moving in their direction.

Suddenly, wispy faces and ragged bodies appeared luminous against the darkness, all hovering a few inches above the ground. The clamour of ghostly voices filled the garden again. It seemed as if the ghosts had simply paused for a long, long intake of breath, all the better to howl louder.

'Help me!' and 'For the love of all that's good, save my soul!' cried an old woman in an apron. 'Please tell me all is not lost, please, kind children. You *look* kind . . . I am sure that you *are* kind . . . especially after what you've been through, little girl. And what you have witnessed.' This, from a man in prison pyjamas.

'*What* have you been through, Teo?' asked Renzo suspiciously. 'What have you seen?'

'Can't imagine what they're talking about,' Teo lied.

'Tell us that Venice forgives us!' pleaded a child's voice by her ear. Teo spun around. A little runaway boy hovered there, his hands clasped together beseechingly.

'We would,' said Renzo in a tremulous but sympathetic voice. 'We would, if we could, but we're just ordinary children.'

'*If only*,' thought Teo.

There was a long chorus of heartbroken groans from the ghosts. The children stood silently, not wanting to disturb such terrible grief, not knowing what to do next.

Now a new voice could be heard above the others. It was a rough, girlish voice, and it was singing. The book inside Teo's pinafore lurched, pulling her in the direction of the song.

At the same moment, the children's lanterns went out with a conclusive little fizzle. Pulses of fear ran up and down Teo's spine. She clutched for Renzo's hand, to find his blindly groping around for hers. Discarding the useless lanterns, Teo and Renzo stumbled hand-in-hand towards the place from which the singing seemed to come. Four tall slender columns appeared in the gloom, then an arched doorway.

'Where are they going?' cried the desolate voices of the ghosts. 'Oh, don't leave us, never leave us!'

It was as if the voices had fingers, and that they pulled at Teo's shoulders and feet. She was so sorry for them, but the power of their misery terrified her, and she was afraid, more than anything, that they would claim her for their own.

'Put your hands over your ears,' whispered Renzo.

The keening of the ghosts grew dimmer when she did that, but she could not quite block out their cries. The last thing she heard was, 'No, do not go down there, never down the-e-e-re . . . stay with us . . .'

Teo and Renzo shuffled into an old chapel, covered with dim frescoes of a stormy, foggy sea, which were illuminated by the moon reflected in the water. For although the garden outside was perfectly dry, inside the chapel the floor was covered with water and seaweed that wrapped around their feet and threatened to trip them up at every step. *The Key to the Secret City* started to vibrate wildly in Teo's bodice until she exclaimed, 'I was definitely planning to open you sometime very soon.'

As soon as she did so, a great silver key jumped out. Teo, clumsy as ever, missed it. Dappled moonlight lit up the key as it arched and dropped into the water, to be immediately hidden among the dense seaweeds. Renzo sighed.

Teo thrust the book back into the top of her bodice. The children knelt down in the water, combing their fingers through the soft fronds, trying to find the key. All the while the singing voice grew more and more urgent. The strangest thing was that it seemed to be rising up from underneath them. Eventually Teo's hand closed around the key, just as pain tore through her knee. She cried out, feeling her skin open up in a deep cut. The moon must have emerged from behind a cloud, for suddenly the chapel became clear as day and the water grew transparent.

Teo could see her own blood wafting out around the dark green seaweed. She had shuffled straight onto the sharp hinge of a great lock.

'Blood,' she thought in a daze of pain and shock. 'Do ghosts bleed?'

Renzo and Teo saw a beautifully carved door shimmering beneath the shallow water, placed flat in the floor, as if it opened straight down into the sea. Teo pushed the key into the lock and pulled at the door with all her might. It gave a little, just enough to let her know that it might possibly open.

Renzo had put his hand on her shoulder. She could feel him trembling. Clearly, he shared her own fear, that they would be sucked into some kind of deep pool below the lagoon. If even the ghosts were afraid of what was down there . . .

'I'm not . . .' Renzo struggled to admit it, 'not really a good swimmer. You see, we don't always learn to swim in Venice.

It's an old superstition we have here: "what the sea wants, the sea will have . . ."'

'Don't worry, I am.' Teo was a surprisingly good swimmer, happily in her element and graceful as a ballerina under water. Her adoptive mother sometimes called her 'my water-baby'.

Renzo intoned, 'A drowning man should not be helped, for the sea will only claim another victim in his place. It is considered by some scholars that this belief dates back to pagan times, when the gods of the sea had to be appeased by occasional human sacrifice . . .'

'What nonsense!' Teo said briskly. 'Now, we need to pull this door up together.'

Embarrassed, Renzo knelt down in the water beside her and took hold of the other half of the handle. Teo held her breath, closed her eyes, and wrenched. She waited for the big wave, the swell of cold water, the blackness pulling them down.

When she opened her eyes, instead of darkness and sea there was light and music and a dry stone staircase that descended steeply to what distant echoes told her was a vast chamber far below. The walls of the staircase were covered in frescoes of underwater scenes and lit up with candles on sconces made of scallop shells that had been dipped in gold. The perfumed salt smell wafted around them, as did snatches of song, both stronger than ever. There was no doubt that they were coming from wherever the stairs ended, somewhere deep below the garden of the House of the Spirits. The children hesitated at the top stair.

'Renzo!' urged Teo. 'We've come this far . . .'

The stairs wound down and down. The frescoes were replaced by gilded shields, each showing a mortar-and-pestle, and the scallop sconces by exquisite candelabra decorated with all kinds of sea creatures made from glass, glittering in the light and tinkling slightly as the children passed. Teo's injured knee throbbed with every step, and the blood straggled down her leg. The smell of perfumed salt had given way to something else, something warm and spicy, something that didn't really seem at all possible.

'Can you smell . . . *curry*?' asked Renzo.

'Well, something very like it.'

'What do you think it is?'

'Well, it's definitely not a curry house, not down here.'

'Seriously, do you think *The Key* would take us anywhere dangerous?'

'Everywhere is dangerous in Venice now.'

'That's a comfort. Thank you for that. Oh, can you hear something?'

A thumping noise grew louder and louder as they descended.

Finally, the roof gaped open into a great archway, from which they could see a larger space blazing with light.

At the bottom of the steps was a broad stone balcony that rimmed a vast pool, which resembled a Turkish bath. It was tiled all over with tiny gold mosaics like the Basilica of San Marco. Arches opened in all directions to more golden caverns and canals. The golden walls were lined with airy shelves hung with garlands of flowering seaweed thick with pearls. Above the garlands, in neat rows, glittered hundreds of golden mortars-and-pestles. The cavern was lit by enormously thick and tall candles dripping white wax tears, which every few seconds floated away as discs of light in the still, clear water.

The chamber was not empty. It was full of clattering life and song. Rainbow-coloured parrots squawked in gilded cages. And someone was exceedingly busy down there.

Those someones were mermaids.

20. Blood for breakfast

just past midnight, June 8th, 1899

Teo had heard the words 'coral lips' many times. Now, for the first time, she understood that such a description could actually be true. The lips of all the mermaids were a most exquisite moist red, and completely smooth, just like coral. The mermaids' sea-green eyes slanted slightly upwards, fringed by luxuriant lashes. When they looked down, their eyelids resembled white cowrie shells. Their long curly hair was fluffy and tousled. Each wore a single gold earring in her left ear, like a sailor. None looked more than sixteen years old.

Teo and Renzo cowered in the darkness of the stairs, too dazed to exchange even a whisper. Renzo gaped at the lovely creatures with a mixture of fear and admiration. Teo noted with approval that these mermaids showed no sign at all of sitting around gazing at themselves in mirrors like the mermaids in children's stories. Instead, they were all busy with a complicated, highly technical task that was extremely familiar to Teo.

The mermaids were *printing*.

Different mermaids worked in teams to perform all the

functions of the press. But this was not printing as Gutenberg once did it, nor printing like Teo had done in her classroom at school. No, this was a different manner of printing entirely.

Some mermaids were halving oysters and flicking out the pearls. Others were grinding those pearls in mortars-and-pestles. Some were making paper, pressing down moulds on the pulp of pearls crushed together with silky white seaweed. More carried the damp, newborn paper to the drying racks arranged over neat little fires; then others ferried dried sheets to the printing press, which had its own little island in the middle of the submerged cavern. The printing press itself was a beautiful device, more like a giant jewel box than a machine. It was studded with carved oyster shells and pearls. The levers were the bleached bones of some vast ancient sea creature.

And the ink? Teo heard a splashing noise and turned around to see the ink being gently tickled from squid by some mermaids wearing black-splotched aprons, using gloved hands inside a tank. After their ink was milked, the mermaids released the soft, fleshy squid back into the water of the cavern. The squid swam away fast, looking over their pink shoulders rather anxiously, but unhurt.

The printing press swooped down on the paper, and sent out large sheets that were laid on a table where yet more mermaids deftly cut them up into small squares, using scalpels made of sharpened stems of coral. Other mermaids stacked the squares into bundles and tied them with twine made of dried seaweed tendrils. The bundles were loaded onto miniature rafts.

The mermaids sang as they worked, those same jaunty sea shanties that Teo had been hearing for days. And the parrots squawked along too, cheerfully out of tune and full of gusto. There was an atmosphere of intense urgency throughout the whole extraordinary operation.

Renzo shook his head slightly, as if there was something in his ear. He looked at Teo for a moment, and tried to open his mouth, but his eyes were instantly drawn back to the scene in the cavern.

Some mermaids called out instructions to each other, using a strange sort of language, which sounded as if it came from some old sailor's locker. 'Rouse out, rouse out, rouse out. Lash and carry, lash and carry, show a leg!' they shouted.

'Show a leg!' screeched the parrots.

This last was particularly odd, as the mermaids had not a leg between them. Their language was not always easy to understand, but it was very pleasing to listen to; a kind of rude poetry.

'If you love me, move your dome,' one called, when she wanted her companion to bend her head in order to avoid collision with a spoke of the press.

Teo saw those words written in a fine, free handwriting, in deep blue ink.

One of the sheets flew off the press and on to the floor near Teo. She bent down to pick it up, and handed it to the transfixed Renzo without a word. It looked familiar. And it smelt of fish! Angry warnings filled the page. **'Venetians, watch that Mayor of yours. Something's come over him like a pig falling from the sky. Remember the Butcher Biasio and the skin of Marcantonio Bragadin!'**

Suddenly everything became remarkably clear. The mermaids were Signor Rioba!

All this while the mermaids had shown no sign of having noticed their visitors. Renzo and Teo stood in the shadows of the great chamber, their hearts thumping like the press itself, not knowing whether they would be welcome visitors or if they had stumbled in on a secret that could cost them their lives.

They did not need to wonder long. Teo's clumsiness betrayed them. Signor Rioba's sheet slipped from her shaking hand and sailed out of their hiding place, coming to rest on the head of a mermaid who was sweeping small torn pieces of paper into a vast clamshell. She turned and pointed to the children, her finger quivering in the air like an arrow. A little cry escaped from her lips, but nothing more.

One by one, the mermaids noticed the intruders, and each stopped short in her task. In seconds, the printing press had ground to a halt, and hundreds of mermaids were erect, still and silent, each clutching the tools of her particular trade, and staring at Teo and Renzo.

'Human children!' gasped one of the mermaids. 'Blood for breakfast!'

The parrots echoed happily, 'Blood for breakfast, blood for breakfast, blood for . . .'

'Avast heaving, there!' shouted the mermaid's colleague, who was still too busy counting sheets of paper to look up. This seemed to mean, 'Stop teasing me!'

A third mermaid, who had also caught sight of the children, insisted, 'My gib was atwitch, I might of knowed it. Human childer smell most peculiar, I do declare freely.'

The other mermaids immediately chipped in to declare that their gibs – noses, it seemed – had also detected something odd. 'But I dint like to air it, ye know.'

'And now dey have crippen up upon us, bless my owld soul!'

Renzo and Teo felt exceedingly uncomfortable. So many pairs of wide green eyes fixed on them, with so much commentary and without a great deal of approval.

But then the atmosphere changed dramatically, and much for the better.

'You have come, Children,' said a low, graceful voice. 'At Last.'

Teo recognized the owner of that voice at once – for she had the same face as the beautiful, sad girl on the cover of *The Key to the Secret City*.

'It's you!' she gasped.

'Yes, indeed, You are most welcome, Teodora & Lorenzo,' purred the mermaid, who sat on a half-submerged throne. They had not noticed her before because she had been quite still while the other mermaids were a blur of activity. Her azure tail was mostly underwater, its shimmering scales visible in the candlelight.

There was a hubbub among the other mermaids. Amidst their chattering, Teo thought someone exclaimed, 'Avast! 'Tis Teodora! 'Tis the Undrowned Child!'

The Undrowned Child? Where had Teo heard that before?

There was a general splashing as one mermaid rushed forward to lay her hands on Teo's feet, shouting, 'Gangway! Let me touch her for luck!'

'Let me! I saw her first!' clamoured another. 'Who'd a thunk the little maid would look so natural?'

'D'ye think she could do the Hopscotch for us? D'ye have a notion of how the Hopscotch works, Undrowned Child?'

Renzo took a step backwards as the mermaids stroked and groomed as much of Teo as they could get their hands on.

'Now, Pretty Ladies!' reproved the mermaid on the throne. She calmed them with words that seemed familiar, but in unusual combinations. The lettering Teo saw when this mermaid spoke was elegant and quaintly old-fashioned, using the symbol '&' for 'and' in the way of old books she had seen in the library.

The mermaid smiled at Teo. 'I am Lussa. This,' she gestured at the gilded cavern, 'is my Queendom. And these Pretty Ladies,' she pointed to the assembled mermaids, 'are my Subjects.'

Teo noticed that only Lussa among the mermaids spoke with capital letters at the beginnings of her words. It must be a royal prerogative, she guessed.

Lussa added sympathetically, 'My Speech is Strange to You? My Race learnt to speak in Humantongue by eavesdropping upon Sailors who came to these Waters from the Indies & Beyond. I fear this Primitive Education has left its Mark: We oftimes speak as Rough as Guts. Your Shore Parlance is indubitably Difficult for Us, too. About the Hopscotch, 'Tis a Mythical Pursuit among Us. The Ladies are a little Infatuated with the Notion of It, being a Game We ourselves shall never be able to play.' Lussa pointed to her tail.

The mermaid motioned for the children to approach her along the walkway that ran along the edge of the cavern's pool. A pair of carved chairs was placed behind them by two younger mermaids wearing maids' caps and aprons on the top halves of their bodies.

Their mistress bestowed a benevolent look on the stupefied children. 'Teodora, I see You have sustained an Injury. We cannot have our Lost Daughter under-the-Weather!'

'Lost Daughter?' thought Teo vaguely. 'That definitely reminds me of . . . '

Lussa pulled on a long velvet cord hanging from the roof of the cavern, her coral nails flashing like rubies. A red-haired mermaid in a butler's outfit bustled into view. Lussa whispered something in her ear, adding, 'Roundly, Chissa!' A few moments later, the butler-mermaid reappeared with a roll of soft, dried seaweed and an ointment that smelt strongly of . . . *curry* as she squeezed it out of a little leather bag.

'Fermented Chilli Jelly, that purifies the Blood & Heals,' explained Lussa in a soothing voice. 'Those Sailors who taught us Humantongue also brought Us a Taste for piquant Eastern Spices. We use Them in all our Food & Medicines.'

Chissa rubbed a wobbling fingerful gently into the cut on

Teo's leg and then wrapped the seaweed bandage around it, fastening it with a little spike of coral. Teo's knee felt as if a cosy fire had been lit inside it. The pain vanished.

'Why are you printing?'

Of all the questions that Teo needed to ask, this seemed one of the least important. But it was the first one that made its way out of her mouth. Renzo remained in a state of silenced shock.

'You are a Child with both Oars in the Water,' observed Lussa approvingly. It seemed that Teo had asked the right question after all.

'We have recourse to the Seldom Seen Press & Signor Rioba when Venice is in Danger.'

'Why "Seldom Seen"?'

'We are named So because the Press & its Servants are seldom seen by Humanfolk.'

As Lussa spoke, the other mermaids had gradually drawn closer. Hundreds of slanted sea-green eyes were fixed upon Teo and Renzo.

'Pray forgive the Staring. Some of my Younger Sisters have never seen a Human before, Humanfolk not being in general much Use to Us in the Sore Matter of protecting this City.'

'Not much use?' asked Teo.

'No more Use than a Feather Anchor. Only rarely do We summon Humanfolk to help Us. But this is One of those Dread Times.'

Teo wondered if Lussa would now say 'my Hearties'. She did not. 'For many Days I have sought to summon You here. That was our Singing that You heard upon the Streets, Teodora. Those Mermaids of Wax & Carrot & Glass & Tin – They too were My Messengers. In the End I drew You to Me by the Book. I must confess that 'Twas I who caused the Volume to fall upon your Poor Head in the Shop of Books,

Teodora. 'Twas also I who lured You to the Shelves with the Many-Scented Stories.'

'Which included *Mermaids I Have Known* by Professor Marìn,' recalled Teo. 'Did the bookseller know something about this, then? He kept staring at me, as if he knew me, or recognized me from somewhere.'

'He is no Stranger to the Saving of Venice, our Friend the Good Bookseller—' there was a warm affection in Lussa's voice '—otherwise known as Professor Marìn.'

'So he actually *wrote* the book about mermaids?' Teo asked, remembering the mortar-and-pestle on the shop counter instead of a till. 'Do you know . . .?'

'About the Ransacked Shop? The Talk of Murder? Yar, Indeed,' Lussa spoke comfortably, 'but Teodora, You shall soon learn that Everything in Venice is not always what It seems. Nor is Everyone always quite Who They say.'

Amid all her bewilderment, a new feeling was now creeping into Teo's heart, a strangely pleasant one. There was no denying it, she felt enormously flattered that she'd been sought out by the mermaids – she, Teo, who was always picked last for every game at school, who was largely ignored by everyone except her parents and the school librarian. And treated as an inferior being by Renzo.

Surely Renzo must be just a little impressed that the mermaids had picked Teo, too?

Renzo cleared his throat sulkily. All this attention to Teo was clearly making him feel somewhat surplus to requirements. Lussa threw him an understanding look, saying. '*The Key to the Secret City* had a Double Purpose. You see We had our Eye upon Young Lorenzo as well, and knew that such a Book would serve as Irresistible Bait to reel Him in.'

'What mission?' demanded Renzo, visibly more pleased.

Lussa immediately looked serious again, almost grown-up. 'I am most Sorry to tell you, Children, that there is a *Creature . . .*'

Teo felt sticky and faint. Lussa was still talking in serious tones: '. . . Yar, our City is threatened by a Creature that lurks Beneath, a Creature thousands of Years older than the Lagoon itself. 'Tis this Creature who presently heats the Waters . . .'

'Causing the old wells to blow up into geysers?' quavered Teo.

'And sending the High Water into the wrong places?' Renzo's doubtful face showed that he too was struggling to believe what he was hearing.

But now, with the living book, the mermaids in front of them, the garden full of wretched ghosts upstairs, the strange happenings in Venice . . . but above all seeing the distress on Lussa's beautiful face – Teo felt a cold certainty spreading through her that anything was possible at this moment; particularly terrible things.

'How big is the . . . Creature?' asked Teo self-consciously.

''Tis hard to convey how Big the Creature is. Let us say that 'Tis at the same time Tinier than Anything You could see with your Naked Eyes, but also Vaster than Venice Herself. You could try to envision It as a Cancerous Tumour that spreads its Web of Unwholesomeness around and under the City.'

Lussa continued, 'It has no Substance that a Body can really lay a Finger upon. 'Tis more like a *Feeling* than a Living Being. Or a Group of miniature Un-Creatures that can be organized together – for the Good or the Bad. In Itself, 'Tis however Meek & Timid as a Four-legger.'

'A four-legger?' asked Teo.

Chissa growled in a warning tone, 'A coney, underground mutton . . . *you* know.'

'I'm sorry . . .' Teo was still lost.

Renzo interrupted in a low voice, 'She means "rabbit" –

sailors are supposed never to utter that word aloud. It brings bad luck.'

One of the mermaids shouted at him, 'Belay that loose talk, stripling!!!'

Another chimed in, 'Keep yer noggin' mouf shut, ye great dafty!'

'Avast! – Hold! Enough!' Lussa held up her hand, 'The *Creature*,' she reminded the children, 'is the Subject in our Net at this Moment. It has manifested. Now even Humanfolk can see its Parts arranged in Tentacles above the Water.'

Renzo and Teo looked at each other with dawning understanding.

'Yar,' confirmed Lussa. 'The Striped Poles in the Grand Canal. The Creature has been Asleep for Centuries. The Tentacles solidified in the Dormant State to the Extent that They seemed like Trunks of Wood. Humanfolk even started using Them to moor their little Boats, Poor Ignorant Ones. Of course, Humanfolk are notoriously Bad at noticing Things.'

'I've seen the poles move!' exclaimed Teo and Renzo in the same voice.

'You never thought to mention that?' Teo muttered to Renzo.

He looked away, embarrassed.

Lussa continued, 'Soon They shall do a great deal More than move. We Mermaids have been able to keep the Creature aslumbering for ten Centuries with our Singing, but now 'Tis roused once more.'

'Why has it woken up now?'

'There are two Reasons. One is Human-Made. Too many Humans and too much Boating Activity made the Lagoon Warmer & Dirtier than Nature intended. When the Water below the City was Fresh & Cool, the Creature, who is cold-blooded, stayed safely in a State of Suspended Animation, all its Miniature Parts separated. But now the Water grows ever

Hotter & Filthier, and so the Creature stirs. It gains in Strength & commences to act in a Unified Way. 'Tis not fully awake yet, thank the Deep; else our Beautiful City would already be just a Memory.'

Renzo, pale as snow, asked, 'What is the second reason?'

Lussa answered in a sombre voice, 'Bajamonte Tiepolo.'

Silence fell on all the mermaids in the cavern. The parrots shuffled uneasily in their cages.

To Teo this name meant nothing. Even so, her chest clenched and her hands balled up into fists.

Renzo whispered, 'Bajamonte Tiepolo, *"Il Traditore"*?'

Lussa repeated, 'Bajamonte Tiepolo, the Traitor.'

Chissa nodded grimly. 'Yar, Bajamonte Tiepolo, the Orphan-Maker.'

Something stuck in Teo's throat. She choked.

Renzo groaned, 'Oh my God, it's not possible!'

21. A traitor's tale

one o'clock in the morning, June 8th, 1899

Lussa nodded sadly. 'Yes, Bajamonte Tiepolo, who tried to destroy the Republic of Venice and kill the Doge.'

Renzo protested, 'But that was hundreds of years ago, in 1310. The Doge was a Gradenigo. It must have been Pietro, yes, Pietro Gradenigo.'

'Bag o' nuts!' cried a mermaid admiringly. 'Suave as a rat with a gold tooth!'

Another chimed: 'Weren't behind the door when the brains was give out, 'im!'

Lussa smiled. 'You do not disappoint Us, Lorenzo, with your *relentless* Knowledge of Venetian History. Now kindly explain *Il Traditore* to Teodora. I see from her Face that she *hurts* to know of Him.'

Renzo cleared his throat in the way that Teo had come to learn meant that a long historical lecture was in the offing. She sighed.

'Bajamonte Tiepolo,' he began portentously, 'was a rich and spoiled nobleman who wanted to be absolute ruler of Venice. He'd been humiliated by the Venetian Council for robbing the people of the province he had governed. He was bitter as poison about it. He believed that the old ways of the aristocracy were being trampled by upstarts like Doge Gradenigo . . .'

Teo interrupted, 'According to him, the *Doge* was an upstart?'

Renzo raised his eyebrows. 'He considered *everyone* beneath him.'

Teo thought, 'Bajamonte Tiepolo's not the only Venetian who's felt that way.'

Renzo continued, 'So Bajamonte Tiepolo and some of his noble friends raised a secret army, planning to kill Doge Gradenigo and seize power for themselves.

'On the appointed night, just before dawn, three groups of armed men set out from different points of the city towards San Marco. Marco Querini's group was to arrive via the Calle dei Fabbri. The second party, led by Bajamonte Tiepolo, would come down the Mercerie. And the third group, led by Badoero Badoer, would arrive by water.'

'So many of them! How did he . . .?'

'It was rumoured that Bajamonte Tiepolo possessed magical powers and had woven a spell around many good men. Afterwards they claimed he had drugged the drinks with which they toasted their victory. Even his crest was said to have hypnotic properties.

'But at the last minute,' Renzo paused for effect, 'everything went wrong for Bajamonte Tiepolo. Some of his men had a dramatic change of heart and turned informers for the Doge.'

The mermaids smiled proudly then and Teo guessed that might have had something to do with changing the men's minds.

'So,' continued Renzo, 'when the conspirators led by Marco Querini arrived in San Marco, the Doge's loyal army was waiting for them . . .'

Teo privately thought that Renzo could have speeded up

his recounting of the story at this point. But Renzo was enjoying his human and half-human audience too much, drinking in the admiration of the young mermaids. Teo had a sudden sense that perhaps Renzo, like herself, was considered an oddity at school because of his passion for things in books. Perhaps he'd never had anyone to listen to him like this before?

'Well, meanwhile, Bajamonte Tiepolo's men were held up at the Rialto Bridge. They looted the public treasury and set fire to the bridge itself. It was wooden, in those days, Teo. Then the Badoer fleet was caught in a storm that came out of nowhere.'

The mermaids looked smug again.

Chissa muttered impatiently, 'What a drivelswigger! Drags on like a sea cow's saliva!'

Renzo blushed and stammered to a halt. To help him out, Teo said encouragingly, 'But do tell us what happened next!'

'Eventually Bajamonte Tiepolo's party tore themselves away from their looting and made their way towards San Marco. The troop was led by a dwarf carrying a flag emblazoned with the Tiepolo crest. Just before they reached the entrance to the square, an old lady, a baker's wife, took matters into her own hands.

'She leant out of her balcony and dropped her heavy mortar-and-pestle on the dwarf flag-bearer's head. Bajamonte Tiepolo's glittering armour was spattered with dwarf blood and brains. Suddenly he didn't look like an invincible leader. He looked a man who would ruthlessly spill Venetian blood.

'Someone shouted, "Bajamonte Tiepolo, Orphan-Maker!" Someone else screamed, "Bajamonte Tiepolo, *Il Traditore!*"'

'Now he's really telling it well,' judged Teo admiringly. Her eyes flew to the gold mortars-and-pestles that decorated the cavern.

'The spell was broken. The rest of the men suddenly woke

out of their enchantment. Marco Querini had already been killed in the battle at San Marco. Bajamonte Tiepolo fled to the safety of his family palaces, which was like a fortress. The conspiracy was over.'

Renzo paused: 'Except for the punishments. They hanged Badoer between the columns in the Piazzetta.'

Teo asked, 'And Bajamonte Tiepolo too?'

Renzo explained that the noble Tiepolo name still counted for a great deal in Venice. 'The Doge thought he would gain the people's favour if he showed mercy. So he negotiated a treaty by which the conspirator would go into perpetual exile: the worst thing you can do to a Venetian.'

'Except for killing him,' observed Teo.

'The Doge wanted to appear merciful, but he had hatred in his heart for the man who'd wanted to murder him. So he ordered his men to raze the family palaces of Bajamonte Tiepolo at Sant'Agostin and on the Grand Canal. Where there is now the modern Hotel degli Assassini.'

'That's where I am staying!' exclaimed Teo. 'And there's a Bar Tiepolo in there!'

'We do not think that is a coincidence, that ye should be abiding in that establishment,' muttered Chissa, worry creasing her forehead.

Teo felt the air squeezed out of her chest. Until this moment, the violent story of Bajamonte Tiepolo had seemed rather like a fairy tale gone wrong, something to read in an old book curled up on a rainy day, and nothing to do with Teo herself. Suddenly, it felt personal. And she remembered something else. Her parents were sleeping in that hotel now, after a hard day's searching for Teo and meeting with other scientists.

Lussa continued, 'Doge Gradenigo erected a "Column of Infamy" in the Place where the Palace had stood. To remind the Populace of his Crimes.'

'There's no column there now.'

'Sadly not – and nor at Sant'Agostin. Its Absence has allowed Venice to forget what She should most diligently remember.'

Teo asked, 'But what happened to *Il Traditore* himself?'

Renzo replied, 'I believe he died in exile. As far as I know, that is the end of the story.'

Lussa sighed bleakly, 'I'm afraid that was not the End of the Story at all.'

Chissa wound a tendril of dark red hair around her finger and intoned, 'No indeed, Undrowned Child. Ye should know there was an even darker side to the tale.'

22. A long, bitter grudge

two o'clock in the morning, June 8th, 1899

Two of the mermaids swam up with an enormous turtleshell. They turned it so the hollowed side was facing Renzo and Teo. All they could see was a curved, cloudy mirror.

'Look *deep* inside,' urged Lussa. The mirror cleared and became like a kind of moving storybook, rather like *The Key*. It showed a dark-haired man going about his life. From the costumes of his companions, and his own words, there was no doubt that this was Bajamonte Tiepolo. The scene was always shown from his point of view, with the back of his head in sight, but never the front.

The turtleshell played out the conspiracy, the death of the dwarf, the ignominious flight back to his palace and *Il Traditore*'s final departure from Venice in the teeming black rain, with his fellow citizens turning tight-closed faces silently against him. No one bade him farewell. Young gondoliers competed to spit at him. Men cursed him in filthy language. Women held their aprons up to their eyes rather than look at him.

'You're no Venetian,' snarled a fisherman.

123

A child cried, 'And *don't* come back! No one wants you here, Bajamonte Tiepolo.'

Teo and Renzo heard *Il Traditore* cry out, 'But I was Venice's saviour! I wanted reform! Now you treat me like this!'

There was the sound of something wet slapping on his back: another Venetian had spat on him. Then someone tore in half a flag bearing a red, yellow and blue crest. He hunched his shoulders, which shook as if he was weeping beneath his cloak.

But the turtleshell showed that Bajamonte Tiepolo learnt nothing from his defeat. He set himself up on the mainland and started dealing with Venice's enemies, hoping to find other people to help destroy the city that had humiliated him. He talked obsessively of making his former home sink back beneath the waves. News of his plotting filtered back to Venice. In private, Doge Gradenigo summoned his secret police, the *Signori di Notte*, and sent them to murder Bajamonte Tiepolo. He was captured, put in chains, and strangled by a dark-robed state assassin in a mask.

Teo looked away at this part. It was like a horror-story; like something Mr Poe would write, or Mr Dickens. When she looked up, the corpse of Bajamonte Tiepolo was being bundled into a sack. There was no funeral; no prayers were said over his body. The sack was hastily thrown into the lagoon, weighted down with stones threaded among the chains. It sank fathoms deep through the water. Down, down, down it went, landing gently on a bed of seaweed.

The shell clouded over as Lussa told them, 'The Location of his Body was a Sworn Secret. To Humanfolk. We Mermaids of course watched and knew Everything.'

Everyone in the underwater chamber fell silent for a moment, thinking of Bajamonte Tiepolo's fate.

'But he's quite dead, is he not?' asked Renzo, looking at

the mermaids for reassurance. 'And buried out in the lagoon. Why do we need to worry about him now?'

'*Il Traditore* is dead, but, like all Traitors, He does not rest in Peace. His disembodied Spirit has passed the last Six Hundred Years hunting for his Bones in every Corner & Crevasse of the Lagoon. We Mermaids have for Centuries made regular Inspections of his Sea-Grave to ensure his Body was still Enchained & Hidden.'

'But *why . . .*?'

'We fear that if – by the use of Baddened Magic – his Spirit was ever reunited with his Body, then He could grow back to his Former Strength.'

'*Baddened* magic?'

'All Magic is born Good. But Good Magic can be twisted to Evil, perverted for Killing & Cursing.'

'So it was true that he had magical powers?' asked Renzo.

'Yar, *Il Traditore* had Access to certain Mystical Knowledge. His Studies continued in his Exile. Even after his Death. Though his Memory lacks perfect Function.'

'So he's never found his bones, at least?' asked Renzo hopefully.

Lussa's lovely face darkened. 'Two months ago, One of our Number went to look on the Secret Spot where his Body was placed. She never returned. Then I Myself went with my Attendants, and We discovered that the Chains were broken. Someone, Some Human Fisherman or Treasure-Hunter, had found the Body of *Il Traditore* and had taken a Souvenir: the Left Hand.'

'Why would anyone do that?' asked Renzo, wrinkling his nose with distaste.

'No doubt because It bore Bajamonte Tiepolo's Ring. A priceless Emerald from the Ganges that Marco Polo brought back from his Travels. *Il Traditore* had got hold of It, hearing of its Magic Powers. It never left his Hand, not in Life or Death.'

'So the fisherman *cut off* the hand?' Teo whispered hoarsely.

'Indeed. For a Human could never have pulled that Ring off the Finger, whereunto 'Twas bound by a Magical Force.'

Teo murmured, 'A ring, a big green stone in it? Oh no, please.'

Into her mind came the unwelcome image of Maria standing beside the boy with the perfect mole and the large green ring she'd thought was glass.

'Of course We took Immediate Steps. We removed the Rest of the Bones to a new Place of Safety. Fortunately, We were able to do That before the Spirit of Bajamonte Tiepolo became Aware that his Body had been Discovered. And before He had hunted down the Unfortunate Human who found It.'

Teo shuddered, 'I hate to think what happened to that fisherman . . .'

Renzo finished for her, 'And who was no doubt forced to take *Il Traditore* to the original resting place . . .'

Teo guessed, 'Only to find the bones were gone!'

Renzo interrupted, 'But I think I know! There was that story in the newspapers of the fisherman from Pellestrina found drowned with strange marks around his neck – that must have been in the newspapers around two months ago? Before you came to Venice, Teo. The police said it looked as if he'd been strangled, but with just one hand, and no one could have the strength to do that.'

'No Human, 'Tis Certain,' said Lussa bluntly. 'But Whatever happened there, We are now Certain that the Hand is back in the Possession of its Original Owner. The Signs of It are all over the City.'

Teo asked, 'The fountains, the High Water in the wrong place? The lights going out? The Brustolons?'

'All That & More. Just One Week after *Il Traditore* got his

Hand back, the Creature started upon Its Mischiefs.'

'And the sharks?' asked Renzo.

'Aye, 'Twas Bajamonte Tiepolo who sent for those Dogs of Fish. The Sharks are merely a Beginning. He's presently summoning the Forces of Evil to help Him – All the Enemies of Venice from the Present & the Past. Behold how They are gathering.'

The turtleshell filled with cloudy liquid again, and inside it the children caught terrifying glimpses of ghastly creatures, men in bloodstained armour and fearsome helmets, white-robed women who looked beautiful until you noticed their hairy goats' feet – all streaming across the sky with Venice visible in the distance.

Then, in the turtleshell, appeared the image of a solitary white eel weaving through black water. Two long, curved teeth hung outside its sneering jaw. White fins folded like a bat's wings on its back.

'A Vampire Eel,' breathed Lussa. 'The only Natural Enemy of the Mermaids.'

The children and the mermaids watched in silence as the Vampire Eel stalked and fell upon a baby dolphin from behind. It used its forked tail to hold down its struggling prey while it struck again and again with its deadly incisors. As the little dolphin grew still, the eel fixed its jaw on its prey's neck and visibly gulped for minutes on end. All the while its milky eyes, rimmed with black, turned here and there in search of new victims. The eel's gills, clustered on the outside of its diaphanous skin, now swelled up like branches of red coral.

Teo remembered the music box with the terrified tin mermaid and the pursuing serpent she had seen at the toy emporium. It had been a Vampire Eel, not a snake, chasing the mermaid round the carousel!

Lussa continued, 'The *magòghe* have gone over to Bajamonte of course, but the Little Black-Headed Ones, the

Cocai, are still Loyal. Meanwhile, we too are summoning Support. We await some Dolphins from the South Seas. But They are delayed by a Spillage of Oils & Ambergris from a Merchant Ship in the Spanish Straits. Hopefully They shall be ridden by our Old Friends, the Nereids. We sent Sea-Shells for Them.'

'Shells?'

'We inscribe our Messages upon Seashells and send Them out with the Retreating Tide. The Sea is a most Reliable Courier. With the Shells We have recruited the staunch English Melusine, the Little Steeds of Neptune, and the London Sea-Monks and Sea-Bishops.'

Lussa noticed the children's puzzled looks. 'That is, Two-tailed Mermaids & Seahorses, and two very large Species of Squid, respectively. And here in Venice, We have tamed as many of the Wild-but-Good Faeries as 'Tis safe to parley with. Also on our side are the Herons and the Egrets. The Parrots, It goes without Saying. And even the Pigeons. Naturally, the Doves have remained Pure of Heart.'

'And the insects?' Renzo shuddered.

'Alas, gone over to the Enemy in the main, which could prove Problematic.'

Teo asked, 'What about people's pets?'

'The Cats, who cannot abide a Dictator, are with Us. The Dogs are confused. Each Breed is of a different Mind. A friendly Circus-Master currently parleys with Them, Dog by Dog, and has commenced Negotiations with the Winged Lions.'

'The Signor Alicamoussa!' cooed the mermaids, and extremely flirtatious expressions stole across a hundred pretty faces.

Lussa held up her hand, 'To return to our Main Drift – the Danger grows acute. The Beasts know It. The Birds know It. They have their Instincts to guide Them. Only Humanfolk remain in Blissful Ignorance. But soon Venice shall start to sink, not evenly & slowly, but in Catastrophic Chasms. The Backbones of all the Weakest & Oldest Buildings shall fail first. Then shall occur a Chain of Collapse, all the Palaces Astagger & Afall like the Pieces in your Human Game of Dominoes.'

Renzo was pale as a glass of milk. Teo felt cold worming through her bones.

And there was one more thing, Lussa told Teo, looking straight into her eyes: 'The Girl Maria. You must give Her a Wide Berth.'

'Who's Maria?' asked Renzo, in a tone that insinuated that Teo had deliberately contaminated the city. 'Some *Napoletana* friend of yours?'

'She's not my friend,' protested Teo.

'*She* has a Friend, however,' said Lussa. 'Most misfortunately Maria has taken up an Amicable Alliance with the Spirit of Bajamonte Tiepolo, who can show Himself – for just a few Minutes at a time – as a nice-looking Young Man. More often He's to be seen as a gargantuan White Bat. He struggles to fix Himself in any one State. Only the Hand & the Ring remain constant . . .'

'I've seen him,' Teo shivered. 'Both ways.'

She explained what she had witnessed in Santi Giovanni e Paolo: the terrible white bat and the headless butcher and the skin of Marcantonio Bragadin ripped out of its tomb. Then she described the boy she had seen with Maria and the white fur growing out of the back of his neck. 'I suppose he was changing back into the bat. That was why he had to disappear so quickly.'

Renzo, just as she'd feared, demanded angrily, 'Why didn't you tell anyone, Teo? The police? Me, even? It's the *responsibility* of a witness . . .'

Teo tried to pretend she hadn't heard. She continued

shakily with her account of the young man with the perfect oval mole and how *The Key to the Secret City* had showed her that the mole meant 'murderer'.

Lussa observed grimly, 'And the First Person to know That shall be Maria Herself. Once a susceptible Human is under his Power, there is but Little that can be done to save Him or Her, short of releasing the Victim from their Misery.'

'You mean they have to *die*?' asked Teo, feeling a stab of nausea. She could have tried to intervene in Maria's friendship with the young man. Instead, she had stayed selfishly silent so as not to lose her delicious days of freedom.

'Alack, a Quick Death is the Only Choice. Unless They can redeem Themselves by betraying their Evil Master. In that Way, Maria *could* be saved.'

'So long as it wasn't a trap,' muttered Renzo. 'Obviously, you can't trust anyone from Naples.'

'In the Meantime, You must avoid Maria like the Very Plague, Teodora. She must never hear of Us. As yet, Bajamonte Tiepolo knows Nothing of this Cavern; indeed He does not know that We even exist, or that Anyone is working against Him. This Secrecy is our Strongest Protection, and 'Tis most Fragile.'

'What about Signor Rioba? asked Renzo.

'*Il Traditore* cannot know Signor Rioba is the *nom de guerre* of a School of Mermaids. We have sought to make Signor Rioba's Tone authentically, well, *Male*.'

'No one would think he was a *girl*,' smiled Teo. Those insults he'd piled on the Mayor were rather too ripe for that.

'You can be sure Bajamonte Tiepolo is hunting for Signor Rioba, with the Aim of silencing Him.'

'How can a disembodied ghost do that?'

Chissa observed, 'He has his henchmen. And his hand back. He can kill.'

Lussa added, 'And He has a poor Human Skin that he

hopes to make Use of. A Hero's Remains, whose Heroism He hopes to steal thereby.'

'Marcantonio Bragadin!' exclaimed Renzo, glancing disapprovingly at Teo.

'And He seeks One More Thing to swell his Strength: Something He lost when He was driven out of Venice: his Spell Almanac. 'Tis a most sophisticated Volume, a vast Repertoire of Baddened Magic. His Spells will have included The Transference of a Bad Old Spirit to a New Body & The Reviving of the Wicked Dead. Also Food-Potioning & Fear-Twisting the Brain & many, many Death-Curses.'

'Surely he'd remember his baddened spells? Why doesn't he just use them?'

'Remember, his Form is still Evolving. It sheds its Memories each Time He transforms. He cannot retain the Necessary Spells for Long enough to make Use of Them. The Brustolons, for example, would be a Fine Brutal Army for Him. But He can for now animate just One at a Time and then only for a few Scant Seconds.

'They shall stay Inanimate, as long as Bajamonte Tiepolo does not obtain the Almanac. And even then . . . He absolutely needs his Full Strength back to utter the Spells Themselves. A Spell, as You know, is not simply a Set of Words.'

Teo and Renzo tried hard to look as if they *did* know that, but Lussa tactfully filled in, 'The Being who casts a Spell must send out some of his Soul with it. 'Tis knowing how to harness Soul & Words & Time & Desire that gives a Spell its Power. Of course, One must first be in Possession of the Words.'

'So why hasn't Bajamonte Tiepolo got his Almanac back?' asked Teo.

'Answering that Very Question is exactly how You Children shall prove Your Usefulness.'

23. Ninny-broth

half past two in the morning, June 8th, 1899

Teo and Renzo gazed at Lussa apprehensively.

'We nourish Strong Suspicions that the Spell Almanac is now stored in the State Archives of Venice, with the Hatches battened down upon It for Safety. It might even be disguised as Something Else. You must go to the Archives & bring It back to Us. Here We can, We hope, study the Spells & turn *Il Traditore*'s Magic back against Himself. Teodora – You are specially charged with this Mission.'

Teo stared at the mermaid. The word '*why?*' formed on her silent lips.

'You must invent some Manner of Scholarly Pursuit that will disguisingly account for a Visit there. Lorenzo, You must smooth the Waters with the Archivist. She is a Formidable Piece of a Woman, We hear. Though unlike Mermaids in that She is reputed not particularly fond of Children. You must charm Her, Lorenzo, in the Venetian Style. It shall not be easy for You. You must be Crafty as Cuttles.' If It comes to the Attention of Bajamonte Tiepolo that Someone Else is hunting for his Spells . . .'

Lussa's expression said more than any words could ever express.

'But,' stammered Renzo. 'We are not . . . magical creatures like you. We really couldn't . . . We have no special powers . . .'

One of the mermaids muttered sarcastically, 'Aren't ye the plucky fellow?'

Another asked, 'Have ye been a-sipping at da ninny-broth, eh?'

Renzo flushed as the parrots chorused, 'Ninny-broth! Ninny-broth! Ninny-broth!'

Avoiding Renzo's humiliated eyes, Teo said politely to Lussa, 'We'd like to help, of course. But why do you need *children* for this mission?'

Lussa explained: 'Children will arouse less Suspicion than Adults. Our Enemy has surely mounted Guards outside the Premises. We have Reason to think that *Il Traditore* suspects that his Almanac lies inside. There have been Attempts . . .'

Chissa smiled, 'Thwarted until now . . .'

Lussa continued, 'But the Main Reason for your Employment is so Simple that It has obviously escaped You. We Mermaids have no Lubbersome Legs – We cannot walk into the Human Police Station or the Town Hall and explain the Danger. Nor can We swim into the Archives.'

Teo and Renzo nodded.

'Adult Humanfolk in any case have Limited Vision. Once They pass the Age of Thirteen or Fourteen, They can no longer see Mermaids or Ghosts. We need some Children to act as our Ambassadors. All through History, We have found Children our Best Allies. Children & Nuns.' She cast her eyes upwards.

'So the Nuns upstairs in the House of the Spirits know about you?' asked Renzo, 'But you are . . . forgive me . . . pagan creatures. There are no mermaids in the Bible. Surely the nuns would not even *want* to believe in you?'

'They understand who We are, and They help Us in Subtle Ways. The Nuns of the House of the Spirits are Special Ladies. They are quite Antique, some having nearly One Hundred Years. Although deeply Religious, their Minds are Open because they are Clean of all Manner of Things that clutter up the Consciences of Ordinary Humanfolk. Living long & purely good has given Them an Innocence & a Vision like That of Young Human Children.'

'Can the nuns see ghosts too?'

'O Yar indeed! They look after the Garden Ghosts, comforting Them as best They can. They never reproach Them.'

'That's another thing! Why are those ghosts so sad?'

'Aye, Surpassing Sad. They are Humanfolk who were in the Process of mending their Wicked Lives when Death overtook Them. Our Garden Ghosts are caught between States of Being. Until Someone finds a Way to help Them.'

'Are they between-the-Linings?' asked Teo urgently.

'Between the *what*?' snapped Renzo.

'Nay,' Lussa frowned. 'They are not so Fortunate. They are Ghosts who are in-the-Cold.'

'*Fortunate?*' speculated Teo to herself. 'Then it's *good* to be between-the-Linings? I suppose Pedro-the-Crimp is in-the-Cold? He was sad and sorry too.' Aloud, she asked, 'Will they ever get out?'

'Perhaps. They may redeem Themselves by a Selfless Act in Time of War.'

'Is the Butcher Biasio in-the-Cold too?'

'Nay. The Butcher never repented his Crimes. He's another Tribe of Ghost. A Badder Kind. We call Them "in-the-Slaughterhouse."'

'How do you pick them apart from . . .?'

'Easily. Their Spirit-Forms are Mutilated. If You see a

134

Ghost carrying his Head, or with his Hands cut off – avoid Him! Those like Butcher Biasio feel Nary a Drop of Guilt for the Harm that They did. They desire to keep doing the Very Same.'

'So the Butcher wants to keep killing and eating children?' gulped Teo.

'He's *ravenous* for Them. Though of course 'Tis an untidy Process, his Digestion. He must balance his Head on his Neck and hope that no Morsels leak out of the Gappy Hole . . .'

Renzo interrupted, white-faced, 'And Bajamonte Tiepolo is in-the-Slaughterhouse too?'

'No, he's a third Manner of Ghost, the Worst & Rarest. Such Ghosts have lost their Original Form entirely – all that is left of Them is their Boiling Anger. We say this Kind are "in-the-Meltings". For, like Anything that boils, They cannot settle, as We have seen with Bajamonte Tiepolo. Their Obsession is Bloody Revenge. If One of Those Ghosts should escape his Fate, become Solid & Fixed, then the whole World, and not just Venice, stands in Danger.'

'But,' said Teo slowly. 'I still don't see why . . .?'

'Why You Two? You each have your Special Qualities. Lorenzo's talent for History & the Fact that he's a Gondolier's Son – these Items mean that He has Special Knowledge of Venice that shall be Vital in our Task. Venice is in his Blood and He has Abilities inside Him of which even He does not yet know.'

Renzo stood a little taller.

'But,' thought Teo, 'what can an undersized and possibly dead orphan from Naples do to help Venice?'

Lussa continued, 'You, Teodora are Clever with Languages & Working out Puzzles, and You are Blessed with a Memory that operates like a Human Photographic Machine.'

'But I'm not Venetian. Actually,' protested Teo, full of self-pity. 'I am adopted. I don't know where I come from, so I don't belong anywhere.'

Renzo exclaimed scornfully, *'Adopted!'* in a tone that sounded as if 'adopted' was even worse than 'from Naples'. He rolled his eyes. 'Didn't you ever think of asking the people who adopted you where you actually came from?'

'I didn't want to hurt them,' said Teo steadfastly. 'It's not their fault that I never quite feel at home anywhere. It's not their fault that I am clumsy and I don't fit in. It's just that I am rather odd, I suppose.'

Teo was trying to fight off tears, but one sneaked out of her eyes anyway.

Lussa looked at her seriously. 'Teodora, 'Twas our Intention to spare You This, a While, but . . . Did You ever wonder how You got your Name?'

Teo shook her head, and the tear flew away.

'Well, Lorenzo will know that your Namesake – Teodoro – was the Ancient Protector of Venice. Before Saint Mark was our Patron Saint We had Saint Teodoro to watch over Us.'

'What a coincidence!' remarked Renzo.

Lussa answered, 'In fact Not.'

'Do I have something to do with Venice after all?' asked Teo eagerly. 'Is that why I feel so at home here? Why it has been so easy for me to learn Venetian . . .?'

'A *smattering* of Venetian,' interrupted Renzo.

'Very well, a smattering of Venetian. But it's more than that. I love to be here. I always wanted to come. I kept plaguing my parents . . .'

Renzo opened his mouth, but Lussa held up her hand. 'There is no Need for You to swagger so with Teodora, Lorenzo.'

'Ninny-broth!' clacked one parrot quietly.

'Teodora,' Lussa spoke again. 'Now 'Tis Timely to explain an important Part of your Own History to You.'

Teo swallowed loudly and nodded, feeling rather as you do in that moment before you are asked to turn over the paper in an examination. She was not at all prepared for the next question.

Lussa asked, 'So, Children, are You ready for a Dip in the Drink?'

'The Drink?'

All around them, young mermaids chorused, 'Da Ditch, da Pond, da Oggin, Sir Briney, Harry Hogwash, da Old Grey Widow-Maker. Da SEA!'

'In other Words,' smiled Lussa, 'Children, are You ready for a Swim?'

Teo felt goosepimples raise themselves up all over her body.

Renzo whispered, 'A sw-w-w-im?' and Teo noticed that he could not keep the trembling out of his voice or the pallor off his skin.

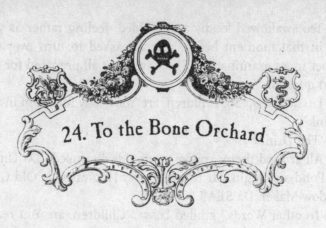

24. To the Bone Orchard

three o'clock in the morning, June 8th, 1899

'Ahoy! To the Bone Orchard!'

Teo had no idea what or where that was, but it did not sound very cosy.

Renzo hissed, 'It's an old sailors' name for a cemetery. Venice's is on an island. San Michele. You can see it from the garden of the House of the Spirits.'

'We're going there?' asked Teo nervously.

A *cemetery*? In the middle of the *night*? In a city where everything was going seriously wrong? And the word 'swim' had been used. Swim through the shark-infested waters? Where Vampire Eels had been sighted?

Lussa seemed to read her thoughts, 'The Eels have no idea where We are. Meanwhile, the Sharks cherish no great Amity towards Mermaids. The Concept of protecting a City, or even looking after Other Beings – that is Unknown in their Primitive & Nasty World. So They do not understand what We are for.'

'Wouldn't they just eat you anyway?'

'The Rumour among Them is that Mermaids are tough & taste abominable. I suppose 'tis the Vast Amount of Curry

138

that We consume. Also, Sharks do most viscerally detest Mermaid Voices. If We sing in High Pitch, It hurts their Ears terribly, whereupon It drives Them away. Usually.'

Renzo suggested, 'Er, couldn't we take a boat?'

'We have only Rafts for distributing Signor Rioba's Handbills. We shall give You some Cauls, however.'

'Cauls?'

Chissa explained, 'The net that covers some human babies' heads in the womb. Sailors believe that those nets can save people from death by drowning. Mind ye, sailors also think warts can be cured by rubbing 'em with eel blood! Foolish coddles! But lately we always keep some cauls at hand. Just in case the stink of 'em puts off the sharks.'

Lussa tied a little dried packet around the neck of each flinching child. Teo caught a whiff of something sour and salty. Two mermaids flopped over in the water; Chissa told Renzo and Teo to walk down into the pool and climb onto their backs.

'Handsomely!' the mermaid urged the children.

'We cannot change the way we look,' said Teo defensively.

Chissa laughed delicately, 'I am sorry. By us "handsomely" means "with caution". Which brings to my mind the book. It will not serve as ballast when ye swim, Undrowned Child.'

Teo did not like letting go of *The Key to the Secret City*, but she handed it to Lussa who placed it carefully on a dry cushion of moss. 'It will be safe as a Shrimp in its Shell here.' She smiled reassuringly.

Teo felt curiously empty. She had grown so used to the feel of the book between her bodice and pinafore where she usually hid it. The mermaids seemed kind, but she didn't *know* them, not as she knew *The Key to the Secret City*. And now these mermaids were asking her to swim across the lagoon and did not appear to be offering any choice in the matter.

The water was surprisingly warm. Of course, Teo remembered, the Creature had been heating it up. Lussa did not need to remind her not to swallow any of it. They set off through a torchlit gilded tunnel, emerging under the House of the Spirits, on the edge of the lagoon. They pulled out into the stretch of velvety black water that lay between the House and the island of San Michele, where the white stones of the cemetery gates glowed encouragingly in the dark.

''Tis a Ladies' Sea tonight,' murmured Lussa. 'Calm & Fair.'

Teo and Renzo clung to the backs of their mermaids, trying not to tangle their fingers in the lustrous curls that hung down their backs. Lussa and three others accompanied them, holding burning brands above the water to light their way. Everyone was silent, keeping their eyes fixed on the approaching shore.

'Shouldn't you start singing now?' asked Renzo tensely. 'You know, to keep away the sharks?'

'We *are* singing,' smiled Lussa. 'A special Melody for the Sharks. In this Case, 'Tis simply too High in Pitch for Human Ears to register It.'

'How does it go?' Renzo asked suspiciously.

Untroubled by sharks, they arrived at the cemetery island. Lussa handed Renzo one of the burning brands. 'Hurry now, walk straight past Three-and-Thirty Graves, then to the Right past seven Graves, and then Left past four Graves. Then You shall find what You need to see in the Bone Orchard.'

In the graveyard, leaves were rustling in the wind, and strange shadows shifting in the moonlight. It was hard to count the graves in the nearly total darkness. The wavering light of the brands swept over weeping stone angels, broken urns and the faces of dead Venetians daguerreotyped on little china discs. Many recent ones showed the faces of children. The mermaid's instructions led them to the far edge of the graveyard, away from the main lanes. Eventually they pulled up short. Exactly where they should walk now was an overgrown clump of flowering bushes.

'There's nothing here,' sighed Renzo. 'The mermaids must have made a mistake.'

'I don't imagine Lussa has made a mistake in a thousand years,' remarked Teo. 'Hold this.'

She handed Renzo her brand and used both hands to stretch apart the branches of the bushes in front of them. Renzo shone the light through the parting. A small gravestone glowed eerily white among the green foliage.

Teo ripped at the branches, snapping off leaves and clumps of flowers until she'd cleared a space big enough to kneel down. 'Now give me the brand, Renzo.'

It was a small, fairly new grave, just eleven years old – the first thing Teo noticed was the date carved on the top of the stone: JUNE 15th 1888.

Then Renzo, leaning over her shoulder to read the mossy writing, whispered, 'No! I simply don't believe it!'

Teo forced herself to read the rest of the tombstone. Carved into the flecked granite were the following words:

JUNE 15th 1888
MARTA AND DANIELE GASPERIN
DROWNED IN THE WATERS
OF THE LAGOON
SURVIVED ONLY BY THEIR
INFANT DAUGHTER TEODORA.
MAY THEIR LOVING SOULS
REST IN PEACE.

Renzo noted, 'June 15th! The anniversary of Bajamonte Tiepolo's conspiracy!' Then his face changed. 'But, the thing is . . .'

'Their infant daughter Teodora,' repeated Teo. 'I was a baby in June 1888.'

Teodora-of-Sad-Memory, that was how the book had first greeted her. Teo suddenly remembered the expression on her adoptive mother's face when she called her 'my water-baby' – it had always been sad, not joking. She felt sick and yet unbearably excited at the same time. Renzo's incredulous eyes showed her that his thoughts were hurtling in the same direction.

'That seems to be what the mermaids are trying to tell you,' he said.

'How could Marta and Daniele Gasperin have drowned? Renzo, I know it's not exactly historical, but do you know anything about it? Of course you were a baby then too . . .'

From Renzo's waxen face, Teo understood that he did indeed know something and that something was going to hurt, very badly.

'June 15th, 1888,' said Renzo gently. 'All Venetians know that date, Teo. That was the night of a terrible ferry accident in this very part of the lagoon. A *vaporetto* rammed a gondola accidentally in the fog. Ten people died. The captain of the *vaporetto* didn't see a thing – he was set upon and murdered by a flock of seagulls that had gone mad in the mist. None of his passengers saw a thing either. So the accident was not reported straightaway. It was too long before anyone realized what had happened. It was also odd because the gondola sank to the bottom of the water – normally the wreckage would float. The fog didn't lift for ages. And then it was a day before the bodies were washed ashore. They were all Venetians. It was one of the worst accidents of modern times.'

He spoke again, after a few seconds, 'From what I

remember about it, an entire family, several generations, died in that accident.'

He parted the nearby bushes, shining the brand on graves to the left and the right – more Gasperins, all with different ages but the same date of death. 'The infant daughter Teodora' had lost her grandparents, her aunt, her uncle and two cousins.

'I am not an orphan. I come from a large family!' whispered Teo, with a sudden exhilaration. But that little flame of happiness was directly extinguished by a rush of sadness.

'No,' she thought. 'My family lives in the Bone Orchard! I am still an orphan, just lots of times over. Maybe even just the ghost of an orphan. Nothing. Less than nothing.'

She had to ask, 'So what happened to me, Renzo? How did I survive?'

Renzo's lips were set in a tight line. There was something he did not want to tell her. 'The thing is, Teo, nobody thought that the baby *did* survive. They found all the bodies except hers. For days people said that she was so small that . . . that . . .'

'Why do you keep saying "the baby" and "her"? Why don't you say "you"?' demanded Teo. 'It's perfectly obvious that I am that child.'

'It's difficult, Teo. You see, the thing is . . . they said that the bab— *you* . . . had been eaten by fishes.'

'*Eaten by fishes?*'

'I'm sorry, Teo, that's what people always said. If that baby was you, I don't know how you survived or how you ended up in Naples. I don't remember anyone ever talking about it. Look at how this gravestone is tucked away in a far corner of the graveyard. Hidden in the thick bushes. It looks as if someone planted them deliberately, if you ask me. No one comes here. I don't know . . .'

Reading his thoughtful face, Teo urged, 'But I think you have an idea?'

'Well, I can take a guess. Say, you were so little and light – after the shipwreck you floated away to safety and someone found you. Perhaps whoever found you didn't know who you were. Or, if they did, well I'd lay money on it that the Mayor rushed through your adoption to get you out of the city . . . he wouldn't want you here in Venice, attracting the attention of the papers, with anniversary stories every year to remind his beloved tourists of the tragedy. That's not the type of publicity he likes. If my guess is right, then no one in Venice even knew that you survived.'

Given what Teo had read in the papers, and in the absence of any other theory, Renzo's sounded all too plausible. The Mayor was ruthless with the truth. He would do anything to keep the image of Venice bright and shiny. Teo imagined herself passed from hand to hand and out of Venice, her birthplace. Her life had been decided on the whim of the Mayor. She'd been inconvenient, and for that reason he had sent her away. A little baby, she'd had no rights.

A hot red haze descended over Teo's brain.

Renzo did not see the dangerous look in Teo's eyes. He was musing, 'And it's probably why your adoptive parents didn't want to bring you here. Didn't you tell me that it took years to persuade them? They must have been afraid you would find out.'

Teo tried to breathe more slowly, but her blood was raging around her body. So many questions – including questions she'd not even asked – were answered by this sorrowful little gravestone. Teo remembered the poem in *The Key to the Secret City*, the one that had written itself on the page when she saw Maria together with the perfect young man who had turned out to be none other than Bajamonte Tiepolo.

'Renzo! There was something the book told me, before I

144

met you. It was a poem about this place, about a secret hidden in the old Bone Orchard.'

'Can't you remember it? Aren't you supposed to be able to remember everything?' Renzo challenged. 'You know, like a camera.'

Teo knelt down and closed her eyes. She focused all her thoughts on the poem that had printed itself inside *The Key to the Secret City*. Single words and lines tugged at her memory. Then her photographic memory framed the whole page, and she could read it as if it were written out in front of her. With her eyes still closed, she recited the poem to Renzo, faultlessly, including all the rats, the wells, the lions, the Plague spores, the Butcher, concluding triumphantly . . .

Where's our Studious Son? Who's our Lost Daughter,
Our Undrowned Child plucked from the water,
Who shall save us from a Traitor's tortures?
That secret's hidden in the old Bone Orchard.

Teo repeated the lines: 'Who's our Lost Daughter, our Undrowned Child plucked from the water?'

Renzo whispered with a stunned expression, 'Where's our Studious Son?'

There was a new softness in his voice. Renzo knelt down beside Teo and awkwardly put his wet arm around her. Instead of his usual lemony, soapy scent, he smelt of the sea and of smoke from the brands. He said quietly, 'Poor Teo, you've had the most enormous shock.'

Teo pushed his arm away. 'I see, now that you know I am a *Venetian* like you, it's fine to be nice to me. *Before*, I wasn't good enough to tie your shoelaces! Is that it? I suppose now you think it's all right for me to have the book?'

Renzo stared at her, frozen with confusion and

embarrassment. Teo stormed off towards the far end of the cemetery. Her heart was pounding, full of a thousand emotions, about her unknown dead parents, about the crafty Mayor. And about Renzo, who suddenly liked her, just because she was a Venetian!

She pulled up short, sobbing, at the end of the cemetery garden, by the edge of the lagoon. She saw Venice just a little way off, and suddenly she just wanted to be alone, to walk the streets of this city that did indeed belong to her. No matter that she was dripping wet, crying, and furious.

'Teo Gasperin. That's who I am,' she thought. 'Or *was*.'

Gasperin: she was sure she'd seen that name on doorbells. She was going to run around Venice, ringing the doorbells of any Gasperins, to ask if they were distantly related to her. She would find her real parents' house! She could not be totally forgotten in Venice! She'd show that smug moustachioed Mayor! *And* his Minister for Tourism and Decorum! She would not let the city forget her or her dead parents! The mermaids were waiting for her and Renzo at the main entrance to the cemetery, but she wasn't accountable to them! Really, she couldn't start too soon!

She stared at the restless water that lay between her and Venice. As a baby she must have been able to breathe underwater to survive when everyone else around her drowned.

'I think I'll try that again!' she said to herself wildly, and dived into the black waves of the lagoon.

The warm water embraced her body. It was easy to hold her breath. Under the waves, she didn't hear Renzo running and shouting after her. At the edge of the cemetery, he hesitated a moment, and then threw himself into the water. Renzo's swimming was even weaker than he'd admitted. He trailed far behind Teo, who was still skimming under the surface at a furious pace. When she finally came up for air, the first thing she saw was Renzo, flailing his arms, fifty yards away. The sound of the waves drowned out his voice, but the moonlight fell starkly on his terrified face.

He mouthed the word 'S – H – A – R – K!'

Behind him, and cutting through the waves much faster than Renzo, the tip of a shark's jagged fin appeared in dark silhouette.

Too late, Teo remembered the sharks. Absurdly, it flashed through her mind – *Crafty as Cuttles!* She had been not crafty but just about as stupid as she could be. As Renzo panted to her side, the sharks surrounded the two children, milling in circles.

A long grey form pushed between them, gashing their legs with its serrated hide. It was the most agonizing pain Teo had ever felt, as if her skin was being branded by hot tongs. And the sharks had not even used their teeth yet – teeth that curved visibly backwards inside their open jaws, ready to tear. From those jaws came an overpowering stench of rotten meat. Teo thought of the tourists gone missing since the lights went out in Venice.

One shark tugged experimentally at the sash of Teo's pinafore and then ripped it right off. Immediately other sharks challenged it: in seconds the white sash was reduced to fragments of thread churning in the water. The same shark closed in on the cuff of Teo's sleeve. She snatched it back and wrapped her arms around herself, frantically treading water. Another shark was butting Renzo's shoulder, pushing him under the water. A third wrenched the caul off his neck . . .

'Does it prove that I am not a ghost – if I am edible?' wondered Teo. And then, 'But even if I'm alive I soon shall be a ghost, a mangled, eaten one.'

'I'm sorry, Teo,' sobbed Renzo. 'I was horrible to you. A snob. So uncivil! Forgive me . . . You deserve better . . .'

'No,' gasped Teo. 'I am sorry I lost my temper. You were my good friend. I would have loved to have seen the Archives with you. It would have been a pleasure.'

Were. Would have been.

The sharks jostled around the children, nudging them further away from the meeting point where the waiting mermaids might see them. One of the sharks ripped the seaweed bandage off Teo's knee. Her wound was bleeding again. The smell of her blood seemed to rouse the sharks to an even more terrifying level of excitement. A grey monster snapped the caul off Teo's neck and tossed it down its gaping throat. It appeared to find the caul appetizing, for it immediately loomed in closer again.

'I am meeting the same Fate as my parents,' thought Teo. 'I shall die in the water of the Venetian lagoon. Though in a different way. A worse way.'

A shudder ran through her whole body, like an electric shock. What were the sharks waiting for? Why had they fallen so still? She almost wished they would just get on with it, so that it could be over. She turned to give one last look to Renzo, too numb to cry, just wanting a familiar human face to be the last thing she ever saw.

25. Fish food

just before dawn, June 8th, 1899

It was another face Teo saw. Not Renzo's, and not the grey snout and cold eyes of a shark.

No, a beautiful face.

Ten foaming, crashing, screaming minutes later, Teo and Renzo were back in the underwater cave in the House of the Spirits. Teo was bleeding profusely from the shark scratches. Renzo was holding his shoulder, and grimacing with pain. Neither of them could quite bear to look at the other, remembering what they had said out there in the water, when they had believed they were about to die.

In moments Chissa was applying fermented chilli jelly to their wounds with a gentle hand, while Lussa explained what had happened. 'I grew Suspicious when You did not return after Twenty of your Human Minutes. So I sent out a Patrol. My Scouts sighted the Dog-Fish gliding towards Teodora and summoned Reinforcements from the Cavern.'

'What happened then?' asked Teo.

'A Hundred of my best Warrior-Mermaids closed around the Sharks, even as the Sharks were closing around You.

They sang at the Tops of their Voices to stun the Beasts into a deep Trance.'

Chissa continued, 'That's when we moved in amongst them to take ye in our arms. I myself had the honour of reaching ye first, Undrowned Child, ye'll remember.'

'The sharks didn't wake when you swam among them?'

Lussa laughed, 'Contrariwise, They were dreaming. Indeed, Some of Them were snoring in a most Unattractive & Chortling Manner.'

'But I remember splashing. And shouting.'

'Unfortunately, Some of the Hungrier Sharks lurched back to Life just as Their Supper was being taken away from Them.'

Chissa described how it had come to blows between the mermaids and the monstrous fish. The mermaids had thrashed with their vast tails, making a great white wedding cake of waves in the lagoon. Under cover of this she and Lussa had carried the children back to the secret submarine tunnel under the House of the Spirits.

'Are the other mermaids safe?' asked Teo, reaching for *The Key to the Secret City* on the moss cushion where she had left it. She hugged it to her chest.

'Oh Yar, all accounted for,' affirmed Lussa cheerfully, ''Tis, in True Fact, a Relief of Sorts to meet the Enemy's Vassals in Open Conflict.'

Renzo frowned, 'But won't they tell Bajamonte Tiepolo that they were attacked by mermaids? Won't that alert him to your existence? And where you are?'

'Fortunately, Sharks think only of Food. It would not enter their Brute Heads to ponder on subtle Matters like Revenge, or even to calculate what robbed Them of their little Feast. They will already have forgotten about Us, and be warring among Themselves over some Scrap of Seagull or Fish. *Il Traditore* keeps Them only for the Crudest of Work. If He wants some Spying performed, He sends up One of the *magòghe*. Or an Insect. Or a Bat. They are always up for Improperness.'

Mermaids brought the children dry towels and delicious hot drinks, salty and sweet and very spicy at the same time, served in beautiful Venetian glass goblets, and then, in bowls made out of scallop shells, a thick creamy soup, with crunchy croutons floating in it, and some soft bready cakes, dusted with a white powder.

'Down the hatch!' urged Chissa. 'Do ye good.'

Teo and Renzo gulped and munched and held out their scallop shells for more.

'What is this?' Renzo asked. 'It is absolutely delicious!'

'You are drinking Seaweed Cocoa with Cayenne Pepper. The Soup is Curried Lagoon Samphire, of course. And those are Deep-Fried Algae Croutons. The Bread is stuffed with River-Ripened Sea Semolina and the Savoury Powder is Stone-Ground Mud Myrrh.' Lussa licked her pretty lips.

'I wish you hadn't told us that.' Teo put her scallop-shell down. It immediately fell off the table. 'I don't think I eat most of those things.'

'Perhaps you have not been Fortunate enough to taste Them prepared properly before.' Lussa looked proud. 'As You see, Mermaids dine well. We are known for being Uncommonly Fussy & Exceptionally Greedy.'

'So,' wheedled Chissa. 'Undrowned Child, shall ye not partake of a little Potted Duff? With a snattock o' Beetle Bait?'

'Really, I couldn't manage another morsel,' said Teo politely. 'Also, I don't eat fish.'

'But Nor do We!' cried Lussa. 'What did You think We dined upon – raw Barracuda Hearts & Cod Liver? Nay, We do not eat our fellow Sea Creatures. That would be what You Humanfolk call Cannibalism. Chissa uses a Sea Expression for Steamed Pudding and Jam. In our Case, served with Cumin Custard.'

Chissa held out the platter so the smell wafted over to the children. Potted Duff had a delightful sweet fragrance. But Renzo and Teo were really not hungry any more. Now that they felt warm and safe again, their minds had started to return to the subject of Bajamonte Tiepolo.

Teo blurted out what she had been thinking ever since she saw the graves of her parents and relatives, 'My mother and father . . . Was it really an accident?'

Chissa's eyelids dropped down. Lussa stated, 'Sadly, nay, 'Twas no Accident. It had been a decidedly Hot Summer that Year. A Pipe broke at a coastal Manufactory. A Tide of Filth & Poison swept into the Lagoon. The Mayor tried to keep It hushed.'

At the mention of the Mayor, a mermaid shouted, 'Scoundrelly rectum!'

Lussa threw the parrots a warning glance, and continued, 'But the Water of the Lagoon waxed warm and the Creature started to stir. We were not able to pacify It completely, no Matter what We did. It may have been the first Time that the Spirit of Bajamonte Tiepolo tried to harness the little Creatures that make up the bigger One, because It had never killed Humanfolk before.'

'But *why* did my parents have to die that night?'

'Let Us just say that Bajamonte Tiepolo has always sought to kill Gasperins when He could get Them. That night They were taking You to your Christening by their Family Priest on the Island of Murano.'

'Why Gasperins?'

Lussa continued as if she had not heard: 'By the time We arrived There it was too late to save the Adults: They were already drowned. There was No one left to save except You, Teodora, the Undrowned Child of the old Prophecy. You alone, by a Miracle, were able to survive some Time under the Waves. Of course, being the Daughter of Such Parents had left You with some Particular Talents. I understand that You are a *Vedeparole*, for Example.'

'A what?'

'A *Vedeparole*, meaning that You see Spoken Words as Written upon Air. By which You can learn much about Him or Her who utters Them. And furthermore, You are a *Lettrice-del-cuore*, are You not? You can read People's Hearts by touching their Chests.'

Teo remembered what she had felt when she had put her hand on the stone chest of Signor Rioba. She wondered, 'Does that mean that I can do it with anyone?'

Aloud, she asked, 'But how did I survive?'

'We suspect the Fish helped You.'

'The . . . fish?'

'It would be just like Them. Such slandered Little Beasts. Humanfolk think Them mere Swimming Machines. I understand You Humanfolk even have an Expression "as cold as a fish". Never was Anything more Untrue. Fish are verily the Kindest-Hearted Things in the Sea. Particularly the *Branzino* and the *Sgombro* . . .'

'But how . . .?'

'One day We shall perhaps know the Entire Story. For now All We can tell is This: the Fish came Here to warn Us of your Plight, all by Signs & Motion, being Mute. Somehow – We know not How – They kept You alive until We reached You. We hastened to fetch You to the House of the Spirits, and made Sure that the Nuns found You. And Those Ladies looked after You here until a new Home was found for You by the Mayor.'

Lussa's laugh tinkled scornfully around the cavern, 'Of course, that Pompous Monkey knew Nothing of Us! Given What had happened, We agreed – our only ever Agreement with Him – that it was safer for Teodora to be taken away from Venice, at least for a While. We even approved of his

153

sneaksome Plan to let the Flowering Plants grow over the Graves of Marta & Daniele Gasperin. For That hid from View the Fact that their Daughter had been found and was Alive.'

Renzo exclaimed triumphantly, 'So I was right – the Mayor wanted to get rid of Teo, and even the memory of Teo, to avoid bad publicity for his precious tourists!'

Teo's voice trembled, 'And that's why I felt strange when I saw the House of the Spirits. I had been here before. But it feels like someone else's life. I don't remember the nuns . . . I don't remember my *parents*.'

'Your Parents adored You, Teodora. Then the Nuns loved You,' recalled Lussa. 'You could not have been more loved, or more tenderly taken care of. You were here with the Nuns for some Time, the only Baby who had ever lived in that Great House. I shall not soon forget how They cried when it was Time to send You away. But They understood Why. It was not safe here in Venice.'

Renzo observed, 'And now you've saved her life a second time!'

Lussa replied sombrely, 'Teodora's life is still in Danger, and so is Yours, Lorenzo, and so is That of Every Human in Venice as long as the Spirit of Bajamonte Tiepolo is abroad. But Yar, Teodora was saved for a Reason. Because she *Herself* will be Instrumental in saving Venice, according to the Prophecy.'

'The poem in the book is a prophecy?' asked Teo.

Lussa nodded.

Chissa explained, 'You two childer are short-spliced now.' She plaited two tresses of her red hair together to show them what she meant. Renzo scowled.

'Can . . . can a *ghost* save Venice?' asked Teo. She was tired of pretending to herself, and to Renzo.

'But you are not a Ghost, Teodora. Poor Child, have You

154

been worrying about That? Nay, You are not Dead. You have just gone between-the-Linings for a While.'

Teo's knees and arms felt milky with sweet relief.

Renzo demanded, 'What's that – between-the-Linings? Why didn't you answer me when I asked about it before? Teo, what are you smiling about? What do you know about this?'

Lussa explained patiently, 'Then was not the Time. Now Lorenzo, You should know that Those who live between-the-Linings are Beings who have stepped out of Time for a Space. They are invisible to Human Adults. Children can see Them. Animals can see Them. They breathe, eat, sleep, and have Bodily Functions like Everyone Else. But They cast no Shadows, leave no Fingerprints and Whatever they write is also invisible to Others. To Adult Humanfolk, the Air feels a little colder around Them. 'Tis a State that usually falls upon People in Times of Crisis, to protect Them from their Enemies, Including Enemies who are Ghosts in-the-Meltings.'

She turned to Teo, 'You see, Child, 'Twas once again Necessary to take You away from your Old Life, and from the Supervision of your Adoptive Parents, in order for You to do what is now required of You. So We put You between-the-Linings.'

'How did you do that?' asked Renzo.

Lussa explained serenely, 'We sing People into that State.'

Teo remembered the singing she had heard in the hospital, before she fell unconscious and woke up in the graveyard.

Teo, who had not cried when the sharks closed in, or when she saw her real parents' grave, now burst into undignified tears. 'So I can't tell my parents, I mean my Naples parents, that I am safe? They think I might be dead. You can't imagine how they suffer.'

'I regret not. We must wait till This is over before You can appear to Them again.'

Renzo looked disgusted. 'So you thought you were a *ghost*, Teo? Is that why you risked *my* life, jumping into the water like that? Because you had nothing to lose? Because you were already *dead*?'

'Hush, Lorenzo!' Lussa's voice was firm. 'There are Many Matters that You do not yet know about Teodora, indeed that Teodora does not know Herself. Remember, this is hard for Her. She has been Most Mournfully Lonely between-the-Linings – and I daresay, even before That. 'Tis a Lamentable Truth that Children who are Marked Out by Destiny are generally sadly Alone.'

'That is exactly it,' reflected Teo, remembering her solitary walks around Venice. Most Mournfully Lonely.

'You must stay Secret & between-the-Linings, Teodora,' Lussa repeated. 'For your own Safety. It will be harder for Bajamonte Tiepolo to find You there.'

'But why . . . why would *he* be looking for *me*?' asked Teo, in a shaking voice.

'You are a Gasperin, Teodora. Bajamonte Tiepolo likes not to leave any Unfinished Business. And of course the Old Prophecy will be in *Il Traditore*'s Mind. If He knew that the Undrowned Child had come back to Venice, He would be looking for Her,' said Lussa simply. 'That is why You must keep Yourself away from his Little Henchwoman Maria, who might lead Him to You.'

She concluded firmly, 'Now That is all You need to know at this Time. We have frightened You enough for Today, I believe.'

She asked Renzo to take Teo back to her 'cabin' at the hotel. Renzo's anger had evaporated. He looked as frightened as Teo felt. A light aperture in the roof of the cave showed that the moon had gone behind a big black cloud. How could they walk back through the city without light?

Renzo, with a wary eye on the parrots, explained, 'Our lanterns keep dying.'

Lussa nodded, and clapped her hands. A pair of slightly oily mermaids, whose apron pockets were bulging with tools, now appeared. They held aloft two tattered old kites in the shape of plump red and blue fish made out of lacquered paper.

'Tested and in full working order, Your Majesty.' The engineer-mermaids bowed to Lussa, and then handed one to each of the children. The fish jerked upwards on their strings. They bobbed in the air, their eyes blank and their mouths open.

'Kites?' observed Renzo dubiously. 'Children's kites?'

'Tie Them to your Wrists,' Lussa suggested. 'Ask Them nicely.'

Feeling self-conscious, Teo spoke softly to her fish, 'If you please, give us light.'

Inside the kite a jewelled candle burst into life. Suddenly the eyes of the fish glowed with alert intelligence.

'Now snap your fingers, Teodora.'

The flame extinguished immediately. Renzo and Teo climbed up the stairs, wading through the seaweed, out of the chapel and through the garden, where all the ghosts were silent now, watching them pass with a sort of respect that suddenly made the children more nervous than before. After hauling themselves over the wall and the row of boats, they found someone waiting for them on the path at the water's edge.

For some reason *her* lamp hadn't gone out but shone a bright dirty yellow.

Maria whistled when she saw Teo. 'Ain't *you* in trouble! Wait'll I tell your parents! I shouldn't like to be in *your* shoes when they hear about this.'

26. Who's your friend?

the first glimmerings of dawn, June 8th, 1899

Renzo and Teo regarded her in stupefied silence while Maria chattered like a budgerigar.

'Te-Odore, where did you get those stupid old kites? Very dainty you look, I must say. What happened to your skirt? It's all torn! Have you been swimmin'? Ugh, you stink like a canal! And have you been eating curry? Ugh! But who's your friend?' Maria simpered. 'Where did you find him? And by the way, *Dora*, I've seen you two together these last few days, lookin' in that crazy old book . . . I should think your parents are going to *kill* you,' she added happily. 'Their Little Miss Perfect has really gone off! Upsettin' them like that!'

All the while Maria twisted the emerald earring in her ear, which had visibly swelled and was now discoloured with a black and yellow bruise.

Renzo looked at Maria with fascination, as if she was a particularly repulsive spider. And indeed, while Teo watched Renzo watching Maria, a large brown insect crawled out of Maria's pocket, unseen by her, and scuttled off.

With relief, Teo realized that Maria herself was not really

interested in *The Key to the Secret City*, or what they'd been doing. The thing was that Renzo was a *boy*. For the first time Teo noticed that Renzo, even wet, injured and in a state of shock, was probably what most girls would describe as handsome.

Teo thought, 'Well, at least Maria isn't in love with Bajamonte Tiepolo, if she's trying her so-called feminine wiles on someone else. That's one good thing.'

Maria's face was plastered with rouge and she was wearing high-heeled boots that made her lurch from side to side like a baby giraffe. She obviously believed she looked like a fashion-plate. But her skin was a strange greenish colour under the rouge, and there was something wrong with her shoulders. It couldn't just be the ruffles of her bodice. Maria was also wearing more crests than ever, and they were all the same – red, yellow and blue.

Renzo continued to stare at Maria, who was making great big eyes at him. Renzo bowed like a courtier and formally requested permission to see 'you delightful young ladies' back to the hotel. All the way, Teo endured Maria's squeals and giggles, wondering how Renzo could be so blind as to respond so gallantly to them. Maria was a *Napoletana* – not a Venetian. Why was Renzo treating *her* like a princess? Maria's inane flirting rattled Teo's nerves. At the door to the hotel, Maria announced that she was going inside for her 'beauty sleep'.

'Not needed at all!' purred Renzo with an approving smile.

Maria gave Teo a half-lidded triumphant glance that announced *I got him*.

Renzo bowed, 'It has been the greatest of pleasures to meet you, Signorina Maria. Naturally I trust we can count on your discretion. Given the delicacy of the situation, it would be advisable *not* to mention to anyone that you have, as it

159

were, *encountered* young Teodora. I'm confident you comprehend perfectly . . .'

'What?'

Teo practically snarled, 'Sorry Maria, Renzo doesn't speak baby-talk. Let me translate. You're not to tell anyone you've seen me. Did that sink in?'

Renzo looked daggers at Teo and beamed at Maria, 'If you would be so kind, dear girl.'

'Who? Dora? I've forgotten her already! That's not hard!'

Maria gave Renzo a coquettish wink and flounced indoors.

As soon as Maria was gone, Teo – although she'd sworn that she would deal with this in a cool, collected manner – simply could not stop herself.

'How could you?' she hissed. 'Carrying on so disgracefully with Maria! She's not a great lady, and you're certainly not a courtier. Not only is she mixed up with Bajamonte Tiepolo but she's nothing more than a stupid flirt. With the inner life of a hairbrush, or maybe a comb . . .'

Teo did not stop for breath. There was so much to spill, so many incidents, so many slights in those eleven long years of being forced into Maria's company because of the friendship of their parents. At the end of her recital, Teo felt empty but also somehow dirty and ashamed, even though it had been Maria whose character and intellect she had just torn to pieces.

Renzo met her outburst with silence.

'Well?' she challenged, leaning back against a lamp-post with her arms folded. 'Do you disagree with me?'

Renzo looked astonished. 'Oh Teo, I'm no more captivated by Maria than you are.'

Teo's face blazed like a sunset. She was grateful for the cover of darkness.

'Though clearly she's not such a *consuming* subject for

me, ahem! Don't you see? We have to keep Maria "sweet". We don't want her running to Bajamonte Tiepolo, to tell him about her two friends wandering the town at night, do we? Given the prophecy, I'd say her friend *Il Traditore* might be quite interested to hear of a pair of children, an orphan girl and a rather clever, that is to say, *studious* boy . . .

'And before I err, *worked* . . . on her, she was also threatening to tell your parents that she'd seen you,' Renzo continued in his lecturing voice. 'Your parents would be devastated. They would think you'd been playing some kind of cruel game of hide-and-seek. By being polite to Maria, I've persuaded her to promise not to tell them either. Now, isn't that better than the alternative?'

Teo was forced to admit that Renzo had been clever. But a sliver of left-over resentment made her say, 'Still, aren't Maria's clothes unbearably ridiculous?'

Renzo surprised her. 'At least she makes an effort with her appearance. It may be misguided, but an effort is always appreciated here.'

Teo looked down on her damp dress, crumpled pinafore and scuffed shoes. Remnants of seaweed bandage trailed from her bloodstained leg. Her hair was surely standing on end: her curls always frizzed up when she swam. For the second time she noticed that Renzo, even a little chewed up by sharks, wet and exhausted, still had a kind of elegance in his appearance.

Renzo said benevolently, 'Well, if you're to be a proper *Veneziana* now, there are some things you must learn, Teo. We Venetians hate the way tourists wear seaside-holiday clothes in our churches and museums. Men walking around with their cravattes untied, as if they were at a bar in a seedy port.'

Teo protested, 'But some people cannot afford nice clothes. You can't be such a snob. Just because someone doesn't dress well doesn't mean that they're Venice's enemy.'

'It's a question of respect! Look at how Venice dresses for *us*! So beautiful, every day, every hour. We Venetians try to keep up appearances. There's so few of us now that it is even more important. We've lost half our citizens in the last fifty years.'

'If they love it so much, then why are so many Venetians leaving?'

'Love *her* so much. Venice is always referred to in the feminine, Teo. You must learn that now.' Renzo sighed. Educating Teo to be a proper Venetian clearly seemed an enormous job of work to him.

Teo persisted, 'So why are the people abandoning *her*?'

'It breaks their hearts. But now the salt is eating the ground floors of the buildings, so you just can't live in the cheaper housing. It's too bad. The damp gave my father bronchitis . . . The steam ferries drench the gondoliers ten times a day.'

As if to reinforce his point, at that moment a gondola passed by on the other side of the canal, and the gondolier gave a hacking cough into a white handkerchief.

Renzo flinched but continued, 'Even young people get rheumatic illnesses. Listen . . .' He stretched out his arms and turned them around. His shoulder joints clicked loudly.

'Oh! Does that hurt?'

'Not yet. But so many of the real Venetians, who stay on, grow ill. It's like a tax on their health. And diseases spread like wildfire here, because we live so close together. The Bubonic Plague killed a third of the population. But no one wanted to leave.'

Renzo wrinkled his nose. A whiff of something rotten had floated in off the canal. Teo decided it was safer not to remark upon it. Renzo might take it as an insult to Venice. Instead, she exclaimed, 'So if you are loyal to Venice, you'll suffer for her? Even the Bubonic Plague?'

Renzo said warmly, 'Teo, you are . . .' Then he shoved his hands in his pockets. He pulled out his hand with a wry expression; it was still full of gravel from their fall in the garden of the House of the Spirits. He tossed the stones in the canal.

So deep were they in conversation that neither Renzo nor Teo noticed that, just where the pebbles had fallen, the water was starting to stir in circular motions. Behind Renzo's back one of the striped poles began to quiver. Then it flexed upwards and slowly spiralled down into the water. The foul stench immediately disappeared.

Teo offered shyly, 'I would suffer for Venice, if I had to. If I could help her.'

A splashing noise drew Teo's eyes to a sudden blur of movement behind him.

'Renzo!' she screamed. But it was too late. The tentacle that had pretended to be a *palina* surged out of the water and wrapped itself around Renzo's left leg. A second, more slender feeler slid forth to take his neck. Renzo toppled over, screamed and pulled at his throat, around which the living noose was tightening. The two tentacles started to drag him towards the water.

Renzo could not utter a word, but his agonized eyes implored Teo for help. She threw herself on the ground and wedged her own ankles around the lamp-post, at the same time grabbing Renzo's right leg and clinging with all her might.

'Take my arm!' she cried. His trembling hand reached and gripped her elbow.

The larger tentacle was thicker than Teo's waist, and powerfully muscled. But it was not expecting resistance. Or attack.

With her free hand, Teo pulled *The Key to the Secret City* out of her pinafore and struck out again and again with the book's sharp corners. The small tentacle recoiled and slid back into the water. The larger one released its grip for a moment, and then grabbed the fabric of Renzo's trousers at the ankle. This was its mistake. With a retching noise, the flannel came away to the knee, and Renzo kicked himself free and rolled over on his back.

Teo dealt one final blow to the striped tentacle. This time the corner of the book pierced the slimy skin, and a reeking ooze of yellow and black slime exploded over Renzo's shin, bare from where the fabric had torn away. Renzo screamed as his skin fizzed and smoked, as if acid had been thrown on his leg.

But the tattered tentacle at last withdrew back into the water.

Renzo, barely conscious, lay on the paving, gasping shallow breaths. Teo dragged him back to the lamp-post and propped him up against it. She ran into the hotel and snatched a jug of water from the deserted kitchen. Back by the canal she rinsed the slime off Renzo's leg, revealing three angry raised blisters, each the size of a small egg. Her own lip burned; a drop of the stinking viscera had splashed onto her mouth. She could taste its rottenness. She upended the jug over her face, so the dregs of the water washed away every trace of it. Then she spat repeatedly into the canal.

Renzo spluttered back to life and into tears of unashamed pain and relief. Teo quietly wiped his eyes with the corner of her pinafore, and held his hand until his sobs subsided.

'You saved my life,' he whispered eventually. He did not let go of her hand.

'I owed you for the sharks. Does it still hurt?'

'Less.'

Teo knew he was lying. She asked, 'Do you think you can walk?'

Renzo clambered to his knees, with a brave, false smile.

'Look at me!' he grimaced, pointing to his ripped trousers. 'After my great speech on Venetian elegance, I've turned out a very poor example, haven't I? Well, must get myself home and deal with this *shambles*,' he added, with a brightness that did not deceive Teo for a moment.

'Shall I come with you? You can lean on me.'

'I can walk perfectly well.' Renzo took a few steps, wincing.

'You're limping!'

'I am not. I'm just a little tired. Good night, Teo. Or I mean good morning, I suppose. We'll meet at the usual place? Then the Archives, yes?'

She nodded. Renzo walked normally until he reached the edge of the courtyard, when he thought he was out of her sight. Then he sagged, and she saw his shoulders shaking. And finally he limped away, slowly and awkwardly.

She slipped inside the hotel and up to her room and rinsed the blood out of her clothes.

Then she washed and combed her hair. And thoughtfully looked through her armoire for a fresh pinafore and some rather tidier clothes to wear to the Archives later that day.

27. A sick day

June 8th, 1899

Teo woke suddenly with a high temperature and a streaming nose. The sore spot on her lip throbbed and burned. She couldn't help wondering if she had caught something from the entrails of the tentacle – perhaps she had swallowed a drop of that stinking slime? The very notion brought on a wave of nausea. Meanwhile, the water from her swim in the lagoon had got inside her ears and they echoed like a cave.

'No, it's just a cold,' she told herself. When she thought she was dead, at least she had not caught any human colds.

She dressed quickly and hurried over to Maria's room. Much as it irked her, she knew she should reinforce Renzo's flattery from last night. But the door was locked, and her frantic whispers raised no answer.

In the dining room, Teo watched her parents eating their miserable, rushed breakfast. They were going to the gathering of scientists: she could see that from their satchels. Of course they could not spend all their time looking for their daughter.

Teo guessed, 'They must be beginning to believe I am

166

dead. It would be just their way to try to work themselves to distraction.'

Teo felt doubly guilty. Her absence was causing all this pain – not that she could do anything about that. But it also made her uncomfortable that she now knew who her real parents were, and who she was herself. And even if she could speak to her adoptive parents now, she could not talk of Daniele and Marta Gasperin, not without hurting them terribly.

She followed them out of the dining room, listened to them urge the manager to send a messenger if even the smallest piece of news came in about Teo.

'Even a false alarm,' said her father.

'Even a rumour,' whispered her mother.

Teo climbed up the stairs back to her bedroom and lay on the bed. A dry pain seared her throat and she snuffled pathetically. A cold seemed almost a joke after all the danger she had passed through. But it was a tiring joke. Gradually her eyes grew heavier.

Well after nightfall she woke again, her throat on fire and her head thumping. A wistful memory came to her, of that delicious seaweed cocoa down in the cavern. Consulting the wall-clock, she calculated that she had been asleep for at least twelve hours. Had Maria betrayed her yet? Or had she kept her promise to Renzo? She certainly wouldn't do it for Teo's sake.

Lying in her hot bed, Teo's next thought was of her real parents, her dead parents, hidden in their leafy graves on San Michele. She pictured the family funeral, and wondered if she was there, perhaps held in the arms of one of the white-clad nuns from the House of the Spirits. Had she cried? Babies cry; they understand things.

Then there came into her mind an image of Renzo being dragged towards the canal by the two tentacles. Renzo!

He had not hesitated to jump into the water to follow her. She had practically led him to a ghastly death in the jaws of a shark! Teo lurched out of bed. Renzo must have been wondering what had happened to her. She hurried downstairs to the kitchen in her petticoat. Who would see her to notice? After two jugs of water, she felt much better. She helped herself to a spoonful of honey for her sore throat.

Back in her room she washed and dressed with care, choosing her best skirt and a clean blue bodice, and even brushed her shoes. Running a comb through her hair, she experimentally changed the parting. She tried to look at herself through Renzo's eyes: did she pass muster as a Venetian? She hoped so.

As she stole out of her room, she noticed light under the door of Maria's. Muffled shouts leaked out into the corridor. She ran to put her ear to the door, and soon realized with horror what was going on.

Maria's parents had finally noticed their daughter's new slippers, jewels and scarves. Jumping to the worst conclusion, as was their wont, they had accused her of stealing and of being a superficial little girl, obsessed with fripperies and chasing boys.

Maria whined, 'Everyone's got these crests, Pa. You ain't interested in fashion. You only care about the laboratory! But there is a life outside, with pretty clothes, and boys, and . . . lots of lovely things. You just never see it!'

Teo flinched as Tommaso Naccaro stated coldly, 'We've never been impressed with you as a daughter. Now you have proved what a worthless child you are.'

'Poor Maria,' Teo thought. But her compassion evaporated the next minute.

For now Maria whimpered that it was Teo who had given her the money for her finery! 'It was a bribe so *she* could run around in secret with a dirty Venetian boy. No, I don't know where Teo got the money! Probably stole it. You know Teo, Ma, Pa! She ain't got any friends. She'd do anythin' for attention. That's why she's run away. She's perfectly well – just havin' a good laugh at everyone else's expense.'

'You've seen Teodora! You nasty, nasty child, why didn't you tell anyone before?'

Teo heard the sound of teeth rattling. Maria's mother must have been shaking her.

'Leave me alone!' shouted Maria. 'I only saw her last night. I was going to tell you but you started on about the clothes. You didn't give me a chance to speak!'

Teo heard a face being slapped, and a storm of tears from Maria.

How badly Maria's parents must be thinking of Teo herself now! And soon her own parents would be thinking the same thing. And if Maria could betray Teo to her parents, she was perfectly capable of running to Bajamonte Tiepolo.

Then Maria's father harrumphed, 'We'll not upset Teodora's parents with the lies of a malicious little girl! We won't tell them one word, unless we can verify that it is the truth, Miss.'

'Yes!' snuffled Maria. 'You do that, why don't you?'

After a few more harsh words they left their daughter sobbing into her pillow. Teo watched as they swept out of the room, stiff with indignation. Maria turned the lock ostentatiously from the inside. Teo darted out and beat on Maria's door without mercy.

'It's me!' she hissed through the keyhole.

'No! Leave me alone!'

Teo thought quickly. Adults could not see or hear her, but Maria probably didn't realize that. She bluffed, 'Shall I tell your parents *my* side of the story? On past record, whom are they more likely to believe – you or me, Maria? Let me in!'

A snuffling noise approached the door. A red-eyed Maria

opened it a crack. Teo briskly pushed her way in. Maria's swollen eyes glowed hotly with tears. Her clothes were all crushed. She seemed bedraggled, small and vulnerable, afraid of Teo, even. And that frightful perfume smelled stale and sordid.

Maria took Teo's hard words without protest. And they were very hard; after all her reading, Teo was equipped with a vocabulary that could cut rocks. Maria seemed abjectly sorry. When she finally spoke, it was in a tiny, tearstained voice. 'Teo, what was I thinking of? I just panicked. I humbly beg your pardon. I said all the wrong things. I'm not smart, you know. You must hate me.'

Maria's words appeared above her head to Teo as usual, but the strange thing was that they were not written out in Maria's usual babyish handwriting. They looked *older*, somehow, as if Maria had aged by hundreds of years as a result of her parents' cruel scolding. Teo could not stay angry with someone who was so clearly in such awful trouble. Maria must be tired and lonely from all that sneaking around. Teo knew from her own recent experience how simply exhausting it was to have secrets and to be forced to protect them. 'No, of course not,' Teo reassured her. 'I don't hate you.'

Maria mumbled, 'That's very decent of you, Teo. Aren't parents beastly? How's a young person to do anything without getting shouted at and insulted?'

'You've been up to some things that worry yours,' Teo reminded her gently, uncomfortably aware that she was in no position to criticize.

'A few new clothes? That isn't it. It's because they just despise me.'

Maria was so cast down that she forgot her fashionable slang. 'I never knew you were so nice, Teo!' she pronounced wonderingly. 'I always thought you were stuck-up. And that you thought I was a cretin. All this time we've known each other, we should have been friends. I know I'm not brilliant like you and Renzo, but *couldn't* we be friends now? Please, Teo.'

Maria was behaving so sweetly and persuasively that Teo felt the remnants of her old dislike melting away. And the more her dislike crumbled, the more her fear for Maria grew. Lussa had been categoric: anyone who befriended *Il Traditore* would have to be . . . sacrificed.

'But Maria did it in all innocence,' Teo thought.

Maria edged closer to her. The smell of that musky perfume flew right up Teo's nose. Maria chattered on, dwelling on affectionate memories of their joint childhood. Teo kept a simultaneous monologue going inside her own head. Maria really had had the worst luck! Utterly rotten parents! When they were not ignoring their daughter, they were criticizing her. No wonder Maria needed to get boys to smile at her. Now, driven straight into *Il Traditore*'s clutches by outright mistreatment, Maria faced death as his hoodwinked accomplice. The poor girl did not even have the wit to know she had made a dangerous mistake.

Maria's hand inserted itself around Teo's elbow. Maria had linked arms with her! The way the girls in the fashionable crowd walked around together!

Renzo and the mermaids had been so quick to dismiss Maria, and abandon her to a terrible fate. But they hadn't known her for years, had no conception of what a troubled creature she was. They were not being fair. Maria should be given a chance to redeem herself before it was too late.

'I know,' Teo thought, 'I'm supposed to go to the Archives but . . .' Maria's perfume really was *very* strong. It was quite impossible for Teo to think clearly with that over-sweet scent flooding all her senses and making her feel positively dizzy.

What if Maria changed sides? Given the girl's friendship

with *Il Traditore*'s spirit, Maria was in a perfect position to find out his plans. If Maria truly understood the situation, then of course she would want to help the forces of good. Why, Maria might even be the key and not the obstacle to everything!

Lussa had said, 'We have always needed Children as Ambassadors.'

Surely *three* ambassadors would be better than two in the present danger?

And of course, if Maria was on the right side, then she would never dream of hurting Teo's adoptive parents with the story that their daughter was alive and well, and simply hiding from them.

Teo turned to Maria with a confidence-inspiring smile. 'Get dressed – we're going for a little walk.'

Maria's eyes sparkled. 'Of course, Teo,' she spoke brightly. 'Whatever you suggest. Wonderful!'

Maria complained a little about walking through the dark. She insisted on wearing her high-heeled boots. She kept looking behind her and grimacing, then hurrying forward a few steps as if something was chasing her.

Teo had a good stare behind them each time this happened. There was no sign of the Butcher, or indeed any human. But she caught a glimpse of something small and dark with many legs scurrying furtively along the wall beside them.

Beetles! She shuddered. The insects had gone over to the enemy.

The strange thing was that even in the high heels Maria seemed to be shrinking, and her shoulders were sticking out at an unnatural angle. The moonlight further distorted her shadow to a curious squat shape. She kept a fast grip on Teo's elbow. Walking alongside her, Teo had to turn her head to avoid breathing in the waves of perfume that billowed off Maria's skin.

At the House of the Spirits, they clambered over the boats and scaled the wall, Maria with many squeals and 'ouches'. In the garden the ghosts remained both invisible and silent. Teo couldn't help taking the ghosts' sullen silence as a bad sign, even though it was something of a relief to not have everyone beseeching her like last time.

At the chapel, the key failed to jump out of *The Key to the Secret City*.

'The book doesn't want to bring Maria here either,' Teo realized guiltily.

But she and Renzo had not locked it last time. They'd been too dazed by what they had discovered down below. The door was even heavier than she recalled. An uncomfortable idea crossed her mind: perhaps it too was trying to keep Maria out. Teo grunted, strained and finally wrenched it open.

'Come,' she urged an apparently dumbstruck Maria. At least the girl was not whining or protesting. She really did seem to be making an effort to behave better.

She led Maria down the stairs towards the mosaic pool of the mermaids. With every step down, Teo's misgivings rose. She wasn't looking forward to this encounter. Not only was she revealing the mermaids to a person known to associate with Venice's worst enemy, but she was arriving in the company of the one person they had told her to avoid at all costs.

'Wait here,' she told Maria as they neared the bottom of the steps. 'It will be better if I come and get you after I've explained.'

28. Beware Mahogany Mice

late at night, June 8th, 1899

Teo had not picked a good time to visit the mermaids. They were gathered around coral tables, eating greedily. Interrupting mermaids at feed always tends to produce somewhat snappy results.

'Who goes there?' thundered a disgruntled voice.

''Tis da Undrowned Child!' called out one of the mermaids indistinctly, as she had a rather full mouth, 'Make way for da Undrowned Child, Lord love 'er heart!'

'Teodora Gasperin!' exclaimed Lussa, 'Come and join Us.'

Chissa held out a chair. Teo sat down, feeling dreadfully awkward. Would the mermaids be so hospitable if they knew whose little helper was waiting around the corner?

A mermaid in a white chef's hat piled fragrant parcels of food onto a scalloped plate in front of her.

'What is it?' Teo asked, just in case, though her fork was already impaling a fragment. She had not eaten a thing for more than a day.

'Coriander Pea Cakes in Coconut Curry. Twice-Fried Chilli-Cucumber in a Pool of Amber Sauce. Perfectly toothsome.'

Delicious as it was, Teo could not force more than a mouthful down. How would Renzo handle this? she wondered. Then it struck her, hard and horribly, that she hadn't even consulted him about her plan to save Maria. Now that she was a few feet away from Maria's perfume, everything seemed sharper and clearer. She was starting to feel not just guilty but also a little sick.

'Are ye not hungry, Undrowned Child?' asked Chissa. 'Do ye have a rumpus in your chitterlins? Eat up and tell us about the Archives!'

Teo stammered. 'I have taken the liberty . . . I have brought . . . someone to see you.'

'Yoiks, can you smell somethin' proper 'orrible?' asked one of the mermaids, sniffing disgustedly.

''Orrible, 'orrible, 'orrible,' chorused the parrots. It was not necessary to explain any further because at that moment Maria herself appeared at the threshold of the cavern, staring at the assembled mermaids with more distaste than surprise.

'I got bored,' she whined at Teo. 'And here you are fillin' yourself with food. Did you forget about me?'

The whole chorus of mermaids turned as one to look at her. Someone cried, 'What in da name of curried samphire is *that*?'

'Teodora, is This Who I think It is?' asked Lussa in a voice quiet but menacing.

Teo nodded miserably. The mermaids erupted in salty expressions of disgust.

Lussa spoke over the hubbub in a voice heavy with disappointment, 'Teodora, We expressly ordered You to Keep away from that Girl. We had our Reasons for It.'

'Yo-ho, Undrowned Child, why did Ye bring dat hunchback dwarf in here?' a very young mermaid shouted.

'Hunchback? Dwarf?' screamed Maria. 'Are you talking about *me*?'

Chissa spoke out now, 'And who else, pray?'

'Yer got it on the nob, girlie!' someone hissed.

Other mermaids hubbubbed, 'That's a plain piece of goods! Look at that forehead – narrow as an eel's bed, not much room in there for a brain!'

'Aye! This girlie is depriving a village somewhere of an idiot. Drown da brute, say I! At least give her a good pinching! She's got no business here!'

The mermaids lashed their tails at Maria, and bared their teeth and looked more like sharks than beautiful girls for a moment. Lussa swam into the middle of them, and calmed them with a few sharp words. But when she turned to Teo, her lovely face too was distorted with anger.

'Do You not remember,' Lussa demanded, glaring at Teo, and pointing at Maria, 'that Bajamonte Tiepolo's familiar was a Dwarf Who carried his Flag? Don't You see that He's turning this Foolish Little Girl into his Old Accomplice? Look at that suppurating Hole in her Ear! Ready for Him to lead Her along with a Chain! Dwarves are known for their Weakness for Precious Metals & Jewellery,' Lussa added contemptuously, 'so 'Tis easy to lure Them with a Bit of Fool's Gold.'

Chissa screwed up her face, 'And that repulsive stench of musk – 'tis no doubt the potion he has employed to effect her transformation.'

'And deprave the Brain of our Undrowned Child, I fear,' added Lussa.

One of the mermaids held up a turtleshell to Maria, and its surface dissolved into a cruelly clear mirror. Suddenly it was obvious even to Maria what was happening to her. She was shrinking to the size of a dwarf, with a definite hunchback as well.

Maria launched into noisy hysterics. Lussa spoke with a reluctant touch of kindness, 'Quieten Yourself, Child. Most

Humanfolk will not notice. Magical Transformations are invisible to Adults, for Example.'

Teo cleared her throat, 'I have had . . . an idea.'

All faces turned to her.

At that moment came a shriek from the back of the cave. 'Sufferin' seahorses! It's the Mahogany Mice agin! All hands to deck! Fetch the noggin' boots!'

Teo spun around, expecting to see small furry – or even wooden – creatures scampering around the cavern. Instead, the golden walls were suddenly dark with extremely nasty-looking brown beetles, of an appearance halfway between the largest cockroach Teo had ever seen and a centipede. All over the cavern mermaids were seizing strange weapons – long sticks, each with an old boot mounted at one end.

'They're not mice then?' Teo asked one mermaid rushing past her.

'Nay! They're *scolopendre*, hundred-leggers. We hates 'em like poison. They bites. And keep ye away from 'em, Undrowned Child. They likes 'oomans. Ye know where they likes to hide da best of all? Inside 'ooman clothes!'

Teo and Maria hastily stepped backwards, away from the crawling walls.

With a mighty blow upwards, the mermaid smashed her boot on three *scolopendre* at once.

'Yoiks!' the mermaid shouted, as the dead insects dropped onto her beautiful curls. In seconds the cavern was full of mermaids beating the walls with their boots-on-sticks and shouting 'Yoiks!' with every kill. Chissa armed herself with two boots and destroyed twice as many *scolopendre* as anyone else.

Dead insects rained into the water. Mermaids from the printing press scooped up the brown corpses with nets and flung them on the fires that dried the paper sheets. The *scolopendre* writhed and crackled in the flames, sending out a nose-wrinklingly sour smell.

Two minutes later the swarm of Mahogany Mice had been all but vanquished, and the storm of shouting had subsided to a quiet chorus of 'Well, that one's hung up his galoshes!' and 'Take that, ye lingering beastie!'

Lussa looked self-possessed as ever, but her face was set in tense lines, 'Don't let any escape!' she urged. 'You must get them all.'

Chissa growled, 'Some say the *scolopendre* are the spies of Bajamonte Tiepolo.'

She waved a barnacled boot at Maria, 'This is how we deal with spies down here.'

Maria pouted. 'Teo, what's she talking ab—?'

'Where do you get those old boots?' interrupted Teo quickly.

Chissa looked down, 'Well . . . er . . . shipwrecks happen, ye know.'

Lussa gave Teo a glance that seemed to penetrate her skin. 'Teodora, Something Compelling must have driven You to bring Maria amongst Us. Pray explain Yourself. I hope for all our Sakes that your Reason is surpassing Good.'

With many 'um's and 'so's, Teo stammered out her idea. How feeble they appeared now, all the plans that had seemed so excellent back at the hotel. Her halting phrases sounded unconvincing even to herself. '. . . forced to take a wrong path . . . cruelly treated at home . . . truly eager to do better . . . shouldn't she be allowed to have an opportunity to redeem herself?'

She glanced from time to time at Maria, who stood with her mouth open.

'It's only fair,' Teo concluded lamely. 'And Maria could help us, as a double agent. She could *pretend* to be friendly with Bajamonte Tiepolo and keep us informed of his plans, helping our cause at the same time . . .'

Her voice trailed away.

'That Lubbery Dwarfess won't help you, Undrowned Child!' shouted an aggressive-looking mermaid who wore an inky apron. 'You might as well whistle psalms to a dead dog!'

'Bilge-water!' jeered another.

There was a simultaneous chorus of 'Pig's Ribs!' and 'Codswallop!'

Lussa raised her voice, 'Ladies! *I entreat you to behave Yourselves before Folk.*'

She turned to Teo, 'My young Colleagues rightfully, if inelegantly, express Doubt in your Idea. And what, may I ask, did Young Renzo make of It?'

Teo hung her head and mumbled, 'He doesn't know. I didn't ask him.'

Lussa said pointedly, 'Does That not tell You Something?'

Desperately, Teo turned to Maria, 'You *could* help, couldn't you? Now you understand how serious this is? You understand that Bajamonte Tiepolo is not a nice young man. He's a dangerous criminal. You understand I have to stay hidden for a while? So will you keep quiet about *this*, and me to my parents . . . to *everyone*?'

One last *scolopendra* ran over Maria's foot, pausing to dig its pincers into her ankle.

'Ooow,' she wailed. Then her blank expression changed, as if she had just received a transfusion of fresh, sweet blood. She smiled from ear to ear, 'Whatever you like, dear Teo. Why certainly, I shall.'

Teo looked down at a sea of angry mermaid faces and sternly crossed arms. The silence was worse than all the rowdy abuse. All eyes were fixed on Maria, with cynical expressions. So only Teo saw that last *scolopendra* sneak away behind Maria's foot and crawl over the struts of the Seldom Seen Press. Finally it scuttled out of the cavern unmolested by a single boot.

It was Chissa who finally broke the dreadful quiet. 'Here's the thing – what choice have ye left us, Undrowned Child? Now that *Il Traditore*'s scurvy dwarfy minion has seen us and knows where we dwell?'

Lussa stated quietly, 'You have been undone, Teodora, by your Soft Heart. And by the Perfume this Girl wafted on You. No Good will come of This. Maria is Cleverer than You think, or at least She is Manipulated by Someone Cleverer than Herself. She is merely pretending Meekness.'

'Plank her, says I,' hollered someone else. 'Be a kindness, really. If *Il Traditore* hears she's with us, he'll give her straight to the Butcher, don't ye know.'

Clearly Maria had no idea who or what the Butcher was. Her face was still suffused with the blank smile that had come over it when the *scolopendra* bit her. Now she strolled over to give Teo a big warm hug. Teo flinched away from the stink of the perfume. It made her feel vague again, and not quite steady on her feet.

'Just tell me the plan, Teo, and I'll help!' Once more Maria blinked like a doll.

'What a lot of fanny nanny!' muttered the mermaid with the inky apron.

'Do not trust her, O Undrowned Child! She's hornswaggling ye, good and proper!'

Maria's perfume was suffocating. Teo pushed Maria away gently. Her hand, touching Maria's chest, was shot through with a terrible pain as if darts pierced every one of her five fingers and sent fiery poison up to her own heart.

Maria cooed, 'Dear Teo, did you snag your finger on my crest brooch? So sorry!'

Teo looked over Maria's shoulder towards Lussa, hoping

to see at least a small smile of acceptance. Lussa and Chissa were watching her with expressions of extreme disquiet. 'Beware, *Lettrice-del-cuore*, Reader-of-Hearts, beware.'

29. A betrayal

in the hotel dining room, early morning,
June 9th, 1899

Teo's mother looked deep into Maria's eyes and spoke, 'Dear, your parents here have been telling us something very serious. That you have seen our Teodora, and that she is *hiding* from us? Maria, is this true? Have you seen our daughter?'

Maria's dwarfish transformation, like Teo herself, was, of course, imperceptible to the adults. Since the girls had arrived back at the hotel, where they found both sets of parents just sitting down to breakfast, Maria's sweetness had evaporated like dew. She now threw Teo a mocking glance.

Teo stood mutely watching her parents. It broke her heart to see how much thinner they had become. She was haunted by the dark circles under their eyes. She longed to rush to them and hug them, to be folded into their arms, to comfort them.

Instead, Teo's mother reached out a gentle arm towards Maria, and drew her close. Teo felt a stab of jealousy.

Now Teo's father pulled up a chair in front of Maria. His voice was incredulous. 'You told your parents that Teodora has been stealing money and running around with a Venetian boy. Now that just isn't like Teodora, is it? Tell us it's not true, Maria. No one will be angry with you.'

Maria's father snorted loudly; her mother sniffed.

Teo's mother coaxed, 'Perhaps you have been a little confused, dear?'

Confused? Teo hoped desperately that Maria would say something to defuse the explosive atmosphere.

But Maria was smiling sarcastically, 'Oh yes, Teo's fine and well, and runnin' all over Venice like a giddy goat! She told me it's the best fun she's had in years. Truth is that she's tired of all your mollycoddling!'

Teo's parents stared at Maria as if she was a demon speaking in tongues. Teo yearned to put her hand over Maria's lying mouth.

'And as for the boy,' trilled Maria. 'Oh yes, I've seen him. A perfectly foul street boy, who can barely speak proper Italian. We've just been playin' cards with him – that's why we were out all night. Teo's a real wizard at gambling. She's cleaned me out. I suppose an advance on my allowance is out of the question . . . .?'

Tommaso Naccaro turned purple and his slicked-down hair bristled up like a mane. Maria glanced round at the stony faces of the adults. Seemingly impervious to her father's spluttering fury, she now gave a smile that made Teo's teeth ache. 'Now can I have some hot chocolate? . . . You know, when that book hit old Teo on the head it really made her brain go strange. You'll see her, soon enough, when she feels like it. Next thing she'll be telling you that she's been for a swim with some mermaids! That would be a good laugh, ha ha ha!'

Maria giggled hysterically. 'If Teo was here right now, I just know she'd be laughin' too!'

Teo recoiled from the sight of her. Maria had betrayed her,

183

just as Lussa warned she would. And not only that, but Maria had uttered all the most hurtful things that could possibly be said to Teo's grieving parents. That pain in her fingers, when she touched Maria's chest: she had read Maria's heart, and she should have taken heed. And the writing above Maria's head – of course it did not look like Maria's childlike scrawl any more; it looked like her master's, like Bajamonte Tiepolo's! All the signs had been there. Teo had simply failed – or refused – to take them in.

Teo shouted, 'Maria! The mermaids were right about you, you hunchbacked dwarf!'

No one heard her, of course, except Maria herself, who turned to give Teo a slow smile of triumph. 'Sticks and Stones . . .' she sang. 'La la la.'

Then Teo's mother raised her voice, something that almost never happened. 'Maria! How can you be so cruel about your friend? And what about this boy? Is he older than you? What have you done with our daughter, *you little minx*?'

Teo winced as she heard the anger and tears in her mother's voice. She thrust her hands into her pockets, only to send three playing cards fluttering through the air. Maria must have planted them in her pinafore when she gave Teo that hug – that *traitorous* hug back at the mermaid's cavern.

Once they left Teo's body, the cards ceased to be invisible. They tumbled to the floor, for all the world like tangible evidence of the truth of all Maria's dreadful lies.

In silence, everyone looked at the cards. One had fallen face down . . . the back showed a crest that Teo recognized from somewhere, though in her misery she couldn't work out where.

Maria smirked and quietly backed out of the room.

'Hey! Where d'you think *you're* going?' shouted Teo, trying to grab her.

But Maria had already been seized by her father's strong

hand. He hauled her shrieking up the stairs.

Teo's parents were holding each other and shaking with emotion.

'Could it be true?' whispered her mother. 'That Teodora's alive?'

'It is logically speaking possible,' mused her father. 'They have not found a . . . a . . . body. Though the authorities already talk of a funeral. To "lay the matter to rest", as they put it. And the damnedest thing, Leonora: the police told me that the Mayor insists on children's funerals by night.'

A funeral? Teo felt hot and cold all over.

'What has logic to do with it?' wept Teo's mother. 'Do you mean that I should start wearing mourning now? No, I shall not do it! Oh Alberto, do you remember how Teodora begged to wear mourning for Nanny Giulia?'

At this, even Teo's father broke down.

As Teo stumbled outside, half blinded with tears, she noticed something strange. The windows of the hotel had changed shape. They used to be neat rectangles – instead they had shambled into tall, rickety arches that looked as if they were perching on stilts. She could have sworn that the building seemed bigger today than it had been yesterday. The corridors seemed wider and the ceilings higher. And the outside of the building – it used to be a smooth creamy plaster. Now the paint was falling away like great scabs to show old stone underneath. The shabby walls were studded with round sculptures.

She had seen those sculptures on walls all over Venice. The ones she remembered showed hawks carrying rabbits, and saints attacking dragons. But these sculptures were different. The rabbits had grown huge fangs and were biting hawks. In a strange reversal of all the Biblical stories, the dragons were now winning in the battles with the saints. All over Venice, the forces of evil were conquering the forces of good. She shuddered, and tried not to look at them any more as she hurried to Renzo's house.

Her thoughts were as violent as the sculptures on the wall. Not only had Maria disgraced her in the mermaids' eyes, and promptly betrayed her, she had made Teo forget the one true task that had been set for her: to find the Spell Almanac of Bajamonte Tiepolo. The Spell Almanac! Teo remembered with relief – that was one piece of information she withheld from Maria, at least. She had to go to the Archives as quickly as possible, and accomplish the mission Lussa had set – that was the only way she could undo some of the harm she had done by foolishly trusting Maria.

And she had one more unpalatable task too: to confess her stupidity to Renzo.

'For once, I'll deserve all his scorn,' she thought.

By galloping through the streets, she managed to arrive just at the time when Renzo should be leaving the house to make his way to their usual rendez-vous. But half an hour passed and Renzo still had not come out. No one came out at all. After two fruitless hours she abandoned her post. For the rest of the day she wandered around Venice, trying to work out what to do. Perhaps Renzo's parents had caught him creeping back in during the early hours – and locked him in his room as punishment?

Without the Spell Almanac to bring them, Teo couldn't face going back to the mermaids: not to tell them that she had been completely wrong about Maria, and that she had jeopardized the one advantage they had over Bajamonte – secrecy. She thought of the one *scolopendra* that had escaped the cavern. Was that vile insect even now informing Bajamonte Tiepolo of the mermaids, the cavern, and the

Undrowned Child returned to Venice?

That night Teo was as lonely as the dreadful days when she believed she was a ghost. She tossed and turned on her bed, tortured by a thousand wretched and guilty thoughts, each like a painful pin-prick to keep her awake in the midst of her exhaustion.

30. Green gelato

June 10th, 1899

Teo's parents refused to go to the meeting the next day. They declared that they would spend the entire day looking for her. Her mother was dressed in defiant, hopeful yellow, with a flowered straw hat, ignoring the pitying looks of the other hotel guests.

It was still very early in the morning when a desperate Teo followed them to the square of San Marco where the torture instruments still hung on the lamp-posts. Workmen had been despatched to remove them, but they had been unable to cut through the chains. Then the Mayor had lit upon a happy idea. Posters were now affixed to each entrance to San Marco:

NEW ATTRACTION! OPEN-AIR CHAMBER OF HORRORS. 5 LIRE ENTRANCE FEE.

Teo's parents paused on the edge of the square to watch a workman fixing a newly-painted sign to the wall. Teo read over her mother's shoulder:

Incredible New Exhibition begins June 15th!

'So what is this new show about?' Teo's father asked the workman.

'Something about some chap called Baja – Bargaminty Tiepolo,' the man answered. 'Whoever he is.'

'Whoever he *was*, presumably,' laughed Teo's father. 'Name like that, must have been some kind of clown.'

Under the arches above the square an ice-cream trolley had set up for business.

'Would you care for a *gelato*, Leonora?' asked Teo's father.

It was clear that Teo's mother felt far too wretched to be hungry. But for her husband's sake she exclaimed cheerfully, 'Oh yes, Lovely! Vanilla, please.'

But it seemed that the vendor, a pallid human skeleton, had only one flavour to sell. The *gelato* was a vivid emerald green that glinted in the sun.

'That looks refreshing,' said Teo's father. 'Mint flavour, I dare say.'

'That sounds nice,' thought Teo, drawn to the strong sugary smell that came from the trolley. Pillowy mounds of cool green *gelato* were piled up in metal trays. Teo squeezed herself between the people queuing up to buy it under the beating sun. Some were coming back with empty paper cups for second helpings. They had an aggressive glint in their eyes.

'I don't think so, after all, Alberto,' her mother said, uneasily. 'It's too crowded. Let's just go back.'

'Leonora, look!' called her father. 'This ice-cream is to promote the new exhibition.'

'What do you mean?' asked Teo and her mother in one voice, except that Teo's was unheard.

'See the sign on the side of the trolley. It's called Baja-Menta *Gelato*. Don't you see? Menta as in *mint*.'

'It's certainly going down a treat. Look at those people trying to get more,' exclaimed Teo's mother. 'They're going mad for it! We should make ourselves scarce.' They hurried away.

The queue had turned into a clamouring mob. Intent on *gelato*, adults were pushing and elbowing and trampling little children. Teo burrowed among the customers. As she reached the front of the crowd, a strong whiff of the ice-cream caught her. It made her dizzy, like Maria's perfume did. There was a sour undertow to that sweet smell. That green! It was exactly the same shade as Bajamonte Tiepolo's emerald ring. The trolley was emblazoned with the Tiepolo crest! Now that she stood within two feet of the trolley Teo was chilled by a cold gust of air. The ice-cream vendor was a ghost! And from the look of him, the ghost of an experienced poisoner, an in-the-Slaughterhouse ghost who was happy to continue with his crimes in death as in life.

'Stop!' she screamed at the eager throng. 'Don't eat that ice-cream! It'll poison you. It'll do something to your minds. Just leave it alone!'

None of the adults heard a word, of course. But the little grey pigeons of San Marco seemed to understand Teo's plight. Normally they waddled complacently around the square, but now they took to the air, wheeling around the customers of the ice-cream trolley, flapping and pecking.

No one took the slightest notice of Teo or the pigeons. Even the children had eyes only for the green *gelato*. Teo took a little girl's hand and pleaded, 'Please, don't eat any more. You'll be terribly ill, I'm sure you will. For your mother's sake, don't . . .!'

But the little girl snatched her hand away and pushed closer towards the trolley. She already had green *gelato* smudged all around her mouth.

Teo cried out, 'It's as if you've all been *enchanted* by this ice-cream!'

She sat on the steps of San Marco and put her head in her hands. A dull rumble forced her to look up. The tall brick Campanile was shaking like a blade of wheat in the wind.

Lussa had told the children that the Creature's poison was decaying the poles that held up the city. Was this the beginning of the end? People screamed with terror as the pavement shook beneath them. In two seconds, the vast square emptied.

So it was that Teo, unimpeded by the usual tourist hordes, witnessed the dreadful sight of the Campanile swaying from side to side. The bells of the poor clock tower clanged tonelessly. The ground groaned, and the tower seemed to sigh. The brickwork opened up, the steeple and its gilded angel dropped down through the centre of the tower. Then the whole building telescoped neatly into itself, collapsing into a jagged heap from which a vast cloud of dust rose up. Café tables overturned, glass shattered, pigeons tumbled through the air and a dusty cat streaked away.

When the dust settled, the angel was lying with broken wings on the threshold of the basilica. Then a vast wave crashed into the square, filling it with foamy, dark water dotted with top hats, torn parasols and the baskets of the flower-sellers. Teo backed up the stairs, splashed and buffeted.

After a moment's stunned silence, soaked Venetians huddling at the edges of the square burst into tears, keening, '*Il povero morto*,' 'Our poor dead one'.

From the back of the basilica came a terrible sound of low, unearthly screaming.

'What is it?' a petrified tourist asked. 'Where is that coming from?'

An old Venetian flower-seller, her face wrinkled like the sea, called out, 'That will be the old graveyards, dearie, the *campi dei morti*, around the city. And that is the sound of all the skulls buried beneath this earth since the Campanile was first put up a thousand years ago. They are mourning *il povero morto* too.'

Teo clamped her hands over her ears and fled.

And the people around the edges of the square clutched their cups of green ice-cream, seeking comfort in its sweet taste. Their eyes were glazed with craving. They pushed it into their mouths greedily. The more they ate, the more they wanted.

31. Venetian Treacle

night-time, June 10th, 1899

The Key to the Secret City had insisted that their journeys must be by night. That was Teo's excuse for waiting the whole of the rest of the day until she went to tell Renzo all that had happened. With the sound of the screaming skulls echoing all around the city, and her own spirits so desperately low, it was easier to stay indoors with a pillow over her head.

When a wan moon finally rose, Teo quietly left her room. She listened briefly at her parents' door. They were discussing her in low, sad voices. But their typewriting machine clicked away. They were working on the next day's lecture, even while they grieved.

Teo made her way to Renzo's house. The screaming skulls now sobbed quietly but inconsolably for the Campanile, making the air throb with their pain. Teo's mood matched their misery. She was, she realized, a very different girl from the one who had arrived in Venice just two weeks before, tougher and about a hundred years older. She would have given so much just then to be one of those ignorant top-hatted tourists sitting in cafés complaining equally hard about the price of coffee and the screaming of the skulls, all absolutely ignorant of Bajamonte Tiepolo, the Creature, the ancient prophecy and the true danger to Venice.

She was Venetian; she belonged at last, but to something so fragile that it might not even exist very soon – it did not seem fair.

'Fair and unfair are for children,' Teo reflected, arriving at the courtyard in front of Renzo's house. Her plan was to climb the wisteria vine right up to his room and find out what he was up to.

But it seemed that Teo was not alone in wanting to know Renzo's whereabouts. She watched from a shadowed doorway across the narrow alley as two boys arrived at the door – not very nice-looking boys, who cuffed and nudged one another while waiting for their knock to be answered. A pretty woman with an anxious expression opened the door.

'Where's Renzo?' one boy asked. 'Teacher sent us, didn't she? Why did he miss school today? And yesterday, isn't it?'

They shifted from foot to foot, not quite meeting her eyes.

The woman seemed upset. 'You're out very late, boys? Poor Renzo has a fever. I think he might not be going to school for a while.'

The boys gave each other nasty smiles that did not reach their eyes. They swaggered off, passing close by Teo. They didn't look clever. They looked mean. Mean and stupid hates clever, as Teo had reason to know. So these were the school bullies come hunting their prey. Well, given his studious habits, Renzo was hardly likely to be in with the fashionable crowd, was he?

She made her way round to the back entrance to the house. The craggy wisteria vine climbed up to the first floor, offering a sore trial to someone as clumsy as Teo. What choice did she have, though? Gingerly, she pulled herself up to her full height, clambered onto the thick stalk, and then

194

shimmied ungracefully along the winding branch until she found a room, entirely lined with books, where she could see the unmistakable outline of Renzo lying in his bed. He looked small and vulnerable. She tapped at the open window to warn him of her arrival, and climbed in.

Strangely, Renzo made no motion to get up, or even raise his head. His eyes glittered: he was awake. His blankets were weighed down with open books.

With all the drama, Teo had forgotten her own cold. Renzo had probably been suffering from the same sore throat and snuffling nose.

The first thing he said was, 'You look very nice, Teo. Have you done something with your hair?' His voice was strained.

'I listened to what you said the other night.'

'I was worried you would take it the wrong way. Very decent of you not to.'

These pleasantries were ridiculous, but Teo was so embarrassed to be in Renzo's bedroom that she could not stop herself gabbling. Renzo, on the other hand, seemed like a count or a duke, receiving a minion in his bedchamber.

Teo turned to the more serious matters. She explained her news in whispers, with Renzo exclaiming aloud about Maria's betrayal, the Baja-Menta ice-cream and the exhibition at the Correr Museum.

'But Teo – I don't understand one thing.'

Renzo's question was the one that Teo dreaded. 'Didn't Maria's words look different? You know, when you saw them above her head?'

'I didn't notice properly.' Teo sighed. 'I was bamboozled by her perfume. Lussa said it was like a drug.'

'I see.' Renzo did not rush to support that theory.

When she told him about the fall of the Campanile, he turned his head aside, unwilling to show his tears, 'That I knew. I heard the rumbling. My mother told me.'

'We've got to go and tell the mermaids. I've been thinking about it all day. Don't you see, at least Signor Rioba could warn the people against the ice-cream,' Teo concluded. 'They could print new handbills tonight and get them out by the morning so that no one else buys any more Baja-menta.'

'The Mayor and the Minister for Tourism and Decorum will simply scoff at that. No one will listen.' Renzo's voice was painfully hoarse. 'I'm more concerned about Maria anyway. What's she up to? What if she told Bajamonte Tiepolo about you and where the mermaids are?'

That thought haunted Teo too, but she still could not bear to confront it. Anyway, Renzo wasn't the only one wanting explanations.

'And why,' she hissed, 'didn't you get out of bed and come to find me? I'm sorry I wasn't there the first day at the usual time, but honestly, I was sick too . . . you shouldn't sulk with me.'

In answer, Renzo lifted his collar and showed Teo such a hideous sight that she had to put one hand over her mouth so as to hold in the scream. On his neck was a throbbing lump the size of a small apple. It was black.

'What is *that*?' All this time Renzo must have been in agony, and he had listened to her patiently, without saying a word about his own problems.

Renzo pointed to the books spread out on his bed. Each of them was open at a page about the epidemics of the Black Death in Venice.'

'Renzo! Do you think you have the *Plague*?'

'The Bubonic Plague. Otherwise known as the Black Death. And this,' he said heavily, gesturing to the swollen lump on his neck, '*this* is a plague bubo. And so's this one on my leg. Remember the prophecy in *The Key to the Secret City*?'

'*Come to life are Black Death's ancient spores.*'

Renzo nodded. 'I think the Creature carries the spores of

the Black Death in its tentacles, and I believe that Bajamonte Tiepolo plans to infect all of Venice with it. That's how he will empty the city of Venetians. Listen.'

Renzo struggled to pick up one of the heavy books. He moved a lamp closer to him, and read: 'The spores of the Bubonic Plague can live for centuries. Symptoms usually appear two to five days after exposure to the source of infection. The onset manifests in chills and a high fever.'

Teo thought of her own fever, and flinched. Renzo continued, 'Swollen lymph nodes called buboes appear in the armpit, neck or thigh along with the fever . . .'

'Do you also . . .?' interrupted Teo fearfully.

Renzo nodded, and turned back to the book, 'The buboes may fill with pus and turn black. Then death is usually not far away.' His voice trembled.

'What can we do, Renzo?' Teo remembered what the doctor had said, that the hospital was full of children with mysterious high fevers. The little boy who had run into her room – he'd had a swelling on his neck, just like Renzo's. The doctor had checked her neck and arms – now she knew why. Lussa had explained the Plague was already starting to spread among the children of Venice. And the Mayor, of course, was covering it all up.

Renzo read from the book in a monotone: 'More than sixty per cent of untreated people die. The mortality rate is higher in children.'

'We have to get help! We'll get a doctor! No, we'll go to the mermaids! They'll fix it with that chilli jelly. Or the book! *The Key* will tell us where to go for help, I'm sure of it. Can you walk?'

'I haven't tried yet. I didn't want my mother to see me out of bed. I told her that I had a bad head and an upset stomach – so I had to go without dinner – anyway, it worked and she hasn't seen the buboes.'

Renzo staggered out of bed, leaning heavily on Teo's arm. He was weak and sore, but he could do it. What he could not do was put on any trousers. When he tried he made the kind of noise one generally hears when someone sits on a cat. The blisters on his legs were still too raw.

'You'll have to wear your long-johns and nightshirt,' insisted Teo.

Renzo gave her a look of horror. A Venetian out on the street in his nightshirt? But the swelling on his legs were so painful that even Renzo admitted that he had no choice. He carefully rolled up a pair of clean trousers in a beautifully pressed shirt and folded them into a satchel he slung over his shoulder.

With many groans from Renzo, and much fumbling by Teo, they climbed out of the wisteria and down into the street.

Teo reached inside her pinafore, hoping for the best. On the cover, Lussa smiled at her encouragingly, and nodded.

The Key to the Secret City opened to a map of the ancient apothecaries of the city. Some, like the *Al Lupo coronato* – the Wolf-in-a-Crown – showed a skull and crossbones hovering over their names and symbols. Others, like the *Testa d'Oro* – the Golden Head – were surmounted by the Venetian flag of a golden winged lion on crimson silk. Under its red flag, one of the apothecaries glowed brightly. Its name: *Alle Due Sirene scapigliate*, the Two Tousled Mermaids.

Teo grinned, 'Of course!'

'Oh no! That's near the Ghetto, it's miles . . .' groaned Renzo. Teo offered her arm, and he took it gratefully, asking, 'What's that noise?'

'They say it is the skulls of the dead weeping for the fallen Campanile.'

Fifteen minutes later they found the door to the Two Tousled Mermaids open, revealing candles burning inside. The smell of fresh medicinal herbs prickled their noses, but the apothecary was empty of human or ghostly life. The walls were lined with dark wooden shelves. Just as in the mermaids' cavern, the uppermost shelves held rows of golden mortars-and-pestles. Below them, the candles illuminated squat glass bottles in which mice, two-tailed salamanders and cuckoos floated in dreamy ballets.

Next came rows of big china jars painted in yellow and blue. The names of their contents were spelt out in ornate scripts. 'Majolica,' Renzo told Teo wearily. He slid down to the floor, and leant up against a dark glass tank.

The labels bore names like 'Four Thieves Vinegar', 'Rabbits' Feet', 'Sneezewort' and 'Devil's Shoe-String Roots'.

'It's just a museum,' sighed Renzo, cruelly disappointed. His face was pale and set with pain. 'No one takes those things seriously now. What does the *The Key* say?'

Teo opened the book on a picture of a beautiful majolica pot labelled *'Theriaca'* in a curly blue script. *'An ancient medicine,'* she read out loud, *'popularly known as "Venetian Treacle". It contains sixty-four ingredients, including ground-up vipers.'*

'Ugh!' winced Renzo. 'I absolutely detest snakes.'

'Then you're not going to be very happy about what's behind you.'

32. Vipers and hot chocolate

the early hours, June 10th – 11th, 1899

Teo had just caught sight of a sign on the tank against which Renzo was leaning. It said, 'VIPERS FOR THERIACA. DO NOT TOUCH THE TANK.'

Behind Renzo's head Teo could make out something flickering. Renzo followed her eyes just in time to come face-to-face with a pair of black jaws lunging at him. The tank rattled as the hissing snake spent its venom in two spurts that trailed mistily down the glass. Renzo rolled onto his back and lay there panting.

'Teo,' he gasped. 'Tell me there's a lid on this tank.'

'It's nailed down,' she reassured Renzo. 'That snake's not going anywhere. Except ground up in the *Theriaca* jar, some time soon, I hope.'

'Wishful thinking. These jars have been empty for centuries. I feel dreadful! Aren't there any Dottore Dimora's Tasteless Ague Drops? My mother gives me those.'

Teo checked the shelves. 'Nothing like that.'

The Key to the Secret City stubbornly showed the lid floating off the jar of Venetian Treacle with a whiff of violet-coloured smoke. Inside glistened a liquid thick as honey and black as coal.

'I *suppose* . . .' muttered Renzo unwillingly, 'if there's some here . . .'

Teo clambered up a set of steps. In her haste she sent a jar of Sans Pareille Powder crashing to the ground alongside another of Compound Syrup of Poke Root.

'Oh, sorry!'

Renzo lay spattered with powder, broken glass and syrup. He sighed. 'Do you think you could get the Venetian Treacle without actually killing me first?'

Teo lifted the *Theriaca* jar down to the floor beside Renzo. She prized open the lid. Violet-coloured smoke gushed out. Gingerly, Teo dipped a finger in the cool dark liquid inside. 'Shall I?' she asked Renzo, pointing to the bubo on his neck.

'Try my leg first. It's further away from my brain.' Renzo lifted the legs of his long-johns about half an inch. Teo let a few drops fall onto one of his damaged ankles.

'Handsomely!' he tried to joke, but all the colour had drained out of his face.

'Ahhhh!' whispered Renzo, as the blisters fizzled, then shrivelled. Seconds later they'd disappeared. He ripped open the seams of his long-johns, reached into the pot and spread fingerfuls onto his wounds until his legs looked entirely normal again. Then he rubbed a generous portion onto the bubo on his neck.

'Um,' said Renzo. Teo realized that he had to deal with the buboes under his arms and on his thigh. She discreetly turned her back, gazing at the labels on the other majolica pots – 'Essence of White Dove', 'Dolphin Spittle' and 'Monkey Business'.

'What do you think "Monkey Business" is?' she asked Renzo.

'Look inside and see,' he said distractedly. 'If you must.'

Teo did so. A foul stench of aged dung filled the room. 'Sorry!'

Teo turned to see Renzo looking his usual immaculate self, fully dressed in the clothes he had brought in the satchel.

After some hesitation the children licked their sticky fingers clean, and the taste was delicious, like caramel-chocolate-lime-strawberry. Even better, the tiredness of their broken night slipped right away from them. They felt ready for anything. Teo decanted a little into a small bottle to take away. 'You never know . . .'

'We should pay,' fretted Renzo.

At this, Lussa's face smiled on the front of *The Key to the Secret City*. Out from between the pages dropped a coin. Renzo picked it up and showed Teo the date – 1867, thirty-two years ago. He shrugged and left the coin on the counter.

A happy idea crossed Teo's mind: 'Let's take the rest of the Treacle to the hospital! For the children!'

As they walked out of the Two Tousled Mermaids, all the candles promptly extinguished themselves, and the door latched itself with a click.

The hospital was close by. Renzo carried in the majolica jar and deposited it with the night-porter, who turned out to be a second cousin.

'So you'll give it to the children's doctor, Mauro? Tell him it will help the children with the fever,' Renzo urged. 'Tell him not to tell anyone where he got it.'

Teo, standing quietly and invisibly beside him, was lost in dismal thoughts.

As they walked back outside, she said abruptly, 'You know it will come to a battle, Renzo? The mermaids against Bajamonte Tiepolo and the Creature.'

'The gondoliers will defend the city too!' asserted Renzo defiantly.

'*Il Traditore*'s army are ghosts. How can the gondoliers fight an enemy they can't see?'

'All the gondoliers' children can row their gondolas.'

'Could you get them all together?'

'Of course, we are around three hundred. But what would we do then?'

'The mermaids will have to help us with that part of the plan.'

'Will they feed us? I am dying of hunger.'

Teo was pulling the book out of her pinafore. 'Probably some curried pumpkin curds and spicy seaweed ice-cream. Oh dear!'

Lussa's face on the cover looked a little hurt. Then she smiled and waved towards the inside of the book. Teo opened it up on an advertisement for hot chocolate at the Orientale café on the Riva degli Schiavoni.

Renzo smiled. 'My third cousin does the dawn shift there. His wife says he's a bit of a lad himself – he won't give me away for being out at this hour.'

At the café, Renzo ordered a huge four a.m. breakfast of buns and hot chocolate.

'That's enough for two!' grinned Renzo's handsome cousin. 'What have you been up to, young man? On the house.'

The buns were all gone but Renzo was still blushing when the early editions arrived with a thud. **'It's all over for Venice!' 'Venice: dreadful death of a city.'** Without knowing anything about Bajamonte Tiepolo, journalists were writing Venice's obituary in grandiloquent phrases.

Teo wanted to shout, 'She's not dead yet! Give her a chance, you vultures!'

To change the subject, she told Renzo about the changes in her hotel, drawing the new windows on a paper napkin. He explained, 'Teo, those are stilted arches, from the

Byzantine period, from Bajamonte Tiepolo's time!'

A line of writing appeared in the foam on the top of her hot chocolate.

And from its ruins the Razed House rises

'We have to get to the Archives,' Teo exclaimed. 'What time does it open?'

'Not for a couple of hours yet. So we *could* have another breakfast.'

'I'm glad you're better,' she said shyly. It must be something about the rich foamy drink, she told herself, that was making the room spin gently around.

And that was the last good cup of hot chocolate that anyone had in Venice.

33. The Venetian Archives

early morning, June 11th, 1899

That very morning something terrible happened to the bakers of the city. All over town Venetians woke up, washed, dressed and hurried to their favourite bars for their coffee or hot chocolate and their sweet brioches, their almond cakes and Margherita biscuits to dip in their frothy hot drinks.

And everyone had a dreadful surprise.

The sweetness in every item of food and drink had been replaced by a mouth-curdling bitterness. Instead of custard cream, the brioches were packed with a nauseating, smelly ointment. The Margherita biscuits tasted of crusty old socks. The almond cakes were solid lumps of nastiness. All over Venice, there was an indignant noise coming out of all the cafés: people screaming and spitting out their breakfasts.

No one could understand it.

Somewhat faded after just four hours sleep, Renzo and Teo met, as arranged, at their usual bar at San Giacomo dell'Orio. But the owner had closed up, and put up his sign that said, '*Chiuso per lutto*' – the words normally used for a death in the family.

205

Renzo had already heard the story from every café between Giudecca and Castello. He told Teo, 'This is the work of Bajamonte Tiepolo. The woman who dropped the mortar-and-pestle on *Il Traditore*'s head – she was a baker's wife. And Bajamonte Tiepolo swore he would one day be revenged on the Venetian bakers. That's bad enough, but the worrying thing is that it means that his powers are growing. A little while ago he couldn't do a curse like that.'

Teo added, 'And of course the only sweet thing left in Venice is the Baja-Menta ice-cream. Everyone will be rushing to buy that when word gets out.'

'What do we do first? Tell the mermaids about the ice-cream or go to the Archives?'

'The Archives are only open during the day . . .'

As they hurried through the white-hot streets towards the Archives, Teo was aware of something strange in the shadows falling along the stone pavements. It was the chimneys of Venice . . . they were all growing to the same shape, the stones and terracotta twisting and turning until each chimney stack resembled . . . the crest of Bajamonte Tiepolo.

'Look!' She pointed up. The chimneys loomed like sinister, massive soldiers.

'And of course, the Mayor will say it's just another Biennale art joke!'

'Biennale?'

'It's our international modern art show, happens every two years,' explained Renzo proudly. 'It's just about to start. Biennale artists are famous for quirky ideas.'

'Yes,' said Teo ironically. 'You can always rely on our Mayor.'

An unnerving thought struck her: 'Renzo, is it possible, do you think, that the Mayor might be on Bajamonte Tiepolo's side?'

'Not really. But I think he will pretend this isn't happening until the last minute. And then simply hand over power to *Il*

Traditore, out of sheer weakness and fear.'

Renzo pointed to a vast building on the other side of the church. 'That's the Archives over there. They say there are ten miles of shelves in there!'

Teo's neck prickled then, for all around the Archives, on every rooftop, on each chimney, stood a huge *magòga*. She whispered, 'Lussa said he'd mount guards outside the premises.'

Renzo warned, 'Don't look at them. Don't show that we are aware. Remember Lussa also said, they would not be expecting "Mere Children."'

The gulls watched Teo and Renzo enter the building, as they watched everyone who went in and out, with their glassy, cold eyes.

Teo's shoulders tensed. What if they were not allowed inside the door? The Archives was a place for serious scholars. Even if Renzo talked them in, how could they find what they needed? Then the delicious smell of old books enfolded her. She felt calmer, and even optimistic. If there was anywhere in the world where Teo belonged, it was a library.

In the lobby, a clerk looked enquiringly at Renzo. 'Young, aren't you? All new Readers are subject to an interview with Signorina Grigiogatta.' He pointed in the direction of a massive door studded with black nails.

When Renzo tapped, a voice purred out, 'Enterrr.'

Teo flinched. Two vast Brustolons flanked the portals of the room.

A woman dressed all in grey was standing over an enormous desk. She had grey spectacles, behind which round green eyes did *not* blink. Her face was heavily made up with thick white cosmetic cream. She wore white gloves all the way up to her elbows. Her skirt was long, covering the top of her elegant black boots. She moved gracefully to the front of the desk, the ballerina effect slightly compromised by the fact that she was at the same time hastily stuffing something back into the hem of her skirt.

She took off her spectacles. The woman's eyes were extraordinarily beautiful: almond-shaped and slightly slanted upwards. But the effect was intimidating.

'Children! We don't often have *children* here. Children don't like booksss, in our experience, and they leave their dirrrty little fingerprintsss all over them.'

Children! Not 'child'! Teo realized with a shiver that this unusual woman could see her. Renzo, clearly sharing her anxiety, motioned to Teo to keep quiet.

The script that floated above the woman's head was not like anything Teo had seen before. She could not make out the words. It looked like scratch-marks in sand, not human writing at all. And her accent was slightly foreign, with a little burr on the consonants, as if she was from the East, or beyond.

Teo cast her eyes down on the desk, reading upside-down the letter on top of Signorina Grigiogatta's pile of correspondence. With a start, she made out the words 'Bajamonte Tiepolo . . .'

Renzo asserted bravely, '*Signorina*, we *love* books. And our hands are clean. We're working on a school project about Venetian history, and we want to see some of the real historical documents . . .'

'Oh, "we *want*", do we?' Signorina Grigiogatta raised an eyebrow.

'Forgive me. We should very much *like*, if at all possible, to see them. In fact we are also working on a – a – historical *origami* project, and we want to see how all the old letters and documents were folded up. Everyone wanted to do this project but we two were given the honour because we were voted the best students in the class. The hardest workers. Best at origami. We are very serious. If you please.'

Teo privately thought Renzo was laying it on rather thick here. Historical origami project! So this was the famous Venetian charm? It sounded a little oily to her.

'Indeed,' purred the Grey Lady, 'And how verrry hard you are working now to impresss me.'

Teo found the lady's smugness quite maddening. Ignoring Renzo's warning glare, she asked boldly, 'And have we succeeded?'

The Grey Lady wrinkled her small nose at the sound of Teo's Naples accent, as if there was a bad smell in the room. 'Frrrankly, my dear, no, not really, not yet.'

Renzo assumed a benevolent tone, 'Yes, my companion is a poor *Napoletana*. The victim of a pitiably vulgar education. My school has founded a charity to help students from less fortunate areas. This girl has been forced to study in badly-stocked libraries in Naples, and now the authorities want her to have an opportunity to study in the . . . in the . . .'

'Yesss?' asked the Grey Lady, licking her lips with a small pink tongue.

'The *cream* of libraries!' exclaimed Renzo triumphantly.

'Oh indeed, the verrry crrream of libraries,' declared Signorina Grigiogatta.

There was a long pause, during which the Grey Lady attended scrupulously to her cuffs, her hem and her very pointed nails. This she did by sharpening them casually on the out-thrust arm of yet another Brustolon behind her desk. Teo winced.

'Well,' wheedled Renzo, in the end. 'May we look? Please?'

'Well, I don't see any harrrm, I suppose,' pronounced the Grey Lady. 'Run along. Make sure you leave before closing time. You wouldn't want to be locked in here at night. The

Mayor has not given us fundsss for a nightwatchman's wages so there would be no one here to let you out, no matterrr how much you mewed.'

'Mewed?' asked Teo.

'Howled, crrried for help,' said the Grey Lady, stiffly.

Renzo bowed like a courtier in front of a queen. 'We shall not forget your graciousness, Signorina Grigiogatta,' he asserted humbly, with his head on one side.

Out in the corridor, Teo whispered, 'Do you think she's a ghost? Is she in-the-Cold? Or in-the-Slaughterhouse? Do you think she guessed what we are up to? You know she had a letter about Bajamonte Tiepolo on her desk?'

'How do you . . .? Oh, never mind. What did her voice look like?'

'Well, not quite . . . human.'

Renzo fretted, 'And it's uncanny that *she* could see you when you're supposed to be between-the-Linings. And that she talked about us getting locked in at night – as if she could read our minds.'

For getting locked in at night was just what they had decided to do. Their plan was to creep back to the Archives when all the scholars had gone home. Then they could hunt through the shelves in private.

After leafing politely through a few boxes of files that the clerks brought Renzo, and making some paper models, the children made separate reconnoitring trips to the rear of the building. Ranks of Brustolons lined the corridors, filling them with the smell of varnish. They were useful for hiding behind, as it turned out. It was Renzo who found a suitable window at the back. Returning to the desk, he sent Teo to unfasten it.

'Close it, but not really,' he urged. 'So it looks closed.'

That mission accomplished, Renzo made a great ceremony of leaving the place so that every possible guard noticed him depart.

'I wouldn't want to get locked in *here*,' he said loudly. To Teo, he whispered, 'See you tonight.'

Back at the hotel, it was too painful for Teo to watch her parents toy with their food in the dining room. She lifted a bowl of fruit and a tall jug of orange juice, and carried them up to her room. She drained the jug and wolfed down the fruit. She didn't bother to take off her clothes, waiting fully dressed and wide awake on top of the covers until sunset. Before the moon was high in the sky, Teo was out of bed, pulling the fish-kite out of the back of her armoire.

Down in his courtyard Renzo was already waiting, his face tense and pale. They walked in silence through the deserted city, towards the Archives. Their fish-kites floated above them, casting a comforting bluish light.

They were in luck. No one had discovered the open window. The children hauled themselves inside and clapped their hands to extinguish the fish.

Even in the sinister moonlight, Teo loved the Archives: that beckoning scent of old books, and the tweedy smell of old scholars, and the tall shelves making order of the chaos of all Venetian knowledge.

'When I grow up,' she thought, 'I want to work somewhere like this.'

The stolen jug of orange juice had its effect on Teo. Noticing the door marked 'LADIES', she waved Renzo on and slipped inside. She dared not turn on a light, so felt her way around. She was washing her hands when she heard footsteps coming in her direction. They were not Renzo's – too light. In fact, they pattered like two *pairs* of delicate feet.

No one should be in the library now! Signorina Grigiogatta had said there was not even a nightwatchman. Trembling, Teo hid in one of the cubicles.

The door creaked slowly open.

Teo drew in her breath.

34. The enemy's enemy

late at night, June 11th, 1899

It was the Grey Lady.

Signorina Grigiogatta did not light the lamp. She looked in the mirror, seeming quite at ease in the moonlight. She licked her wrists and ran them over her face. And then she bent her head and licked each of her shoulders.

Lastly, she pulled a long grey tail out from under her petticoat and licked it thoroughly, and then tucked it back into her voluminous skirt. She turned her attention to her fingers. Long glinting nails like little scimitars popped out. She curved her fingers around and they retracted. Then she drew a large satin purse from her handbag and reapplied a thick layer of white cosmetic paint to her face. Finally, she left.

Outside the LADIES', Teo heard a curious sound, as if the graceful Grey Lady had fallen lightly to the ground. Perhaps she had dropped something? When the Grey Lady started walking there seemed to be enough footsteps for two light pairs of feet.

When the Grey Lady's many footsteps had faded away, Teo rushed out to tell Renzo about the furry tail and curious behaviour.

'Where is she now?' asked Renzo.

'I think she went back to her office. I heard the door shut down there.'

'Perhaps she's just working late.'

The children tried to put Signorina Grigiogatta out of their minds. Lighting up their fish-kites, they roamed up and down the corridors.

The trouble was, clever as they'd been to get into the Archives, they had not really thought about how to find what they wanted. This was made all the more difficult because they didn't have any idea what it would look like. The mermaids had warned that the Almanac might even be disguised as something other than a book.

'But,' reasoned Teo, 'it must be rather *like* a book, or it couldn't be in the Archives, could it? Not without sticking out a mile.'

They went hunting along the shelves till they found the department for the fourteenth century. The Tiepolo boxes were sealed with fearsome padlocks and labels inscribed 'Most Secret' and '*Non Toccare, Pena La Morte*', 'Don't Touch on Pain of Death.'

The children clambered up the shelves on a pair of library ladders and forced open one of the locks with a corner of *The Key to the Secret City*. The lid of the box rose up with a groan like somebody dying.

'Watch out!' yelled Renzo, as dozens of sheets of parchment flew out and formed themselves into arrow-heads, with points sharp as needles.

The parchment arrows wheeled around in formation, like a flock of white bats. Then they swung into the direction of Renzo and Teo, gathering speed for an attack. The children cried out as sharp paper cut their ears, their eyelids and mouths.

'It's worse than the sharks!' screamed Teo.

'Shhh!' whispered Renzo. 'No noise! Signorina Grigiogatta will hear us.'

It was too late to be quiet. The ladders on which the children perched were already teetering dangerously. One more assault by the parchment arrows and they tumbled noisily to the ground. Teo fell on top of Renzo, who grunted in pain. The white arrows were now zooming straight down at them.

'Can paper kill you?' gasped Teo.

'I don't know,' moaned Renzo. 'But I think *that* can.' He pointed.

A colossal grey cat had hurtled into the room. It was bigger than any cat Teo had ever seen. Outside of the tiger-cage in the zoo, that is.

The cat arched its back like the Rialto Bridge and hissed. Then it crouched on the floor, waving its tail violently from side to side. Its rear quarters trembled as it coiled up all its energy to pounce on the children.

Springing high into the air, it howled at them, 'The papers of Bajamonte Tiepolo arrrre touched only on pain of death. Preparrrre your horrrid little selves to die!'

Even as the cat sailed through the air towards them, Teo recognized that voice and the writing above the spitting creature's head.

'Signorina Grigiogatta!' she shouted. 'Don't hurt us!'

The cat dropped back down on her haunches, her tail still lashing. She looked at Teo through eyes narrowed to glassy green slits. 'How do you know who I am? And, morrre importantly, why shouldn't I kill you?'

'I . . . saw . . . you in the bathroom,' stammered Teo. 'And your voice . . .'

'One point to you forrr observation. But that's not nearrrly enough points to save you. Can't you read, children? "On pain of death." And a painful death too.'

She flexed her claws.

Renzo spoke up bravely, 'We are here because all of Venice is threatened with death, Your Grace.'

'*Your Grace?*' Teo started. But Renzo's respectful tone seemed to give the cat pause for thought.

'In what way is the city threatened?' she asked Renzo in a menacing, cynical tone. 'Make this good, little boy, or it will be the lassst thing you say.'

Renzo fell silent. Teo understood: their mission was supposed to be a secret.

'Well? Is it death then? I sssuppose it shall have to be.'

'Was that a purr?' wondered Teo. The Grey Lady seemed uncommonly happy to do them the service of slaughtering them.

'There is something you should know,' faltered Renzo, looking at Teo.

'Yes,' Teo realized, 'we have to tell the truth. It is the only thing that can save us. Plus, if this cat is angry with us for looking for the Almanac, then she must be against Bajamonte Tiepolo.'

Teo gabbled, 'Bajamonte Tiepolo is abroad again. We need to find his Spell Almanac before he does. We think it might be here.'

'In that case it may interest you to know,' remarked the Grey Lady, 'that I myself am entrusted with protecting the Spell Almanac of Bajamonte Tiepolo.'

'So you see! We are on the same side!' cried Teo.

The misunderstanding was explained in moments, and Signorina Grigiogatta turned herself back into a woman. At least, her human face reappeared on top of her cat's body. 'Tell me everrrything,' she commanded.

The children took turns to explain about the hot

215

fountains, the chimneys, the sharks, the Baja-menta ice-cream, the Creature, not in any particular order but just as they remembered it. The Grey Lady listened with her head on one side. Occasionally she interrupted with a question.

'To think that it is a pair of *children* who come to enlighten me! Never liked the little beasssts before. Tail-pullers! Yet now . . .' she marvelled. 'So it's true about what is happening in Venice. Sequestered here, I am never sure what to believe when I hear humans jabberrring. They are ssso unsubtle and they exaggerate ssso.'

Lastly the children told her about the mermaids and *The Key to the Secret City*. Teo produced the book from her pinafore, and Lussa smiled from the cover. This news brought a little wobble to the Grey Lady's deep voice. She stroked the book with a reverent paw.

'Ah! Ssso I am not alone after all!' The cat had tears in her beautiful almond-shaped eyes. 'Merrrmaids in a secret cavern!' she exulted. 'Ha! Bajamonte Tiepolo shall never know of them, till it is too late! Please tell your mermaid friends that the Spell Almanac is safe. They sound like sssplendid creatures. If it were not for the mutual incompatibility of our elements . . .'

'I beg your . . .?' asked Renzo.

Teo explained, 'She means that mermaids live in water, and cats cannot bear water.'

'As I was sssaying, were it not for that mutual elemental incompatibility, I would adore to visit the dear merrrmaids and ssstrategize with them. One candle does not hurt itself by lighting another, as we sssay in Venice.'

A fleeting greedy look crossed the Grey Lady's face. 'Mermaids are a little like fisssh, yes? Like a very large tuna? Fisssh is verrry good for catsss . . .'

The Grey Lady shook out her ears, 'But no, they are my allies! My sisssters!'

'Could you,' Teo asked, 'tell us how . . .?'

The Grey Lady explained that she had been appointed by Doge Gradenigo back in 1310, to make sure that neither Bajamonte Tiepolo nor his followers could get their hands on the Almanac.

'So you are . . .?'

'Yes, I approach my six hundredth birthday imminently.'

Renzo said politely, 'May I say that you look remarkably elegant on it?'

The Grey Lady threw him a flirtatious glance, and delicately licked the underside of one paw. 'You may.'

Teo thought, 'You don't need to keep pouring on the charm now, Renzo.'

Then she realized that it was not an act. Renzo was simply being himself, being a Venetian. Compliments and elegant behaviour were part of it, even in the midst of a crisis. Still, it had been going on too long! There was a real and urgent danger to deal with. She interrupted, 'How did Doge Gradenigo get hold of the Spell Almanac?'

'You children know the ssstory of the conspiracy, I assume? That on that drrrreadful day, Bajamonte Tiepolo, Querini and Badoerrr set off from different pointsss in the city? But that Doge Gradenigo had been forewarned about the attack, ssso he wasss ready?'

Renzo and Teo nodded.

'What you may not know isss that the Doge had guardsss hidden at the back of the Tiepolo palace. As soon as *Il Traditore* left, the Doge sent hisss men in. While Bajamonte was burrrning the Rialto Bridge, unbeknownst to him, the Doge's soldiers were rrransacking *his* own home. The Spell Almanac was among the booty. Doge Gradenigo immediately guesssed that the book could be verrry dangerous if *Il Traditore* got his hands on it again. So it was hidden firssst at the Doges' Palace and then laterrr here.'

Teo asked, 'Wasn't it rather obvious to put the Almanac into the *Archives* of Venice? Surely it would be the first place Bajamonte and his friends would look?'

'It is a worrrthy question, little girl. In fact, it was deliberate. You sssee, anyone interested in Bajamonte and his Almanac would inevitably come here, and then we would know who was still sssupporting him. And indeed we have seen off a couple of, as it were, "copycat" conspirrracies that way,' the Grey Lady said smugly. 'Most recently in 1822 and in 1829 . . .'

Teo interrupted, 'Has Bajamonte Tiepolo himself been here, or his spirit, or one of his servants?'

'*Il Traditore* himself has not set foot here, because he would sussspect a trap. He's not yet strrrong enough to face the spells that Doge Gradenigo borrowed from his own Almanac to protect its hiding place. But our enemy has sssent plenty of his accomplices in search of it over the centuries. Human sacrrrifices, so to ssspeak. It's easy to recognize them, the unfortunate crrreatures – he's usually deformed them in some way.'

Renzo asked, 'Have you had anyone recently, since all the bad things started happening in Venice? I mean, apart from the Brustolons turning up?'

'Ugly brrrutes! Useful for sharpening claws but otherwise they just clutter up the library. But they don't frrrighten me. Inanimate wood.'

'They can move a little,' Teo pointed out.

'Oh yes, just for a second. I hear them crrreaking sometimes. Quite pathetic! And the cleaner is tired of mopping up all that nasssty leech blood. But you refer to other guestsss courtesy of *Il Traditore*? Yes, in fact, yesterrrday. A poor silly little girl who had been turned into a dwarf. Her bluff for getting in was even more risible than yoursss . . . she claimed she was rrresearching dwarves in Venetian history! I let her wander into the fourteenth-century corridor and then rrroughed her up a little with my nailsss, and she fled. Snivelling. I felt quite sorry for her. I imagine Bajamonte won't be ssso gentle when he hearrrs of her failure.'

'Maria!'

'Oh, you know about her? Sssomeone ought to put her out of her misery,' sniffed the Grey Lady casually, flicking the tail which, in her excitement, kept escaping from her dress. 'It'sss the only way.'

'Not the only way,' protested Teo. 'The mermaids told us that . . . people could redeem themselves. Everyone makes mistakes. I've made more than a few myself.' Teo squirmed silently at the thought of the mermaids in their cavern, still hoping that their existence was safely secret from Bajamonte Tiepolo.

Renzo asked, 'Can you tell us where the Spell Almanac is? The mermaids think there might be something inside it that will help us. Anyway, it is no longer completely safe here. Bajamonte Tiepolo is getting stronger. He has a hand now. The one with the emerald ring. He might dare to make a raid.'

The Grey Lady didn't look at all afraid, merely miming the long scratch of one of her elegant fingers. She added airily, 'I have waysss of keeping him out. And frrrustrating him if he getsss in here.'

'So where is it, anyway?' Renzo persisted. 'The Almanac?'

'You'rrre looking at it, young man,' the Grey Lady replied.

'We're looking at *you*,' observed Teo.

The Grey Lady preened. 'Exactly so, my dearrrrr – Doge Gradenigo ordered his court magician to make use of the Spell Almanac itssself to transfer the book to a living thing. Bajamonte was of courrrse a master of magic, though he preferred the baddened kind. He'd found out ways to make his crest work as a hypnotic device, and he was becoming tolerably accomplissshed in transferrring inanimate substances into the fabric of living beingsss. So the court magicians made use of one of those spellsss, and recruited me, the Doge's favourite and most courageous Syrrrian cat, to carry the burden. For centuries I lived among the sssecret papers in the Doges' Palace. Then Napoleon moved all the archivesss to these hallsss by the Frari Church, so I came with them.'

'You mean *you* are the Spell Almanac?'

'The spells are tattooed on my ssskin beneath the fur.'

Teo asked shyly if they might look. The Grey Lady extended a paw and the children gently parted the soft grey fur. Very faintly on the skin, they could see long lists of incantations with magical symbols.

'Bajamonte Tieplo would never guesss it,' said the Grey Lady proudly. 'And anyway, I transforrrm into a cat whenever he or any of his minionsss come near. No one thinks anything of a librrrary cat, who stops the rrrats from gnawing the books. Least of all Bajamonte Tiepolo, who hatesss cats.'

'Does he really?' asked Teo. 'The mermaids said that cats disliked *him*. Because they hate a dictator.'

'Indeed. Cats make verrry poor minions.'

'The words are in different languages,' Teo observed, looking closely at the spells. 'And different kinds of handwriting.'

'This Almanac,' explained the cat, 'is not the original work of Bajamonte Tiepolo. He was never crrreatively brilliant. As a governor of Venice's prrrovinces, he collected baddened magic from arrround the Mediterranean Sea and put it all together . . .'

'Like an anthology of poems?' asked Renzo.

'Like a verrry bad anthology of poems. The poets were the witches who sssmeared the door handles of innocent people with plague spores, or those who grew evil familiars from rock cryssssstals . . .'

'Familiars?'

'Immortal servants who were unutterably loyal because they were crrreated not born. Bajamonte Tiepolo has made himsssself Dark Elves and the *Folletti*. They are a ssscurvy mixture of insssect and wicked fairy.'

'The mermaids showed us those creatures in a turtle mirror,' breathed Renzo.

Teo said proudly, 'The mermaids say that we are their ambassadors.'

'Forgive me, but a *Napoletana?*' The Grey Lady could not quite keep the scorn out of her voice.

Renzo explained, 'In fact, Teo was born here, but she was orphaned and brought up in Naples. Now she is living between-the-Linings for a while.'

'Ah, *poverina*.' Teo wasn't sure if the Grey Lady was sorrier for her being orphaned, living between-the-Linings or having to live in Naples. 'What were your real parents, my dearrrr?'

'I don't know. The only thing I know about them is what I read on their tombstone. Just their names and the date of their death,' whispered Teo. It was hard to keep the self-pity out of her voice.

'Well, we can at least give you that,' offered the Grey Lady kindly. 'We are in the Archives now. Everything that'sss happened in Venice is rrrecorded here. What were yourrr parents' names? We shall consult the ledgersss.'

'Marta and Daniele Gasperin.'

The Grey Lady jolted her head. 'The Gasperins? My dear Gasperins? My poor lost friends! *Che tragedia*! Young lady, do you realize that yourrr parents were both scholarrrs and librariansss, and that they worked here in the Archives – with *me* – for most of theirrr all-too-short livesss?'

Teo sank to the ground. The cat rubbed against her sympathetically.

'It was their dessstiny, poor creatures,' continued the Grey

Lady sadly. 'You sssee, for nearly six hundred years, every generrration of Gasperins has supplied a new pairrr of guardians for the Spell Almanac of Bajamonte Tiepolo. Yourrr parents defended the Archivesss from the incurrrsions of his underlings many times – and they paid for it with theirrr lives, in the end. As will you, little girl, if you come out frrrom between-the-Linings. Forrr Bajamonte Tiepolo will find you then, and I frankly don't care a great deal for your chancesss if he doesss.'

Teo flinched. 'Do you know what happened the night my parents died?'

'Your parents were sssafe with me inside the Archives. But it isss my theory that the night they took you to be chrrristened, sssomeone out in the lagoon must have said sssomething about the Archives, or mentioned that they worked here. The wordsss would have floated on the air and must have been hearrrd by the malignant ssspirit of Bajamonte Tiepolo beneath the wavesss . . .'

The Grey Lady was actually weeping now. 'Marta and Daniele never knew my trrrue identity, of course, but they were kind friendsss to me, whether I appeared as a woman orrr a cat. Sometimes I thought that they, and Professor Marìn too, had guessed that the woman and the cat werrre one, but they never sssaid it aloud. It was too dangerousss. They knew it might compromise me. And them.'

'So Professor Marìn from the bookshop also knew about the Spell Almanac?' asked Teo.

'Of course. He was another of the secrrret guardians. They are called the *Incogniti*, the Unknowns. Your parrrents, of course, werrre *Incogniti*, young lady.'

Teo interrupted. 'Does that mean . . .?'

'Of course, you and yourrr young man are *Incogniti* too. There are others . . . the nunsss at the House of the Spirits, a rrrather delectable cirrrcus-master by the name of Sargano Alicamoussa has come to my attention recently.'

Renzo whispered, 'Lussa talked of a circus-master!'

'But it's sssafer if the *Incogniti* are not known even to each other. Professor Marìn's bookshop has always been a meeting place and a kind of post office for people who needed to exchange information secretly. He has always kept a stock of living booksss that could pass messages more discrrreetly than humans.'

'That's how the mermaids found me,' explained Teo, remembering how the old man had talked mistily of the scholars who used to come to his bookshop. The Professor must have known her parents! Perhaps he had recognized something of them in her? That was why he had been so kind to her?

'The good Professor has not been to sssee me lately. I worry . . .'

'I am afraid,' quavered Teo, 'that your friend Professor Marìn has also paid for his involvement. He too shall be avenged,' she added, with an edge to her voice.

The Grey Lady looked at Teo with dawning respect. 'I can see now why you were called back to Venice. I see great deterrrmination in you. Of course, you will have received certain giftsss, to help you with your tasssk. Are you, like your parents, a *Vedeparole*? You see wordsss written in the air?'

'She is,' confirmed Renzo, struggling to keep the envy out of his voice. 'And a *Lettrice-del-cuore*.'

'She reads heartsss too? Ah, the Undrowned Child of the old prophecy! So you, young man, must be the Studious Son of the sssame!' The Grey Lady bowed low to the two children and offered each of them a velvet paw to press in turn, keeping the scimitar nails well inside. Close up, Teo heard the Grey Lady purring loudly.

She was quivering to ask the cat about her parents, about their lives, what they had worked on in the Archives, where they had lived. She dared only one question.

'If you please, might I just enquire . . . *what were my parents like?*'

'Like candles, joyful like the sssun, tender, clever, quick. Borrrn for each other. When they brought their firssst child to show me – how extraordinary! Now we cats are the earth's tenderest mothers. I had never seen a human child adorrred like that. It was as if that little baby was quite *luminousss* from being gazed at with love.'

Teo felt as if she'd been given the most wonderful unexpected gift, a little piece of happiness that she could pack up and keep by her for the rest of her life.

But the Grey Lady was already guiding them to the door, and holding it ajar with her paw, so that Venetian moonlight spilled in on the stone floor.

'Be safe, children,' she mewed. 'And fassst. So much dependsss on you two now.'

35. Uncle Dog

nearly midnight, June 11th, 1899

Outside the Archives, Teo put her hand on Renzo's arm.

'I *know*,' he agreed. 'We need to tell the mermaids about the Grey Lady. And the Baja-Menta ice-cream. And the Plague.'

They set off at a fast trot towards the House of the Spirits. It was not long to midnight and the next day's newspapers were arriving in the news-stands. The children paused in their tracks when they saw the headlines in the *Gazzettino*: **'THE WINGED LIONS, DRAMATIC CHANGE'**. There were photographs of before and after.

All over Venice, while Teo and Renzo had lain on their beds the previous afternoon, the sculptures of the winged lions had suddenly changed shape. No one saw it happen, but by teatime a general transformation had taken place. The tamest, sweetest lions now bore the fiercest expressions. The ones who had always been fierce were now opening their mouths to roar. The winged lions all had one thing in common. The books on which they rested their paws no longer stood open, showing the words of God to Saint Mark,

225

'*Peace to you, Mark my Evangelist.*' Instead, in every case, the book had snapped shut, showing just a blank stone cover.

In old times, the newspapers explained, this meant that Venice was at war.

'At war?' exclaimed Teo.

'**Yes, at war!**' thundered Signor Rioba in his daily missive, reproduced in full on the front page of the *Gazzettino*. '**Ye aren't worth a pitcher of drowned fleas if ye don't see it, Venetians! Your Mayor's brain has died of overwork with all the lies – don't ye heed his ravings on this subject.**'

For, of course, the Mayor himself was interviewed about the phenomenon. Renzo snorted, reading how the Mayor was reminding the city that Venice's famous art Biennale was just about to start. '**It's a practical joke. There's one every Biennale. This one's a great deal less vulgar than the diamond-studded skull on top of the Campanile in 1895 and far more artistic than the mummified camel in formaldehyde in 1897. Please enjoy your cultural visit to Venice, everyone.**'

Renzo turned to Teo. 'I don't think that is going to be possible any more.' He pointed to the wall of the church in front of them. In dark shadow picked out of white moonlight, were the words from the prophecy:

When the books close under the lions' claws.

A fuzzy brown shadow scampered over Teo's foot.

'Ugh! A *pantegana!*' grimaced Renzo. 'A rat!'

The *pantegana* paused, looking at the writing on the wall. Then it jumped straight up in the air with a squeal, promptly disappearing down a hole in the pavement.

'Where did it go?' Renzo peered down through the crack.

So he did not see a bloodstained, hairy stump of a wrist reach around Teo's shoulder. Nor did he hear Teo's muffled cry of fear.

By the time Renzo straightened up, the Butcher Biasio

had dragged his quarry into a dark alcove at the edge of the square, and had clamped his huge arm over her mouth and nose. It was not just that Teo couldn't scream.

She couldn't breathe either.

'Teo?'

Silence, except for the sound of a rat's paws drumming in the distance.

'Teodora? This is hardly the time for hide-and-seek.'

Trapped under the stinking armpit of the Butcher Biasio, her face rasping against the dried blood on his apron, Teo heard Renzo's voice. But she was suffocating now. Her eyes were closing; her legs were weakening beneath her. Renzo, silhouetted in the moonlight, stood tantalizingly close.

Looking down, Teo saw a white pebble by her left foot. Swiftly, she kicked it out of the alcove into the square.

The slight rattle of the pebble was enough. Renzo spun around to see Teo blockaded in the alcove by the Butcher, who was taking deep appreciative sniffs of his next feed. His hot, greasy hair stuck to Teo's bare arm, the most repulsive thing she'd ever felt. His severed hands dangled on chains in front of her terrified eyes.

'*Porco can!*' Renzo shouted. 'Pig-dog of a coward! Leave her be!'

The Butcher's hideous head was, as ever, under his arm. He now used one wrist to turn that head towards Renzo. His body still had its back to the square, with his back-to-front feet sticking out of the alcove. The Butcher stared at Renzo impassively.

Teo forced herself to bite the wrist held fast against her mouth. It was a disgusting thing to do, but it was that or die from asphyxiation.

227

'Biting a cannibal! What does that make *me*?' Teo wondered as she sank her teeth into the hard, salty skin of the Butcher's wrist. She made little impression on the leathery stump, but it was enough to make the Butcher grunt and hold his arm slightly away from her mouth. She sucked in air, quietly filling her lungs.

In the gap, she saw that Renzo had pulled a penknife out of his waistcoat pocket. It was a tiny, elegant knife, with a handle shaped like the *ferro* of a gondola: a little curve like a wave, and six struts like the teeth of a comb. It was a beautiful thing. It did not look very dangerous.

But Renzo did. Teo had never seen Renzo like this before. His eyes glittered. His elegant clothes now hung on his tense body like the tunic of a gladiator. Instead of his usual lecturing voice, he spoke in a low, threatening tone, and threw out vile insults in pure Venetian that Teo had no trouble understanding.

'You stink like a corpse,' he hissed at the Butcher.

'No, Renzo!' she implored silently. 'Don't provoke him!'

From the Butcher's grim letterbox of a mouth came a long, low growl, a bubbling noise that was barely recognizable as speech.

Teo twisted her mouth free of the Butcher's arm. 'Renzo! What does . . . ?'

Renzo snarled, 'He's offering to scrape out my eyes and eat them in broth. Look at him dribbling at the thought!'

A river of slobber fell out of the Butcher's mouth and spattered on the ground. He stared at Renzo greedily.

'Nice plump boy,' he drooled, clutching Teo tighter.

'By my ancestors, what a dribbling dog!!' responded Renzo. 'And maybe he *did* eat some of my ancestors. His butchery shop was in our part of Venice.'

He brandished his gondola knife in front of the Butcher,

shouting, 'I'll open your head and put your brain in your pocket!'

The Butcher tightened his grip. Renzo moved in half-circles around the alcove, jabbing towards the Butcher with his penknife. Then Renzo rolled up his sleeve. 'Look, Greedy Guts, a nice little cut of boy-steak!' he taunted. 'Lean, good meat.'

'What are you *doing*, Renzo?' thought Teo. 'You'll drive him mad.'

But that, it seemed, was just what Renzo wanted. He rolled up the leg of his trousers and showed a strong calf to the Butcher. 'Fine chewy piece here,' he boasted temptingly.

The Butcher howled with hunger and frustration.

'Enough, Uncle Dog!' jeered Renzo dismissively.

To Teo, Renzo hissed urgently under his breath, 'Do you remember the fable of the dog and his reflection?'

Teo conjured up the page in her own battered copy of Aesop's *Fables* back in Naples. A dog had a piece of meat and was carrying it in his mouth across a bridge. Looking down, he saw his reflection in the water. Thinking it was another dog, with another piece of meat, he greedily decided to attack the other dog and get both pieces for himself. He jumped in the river, losing not just the reflection of the piece of meat, but the one he already had: it dropped out of his mouth and floated away.

'The Butcher wants to eat us both, and he doesn't know how to do it,' realized Teo. She whispered back. 'But Renzo, this is too risky!'

Renzo circled ever closer to the Butcher. 'Why eat one child, Uncle Dog,' he taunted, 'when you could have two?'

The Butcher worked his lips silently, racking his dim, brutal brain for a solution to his horrible dilemma. He needed one arm to hold his head. If he was to grab Renzo, he'd have to let go of Teo. Renzo was indeed more of a meal than Teo, but Teo was the meal in hand.

A conclusion came to the Butcher Biasio, and a horrible smile split his filthy face. Of course, if he put down his head, he'd have two arms free, one for each of these delicious children! Simple! He made subhuman sounds of rejoicing.

Pinioning Teo against the wall of the alcove with his massive weight, he swiftly bent towards the ground, put his head down, straightened up, and lunged. Renzo stepped deftly out of his way.

'Teo, get the head! Turn it against the wall!'

Touching the head of the Butcher Biasio was the worst thing that Teo could imagine. Actually taking it in her hands made her sick to the core of her stomach. Gingerly, she lifted the thing by its ears, trying not to look at the black hairs sprouting from them. She swivelled the head away from Renzo and dropped it back on the ground. The Butcher staggered, his arms reaching out blindly. Renzo leapt in close, kicked the head right across the square like a football and at the same time pulled Teo out from behind the flailing body of her captor.

The Butcher dropped to his knees and began to crawl in the direction of his head.

'Here! Here!' it keened.

It had landed at the foot of a well, and was creating considerable interest among a pack of stray dogs. Renzo dropped his *ferro* penknife back into his waistcoat pocket.

'That's really elegant,' said Teo with admiration.

'I carved the handle myself,' Renzo was starting to say when a scream echoed through the square: 'Pirates!'

Herds of people came running, babbling and shrieking, some still in their pyjamas. 'Run for your lives! They've got swords!'

A plump, dishevelled tourist from Rome stopped to catch his breath alongside Teo and Renzo. Between gasps, he told Renzo what had happened.

An ancient four-rig galleon had sailed in from the lagoon, and thrown down its anchor in front of the Danieli Hotel on the Riva degli Schiavoni. Thereupon a hundred pirates, all dressed in antique costumes, had rushed into the luxurious hotel, where they kicked down the doors, looted the rooms, held all the guests at sword-point and stripped them of their jewellery.

The Roman panted, 'We thought it was some kind of Venetian folkloric event at first, you know, like the historic regatta or something, with actors, and we couldn't understand their dialect anyway. But then we got a sniff of them . . . terrible! Like men who hadn't washed for a year. And those clothes . . . they weren't costumes. They were real. So were the swords. That boat didn't have a steam motor. I haven't seen my wife since they pulled us apart. I have to find her!' He lurched off, weeping.

'And *we* have to find Lussa,' exclaimed Renzo, pulling Teo by her wrist.

Fifteen breathless minutes later, Teo and Renzo were lifting the door in the floor of the chapel in the House of the Spirits.

The heartrending sound of tears and screams flooded up through the well of the illuminated staircase.

36. Consequences

midnight, June 11th, 1899

Down, down, down the children walked, their hearts sinking. The sound of weeping grew louder. Teo recognized Lussa's sobs among the rest, with a small shudder of relief. At least that meant Lussa was alive.

Chissa was not.

The first thing Teo saw as she entered the arch was Chissa's red hair trailing in the water. The mermaid's body was laid out on a cushion of flowering seaweed in a floating bier. Her skin was unnaturally white, her features frozen in an expression of terror. Around the bier, weeping mermaids held up candelabra dripping black wax.

Catching sight of Teo, one of them shrieked, 'Behold your handiwork, Undrowned Child! Better ye had drownded your own self than bring da Vampire Eels among us. Chissa saved ye from the sharks, and *this* was her reward?'

The mermaid laid a tender hand on Chissa's white neck where two punctures still dripped with blood. Then she pointed further back into the cavern. A dozen floating biers, each bearing a still white body, were surrounded by grieving mermaids.

Lussa's voice rose unseen above the sad clamour: 'We were attacked in the Night. Chissa—' Lussa herself broke into a sob '—& her Patrol swam out for Duty by the Lagoon Entrance to the Cavern. The Vampire Eels took Them by Surprise.'

''Twere all up with 'em in the snatch of a moment,' moaned one of the mermaids.

'Because of me,' Teo whispered. 'Because I showed Maria how to get here.'

The parrots, who had been hunched on their perches, took up Teo's words. 'Because of me, because of me, because of me . . .' echoed around the cavern.

Hundreds of green eyes were fixed on her. No one said a word to contradict Teo. Renzo joined the ranks of her accusers, fixing on her a long, unforgiving stare.

'Lussa . . .' she appealed, and then realized that she had nothing to say in her own defence.

Still invisible in the shadows of the cavern, Lussa's voice rang out sombrely: 'Maria brought the *Scolopendre*. At least One must have escaped our Boots. The Insects led the Vampire Eels to lurk at the Entrance of our Cavern. My Mermaids battled bravely but They were outnumbered Two to One. We fought off the Eels in the End, killed Eight of their Number, but Chissa & her Patrol gave their Lives to keep the Rest of Us Safe.'

A hundred slender arms with coral-tipped fingernails rose from the water and pointed at a stinking mass of yellowy-white flesh piled up at the side of the walkway.

'Our Enemy,' observed Lussa. The real Vampire Eels were larger and even in death more terrifying than they had appeared in the turtle screen. Their long teeth hung out of gaping mouths. Their white fins sprawled open, tangled together and impaled on the forked tails of their comrades. Their coral gills glistened bright red.

Those gills were full of the blood of Chissa and the other dead mermaids. Teo turned away, her eyes awash with tears.

Lussa came forward now, accompanied by a group of grim-faced mermaids. They carried tritons of gold and coral. All were wearing military breastplates, each decorated with a mortar-and-pestle picked out in gold and rubies. In a corner of the cavern, other mermaids were practising their archery against a board painted with the crest of Bajamonte Tiepolo.

'We are at War,' stated Lussa with simple dignity. 'We have sent Sea-Shells with the Morning Tide to all our Allies in London & beyond.'

Renzo declared in shaking voice, 'Then we are at war too.'

One of the mermaids shouted, 'Don't much look like it. Dressed for a tea party more like. Ye want to get your fightin' duds in order, stripling!'

Lussa asked pointedly, 'So How have You Two passed these last Three Days? Has Maria, in between her own Missions for our Enemy, proved a Worthy & Useful Double Agent? And meantime, have You brought Us the Spell Almanac?'

Teo stammered, 'Maria . . .' The words dried up inside her mouth.

Lussa nodded. 'It was as I feared. Bajamonte Tiepolo had already found her Weakness for Gold & Silks and bound Her to Him with That. And via her Earring, he dripped his Thoughts into her Ear so She could no longer hear Sense. She was a Double Agent, indeed, but for *Him*.'

As Teo quailed under these words, Renzo seemed to move a little closer to her. His expression had softened. 'You couldn't have guessed all that,' he whispered.

One of the mermaids shouted, 'Loose-lipped little dwarfess has scuppered da lot of us. Should of flogged 'er raw when we had a chance.'

The parrots took up 'flogged 'er raw' with relish.

234

'*Rude Sailors,*' reproved Lussa, 'speak like that. We do not speak like That down Here, Ladies. Birds, desist if You please. Or We shall be forced to look for more polite Pets.'

'Can you curry parrot?' wondered one mermaid aloud. She was shouted down.

Renzo offered, over the din, 'We have other news.'

'He's distracting them from me,' Teo realized gratefully. She stood passively as Renzo explained the Butcher, the pirates, the Baja-Menta Ice-cream and the Grey Lady – she was impressed that he had somehow learnt to be more economical with words, even while he wove a rattling tale. Although she'd lived through it all with him, she listened, fascinated, as if to a story.

In the midst of all the tragedy, Lussa was overjoyed to hear of their ally. 'We Mermaids think very highly of Cats. Even Human Sailors entertain Admiration for Them. There's a Superstition among Them that They must keep the Ship's Cat Happy & Well Fed – 'Tis thought that Cats store Magic in their Tails, and that a lashing Tail can bring on a Storm. Mind you, the same Foolish Sailors believe that the Sighting of a Mermaid indicates a Storm coming on to blow . . .'

'Sometimes it do,' observed one mermaid cheekily.

Lussa ignored that. 'So, the Spell Almanac is Safe, then. We still have that One Advantage. And about the Baja-menta Ice-cream, there is a little Something We can do. We have our Echo!'

'Your echo?' asked Teo.

'The renowned Echo of the Garden of the House of the Spirits,' smiled Lussa. 'Now where's our Choir & Fufu Band?'

Eight young mermaids swam forward and bowed to the children. Another group tuned up their instruments: a little flute, a pig-bladder drum, an oyster-keyed xylophone and a paper-and-comb. Lussa wrote some words on a piece of pearly paper, swiftly annotating them with musical notes.

One mermaid, apparently the choir mistress, pinned the paper to a lectern and lifted a coral baton in her hand. The mouths of the mermaids opened in unison. They took a deep breath and began.

Teo and Renzo heard not one single note.

'It's too high for us to hear?' Teo asked.

Lussa nodded, tapping her fingers to the inaudible words. 'But I'll wager You know the Melody. Humanfolk sing of a Drunken Sailor to this Tune. But our Song warns the Venetians to desist from eating the Baja-Menta Ice-cream, it will disagree with Them. Violently. Consult your Book for the Lyrics.'

Teo opened *The Key to the Secret City*. The words of the song immediately spilled out across the page.

Oh, what shall we do with the Baja-Menta?
What shall we do with the Baja-Menta?
What shall we do with the Baja-Menta?
Early in the Morn-ing?
We'll spew and vomit Baja-Menta
We'll hurl and barf Baja-Menta
We'll puke and chunder Baja-Menta
Early in the Morn-ing
Heave-Ho Up It Rises
Heave-Ho Up it Rises
We'll bare our Guts of Baja-Menta
Early in the Morn-ing

'Repulsive!' remarked Teo, grinning

'Yar,' agreed Lussa. 'That is indeed the Concept.' She turned to the mermaids, 'Good, Ladies! You may also improvise with the Harmonies if You so wish.'

236

The choir resumed singing with gusto, enthusiastically miming the relevant gestures.

'But . . .?' began Teo and Renzo in unison.

'Now They shall swim up into the Goldfish Pond in the Garden, lift the Booby Hatch to the Upper World, and sing. The Echo in the Garden shall carry their Song all over Venice.'

'Won't the people get hysterical?' asked Teo.

'Will they even believe it?' worried Renzo.

'With Ordinary Humanfolk, We must work as We do with the Sharks. There's no Explaining to Them in Rational Ways. Instead, this Song will penetrate their Inner Minds without their knowing that It has entered their Ears. They shall not even need to talk about It. They shall simply stop eating the Ice-cream, for It will taste Repulsive to Them. Weigh your Anchors, Singers! Go take the Wind out of *Il Traditore*'s Sails!' cried Lussa.

The mermaid choir swam off eagerly.

Lussa turned back to Renzo and Teo. Her face was sombre. She was holding a calendar.

'Undrowned Child & Studious Son, do You happen to know the Date?' she asked.

So many nights turned into days – Teo could not be certain. 'June 12th?' she murmured uncertainly. Renzo nodded tentatively.

Lussa opened the calendar to show them. Instead of beginning with January 1st, this calendar showed the year starting on June 15th. '*Vinceremo*' was written in old lettering on the cover: *We will win*. Then the date was repeated, this time illustrated with the Tiepolo crest.

Renzo exclaimed, 'The anniversary of the conspiracy! That is when he plans to seize power again!'

He pointed to a line at the bottom of the page. 'Look, this was printed by the Ca' Dario Press. That's what's been going on at night in that so-called haunted palace. That thumping noise is the printing press churning out this rubbish!'

A host of garish paper objects dropped out of the calendar. Bajamonte Tiepolo was so sure of his victory that the Ca' Dario Press had been set to printing maps, little flags and even postcards, all decorated with his crest. Renzo picked up a map of the city which, ominously, showed all the walkable streets gone.

'Some of the poorer parishes have disappeared entirely,' he fumed. 'What will happen to the people? And why doesn't Bajamonte Tiepolo understand? If he makes the water deeper around Venice, then we are vulnerable to invading fleets. It is only the shallowness of the water that has protected Venice from being attacked over the centuries. Big ships couldn't get in. Otherwise the Ottomans, the Serbs, the pirates, the . . . oh no, I see, he *wants* our enemies to have easy access to us!'

Teo exclaimed, 'And the "Incredible New Exhibition" about him opens in San Marco that day! No doubt on the *first floor* – so it won't be flooded! He's ready to rewrite history and already preparing the story! For those who survive.'

Teo shook Renzo's sleeve. 'Remember when we saw the tusks arriving at Ca' Dario? The Brustolons' eyes are made out of ivory, aren't they? That's what the tusks are for. The smell of sawdust – that was the Brustolons being carved. That smell of varnish around them – it's because they're not antiques – they're freshly made.'

'And you know where the blood comes from, for their leeches? It comes from the Vampire Eels! When they're done, and he's put the leeches in their mouths, he sends the statues out all over Venice, to wait for when he has his strength back.'

'Then he'll make them come alive, and not just for a few seconds either.'

Renzo stared despairingly at the calendar. 'So we have three days to stop Bajamonte Tiepolo.'

The mermaids listened seriously as Renzo and Teo explained their flimsy plan: that the children of the gondoliers take to their fathers' boats to hunt down the Creature and destroy it.

'We're not sure how yet,' finished Renzo, lamely. 'By night, obviously, but . . .' He ground to a halt.

It sounded pathetic even as he said it. How could three hundred inexperienced children overcome so much evil? And how could they destroy the Creature without making its poison spread over the whole lagoon, killing every fish and every mermaid and poisoning the water for the human beings?

The younger mermaids were not impressed. Someone shouted from the shadows, 'Da Common Dog Factor is lacking here!'

'I am Afraid,' Lussa spoke gently, 'the Ladies think that more *Good Sense* should be applied to solving this Problem. Your Stout Hearts are to be commended . . .'

'But?' pleaded Teo.

'More Help shall be needed. Remember, Bajamonte Tiepolo is not Alone.'

37. Persuasion

all through the night of June 11th – 12th, 1899

The mermaids of the Seldom Seen Press were speedily set to printing a handbill that would explain the situation and the proposed plan, which involved 'liberating' a number of gondolas from their posts by night.

Renzo explained, 'I'll speak personally with the oldest child from each *stazio* – every area of Venice has its own station for its gondolas, Teo. That child'll be responsible for distributing the handbills secretly to the others in their *stazio*. I know! They can put the instructions inside the *capitelli* – those tower-shaped lamps by the jetties.'

'Will they believe this?' Teo asked. 'Modern children can be so sceptical.'

Lussa said, 'Lorenzo, I hope that Sons & Daughters of Gondoliers shall listen. We have always thought the Gondoliers believed in Us, even as Adults, for They pass so much Time in our Company, by which I mean, upon the Water, though We are not Visible to Them. Among Adults, only the *Incogniti* can behold Us and parley with Us. Of course, the Children of the Gondoliers can see Us, until They are Thirteen or Fourteen, when They lose that Capacity.'

'I'll *make* them believe.' Renzo spoke fiercely.

Lussa had embraced the children's plan, but she had added to it as well. Each one of the gondolas was to carry ghosts to the battlefield in the lagoon. It would be Teo's and Renzo's next task, Lussa explained, to go around to all the haunted places in Venice and explain the crisis to the city's ghosts and ask for their help.

'Just ghosts in-the-Cold, of course,' said Renzo confidently. 'We shan't be bothering with the in-the-Slaughterhouse ghosts, will we? They won't want to . . .'

Lussa replied serenely, 'They should All be given a Chance to save Venice, and then afterwards, if We succeed, They too may rest in Peace.'

'How shall we find them all?' asked Teo.

Lussa smiled. 'I believe You have a certain helpful Volume.'

'Actually, I have another one too. *The Best Ways with Wayward Ghosts.*'

'An excellent Tract that shall give You some admirably good Advice as to how to handle Them. One of Professor Marin's finest.'

Professor Marìn again!

Teo had one last question, one that she found hard to frame. 'The ghosts,' she asked. 'Is it possible that my real parents might be roused up too? . . . You know, to help?'

'So that you can meet them,' Renzo spoke softly.

Lussa answered, 'Nay, Teodora, I am afraid not. Your Parents died with their Consciences at Ease. They shall rest forever in Peace.'

Teo bent her head so that no one could watch her struggle to absorb her disappointment. She muttered, 'And . . .'

'Your Nanny Giulia also died at Peace, Teodora, and not in Venice, as You know. But the Little Children shall help Us – Those Murdered by the Plague Spores of Bajamonte Tiepolo.

They are now among the Cherubim, and You shall see their Sweet Faces borne by Wings in the Battle. They shall have a Special Role there. And of course the human *Incogniti* shall help us. '

Teo picked up one of the handbills: **'Venetians! Foreigners! Remember 1866. Who can tell what will happen now? Not the Mayor – he lies out of both sides of his mouth at once. Leave the city while you can.'**

Silence enveloped the chamber.

'But what was 1866?' asked Teo in a very small voice.

The mermaids raised a turtleshell and showed Teo heartbreaking scenes of a Venice almost submerged under fast-running black water. It swirled around the basilica, and made a dark, turbulent lake of San Marco. The turtleshell changed to a bird's-eye view of the flooded city. From above, the scene at San Marco was repeated all over Venice: black waves beating against buildings, people fleeing, their mouths open in terror and distress. The corpses of rats and dogs floated down swollen canals. Everywhere, murky water was rising and rising.

Renzo explained, 'On November 3rd, 1866, there was a violent storm, causing the River Po to flood. The surge hit Venice in the night, and filled the city with water two yards above the normal level of the sea. The water should have gone down with the next tide, but it did not, because of the wind and the floodwaters of the Po. Two more tides pushed in . . .'

The turtleshell showed the aftermath: even after the water eventually sank away, it left black oil everywhere, shipwrecked gas lamps, ruined houses. In the dismal light of evening, a solitary father, up to his thighs in water, carried his weeping child across the square of San Marco.

'Venice was crippled for months: churches, hospitals, homes. It took ten years to repair all the damage. Some houses could not be saved.' Renzo heaved a sigh. 'Lussa, are you telling us that Bajamonte Tiepolo had something to do with that?'

'It was his first Attempt to get Revenge upon the City. He took Advantage of the Flood & the Wind. He had by that Time begun to exercise an Influence over the Creature in the Lagoon, purely with the Force of his Disembodied Intellect. The Creature briefly stoppered up the Natural Flow of the Tide when It wanted to Recede. *Il Traditore* could not keep the Tide in Venice for more than Two Phases of the Moon. In fact, his Artificial Flood served Him ill, because It drew to Venice the Attention & Sympathy of Humanfolk from all over the World.'

'Yes, the money poured in,' agreed Renzo, with a cynical look on his face. 'And the politicians. And the scientists. With ideas on how to prevent it happening again. People like your adoptive parents, Teo. And big ideas, like a tidal barrier, in case of another surge. The trouble was, everyone had a different idea.'

'But *have* they actually done anything to protect the city from that kind of storm?' asked Teo anxiously.

'Nay,' replied Lussa. 'For naturally, They are still at Loggerheads about how to go about It, Tens of Human-Years later. That's Humanfolk for You. Many Sovereign Nations have given Moneys to save Certain Buildings beloved of their Particular Citizens. But there's little Point saving the Buildings One by One if They are All to be swallowed up by One great Flood.'

Silence fell again. Renzo pointed up at the mortars-and-pestles, symbol of the old lady who had broken Bajamonte Tiepolo's conspiracy back in 1310 by throwing a humble household object at his dwarf.

'An ordinary Venetian saved us once before,' he asserted defiantly. 'Let's go, Teo. We've got a Ghost army to raise.'

Nevertheless, it was rather slowly that Renzo and Teo climbed up the stairs to the garden of the House of the Spirits.

'We could practise our recruiting speech on the ghosts here,' suggested Teo.

'Good idea. If they don't give us a fair hearing then no one will,' agreed Renzo. 'These garden ghosts are only in-the-Cold, so they actually *want* to redeem themselves. It's the other ones we have to worry about.'

So, to those Garden ghosts, Teo and Renzo gave their first performance of a speech that was supposed to rally an entire supernatural army.

Their first attempt was a humiliating failure.

The ghosts waited until the children had stammered to a standstill, and then booed them roundly. The ghosts complained about their delivery, nitpicked their grammar and jeered at their lack of eloquence.

'Venetians! The pair of you!' scoffed an old miser. 'You'd never think it to hear you mumbling and fumbling and rambling off into the raspberry bushes! You must stay with your point! And you must above all impress us!'

'I am new at being a Venetian,' said Teo defensively. 'Instead of criticizing, why don't you teach us how to do it properly?'

The ghosts relented then, and for half an hour Teo and Renzo were drilled in all manner of rhetorical tricks. They were taught how to pause dramatically, how to raise just one eyebrow, how to lower their voices so that the audience would lean forward to catch every last word.

'And you, young Master Windbag.' The miser poked a freezing finger at Renzo. 'Learn that less is more!'

Finally the children delivered a rousing speech, and the

ghosts awarded them a vigorous round of applause.

'But will *you* help us?' asked Renzo, carefully economic with his words. 'Will you fight Bajamonte Tiepolo?'

'Of course, you stupid boy, we were persuaded the first time. But you've more important and far more difficult ghosts than us to convince, and you must be ready for them.'

Teo and Renzo climbed back over the wall and out into the Sacca della Misericordia.

'Renzo!' exclaimed Teo. 'Do you notice what's missing?'

'The striped poles! All the boats are floating away!'

Not one of the striped poles remained standing above the water. The Creature had pulled all its tentacles down under the water, all the better, no doubt to make its sudden concerted attack.

In three days' time.

38. Supposed to be a secret

a quarrelsome dawn, June 12th, 1899

'I'm off to speak to the gondolier children. Better you don't come, Teo. I'll see you tonight. For the ghosts.'

'It's too complicated to tell them the truth about me, I suppose?' she muttered resentfully. 'Who I am? Or maybe you can't be bothered?'

'It's supposed to be a secret,' he reminded her baldly.

'And you want to play the hero, saving Venice all on your own.' Teo regretted those tart words before she had even finished uttering them.

Ignoring them, Renzo said quietly, 'And I must make an appearance at home. I don't want my mother to get anxious.'

'Or your father . . .?'

'He died five years ago. There's just my mother and me.'

Teo stared. 'Why didn't you mention that before?'

'Well, it's not something I'd say casually, is it? It's not as if . . .' There was a catch in his voice.

Teo swallowed. This explained Renzo's seriousness, the way he seemed so much older than his years. He'd had to be the man of his family all this time. She remembered that Renzo had told her about his father's bronchitis – the night the creature's tentacles nearly took him. He had flinched when the gondolier passed by with that terrible cough. But he had not revealed that his father's illness had been fatal. Even when Teo had discovered the truth about her own parents, he'd said nothing about being half an orphan himself. Until tonight, Renzo had always been so distant with her. He had shared almost nothing about his life. And she'd just been hideously mean to him again, driving him further away.

She said contritely, 'I'm so very sorry for your loss, Renzo.' Seeing his face pinched and closed, she quickly changed the subject. 'I need to study *The Best Ways with Wayward Ghosts*. It's back at the hotel.'

'Meet you there when it gets dark? So we can start on the ghosts?'

Teo was relieved that he was not going to hold a grudge. She nodded and smiled. After so much time with Renzo, it would feel odd to be on her own again. He leant towards her, as if he was going to kiss her goodbye. But at the last minute he jerked his head away, blushed and muttered gruffly, 'For Maria's sake, hope that I don't bump into her in the meanwhile!'

It would be too awkward to walk with him down to San Marcuola now. Teo set off in a different direction, forcing herself to pause and look in shop windows so she didn't accidentally catch Renzo up.

Eventually she found herself at the *vaporetto* stop, and inserted herself invisibly among the crowds of Venetians who poured onto the steam ferry. She chose a spot by the railings and stood there deep in thought. Had Renzo really meant to kiss her? Why had he decided not to? Was it because, as usual, she was a complete fright to look at after the night's adventures? Was it because she had accused him of wanting to play the hero? How unfair and malicious she'd been! What would it be like if he did kiss her? Would she like it?

'I suppose that I rather would,' Teo conceded. And even though no one else saw her, let alone heard her, she blushed just as fiercely as Renzo then.

A shrill toot and a jet of steam announced another ferry approaching from the opposite direction. It was almost empty: just a few old ladies and a single child stood on the deck. The lumpy little girl, dressed in sickly pink and bilious green, clutched a crest-covered parasol. From a distance her whole body expressed utter dejection.

'Maria!' screamed Teo as the two ferries drew almost parallel. If she could have leapt over the water Teo would have done it in a moment, and grabbed Maria, and given her the shaking of her life.

As Maria caught sight of Teo, her face crumpled. A swarm of *scolopendre* was crawling all over her body. Maria seemed too deeply sunk in misery to try to swat the horrible insects away. But she screamed as a *scolopendra* buried its fangs in her neck. That neck was no longer delicate as it used to be, but thick and gnarled, like a dwarf's.

Maria hugged herself with pain. Her hunchback was suddenly clearly visible. Her swollen eyes streamed with fat tears. 'I'm so sorry,' she called out over the churning water. 'Oh Teo, you'll never know how sorry I am. I've run away. I've got to get away from him. I wanted to warn you . . . You've got to tell the mermaids . . .'

At that moment a cold shadow traced its way over the roof of Maria's ferry.

The skeleton of a man-sized bat swept down to the deck where Maria cowered. Its bones were yellowy-white, bare of flesh. Except for the head, which was that of a human being, with a milky, jellified face, like that of a drowned man deep underwater.

The bat grabbed Maria in its claws and flew away with her.

'Help her! Someone help her!' cried Teo.

But no one could hear or see Teo. And Maria, once in the arms of the bat, became invisible, just like an apple in Teo's hand.

All day Teo pored over *The Best Ways with Wayward Ghosts*, staring fixedly at one potentially crucial page after another. She tried to keep memories of Maria's capture out of her head, filling it up instead with useful information for the night ahead. But her tears fell on the pages, gluing some of them together, blistering others.

At ten, when dusk turned into night, Teo was awoken by a shaft of moonlight. She must have fallen asleep over the thick little volume. She rushed to the window. Renzo was already waiting outside the hotel, looking pointedly at the clock tower. She hurtled down the stairs.

When he saw her tearstained face, Renzo hurried forward. Teo explained what had happened to Maria. Renzo's eyes narrowed. 'She doesn't really deserve any better.'

'It wasn't Maria who betrayed the mermaids. It was the *scolopendre!* Even Lussa said so. She's just a prisoner. We have to try to find her. It may not be too late.'

Renzo was stern. 'We've more important things . . . and remember what happened last time you didn't do what the mermaids asked.'

As if Teo could forget Chissa's white corpse and her hair flowing like blood in the cavern! She closed her mouth and led the way back up to her room. She bent over *The Best Ways with Wayward Ghosts*, soaking up the last few pages.

'What are you doing, Teo?' asked Renzo.

'I'm memorizing. You know my memory works like a camera. If I concentrate, I can take in the whole page at once.

This book's so thick! If only I knew which pages we're going to need.'

Renzo said more respectfully, 'Sorry. Forgot that's how you do it. That's not an Undrowned Child skill, is it? Or a Gasperin skill? You've taught yourself that one. Like reading upside-down. One day, when this is over . . .'

'I'm ready.' Teo reached for a jacket and handed Renzo a pullover.

'It's unspeakably hot out there!'

'Page thirty-two, bottom right: *"Make sure you dress warmly for encounters with ghosts in-the-Cold. Such spirits carry a perishing iciness about their persons and diffuse it to others."'*

Rumours of the impending battle had already spread fast among the community of ghosts in-the-Cold. On every corner the children found spirits eager to talk to them. Some positively begged to be allowed to join their enterprise. Others graciously allowed themselves to be persuaded. Few ghosts turned them down.

'Now go to the garden of the House of the Spirits,' the children ordered each converted ghost, 'and wait for instructions.'

When they had finished with the human ghosts, they started on the animals. The children recruited ghost cats that had lived duplicitously with two families; parrots that had frightened old ladies to death with their swearing; dogs that had been cat-killers. All these creatures too had a desire to redeem themselves and to save their city in the process.

No, it wasn't hard to find ghost-defenders of Venice. The children's problem was the chattering of their teeth. Even on this balmy evening, a freezing miasma surrounded them wherever they parleyed with a ghost. Extra clothes were not enough. Soon they were chilled to the bone, huddling close together – somewhat self-consciously – as each ghost told his or her sad story and enveloped them in freezing air.

Arriving at San Marco, they found the water had receded. The Baja-Menta ice-cream trolley lay on its side empty and defaced with angry scribbling. Renzo averted his eyes from the pile of rubble that had so recently been the Campanile.

A new map had opened in *The Key to the Secret City*. It was guiding them towards Marin Falier, a Doge who had once plotted to seize absolute power. Marin Falier had more reason than any ghost in Venice to redeem himself. For he had been decapitated and buried with his head between his knees so that he would never be able to find it again – or threaten the Republic of Venice.

Teo fretted, 'If he's mutilated, then he's not in-the-Cold, wanting redemption. He's in-the-Slaughterhouse – he's not sorry for what he did.'

Renzo grimaced. 'At least he's not a convicted child-eater.'

They found the old Doge's ghost near Santi Giovanni e Paolo, just as *The Key to the Secret City* advised them. Lussa's face on the cover had a warning look.

Teo's first petrified thought was that the headless figure who blocked their path was the Butcher Biasio. But instead of a stinking, bloodstained apron, this ghost wore glorious damask robes lined with ermine. His head nestled between his velvet-covered knees.

'What do *you* want?' he shouted at them. 'A human child and another one between-the-Linings? Why seek me out now? No one has wanted me, no one has thought of me, except with disgust, for all these centuries. I smell a trap!'

Renzo and Teo took turns with the speech, trying to remember all the tricks of oratory they'd learnt in the garden of the House of the Spirits.

The speech was received in brooding silence. Then the Doge demanded, 'And exactly why should I help Venice after what Venice did to me? Anyway, I always was a little bit sorry for poor old Bajamonte. He's really pulling back strongly now, from what I hear. Why, perhaps I should be on *his* side?'

Teo fought down a nervous desire to laugh. Here they were, talking to a head tucked between a pair of knees. The children explained it yet again: if Doge Falier helped he would be redeemed, and even get his head back in the right place.

'Of course, you have to be sorry for what you did, too,' added Renzo reprovingly.

'If I . . . admit I was wrong . . . if I join you . . . shall you get my portrait put back in the Doges' Palace too?' the crusty old man almost whimpered.

Renzo whispered to Teo that paintings of all the Doges lined the walls in the Great Council chamber. But, where Marin Falier's portrait should hang, there was just a frame painted black inside.

'We can't promise to fix *that*, Renzo!' Teo hissed back. Fortunately, the old Doge appeared to be rather hard of hearing, perhaps not surprising, given that his head was so far from its original position.

'I am sure the Mayor will be extremely grateful,' affirmed Renzo aloud. 'He would be absolutely insane if he did not have a famous artist just standing by for the honour of painting your portrait, Sir.'

Teo added, 'Quite off his head.'

Renzo kicked her shin. Meanwhile Marin Falier puffed himself up and started posing in anticipation. 'Very well. You've won me over.'

'But are you *really sorry*?' demanded Teo sternly. The Doge's conversion had seemed rather glib.

In answer Marin Falier burst into tears like a baby. '*Of*

course I'm sorry. I've been ashamed of myself for five hundred and forty-four years. I was just too proud to admit it before.'

Teo knelt and wiped his tears with a corner of her pinafore. The Doge hiccoughed and sniffed, 'But I was never a warrior. I'm more comfortable behind a desk, pushing a quill. The gentleman you need is Enrico Dandolo, even though he's blind and a little eccentric, if you ask me.'

'A little eccentric? He's one to talk!' muttered Teo as the children left Marin Falier practising noble facial expressions for his portrait.

'That went well. Enrico Dandolo next, then!' said Teo cheerfully, wondering why Renzo looked so frightened. *The Key to the Secret City* soon showed her why.

The ghost of Enrico Dandolo had burning brands for eyes, and his restless spirit walked the streets cutting its fingers with a sharp blade. This was a reminder of all the innocent blood he had shed during the Fourth Crusade in 1204. In Constantinople, Ottoman women, children and slaves had fallen before the callous swords of his men.

The burning brands were the first parts of Enrico Dandolo that showed themselves in the gloom of the Barbaria delle Tole. The children made out a stooped, knotty figure, and then the flash of the sword with which he constantly slashed at his own hands. Two servants trailed behind him, remonstrating in grovelling voices. They were both much scarred.

'Try to be sorry for him,' advised Teo in a trembling voice. 'That's what it says in *The Best Ways with Wayward Ghosts*. And if we're feeling sorry for him then maybe *we* won't be so scared. Er, excuse me . . . Doge Dandolo . . . Sir . . .' she called.

'Who's that?' thundered Dandolo. 'Come here and have your throat cut!'

Teo swallowed hard. Dandolo had not scrupled to send

children to slaughter before.

'What do you want with me?' he bellowed, charging past the children, sword aloft. Fortunately the burning brands did not serve as working eyes. He missed them by a yard. The servants dodged wearily, clearly used to the Doge's irascible temper.

'Make it good, whatever you've got to tell,' he ordered, returning for another attack. 'May be the last thing you say.'

This time he passed so close that Teo felt the heat of his burning eyes on her face and Renzo heard the whir of the sword near his ear.

'Oh, I'm *really* sorry for him,' muttered Renzo.

'Sorry for me?' shouted Enrico Dandolo. 'A mere wretch of a boy?'

The ferocious old Doge stood dumbstruck for a moment, and then he dissolved into noisy tears.

'No one was ever sorry for me before,' he sobbed in a broken voice.

The children seized their chance. They spoke soothingly of redemption, and of the glory of saving Venice. Enrico Dandolo snuffled and sneezed, but listened attentively. Renzo spoke economically. Teo practised the dramatic pause. It was one of their better performances. At the end of the speech, he commanded, 'Again!'

At the second rendition, he implored, 'Mercy!'

By the end of the third performance, he had drawn himself up into a manful posture, and spoke with a voice firm with resolve. 'Enough! The Ottomans, you say? Attacking Venice? Kill the Ottoman enemy? That's what I do best! It'll be like old times again,' he sighed sentimentally.

Teo dared, 'But you're supposed to show remorse for what you did before.'

'Don't push your luck, girlie! Would you rather have me

with you or against you?' Dandolo drew himself up, and spun around in a perfect circle with three murderously graceful slashes of his sword.

'With us,' admitted Teo.

'And what do you care if I get redeemed or not? I'll do it, but only if you fetch the Rioba brothers!'

Renzo whispered to Teo, 'The statues on the Campo dei Mori.'

'I *know*.'

The Doge growled, 'They were with me in Constantinople. Signor Rioba's an indispensable lieutenant! Though he would curse the bladder out of a weasel.'

Dandolo had a copy of Signor Rioba's latest missive poking out of a sleeve of his tunic. He dragged it out and waved it at them. 'Now my minions have been reading this stuff to me, and they say there's a lot of fancy doings going on with the lettering. Tell Rioba to desist immediately. Plain soldier style's what's wanted here.'

The thought of explaining the mermaids and the Seldom Seen Press was too daunting to contemplate. Renzo murmured placatingly, 'Certainly, Your Greatness.'

As the children rushed off towards the Campo dei Mori, Enrico Dandolo shouted to them, 'And tell 'em to bring the camel who's carved on the wall of the Palazzo Mastelli. That is one wily beast to have on your side.'

After just ten words of their speech, Signor Rioba creaked to life and jumped off his column full of energy, his chin and nose jutting forward. He smoothed out the pleats in his tunic. Then he spat on his hand and polished his iron nose with his fingers. The chalky dust of centuries flew off him when he flexed his sword arm while listening to the children tell their story.

'My Brothers, Sandi! Afani!' he shouted at the other Moors, who were already climbing down from their pedestals. 'Prepare yourselves for war!'

Signor Rioba had the same gravel-in-honey voice Teo remembered from her first encounter with him all those days – those lifetimes – ago, when she had woken on a tombstone, wandered through the city, come across his silent statue and felt his heart beating under the stone. And Signor Rioba was no more serene than when she'd seen him before. He snarled, 'Typical of this wimbling *woman* of a town! Leaves it to the last lingering minute to summon the folk who can save her!'

Renzo mumbled an apology.

'She's a beauty, but this giddy city has never known what was good for her,' Signor Rioba grumbled. 'Anyway, yes, let me have at him, that *Traditore*! I'll fry his kidneys in a pan!'

He tossed imaginary kidneys in an invisible frying pan in his left hand.

'And as for that scullion-brain the Mayor . . . Where is he? I've a craving to crack his napper and let out his puddings!'

Between violent parries with a jewelled dagger he'd drawn out of his belt, Signor Rioba demanded, 'So where are the saints then?'

'What saints?' asked Renzo nervously.

Signor Rioba thundered, 'Didn't that dunderhead Dandolo tell ye that we'd need the *saints*?'

Renzo and Teo shook their heads mutely.

'Well, I'll be off then to remind the Old Heathen myself then. What are ye staring at? Get on with it! *Saints!* I tell ye! Donato, Nicolo, Onofolo, Taraise, Zaccaria, Anathasios, Marco, Stefano, Damiano and Cosmo. But above all Saint Lucia. Most of her's in one piece! I'll go and get the ghost horses, myself.'

'Horses?'

'The nobles' horses from the Cavallerizza, ye lunar fools!'

'Horses in Venice? With all the canals?' Teo asked. Renzo

mumbled, 'Once there were seventy stallions near the Mendicanti. Horse riding was forbidden at the end of the thirteenth century. I don't think we'll mention that to him, though.'

Teo remembered Pedro-the-Crimp with his horse. That daguerreotype had been taken by the Mendicanti!

Signor Rioba was looking under his tunic. 'The old underwear has stood up well,' he remarked. 'Get one more battle out of that, I believe. And good work with the Press,' he added in a friendlier tone. 'Tell the Mermaids that I am liking the new fonts. They have captured me to a "T".'

'You know about the handbills?' Renzo asked. 'You don't mind that they use your name?'

'Proud as a galleon, actually,' Signor Rioba almost purred.

'But how are we going to find the saints?' called Teo. 'Where *are* they?'

Signor Rioba was at war again in an instant. 'Have ye not got a *book* to guide ye, ye whey-faced girlie?'

'Sorry,' agreed Teo hastily. 'Of course I do.'

39. Night of the bodysnatchers

all through the hours of darkness,
June 12th – June 13th, 1899

On the cover of *The Key to the Secret City* Lussa waved what looked like a little white wishbone at them. The book opened to a most peculiar and rather morbid map – tiny images of the organs, fingers and limbs of saints glowed above churches all over Venice: the leg of Saint Tryphon, the foot of Saint Catherine of Siena, the kneecap of someone else.

'There must be seventy of them. Where do we start?' worried Renzo.

The Church of San Geremia lit up on the page, showing a miniature mummy of Saint Lucy.

'Oh dear!' Teo wrinkled her nose. 'Must we? I feel like a bodysnatcher!'

The church doors groaned open as they approached. They hesitated on the doorstep until *The Key to the Secret City* literally tugged Teo over the threshold. At the back of the church, light streamed from a chapel where the remains of Saint Lucia lay in her glass casket. Above her bloomed trees fashioned from gold, bearing round red lanterns like apples.

Gingerly, they approached the casket.

'Oh!' gasped Teo. Saint Lucy lay with bare feet and hands, dressed in a red robe stiff with gold braid. Her face was covered with a silver mask, as if she'd just been dancing at a *Carnevale* ball.

'Now what are we supposed to do? How do we wake her up?'

The Key to the Secret City spread itself open to a sheet of music with words. A pair of painted eyes danced over the first notes, encouragingly.

'We've got to sing?' asked Teo. Of all the embarrassing things she'd been forced to do since this adventure began – this was surely the worst. Her singing had been compared to a sick toad mourning his mother by a boy at her school in Naples. The most pitiful thing was that the comparison was undeniably apt.

Renzo lifted the book and raised his eyes to the rafters. Heavenly music poured out of his mouth, pure and perfectly pitched.

'I didn't know you could do that,' breathed Teo.

Renzo paused to say modestly, 'Weak swimmer, but I can sing a little, yes. Gondoliers need to, you know.' He returned to his song.

Inside her casket, the skin and bones of Saint Lucy rustled like dry leaves. The saint raised one skeletal foot – with the merest papery covering of transparent skin – and then the other. As Renzo continued to sing, she sat up, hit her head, from which tatters of hair still hung, against the roof of the casket. The mask dropped off, showing the surprised remains of a face with the eyes sewn shut. She lay down again, looking dazed. Then she raised herself more carefully and scrabbled at the glass with her frail, leathery fingers. But the casket was sealed tight.

'Help me!' mouthed the saint. She didn't really have much of a mouth – it was more like a leathery gash in her face. Renzo, still singing, gestured frantically to Teo. 'What are you waiting for?' he hissed, taking breath for another burst of melody.

With the greatest reluctance, Teo approached the rim of the casket.

There were no hinges, no loose seals, and no concealed mechanisms to Saint Lucy's enclosure. The saint tapped impatiently on her window. Then she mimed a hammer crashing down on the glass.

'You want me to smash it?'

The saint nodded vigorously, and curled herself into a ball, ready to shield what was left of her face from the impending fall of glass shards.

Teo seized a chair from the aisle and approached the casket. With all her strength she hurled the chair at a corner of the glass box. Glass rained down and Saint Lucy sprang out, shaking herself like a wet dog.

'I'm ready for war,' croaked the wizened little lady. She immediately knelt on the ground, folded her hands together and started to pray fervently.

'Is this how you do war?' Teo asked.

A clatter of metal and a smell of burning announced a new visitor to the church. The voice of Enrico Dandolo boomed to the rafters. 'Aha! I hear you're making a fine start on rounding up our saints!'

'Go, girl!' he urged Saint Lucy.

'Is that what you wanted?' asked Teo. 'For the saints to pray?'

'For the success of our enterprise, yes. Not much of a one for the praying myself,' explained Dandolo. 'It's always better to have the experts in.'

And so Teo and Renzo turned into reluctant bodysnatchers.

'I'm sorry, I'm sorry,' Teo murmured under her breath as they carefully released the delicate relics of the army of saints from their reliquaries in churches all over the city.

When Renzo sang, the pieces of saints grew their missing parts. From the fragment of a tooth or a toe, entire saints appeared. The reincarnated saints were all just a little smaller than ordinary people, and apart from their mummified appearances, they had one other notable quality – their bare feet never quite touched the ground.

On returning to their full form, the saints did the same thing as Saint Lucy. They fell to their knees (an inch above the floor) and prayed for Venice.

One by one, Teo and Renzo led their seventy saints to the garden of the House of the Spirits, where they arranged themselves on pedestals and niches. They took up their rosaries, and bent their heads. Then they prayed. The echo of the House of the Spirits carried the pure sound of their voices and the soothing click of their beads all over the city.

Just as the last saint had been bedded in among the rosemary bushes, from the near distance came a rumbling sound, like thunder but lasting far longer.

'It sounds like . . .' Teo began.

'Horses!' finished Renzo. 'Signor Rioba has roused the stallions!'

'And here they come!'

The clatter of hooves filled the air. Then splashing drew their eyes to the lagoon.

'And what's that, in the water? They don't look like our mermaids. Look at those double tails!'

'They must be the English Melusine. Lussa summoned them with sea-shells, remember. And those seahorses –

they're called 'Little Steeds of Neptune', aren't they? And those creatures with the long pointy heads . . .'

'The London Sea-Monks and Sea-Bishops!'

The stallions were soon grazing in the orchard, and their warm, farmyard smell floated out through the night mist. At the far end of the trees, Teo recognized the tattered coat of Pedro-the-Crimp who was lovingly tending a dappled mare. He waved at her, and then put his hands together, bowing.

'He's asking my forgiveness, for frightening me,' she realized. She waved and smiled back.

The children left the saints praying and walked wearily down the stairs to the cavern to report their progress to the mermaids.

'. . . and the Doges are with us, Signor Rioba, and his brothers are on our side!' exulted Renzo.

Teo concluded, 'And Enrico Dandolo's agreed to lead the battle party to the Creature in the lagoon. And Doge Marin Falier says he's really sorry.'

If they expected praise, rest and sustenance, they were disappointed. Lussa sent them straight back on the streets. 'Lorenzo and Teodora, now we need Money. And Lions. You need Money to obtain the Lions. The Book will guide You, Children. Our dear Circus-master Signor Alicamoussa has softened the Beasts' Attitudes in our Regard . . .'

'He'd soften anyone, that Signor Alicamoussa,' remarked a young mermaid longingly.

Lussa silenced her with a look. She warned the children, 'Take care. The Lions are known to be somewhat Tetchy.'

And Lussa had turned back to her own work. For the cavern under the House of the Spirits was now engaged in war production. Every surface was covered with jewelled armour, which the mermaids, using tiny tools, were inlaying with slivers of coral. Other mermaids hammered rings into shape.

'Coral protects against Enchantment & Insect Stings,' explained Lussa. 'Rings made from the Nails & the Screws of a Coffin or Seahorse Teeth are said to protect against Drowning, in Your World & Ours. Now off You go!'

She pointed to the stairs, adding, 'Feed the Lions well and They shall follow You.'

'Do we *want* to be followed by lions?' muttered Renzo.

The children climbed back out to the garden. The nuns of the House of the Spirits were moving quietly among the praying saints, tidying the rags of their robes, even dusting them with little feather brushes. The saints continued to pray, but acknowledged their groomers with sad, sweet smiles.

'So gentle!' Teo longed to talk to the nuns, to see if there were any among them that remembered her from the weeks she spent in the House of the Spirits as a baby. But the old ladies were absorbed in their task, their faces lit up with the joy of being kind to so many martyred saints.

On the cover of *The Key to the Secret City*, Lussa rubbed two fingers together impatiently. A map inside glowed with stashes of small black-and-white banknotes.

'*Moneta patriottica!*' Renzo exclaimed. He explained to Teo that this money dated back to the Siege of Venice in 1848, when the Austrians had pummelled the city with cannon balls. The besieged Venetians had pulled in their belts and fought bravely while the Austrians tried to starve them to death. The Venetians had even printed their own currency – the *moneta patriottica*. But then cholera raged through the city, and food stocks dwindled.

'Finally,' Renzo pronounced with disgust, 'the Austrians blocked our supply of fresh water. We had to surrender then.'

He grinned, 'But my mother always told me the Venetians buried their *moneta patriottica* in their wells and gardens in case the city ever needed it again.'

Guided by *The Key*, Teo's and Renzo's fingers grew filthy from poking into secret holes in walls, the backs of dog kennels and under flowerpots to pull out wads of fragile notes. Soon rustling stacks of money filled Teo's pinafore pockets and Renzo's satchel. But all the while both children silently fretted about the same thing. Renzo finally voiced it: 'But how can we use this old money?' No shop will take it now! The siege was over fifty years ago.'

The Key to the Secret City rattled until Teo opened it, to find the words *Give me the money!* written across the page. When she closed the *moneta* inside the book, it turned into modern Italian *lire*, acceptable at every shop.

At dawn, the children used the transformed *moneta patriottica* to buy cuts of meat at the abattoirs. *The Key* guided them to the winged lions in every sculpture, every painting, every relief in the city. Renzo and Teo whispered their well-worn speech in those short, fluffy ears, offering each lion a newspaper cone of minced innards.

The stone lions were the most frightening. On scenting the meat, they twitched their noses. Then they flexed their wings. A few mouthfuls of meat brought them instantly back to life, the stone on their backs softening into luxuriant if slightly musty fur. The children were subjected to suspicious sniffs and even experimental licks.

'Ugh, cat breath!' shuddered Renzo.

'To the House of the Spirits!' the children urged each wakening lion. 'If you please.' The lions nodded, stretched enormously, shook out their ears and set off, brandishing their tufted tails behind them. Teo was pleased to see a few *magòghe* disappearing in mid-air as the lions flew over the city.

Finally, every last lion awakened, Renzo and Teo returned to the House of the Spirits triumphant, hopeful and exhausted. In the garden, a tall, devastatingly handsome man in a top hat was already drilling the lions in battle formations. Their heads on one side, the golden beasts listened respectfully. He, in turn, bowed and spoke to them with warm affection.

Renzo guessed, 'That must be the circus-master. What was his name, Teo?'

'Sargano Alicamoussa, for his pains! The Grey Lady told us he's a member of the *Incogniti*. He might have known my . . .'

'Best not disturb,' said Renzo hastily, as the lions roared. 'Let's go down.'

As they had hoped, a spicy feast awaited them at the end of their labours. They explained their successes with their mouths half full of Hot & Sour Broth, Char-crusted Sea-Gherkin, and Moon-viewing Noodles. Finally, they pushed their bowls aside, feeling satisfied.

'A good morning's work,' Renzo smiled at Teo.

'And we didn't even go to bed.'

But Lussa sighed. 'Children, our Task is just beginning. All your Herculean Labours of this Night have merely *balanced* the Good Magic against the Baddened Magic. We teeter upon a Pivot. And the Signs are all against Us, and against Venice at this Moment.'

From the back of the water chamber came the sound of scampering. Millions and millions of little paws, pounding across the stone above their heads.

Renzo and Teo spoke aloud the line of the prophecy:

'When Rats flee town on frightened paws.'

'Where are the rats going?' Teo asked. 'Whose side are they on anyway?'

'The Rats?' Lussa answered. 'Alas, their Own, Nobody

else's. They leave now because They believe Venice is already Lost.'

'Have you noticed how quiet it is?' asked Renzo.

The skulls in the graveyard were silent now, and that silence was sadder than their sobs.

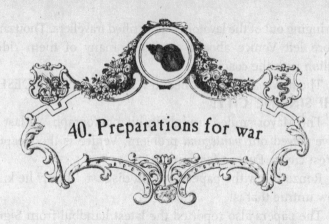

40. Preparations for war

the morning of June 13th, 1899

Lussa told the children to go home and to rest before the exertions of the next day.

'You shall know,' she said quietly, 'when the Battle is about to start, for You shall hear Seven Snorts of the Siren that warns of High Water.'

'The gondolier children shall fight to the death!' growled Renzo. Teo stared at him with surprised admiration.

But Lussa looked sad. 'Let Us hope that It does not come to That. Too many Venetian Boys & Girls have succumbed to the Plague already. Perhaps it is Wrong to send more Children into Battle? We need more Venetians, not fewer of Them.'

To get to the Hotel degli Assassini, Renzo and Teo were forced to walk over a dawn carpet of rats. The rats were all heading in one direction: out of town, and as fast as they could.

The rats jumped onto *vaporetti* and scuttled among the feet of the shrieking passengers. They leapt from gondola to gondola, finding the quickest route down the Grand Canal. They scrambled onto the trains at Santa Lucia station, springing out of the lavatories at terrified travellers. Thousands more left Venice aboard carriages, many of them riding pillion with the coachmen.

The newspapers screamed in war capitals: **'RATS DESERT THE SINKING CITY!'**

The Mayor smiled smugly in his photograph. 'At last we have solved our *pantegana* problem. Venice is the cleanest, safest city in Europe for tourists.'

Renzo threw the paper down in disgust, 'If only he knew how untrue that is!'

The papers also reported the latest handbill from Signor Rioba: **'Flee! Flee the ancient enemy! Your Mayor already has. He's hiding out on the mainland now. Didn't mention it, did he? I thought I would.'**

In the absence of the Mayor, 'out of Venice on business', the Minister for Tourism and Decorum had given an interview under a headline that read: **'SIGNOR RIOBA DAMAGES TOURIST TRADE. INQUIRY.'**

'If all the tourists leave Venice now,' asked the Minister, **'who is going to pay compensation for their ruined holidays? The city would be bankrupted.'**

Renzo said grimly, 'And who is going to pay compensation if they stay and Bajamonte Tiepolo murders them all?'

'Look,' Teo pointed to a single paragraph lost amid the advertisements on the back page. It read, **'An unusual number of fever cases have been reported, with patients complaining of black swellings in the neck, groin and under the arms.'**

'Meet you at ten tonight?' said Renzo. 'We need to go and get some Venetian Treacle for the wounded, and we'll go to the Grey Lady to tell her what has happened, and . . .'

His mouth formed into an involuntary yawn. Teo waved him goodbye, her lids dropping down on her cheeks.

Back at Teo's hotel, everything was in disorder. The palace appeared to be wrapped in a private bandage of mist. Under cover of the soft whiteness, the building's transformation was almost complete. The plaster was peeling inside, revealing old frescoes. Confused waiters arriving at tables with great silver domes opened them up to present repulsive food from older, crueller times. Instead of pasta with tomato sauce, there was a whole pig's head grinning in jelly or a castle carved out of thick white fat.

Teo fell on her creaking bed – it too appeared to be changing itself from a simple iron bedstead to an elaborate four-poster. In her dreams, she rode an antique iron horse into battle.

She was awoken by a shriek outside. It was dark again.

She leapt out of the bed, now hung with towering black drapes. From the window she glimpsed Renzo rushing into the courtyard of the hotel, just as a man ran past him shouting, 'The Rialto Bridge is on fire! And they're looting the Cassa di Risparmio!'

Renzo looked up at Teo, white-faced. Minutes later she was down by his side, and he was explaining, 'That's the biggest bank in Venice. It's started, Teo, just like the night in 1310.'

'How can the Rialto Bridge be on fire? It's made of stone.'

'Remember, Teo, in 1310 it was still made out of wood.' There was no triumph in Renzo's voice for knowing that fact. 'The bridge went up in minutes. Shopkeepers were burnt alive at their stalls.'

Teo exclaimed, 'Let's go to straight to the Grey Lady and see if there are any spells written under her fur that could help us now.'

'But we don't know how to cast spells, do we. It's more than just saying them aloud. You have to say them with your *soul*, or something.'

'We can learn,' said Teo, grim-faced. 'We've learnt a great many things lately that we didn't think possible.'

Sadly, the children had even harder things to learn that night.

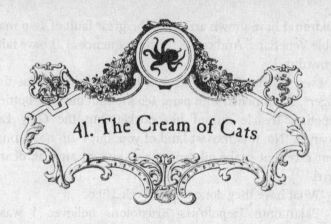

41. The Cream of Cats

night-time, June 13th, 1899

The door was gaping open when they arrived at the Archives. Papers blew about the deserted street. The library looked like the scene of a violent robbery. Shelves had been stripped, with the books lying all over the floor, pages ripped out. Boxes had been emptied over the tables and the contents roughly rifled. The scent of varnish filled the air. The Brustolons, meanwhile, had been rearranged in different postures, all together in the main entrance.

'What's that, on the floor?' cried Teo.

The moonlight shone on smears of blood with four six-toed pawprints dragging through them.

'Bajamonte Tiepolo hates cats,' whispered Renzo.

They followed the trail to the room where Bajamonte Tiepolo's papers were kept. There they found the Grey Lady, lying on the ground, panting shallowly. A thin line of blood coated her lips and nose.

The Grey Lady gasped, 'He has got hisss strength back. He animated the Brustolons . . . and they pillaged . . . And . . . I did not expect that, even though you tried to warrn me, children. I have grown arrogant, the great fault of ssso many noble Venetians. And catsss. In consequence . . . I have failed in my duty.'

Even as the children stroked her with the tips of their fingers, she flinched with pain. Teo brought the little bottle of Venetian Treacle out of her pocket, but the Grey Lady groaned, 'No, it is mossst kind of you, but I am not human. Your excellent snake oil cannot help me, or any cat, dearrrr girrrl.'

'What have they done to you?' cried Teo.

'Bajamonte Tiepolo'sss Brustolons believed I was a common cat,' the Grey Lady spat weakly. 'So the biggest one did not think . . . to look at me closely . . . when he ssstrangled me with one hand . . . and threw me against the shelves. It was just sheer brrrutishness. Childrrren, he did not guess the truth . . . about my role . . . as the Spell Almanac's guardian and bearerrr. They may have dessstroyed me, but that mattersss not. What mattersss is that *Il Traditore*'s bullying minions . . . did not get what he sent them here to find . . .'

The Grey Lady was fighting for breath. The children tried to make her comfortable with a book under her head, but she told them, 'You arrre sweet crrreatures, but you must leave me and tell the mermaids what has happened. They must send messages to the *Incogniti*! And I must . . . imprint the spellsss . . . on another Being . . . before it isss . . . too late.'

'What other Being?'

'A living Being, who can be trusted. A native Venetian beast. A *pantegana*, if necessary, a bird, if I can catch one.'

The Grey Lady was so seriously wounded that she did not seem to realize that catching a rat or a bird was completely impossible for her now. Her voice wandered between a miaow and human speech, as she warbled – as if to some bird in a tree – 'Come here, little one.'

Teo whispered to Renzo, 'Can we catch her a bird?'

'Us? Have you ever caught a bird? And all the rats have left Venice.'

'I'll do it,' said Teo. 'She can use my body to imprint the spells.'

'Are you mad? That will make you Bajamonte Tiepolo's number one target.'

'I'm already Bajamonte Tiepolo's number one target. Someone has to carry the spells. The Grey Lady . . .' and Teo sobbed as she gently held the cat's paw, 'cannot do it any more.'

Renzo exploded, 'Teo! You're not like the Grey Lady. You cannot transform yourself into a cat and cover up the spells with fur! What are you thinking of?'

'I am thinking of my family,' answered Teo, and it felt strangely beautiful to say the words 'my family' to describe her real parents, Marta and Daniele Gasperin, who had also dedicated their lives to saving Venice from Bajamonte Tiepolo.

'Renzo,' she said calmly, *this is what my family does.*'

'And they died for it, Teo.'

'Hush, Renzo! Don't talk about dying now.'

Then Teo whispered tenderly into the cat's delicate ear, 'Can you transfer the Spell Almanac to my body, Signorina Grigiogatta?'

The cat pushed her wet muzzle against Teo's hand, 'Yesss. You are right. Thisss is the only way now. You are a Gasperin. It is yourrr destiny to protect the Spell Almanac, even though you are ssso young . . . and now you may neverrr grow old . . .' The Grey Lady's voice had collapsed to a hoarse rattle. 'None of the Gasperin *Incogniti* lived to an old age . . . but none of them . . . shirked theirrr duty. Neverrr grow old . . .'

'She's fading away,' whispered Renzo. 'It's too late anyway.'

'Never grow old?' thought Teo wildly.

The cat groaned, a low rattling noise deep in her throat.

But she raised her paw and opened her eyes to look directly at Teo. 'Lie down next to me, child, and put your arms around me. Ohhh! No, more gently than that. Now close yourrr eyes.'

Teo did as she was bid, sobbing as she felt the Grey Lady's warm blood on her cheek. She held the Grey Lady as gently as she could, her arms circling the trembling, shattered rib-cage. She felt the breath rasping out of the cat, all unevenly now.

'Concccentrate, little girl,' whispered the cat.

Teo felt her whole body tingle with pins and needles. It hurt a little but it tickled more. She wanted to squirm and scratch, but the cat cried out, 'Be ssstill, young Teodora, or . . . the spells will . . . come out all wrong . . . last thing . . . with the Almanac on your skin . . . you shall come out . . . from between-the-Linings . . . Need to hide the spells . . . Don't . . . forget . . . my cosmetic purse . . . in my office . . . good . . . bye.'

Renzo stared at Teo in horror. She knew what he was thinking – if she came out from between-the-Linings then everyone would be able to see her. Including Bajamonte Tiepolo.

The cat shuddered in her arms. The tickling sensation had gone. Now Teo felt as if her own body had become entirely liquid, and that tides were turning inside her. There was a breathy echo in her ears, and then a sensation as if cold pearls were rolling all over her skin.

At last, mercifully, she fainted.

Teo stirred. The first thing she felt was the Grey Lady lying still and cold in her arms. Teo kept her eyes shut. She could not bear to see the poor cat dead.

Eventually she forced herself, opening her eyes slowly and letting the tears spill out at the same time. They stung her cheeks, which felt extremely tender and thin-skinned. Renzo was looking down at her, his hand poised over her head as if he was about to stroke her hair. When he saw that Teo had regained consciousness, he pulled his hand away smartly.

'At last,' he said. 'You've been unconscious for hours. Listen.'

Birds were starting to sing outside.

'Is it done?' asked Teo. 'Is the Spell Almanac on me now?'

Renzo gingerly raised her arm to show her – very faint like Braille on her skin, the words that were once on the Grey Lady's body were now imprinted on Teo's.

Carefully the children lifted up the limp body of the cat and carried her to a courtyard garden inside the Archives. With their bare hands they dug a grave for her, and tenderly covered her body with earth. Renzo plucked a rose to place on the mound. They stood over it, both of them weeping unashamedly. They were joined by a pair of the small, loyal *cocai* seagulls, who bowed their heads respectfully.

'We should say some solemn words over her,' sobbed Teo. 'She deserves a better funeral than this. She deserves the whole of Venice to mourn her.'

Renzo, as she knew he would, rose to the occasion. 'We consign our dear Grey Lady to the earth. A noble soul, a queen among cats.'

Teo interrupted with a sob, 'No, the *cream* of cats!'

'Very well, the *cream* of cats, who protected Venice from Bajamonte Tiepolo, with the aid of just a handful of human friends. We commend her spirit for ever.'

The children bowed their heads. The birds chirruped mournfully and flew off.

Teo's body felt almost like her own again, but she was weak, as if she had been ill for a long time and had only just

275

come back into the living world once more.

As they re-entered the main corridor of the Archives, an old lady with a smock and a broom bustled past them, sweeping frantically. Over her shoulder, she reproached the children, 'These Archives are closed! Have you not seen the havoc in here? Anyway, you two *bambini* should not be out on your own! Don't you know that the streets are dangerous now? And you're not looking at all well, *carissima*,' she said to Teo. She disappeared down another corridor, still sweeping.

Renzo had turned pale. 'The old lady said "you two children."'

Teo was paler still. 'She could see me. The Grey Lady was right. I have come out from between-the-Linings.' She did not say, as the Grey Lady had, 'So Bajamonte Tiepolo can find me.'

Renzo urged, 'You need to put on some cosmetic paint *now*. Your face . . . I'll get the cosmetic purse from her office. You—' he pointed to the door of the LADIES' '—go in – there'll be a mirror.'

Teo gasped at the writing picked out in white on her face. The spells were inscribed back-to-front and upside-down, like the letters on a printing plate. On Teo's skin the Almanac looked like the worst and ugliest case of measles in the world.

Renzo appeared at the door of the LADIES'. 'Here it is.' He handed her the beautiful purse. Teo burst into new tears touching the soft silk that she'd last seen in the hands of the poor Grey Lady.

'Come in here, I'll need your help,' she told Renzo.

Renzo looked dubious on both fronts. He hesitated on the threshold. 'Don't you even know how to paint your face? I thought girls always knew how to do this sort of thing.'

Renzo's tone mixed irritation with embarrassment. But they both knew that it was not the cosmetics, or being inside a LADIES' lavatory, that were truly bothering him. Teo had shown herself so brave, and he was both worried for her and mortified that he had lagged behind her, merely watching as she took sole responsibility for the Spell Almanac. He mumbled, 'It should have been me.'

'You didn't have a choice, Renzo,' Teo told him. 'Remember the prophecy: the Studious Son shall have his role to play too, and no doubt it will be as dangerous as mine.'

Renzo looked a little sick.

'Though I hope not,' she added hastily.

Teo looked like a clown when they had finished with the cosmetic creams.

Renzo said, 'It'll have to do. Now we'll go back to the hotel and find some clothes to cover the rest of you up, and then we must go to the mermaids and show them what has happened. They will know how best to . . . well, make use of you.'

Warily, they walked back through streets that were almost empty. Teo kept looking behind her: it was strangely pleasant to have a shadow again. Ghosts flitted around excitedly, trailing their cold miasmas, and looting old weapons out of holes in walls, preparing themselves for the battle ahead. Every so often a ghost materialized in front of the children and saluted them, before rushing off.

Flocks of *magòghe* swooped overhead. The dawn air was rent with the commotion of their wings and their hoarse caws. Their blood was roused – their cries were urgent. They flew in and out of windows, scattering papers from people's abandoned desks and dragging books out of bookcases with their yellow beaks.

'What are they looking for?' Teo asked.

'The Spell Almanac, I suppose,' answered Renzo.

Teo flinched, 'You mean – me.'

42. The Games Pavilion

the morning of June 14th, 1899

Renzo and Teo stole past the hotel manager at his desk. It was easy to avoid his attention, for he was deep in a violent argument with Maria's father, who had his back to them.

'I warned you to keep an eye on my daughter!' shouted Signor Naccaro, sounding more like a gangster than a scientist. 'You were uncommon quick to take the tip, my man. So where's the foolish girl now? I can't recall layin' eyes on her in two days. If anythin' has happened to her, I'll hold *you* personally responsible. Got that?'

'We have to save her,' puffed Teo, up in her room. Even though the sun had barely risen, the air steamed hot as ever. All the worse for poor Teo, pulling on shirts and jackets and petticoats in untidy layers, while Renzo managed the feat of glaring at her and averting his eyes almost at the same time.

'You know finding Maria means finding Bajamonte Tiepolo,' he almost shouted at Teo. He put his hands on her shoulders and looked into her eyes fiercely. 'Are you ready for that? And *you* of all people should not go anywhere near him, now that you're wearing what is potentially *Il Traditore*'s greatest weapon.

Why should you save Maria, if it's going to cost your own life, and the lives of everyone in Venice? Is she really worth that?'

Then he looked at Teo's set, silent face and sighed wearily, 'Very well, very well, where's the book? What does it say?'

On the cover, Lussa looked fearful. When they opened *The Key to the Secret City*, the crest of Bajamonte Tiepolo swelled up in full colour on the page.

'That much we know already,' snapped Teo, discouraged and already miserably hot. 'That's no help.'

But on the white page, the crest was slowly sliding apart into its separate elements, a crown, a star, three blue balls, and a red horizontal stripe with diagonal blue and yellow ones below. The children stared at these random shapes and patterns in frustration.

Renzo eventually suggested, 'Could they be the signs to show us where to find Bajamonte Tiepolo's headquarters?'

'Well, obviously,' replied Teo grumpily. She pulled on a crimson jacket with a high neck and a loose front.

In the book the outline of a wolf now appeared under the crown. It wrinkled up its jaws and snarled so ferociously that the children both took a step back.

Teo exclaimed, 'Remember the map of apothecaries? That's the Wolf-in-a-Crown.'

She stuffed *The Key to the Secret City* into a layer between two shirts, splashed some cold water from her ewer down the back of her neck and rammed a straw hat over her curls. 'I'm ready,' she announced. 'I hope you think I am sufficiently elegant for Venice, Renzo?'

Renzo grinned. 'I take your point. Any kind of alive, at this stage, is elegant enough for Venice. I dare say I have been a little bigoted.'

'Just a little.'

At the Wolf-in-a-Crown, by Santi Filippi e Giacomo, a terrible smell was leaking out of the cracks in the cobwebbed windows. The majolica jars in this apothecary bore the titles 'Deadly Nightshade', 'Arsenic' and 'Poison Oleander'. Peering over the sill, the children saw dwarves mixing huge vats of poison and dipping old iron arrows in them. This was the fate that awaited the ghosts and the lions and mermaids in battle!

The children rushed to the Two Tousled Mermaids by the Ghetto, and helped themselves to all the Venetian Treacle they could find in a high shelf that fortunately held a dozen new jars of the precious medicine. The tank that had once held the vipers was empty. Renzo and Teo decanted the scented medicine into dozens of small glass specimen bottles with which they filled their pockets.

'What next?' Teo asked *The Key to the Secret City*, which was busy churning out coins to lay on the counter to pay for the Treacle.

On the page, Bajamonte Tiepolo's crest glowered at them.

Then the three balls from the crest began to bounce around the page. Renzo suggested, 'Maybe it's just this simple: it's about a ball game. Let's go to the Games Pavilion out at Sant'Elena. That's on the north-east edge of the city.'

Hurrying through Castello, the children passed dozens of fleeing Venetians. Others had decided to stay and defend their homes. The sound of hammering echoed through the streets as people boarded up their windows and doors.

'So futile!' breathed Teo.

The people seemed unaware that their door-knockers did not appreciate this treatment. Only Renzo and Teo could see that the miniature brass lions and Moors had suddenly become living things. The lions roared resentfully as the householders nailed crude boards against their doors. And the Moors, fierce as Signor Rioba, berated their home-owners as if each one of them was the Mayor.

'Desist, *pin-heads*!' they called out. 'Lay down Your Foolish Hammer! Our Enemy is Sending *water* and *plague* against

Venice! What use are Nails against that, Ye Unmitigated Noodles!'

Twenty minutes later, the children were gazing through the slats of the pavilion wall, sick at heart. It was horribly clear why *The Key to the Secret City* had sent them all the way to Sant'Elena. Massing inside the Pavilion were all the forces of evil that Bajamonte Tiepolo had summoned for his war against Venice.

There were Lombards and Franks in coarse tunics with hooded falcons on their wrists, the Serbs dressed in filthy red waistcoats with white sashes, the Genoans in their chainmail, the Ottomans with their turbans and scimitar swords, the Dalmatian pirates in lurid rags.

Other enemies were not of this world: bad faeries in white dresses that did not quite hide their goats' feet; Dark Elves with huge leaf-shaped ears; the *Folletti* hovering like human-headed dragonflies; dwarves still dusty from the goldmines of Tartary; malevolent sea sprites in robes of rotting seaweed; and a few ripe-smelling sea monsters left over from the earliest times, which had crawled out of the deep trailing barnacled fins and forked tails.

These soldiers – humans, animals and supernatural creatures – had one thing in common: they had all been killed in battle with Venetians. All bore terrible wounds; some were missing limbs; others were slashed across the face or neck. The human faces were distorted with rage; the semi-humans gibbered angrily. The animals were restive, prowling black metal cages and nipping each other in frustration.

The heat was rising. A sickening stench forced itself out through the slats – of sweat, of old, stale rum, putrefying fish, dried blood, dirt, and of hate.

'Look at them! All in-the-Slaughterhouse,' exclaimed

Renzo. 'They're all mutilated. And they're not exactly looking for redemption, are they?'

'No. They want to kill Venetians all over again.'

A hoarse cry echoed around the pavilion as Bajamonte Tiepolo himself strode onto a stage below the tiers of his ranked troops. He was shrouded in his dirty-white fur cloak. Only his one white hand showed outside his robes.

'He's . . . taller than I expected,' Renzo's voice wobbled. This was the first time, Teo realized, that Renzo had been in the presence of *Il Traditore*.

Even without sight of that terrible milky face, Bajamonte Tiepolo exerted a powerful effect, and not just on Renzo. His minions huddled together. Some of those in the front rows scrambled backwards, trembling. Pirates and Ottomans alike cried out in fear. Dogs bayed, pointing their shaggy muzzles up to the sky. The most blood-curdling howls came from a cage half covered with black sacking. Its denizens were heavily shackled inside.

'Werewolves,' Teo realized, peering towards the gloomy interior of that cage.

Bajamonte Tiepolo, meanwhile, stood impassively while his forces collected their wits again, and calmed to a low hubbub of growling and chattering teeth.

His face was still covered, but from under the swaddling of cloth and fur, *Il Traditore* began to intone an awful oratory. The rasp of that voice, which had whispered in her dreams night by night, brought a bitter taste flooding into Teo's mouth. Every spell on her body rose up in goosepimples. Renzo flinched visibly.

His voice was deeper, but Bajamonte Tiepolo's accent sounded the same as when he had presented himself as a young man – with an edge to it like sandpaper. It was the voice Teo had heard all those days ago in the church, ordering the deaths of the poor little gargoyles. And Teo saw the same

Gothic script in the air, though the letters were thicker and stronger now. He was becoming himself.

'Kill every Venetian who resists!' Bajamonte Tiepolo was telling his troops. 'The streets shall run with their arrogant blood! Did Venetians spit on you? Look down on you like worms? You shall have the joy of humbling them at last.'

The emerald ring flashed on *Il Traditore*'s finger and the eyes of a thousand beings swivelled to follow his jabbing gestures of revenge, murder and triumph. The *magòghe* circled overhead, cawing with fierce joy.

'Lussa must hear about this,' whispered Teo, chilled to the heart.

'Do you think she doesn't already know?' hissed Renzo. 'The mermaids have been protecting Venice for thousands of years. They know all these villains. It's just that they've never faced them all together at one time before.'

'So what are we supposed to do now?'

'*We* haven't finished the puzzle of the crest yet, from *The Key*. If we can find Bajamonte's headquarters, then we'll find Maria. That's what you want, isn't it?'

'And while he's *here*, perhaps we can do something *there* to disrupt his plans.'

Teo opened the book. The crest appeared again. The balls had disappeared: that part of the riddle was solved. The two last pieces of the puzzle were the single star and the stripe of red with the blue and yellow diagonals underneath.

The two children stared at it fiercely, as if their gaze alone could draw its secret out of it. A ripple passed through the diagonal stripes like a breeze.

Teo whispered, 'I know where I have seen that! It's the fabric of those new curtains at the Bar Tiepolo in the Hotel degli Assassini.'

'You mean we have to go back to exactly where we came from?'

'Yes, but at least now we have the Venetian Treacle to help our soldiers against the poison arrows.'

Outside the pavilion, a shadow passed over the children's heads, and then passed again. One of the *magòga* 'seagulls had seen them. The bird circled around, cocking its head, and regarding them with an expression of vicious curiosity.

'It looks like it's sneering!' said Teo.

Renzo giggled nervously, 'Well, you are a bit of a sight in all those clothes!'

An uncontrollable fury welled up inside Teo. '*What*? Even *now* you're carrying on about how I look, Mr Shop-Model? You . . . you . . . Fop! Easy for you to make jokes – *you're* not wearing a Spell Almanac.'

Renzo flushed. 'How dare you? You know I didn't have a choice . . .'

The children turned their backs on each other, fuming. Unseen, the *magòga* landed and sneaked up behind Teo. It cawed noiselessly, opening its mouth up to a red triangle. Then it edged closer, close enough to lift up the sleeve of Teo's jacket and look inside.

Too late, Teo felt the cold yellow beak on her arm. When it saw the writing there, the *magòga* shrieked in triumph, a great coarse belly-laugh, as if the inscription on Teo's arm was the filthiest, best joke it had ever heard. The laugh turned nasty and ended on a threatening note. As Teo wrenched her arm away, the yellow beak lunged at her again, neatly slitting her sleeve right up to her elbow, and shearing through all the shirts underneath to reveal her bare skin. The *magòga* nodded its head vigorously. With a final joyful sneer, it took flight and disappeared over the wall.

'It's a spy,' Renzo grimaced. 'It's gone to tell Bajamonte Tiepolo.'

'Where can we hide?' asked Teo desperately. There was

no shelter. A grove of trees swayed in the wind a few hundred yards away.

'Sant'Elena. Let's run for it. We'll get a *vaporetto* if we're lucky. The steam ferries are still running. Take off that jacket – that red colour is too easy to see. Just drop it. Good, there's a grey one underneath. Now, *run*.'

A church clock struck eleven.

Into Teo's mind came the timetable she had memorized for the *vaporetto*. Her inner eye travelled to the column that said 'Sant'Elena'. She gasped, 'There'll be a ferry in precisely four minutes.'

'How do you . . .?' Renzo almost paused. 'Never mind. Teo, you are incredible.'

Even though the heat was searing, her heart was pounding, her breath was short, and her eyes desperately scanned the lagoon for the *vaporetto*, Teo still felt the impact of those words, 'Teo, you are incredible.' But she did not have time to dwell on them. 'Later,' she promised herself. If there was a later.

Teo and Renzo were only halfway to the trees when the sky darkened. Thousands of *magòghe* swooped down, each consumed with a single desire: to stab at the children with its beak. In the swirling mass of feathers it was impossible to see each other. Teo snatched at Renzo's hand and held on to it tightly.

But the *magòghe* had other plans. Dense packs of thrashing birds hurled themselves between the two children. Their rotten fishy breath was suffocating. Teo closed her eyes; one of those beaks could blind her in a moment. She concentrated on holding onto Renzo's hand, trying to take courage from his warm grip. But more and more birds, an impossible number of *magòghe* – how could there be so many in Venice? – forced themselves between her and Renzo. She felt his hand slipping from her grasp.

'Renzo!' she screamed. 'Don't let go!'

But it was too late. Renzo's fingers were wrenched away. She heard his screams from further and further off. The *magòghe* must have been pecking him, as they were pecking her, making cuts an inch long in her skin. In a few seconds she could hear nothing at all from Renzo.

'They have killed him,' she thought. 'They have torn him apart.' And for a moment she did not care at all what happened to her.

'Just let it be quick,' she begged silently. An even grimmer idea crossed her mind: if the gulls *did* rip her to shreds then the spells on her body would be unreadable. And Bajamonte Tiepolo would not be able to make use of them.

But Teo's survival instinct was stronger than those noble thoughts. She kept beating at the gulls, protecting her face, and shouting at them, in the hope of proving that she wasn't worth the trouble of killing. Finally, she dropped to the ground and bent over in a ball, tucking her head between her knees, with her hands protecting the back of her neck, which felt dreadfully vulnerable. Her bottles of Venetian Treacle felt hard and comforting against her hipbone. She lay folded up like that for what seemed like ages, in a never-ending nightmare of crashing wings and snapping, shrieking beaks.

She almost did not notice when the *magòghe* started to diminish their attacks. They had stopped actually pecking her and were now merely nudging her from time to time to make sure that she stayed on the ground. The first thing that she felt, when her body unfroze from its panic, was the burning agony of all those little cuts.

And Renzo? Where was he? What had they done with him? Teo raised her head, fearful of what she would see. It was not what she expected. The *magòghe* had gone, though they had left enough grey, black and white feathers to stuff the mattresses of an entire orphanage.

'*Il Traditore*, Orphan-Maker,' she muttered disjointedly.

There was no sign of Renzo. Teo worried; Renzo was slight. The *magòghe* might have pushed him into the lagoon. Bleeding like that, he'd soon attract some sharks. Maybe he wasn't even conscious? Then he wouldn't be able to try to swim away.

Teo was fretting so hard about Renzo that she didn't hear footsteps approaching from behind. She was unaware of the tall shadow falling over her, though she felt the temperature plummet, even in the shimmering warmth of the day. Her experience of ghosts should have warned her. But Teo, bleeding and dazed, was not thinking clearly at all.

It was only when she heard his voice that she realized that she was now in the presence of the very last person in the world that she wished to see.

He had thrown off his hood. He was not the handsome young boy that Teo had seen smiling and laughing in the *campo* with Maria, or the albino bat of the Church of Santi Giovanni e Paolo, nor even the human-faced bat-skeleton who had plucked Maria out of the *vaporetto*. His strength was growing, and he had changed again.

In this incarnation, Bajamonte Tiepolo was a tall, gaunt man with a vile face that swam like a half-set custard within a loose, filmy skin. His red-rimmed eyes were still blankly and milkily white, just like those of his minions, the Vampire Eels. Only the faintest green showed where the pupil should be, but a single slit of black slashed down the centre of each white eyeball. His nose was vast, overhanging his lips that wobbled like uncooked shrimps. His coarse white cloak parted to reveal old skin tacked together with red string. The leathery covering hung off his bones in rags. It was a poor fit.

'That,' thought Teo, 'is the skin of Marcantonio Bragadin.'

Instead of the dandyish cane, Bajamonte Tiepolo had a sword clanking from his belt. He drew the sword from a silver scabbard etched with intertwined Vampire Eels.

'Teodora Gasperin,' he said, 'The Undrowned Child.'

43. Six hundred years' hate

the heart of the day, June 14th, 1899

Bajamonte Tiepolo looked down at Teo with hatred. It was a hatred that had been festering for nearly six hundred years.

They both knew that one of her own ancestors, a fourteenth-century Gasperin, must have been the first to frustrate *Il Traditore*'s plans to get back his Spell Almanac. And Teo was the first Gasperin who had been careless enough and foolish enough to fall right into his hands. Worse, she had done so with the actual book clearly tattooed all over her shivering skin.

'So . . .' He lifted her hair with the blade of his sword, peering at the words on her face. 'Ah yes!' He was triumphant now. 'The Insatiable Salt-water Curse! And behold – the receipt for Unquestioning Obedience. That served me well, once upon a time. What's this? The gulls have damaged some lines with their beaks. Clumsy brutes! They shall pay for that with their blood.'

'He can read upside-down and back-to-front,' thought Teo, 'and he can do it better than me.'

He barked at her, 'Now disrobe your feet!'

Teo scrambled to do so.

Il Traditore knelt down to examine her bare toes, separating them with the cold blade of his sword. 'The Moving of Souls from One Body to Another!' he murmured. 'Yes, most useful, that spell. Ah, and Sudden Desire for Drinking Poison. Some of my most unfortunate new subjects shall soon be tasting of *that*.'

Caught up in his reminiscing and planning, Bajamonte Tiepolo seemed to have forgotten that the spells he was reading were written on the body of a living person. Teo hoped against hope that it would stay that way. She did not wish to attract his attention to her own existence. She lay motionless and silent, trying not to flinch from *Il Traditore*'s breath, which stank of stale wine, stagnant seawater and the metallic tang of pure hate.

But Bajamonte Tiepolo had not forgotten Teo at all. It turned out that he was at that very minute thinking about her in dreadful detail. Suddenly he fixed his eyes on her face and Teo's heart felt as if it had been stabbed, so strong was the shudder of fear that went through her.

'The only reason that you are still alive, Teodora Gasperin,' he told her savagely, 'is that it shall be easier for me to read the spells while your miserable, doomed skin is yet moist and plump. I shall need to strip my spells from your skin before I kill you. And there is this joy to consider: that I shall enjoy the killing of you better when I have more interesting ways to do that, thanks to my Spell Almanac.'

He picked Teo up in his bony arms and wrapped his cloak around her. Inside its cold, dusty folds, through the coarse stitching of Marcantonio Bragadin's skin, she saw a greenish heart glowing amid the ribs of his skeleton. *Il Traditore*'s putrid smell was intensified inside the fur-like cloak. Nausea flooded through her, mixing with fear.

Meanwhile, her captor was walking at a brisk pace. Teo

realized that he was carrying her back to the Games Pavilion, where a hundred thousand enemies of Venice were waiting.

Unlike Teo, Renzo had not thought to cover his eyes. He'd been far too busy punching the *magòghe* and tearing at their feathers. A good dozen of them had lost their best tail feathers to this inconvenient boy, who didn't seem to know when he was outnumbered or beaten.

Like all bullies, the gulls were unaccustomed to their victims fighting back. One exceptionally large *magòga* had decided to teach this undersized human a lesson. In a smooth motion it flew past Renzo at eye height, with its claws extended. The gull miscalculated, for it meant to take Renzo's eyes out. It scratched all the way across his eyebrows in a neat line. It was not a deep cut, but it was long, and a curtain of blood cascaded into Renzo's eyes, blinding him. He rolled headlong into a ditch.

The seagulls crowded around the edge of the ditch, peering over. *Magòghe* will eat anything that they can get their beaks on. Pigeons, puppies, fish, squid, bread, rats, peaches, anything. A single notion was now crossing their collective bird brains.

And why not *boy*?

Renzo tried once more to open his eyes. But the blood had clotted with the dirt and matted his eyelashes together. With his sore, bitten fingers, he tried to prise his eyelids gently apart. It didn't work. He felt as if he might tear his own skin if he pulled any harder.

Teo! He could not keep the thought of her out of his mind any longer. Why had he not protected her? He should have thrown his body over hers and let the *magòghe* peck at him. Instead he had selfishly fought for his own life. That was hardly the behaviour of a true Venetian gentleman. Renzo was ashamed of himself to the core of his soul.

Hot tears welled up behind his sealed eyes and burst out, melting away the blood and mud.

Bajamonte Tiepolo had not offered Teo up to the assembled pirates, Lombards, Ottomans, dwarves, werewolves and others who filled the Games Pavilion to its brim. As *Il Traditore* passed through the gates, she had heard the rumble of his troops' voices, and smelt their ancient clothes and that ripe, angry odour that comes from people who are preparing themselves for a bloody battle.

'Are they waiting for a human sacrifice,' Teo wondered, 'to send them off to war in hearty spirits?'

And where was the Butcher Biasio, speaking of human sacrifice?

At the sight of their leader, a great roar had gone up, making *Il Traditore*'s green-black heart blaze with red sparks inside his hollow ribs.

But he did not reveal his trophy. He had raised his one hand to his troops. Then Teo had felt her captor walking through a doorway. She peered out through a gap in his cloak at a room of abandoned desks and typewriting machines.

Il Traditore, without warning, wrenched open his cloak and dropped her on a wooden table in the middle of what appeared to be the ticket office of the pavilion. It was a relief to breathe clean air, but Teo feared her back would break with the pain of falling on the hard surface of the table. The bottles of Venetian Treacle tinkled but did not shatter. She dared not cry out, even when she saw the tank of Vampire Eels by the window. Bajamonte Tiepolo was stalking around the room, looking perplexed at the sight of all the typewriters and stenographers' pencils. He slammed his fist down on the table, shouting, 'This ordure will not serve me!'

Teo's belly clenched up with fear again, shifting the warm weight of *The Key to the Secret City* hidden between her bodice and pinafore. Fortunately Bajamonte Tiepolo had not yet noticed the book.

Il Traditore peered at the machines, and experimentally thrust his skeletal fist through one. He shouted at the jangling ruins of the typewriter. 'Only the forces of ignorance and the rabble could have conjured up an ugliness liken unto this!'

His language, she noticed, was a strange mixture of modern and ancient. He had not quite assumed his old persona, neither was he wholly of the modern world. His form had come to rest as a human being – of sorts – but without the Spell Almanac, she guessed, he could not fix himself in any one time or place.

Bajamonte Tiepolo was still glaring at the typewriters in angry perplexity.

'Girl!' snarled *Il Traditore*. 'Explain to me what these beastly devices look upon, and what they think upon.'

'They . . . don't think,' stammered Teo, surprised at her own ability to speak. 'They make information quick and neat, and people use them instead of writing by hand in books.'

'They no more scribe books? Or consult them?' There was a note of disgust and wonder mixed in *Il Traditore*'s voice. 'Or their own memories? Or their comrades? Or the oratory of their superiors? These guttersnipes speak with the writing machines?'

'I am afraid that it is getting that way.'

'What vulgar education! In my new Venice, the writing machines shall all be smashed. Forthwith.'

Teo did not doubt it. As for the books, she guessed, most of them would be drowned when he flooded the city. The thought of books in danger brought her mind back to her own situation. What was she, if not a book that would be destroyed once Bajamonte Tiepolo had extracted what he wanted from her?

Sadly for Teo, *Il Traditore's* thoughts were turning in an identical direction.

'I must have ink!' he shouted. 'And parchment! You, buffle-headed girl, fetch them me upon the instant!'

Teo clambered down from the table and went to what looked like a stationery cupboard. She felt Bajamonte Tiepolo's eyes burning into her back. Paper there was in plenty, though her captor found it flimsy.

'Poor stuff,' he snarled. 'In my day the parchment was thick and strong. One could lift a stone upon its surface.'

'There's nothing else,' Teo dared, only because it was true.

'Ink! Bluest ink! A pig's bladder of ink now!'

'People don't use pig's bladders any more,' said Teo. 'Ink comes in bottles.'

Teo held one up, but *Il Traditore* knocked it from her hands. It shattered on the ground. Not a drop of ink spilled out.

'Where is the ink? You dare to defy me?'

Unfortunately Teo had picked an empty bottle. She felt the blade of his sword at the back of her neck as she turned to pick up a second bottle.

'I promise you there's ink in this one,' she pleaded, shaking it to make sure. She emptied a wooden tray of pins and poured the ink into it.

Teo was suddenly aware of the craziness of the situation. Here she was, helping Bajamonte Tiepolo to find what he needed to extract the spells from her body and so destroy not just herself but all Venice. But what choice did she have?

The Vampire Eels had caught sight and scent of Teo. They began to splash in their tank. Rows of white snouts now lined up against the glass, following her every motion.

'This ink shall serve, carrion,' said Bajamante Tiepolo, 'lay yourself down upon the table now.'

Bajamonte Tiepolo tore the paper into thick strips. He dipped one strip into the ink and, without warning, pressed it down on the sole of Teo's bare foot. The cold of his fingers sent goosepimples up her leg. Then he ripped it away and pressed it down on another piece of paper. Three lines of writing appeared on the page, the right way up and the right way around. Bajamonte Tiepolo snorted with satisfaction and reached for another strip of paper.

'He's *printing* me,' realized Teo. 'He's printing the spells from my body.'

Slow footsteps slithered into the room. Teo became aware of another pair of eyes fixed on her. Behind *Il Traditore*, she glimpsed a bloodied apron and a stump of a wrist. And again, that awful grunting, bubbling noise that she had first heard in the Church of Santi Giovanni e Paolo. The ankles of the turned-around feet twitched and one struck the wall so the creature who owned it stumbled, causing a flurry among the Vampire Eels.

Bajamonte Tiepolo laughed. 'Ah yes, the Butcher becomes impatient! I have promised him your worthless corpse, when I have done with it and after my Eels have drunk their fill of you. He has already acquired a taste for it, it seems.'

Teo, flattened on the table, was at exactly the same height as the sweating, severed head the Butcher Biasio carried under his arm. For one long, chilling moment their eyes met. Then, bloodshot and bulging, the Butcher's lit up with unmistakable greed.

How long would it take for Bajamonte Tiepolo to print out the contents of her body, and what would happen when he discovered *The Key to the Secret City*?

Because that was exactly how long Teo had to live.

44. Human plans

in the heat of the afternoon, June 14th, 1899

'**I** have nothing to lose,' thought Teo.

She lay staring at the white ceiling while Bajamonte Tiepolo took the impression of the spells on her left ankle. Each touch of his icy hand made her shiver, even in the sweltering air of the close room. She could hear the Butcher Biasio's laboured breathing behind him and the impatient tapping of that hideous backwards foot.

The spells, as far as Teo could see, were written in a flowery old-fashioned Latin mixed with some ancient Venetian dialect. Some were in Greek; others in Arabic. Of course, she now remembered, they had been collected from all over the Mediterranean.

So far *Il Traditore* had extracted a Tickling Malediction, a Pain as if Toenails are Being Extracted Spell and a long curse involving leprosy and fingers dropping off that started '*ulcus acre . . . foedi oculi*'. Teo recognized the Latin words for 'a nasty sore . . . festering eyeballs'. There was a diarrhoea spell, something rather disgusting about *avèr la mòssa*. There was a spell for Making Wood Alive. A very short spell for Sudden Death at a Distance read simply, '*Eminus repente nunc morere!*'

295

Il Traditore was in a fury of impatience, his hands trembling, his eyes straining. He whispered to himself, 'Calm, calm! There's no help for it. I must print the child methodically, from the feet up, or I risk missing the one spell I truly need.'

That spell, Teo knew, was one that would allow his soul to migrate back into a permanent form, in which it could make use of its full murderous memory again.

That spell could be on Teo's other foot, on her ankle or at the top of her head. It could take him all day, dipping the paper in ink and pressing it on to Teo's flinching skin. He had already slashed off the hem of her skirt and pinafore with his sword so that he could print from her feet without anything flapping in his way.

'If this goes on, he'll remove all my clothes!' Teo shuddered at the image of being naked and vulnerable on that table in front of Bajamonte Tiepolo. And the Butcher's head, a step away from her, was already looking at Teo as if she were a nice cut of meat on a slab. In the silence of the room, the sound of the Butcher swallowing was horribly loud.

Desperation stirred a new notion in Teo's mind. 'Surely *anyone* who read these spells,' she speculated, 'could make use of them?'

Bajamonte Tiepolo was busy with her right foot now. Teo tilted her head to the side of the table where he had laid out his printed spells. She could read the Tickling Malediction tolerably well, but he had placed upside-down (from Teo's viewpoint) the spell for a Pain as if Toenails are Being Extracted.

'You can do this,' Teo urged herself silently. 'You have your library trick of reading upside-down.'

A smaller, scared Teo replied, 'Yes, works well in the library. Will it work on a table with a murderer inches away?'

And what of the spell itself? Things were different today. It was 1899, not 1310. Nearly six hundred years had tumbled over and over, smoothing the rules, breaking them. Baddened magic had come to Venice. There were new rules.

Anyway, Lussa had said that it was not as simple as just reading out the words of the spell, Teo recalled. You had to send your soul out with it. She thought desperately, 'I don't know how to do that. *Do I?*'

Bajamonte Tiepolo had his back to her. She inched her hand out towards the Toenail spell and pulled it two inches closer to herself. *Il Traditore* did not pause in his work. She craned her neck over as far as she dared. Now she could read the spell, even though it was upside-down. Fortunately it was a short one.

She felt the desperate beginning of hope, which was in fact more upsetting than blanket despair. Then she thought of Renzo, and of Venice. Almost delirious, she thought she heard the sound of angry miaowing in the distance.

News of the Grey Lady's demise had spread through the town on the wings of the two loyal *cocal* seagulls who had mourned at her grave. The Syrian cats of Venice, after centuries tucked away in the Giardini and Sant'Elena, were not immune to the delicious possibility of avenging their dead sister the Grey Lady. And a fine feed of *magòghe* was a not unappetizing prospect.

So it was that Renzo, lying in his ditch, was the first Venetian in centuries to see that the Syrian cats of Venice were no myth, but absolutely palpable. Moreover, in their long period of seclusion, they had developed useful wings.

Flying cats! Like the winged lions of Venice, only smaller, and in all colours and shades of tabby. Even silvery, like the Grey Lady. And like the Grey Lady, these cats were many times the size of a normal house cat, and carried themselves with enormous dignity, even when swooping down on their furry wings.

At first sight of the cats, the seagulls took off in an undignified and disorganized rabble. They crashed into each other and tangled their wings in an effort to escape the grim-faced felines now just seconds away from them.

A shower of nervous droppings rained down on Renzo in the ditch.

'Yeuuch!' he shouted, as his clothes turned green with slime. Whereupon he realized that it was better to keep his mouth closed.

Suddenly the grass around Renzo's ditch was a mass of writhing fur and feather, a din of desperate caws and angry yowls. The cats rolled over and over, crushing as many gulls with their great bodies as they killed with jaws and claws.

Finally, all was quiet. A hundred birds lay dead, foam bubbling out of their beaks. The cats were sitting up on their haunches, grooming themselves vigorously. They bestowed the odd quizzical look on Renzo. They were acting for all the world as if they had just happened upon a crowd of annoying seagulls and that it was the merest coincidence, nothing to do with them really, that they had saved his life.

'Thank you!' exclaimed Renzo. Then he understood that this hardly sounded impressive, coming from a filthy boy lying in a ditch. He climbed up, clinking his bottles of Venetian Treacle. He bowed low. 'Oh incomparable Felines, you have delivered my almost entirely worthless self from our mutual enemies, and I am eternally grateful.'

The cats stopped grooming and stood with their tails straight up in the air, just slightly kinked over at the tip, an unambiguous sign of satisfaction in the cat world, winged or otherwise.

'I hesitate to ask you another favour,' grovelled Renzo. 'But . . .'

The cats sat back down on their haunches and swished their tails in unison.

Renzo started again. 'Your Feline Majesties, Venice has need of your noble help. Being omniscient, you will already know all about the terrible plot of Bajamonte Tiepolo . . .' Here he was interrupted by loud hissing. 'Well, we must make an urgent plan to stop him and get his Spell Almanac back.'

The cats gazed at Renzo with expressions deeply tinged with cynicism, for cats know that all human plans are exceedingly likely to go wrong.

45. The toenail spell

the afternoon draws on, June 14th, 1899

The words of the toenail spell were complicated, in both Latin and Venetian. Teo knew less than half of them.

'*Pedes* . . .' she read. 'Now that's "foot" in Latin . . . and *ferii* . . . that's "hurt" in Venetian, isn't it?'

Her imagination filled in the grammatical gaps. So she would need to read aloud, from upside-down, a spell that she did not completely understand. If she got it wrong, it might be her own toes that felt the searing pain of having their nails rent off. Or she might simply alert Bajamonte Tiepolo to her idea, and get herself killed even more quickly.

'He wants my body moist and fresh,' she tried to reassure herself. 'But it would stay that way for a while after I was dead, surely? Even in this heat? If the Butcher . . . and the eels . . .'

Outside in the pavilion, she could hear stamping feet. The creatures out there had been promised Venetian blood, and they were in a hurry for a taste of it.

A bead of sweat dropped from *Il Traditore's* bony forehead onto Teo's foot. He muttered, 'Rascals! Cutpurse bungs! Be patient, animals!'

'He's under pressure,' she realized. 'They've no idea that

he's not yet recovered his full powers. He must have lied to them, to get them here; otherwise they would not dare attack Venice like this.'

In the absence of Bajamonte Tiepolo, the crowd outside had evidently found a leader of its own. The harsh accent of a Serb commander echoed through the pavilion. 'Bajamonte Tiepolo, show yourself to us. We have waited long enough. We shall not be denied our chance to raze Venice to the ground, just because you falter in courage and resolve.'

'Human latrine!' hissed Bajamonte Tiepolo. '*You* shall not come home from the battleground, scullion. And it shall not be the pretty fishwives that do unto you.'

Pretty fishwives! Of course, the *scolopendre* had told him about the mermaids.

The wobbling forehead of *Il Traditore* was slick with sweat. His hands shook as he pressed the strips of paper on Teo's ankles. Cowardice, the old rumour, was coming back to haunt Bajamonte Tiepolo. In his first attack on Venice, he had cut and run. His new troops would not let him forget it now.

Teo thought, 'The skin of the hero Marcantonio Bragadin is a poor fit in more ways than one.'

The creatures outside roared in support of the Serb commander, 'Bajamonte Tiepolo, show yourself!'

Teo took her chance. Under the cover of the din, she read the toenail spell aloud as quickly and as clearly as she could, given the violent trembling of her whole body and the feeling of faintness that swept through her. As she spoke the words, she deliberately pictured Venice drowned in black water, Renzo lifeless under the yellow beaks of the *magòghe*, her real parents dragged to the bottom of the sea, all by the evil of Bajamonte Tiepolo. She saw Chissa lying dead in the cavern, the Grey Lady's bloodied muzzle disappearing under the soil when she and Renzo had buried her. A feeling surged up inside Teo like a scream. She could feel it tingling on the end of her tongue and her fingertips.

'*Pedes . . .*' she murmured desperately. '*Ferii . . .*' The words forced their way out of her mouth like drops of blood.

'Is this casting my soul?' she wondered. It felt like emptying her heart. She felt, as she spoke the words, bleached and scoured of every emotion.

'But do I have enough soul to make this work?'

The effect was instantaneous. Bajamonte Tiepolo dropped the piece of paper in his hand and crouched down on the floor, screaming in a high, tortured voice, 'My foot, my foot! Desist! Do not do it, aaagh!'

Teo pulled her legs up and stood on the table, poised to jump. The Butcher too had collapsed onto the floor, where he writhed in agony, emitting high-pitched grunts. The Vampire Eels crowded to the nearest corner of their tank.

But Bajamonte Tiepolo was rising back to his feet. He shrieked, 'May your lips rot off, you cur of a female!'

His sword flashed out of its scabbard. *Il Traditore* plunged it straight into Teo's heart . . .

. . . where it met resistance. Such strong resistance that it arched up and snapped in half, throwing its owner against a filing cabinet. He slumped back to the ground.

For *The Key to the Secret City* was still there, secreted between Teo's layers of shirts. Somehow the book had taken the whole force of *Il Traditore*'s murderous blow. Teo had the sensation that someone had punched her quite lightly in the chest. The little bottles of Venetian Treacle in her pockets had not even shattered.

Hardly able to believe her luck, she hurtled off the table and out of the room. At the end of the corridor were two doors. One, ajar, led out to the pavilion. The Serb commander was still braying his demands, and the roaring from the seats had reached a deafening pitch.

The other door opened on a dark, dank stairwell; not an inviting prospect, but better than the other two possibilities available. Teo ran though, slammed it behind her and started climbing down the steps. She had reached the tenth one when, back at the top, the door opened. Light rushed through the aperture and she could see the silhouette of Bajamonte Tiepolo glaring into the gloom. She flattened herself against the wall, just out of the light.

Il Traditore stood there for a long time.

He too, she calculated, was unwilling to go through the other door, the one that led out to the pavilion.

But the Serb commander's tone had now risen to the imperative. Even from his outline, Teo could see that at that moment something in Bajamonte Tiepolo stirred, a call of his ancient noble blood, that would not tolerate orders from a mere soldier, that would not accept the leadership of anyone else but himself. He was, after all, a Venetian, a lord among men. He shook with anger, raised his fist, and stormed back into the corridor, and out of the door into the pavilion.

Teo crept back up the stairs and peered out across the corridor. Through the open door to the pavilion, the outline of Bajamonte Tiepolo's back was black against the sea of angry faces.

Il Traditore scanned the crowd until his gaze rested on the dark, bearded face of the insubordinate Serb. Then he raised his hand and the emerald ring sent a jet of green light into the man's eyes. Teo heard Bajamonte Tiepolo hiss the spell he had just printed from her body, the one for Sudden Death at a Distance.

As *Il Traditore* spat the final words, '*Nunc morere!*' the Serb commander crumpled to the ground, screaming in agony. His body twitched for a moment, and then fell still. His head lolled to one side.

'Now, those gentlemen whom I am currently permitting to live,' Bajamonte Tiepolo whispered, 'your attention please.'

The very quietness of his voice had an electrifying effect on his audience. All tongues fell silent. All heads turned to him. Down the hallway, Teo strained to hear him.

'Gentlemen,' he lied, 'as you have just seen, I have performed the needful thing to restore every single one of my old powers. Spring is rioting through my veins. I feel a lovely little war coming on!'

Except for the Serbs, who stood sullenly around their commander's corpse, *Il Traditore*'s forces bellowed with joy.

Their leader spoke over them: 'Take your positions and prepare for the destruction of Venice. First, do you all have your *masks*?'

The crowd roared its assent.

Teo turned to look back down the murky stairwell. But what if it was a trap? Just a dead end, a room down there?

Slow footsteps slithered along the corridor behind her. The Butcher!

Teo did not wait to hear any more.

Down, down, down went Teo. Venice floated on water, so there were no basements. She expected to hit rock bottom at any moment. But the stairs descended so low that she was certain that the stone walls were just a thin crust against a lagoon full of water that could at any minute gush in and sweep her away. There was a hollow sound to her footsteps, as though she was in a tank. The cool darkness was welcome, but the shambling, awkward footsteps of the Butcher, just a few hundred yards behind, echoed in the dark, empty tunnel. Her thoughts were just as hollow.

Eventually the stairs bottomed out and she felt her way along a damp, stifling corridor. The rats down here could not have heard the prophecy that had sent their cousins streaming out of Venice. Every few minutes, rough *pantegana* fur brushed past Teo's skirts, accompanied by hysterical twittering.

At last she stubbed her toe on a step. With a new burst of energy, Teo started climbing rapidly upwards. Where did this tunnel lead? Would she emerge right in the path of Bajamonte Tiepolo's forces? Perhaps he had simply set an arduous trap for her, something that would keep her occupied – and exhausted – until after he had subdued his rebellious army. Teo tried to put that idea out of her head but it forced itself back in.

She bumped her head on the low ceiling. Another unhelpful thought crossed her mind – this tunnel was more likely to have been built for dwarves than human beings. And lately the dwarves were the friends of Bajamonte Tiepolo.

She trudged on and on, the Butcher's steps echoing hers. Teo fought to breathe. She simply couldn't walk any faster in the dark.

Another tight swarm of rats dashed past her, heading back into the darkness. She heard the Butcher stumble and fall. There came a slithering sound and a thump, as if he had tried to raise himself and failed. Something rolled audibly down the stairs. With a shudder, Teo realized that it must be the Butcher's head. More of the *pantegane* rushed between her feet, hurtling to the place, perhaps a hundred steps back, where the Butcher now moaned in terror. The rats squealed with delight and hunger.

A fine-rimmed outline of light appeared above her, in the shape of a door. The mere idea of breathing fresh air again was enough to make Teo reach for the handle, whatever was waiting for her outside.

Renzo was not getting anywhere with the cats.

He had tried flattery, courtly manners, low bows. He reinforced his words with the appropriate mimes, acting out the whole situation like a one-man theatre company. He mimed the evil creatures, the pavilion, poor Teo – at best – trapped inside with *Il Traditore*. At worst – that did not bear thinking of.

But either the cats did not wish to understand him, or they understood him all too well, and had taken a silent decision among themselves that thirty winged cats, however efficacious at massacring a flock of *magòghe*, were unlikely to score a notable victory against a hundred thousand bloodthirsty pirates, Ottomans and Serbs, all led by an evil being who was a known murderer of felines.

Finally Renzo shrugged. 'Well, I'll just go on my own then, shall I?'

He secretly hoped that this would appeal to the cats' natural contrariness, and that they would contradict him merely for the pleasure of doing so. But it was just then that events had taken a new turn inside the pavilion: when Bajamonte Tiepolo returned to his forces and pretended that he had regained all his powers by killing the Serb commander. Bajamonte Tiepolo's voice could then be heard grating distantly and at length. Renzo guessed that *Il Traditore* was outlining his battle plan. There was a brief silence, like an intake of breath. The sea gates of the pavilion swung open, and the forces of Bajamonte Tiepolo streamed out. All eyes were fixed on the flag of their standard-bearer. No one saw one young boy and thirty cats standing transfixed on the Sant'Elena side of the peninsula.

The soldiers thundered into their boats, or took to the air, their weapons clattering, and their rough matted hair streaming behind them. In two minutes they were gone, and there was silence. For just a second, you could imagine that it was a normal summer day in Venice, a quiet, sleepy day, the kind of day on which nothing much happens except a slight case of sunburn.

At that moment, high up above Renzo and the cats, in the thick trunk of a tree, a door opened, and Teo's anxious face appeared.

'Renzo!' she shrieked, and burst into tears. Renzo peered up into the branches. Yes, it was really Teo, alive, though with a shortened skirt and strangely blue feet. And – as far as he could tell, for her cheeks were mottled with crying – her skin was still covered in the inscriptions of the Spell Almanac.

'You see!' said the large golden tabby, in a tone that could not be described as anything but cat-got-the-cream smug.

'You mean you *can talk*?' Renzo tried not to scream.

'Oh my, His Numps is rather tetchy, is he not? Of course we can talk. When there is someone worth talking to and something worth saying. We assumed that your friend, if she was worth her salt, would find our passageway to the *pantegana* hunting grounds. As for you, young man, we wanted to keep you here long enough not to get hurt by some foolish act of pointless bravery.'

Teo was struggling out of the tree. There was nowhere to put her feet, and she was reduced to sliding and slithering, all the while trying to wipe her eyes and her nose, and not blubber like a baby. It was all the more difficult under the cool eyes of the cats, which expressed a clear and open criticism of her lack of grace.

Teo hesitated over the last drop. From now on down, the trunk was completely solid, with no knot-holes for her feet or branches to catch hold of.

'Jump, Teo!' urged Renzo, holding out his arms. The two of them tumbled down together in the grass and lay holding one another in silence.

'Are you all right?' Renzo was the first to ask.

Teo buried her head against his shoulder. He was not much bigger than her, and he was covered with bird droppings, and he was shaking like a leaf in the wind. But Renzo's arms felt like a place of perfect safety just then. She sobbed, 'I stopped him, Renzo, he didn't get all the spells. Just a couple of them . . .'

Teo felt his eyes warm and sympathetic on her. He wiped the wetness off her face with a careful finger that still trembled a little. 'I know, I can see the spells are still on your cheeks.'

'And look at *you*! You've got a great stripe of blood right across your forehead.'

'It's nothing. It doesn't hurt at all. *Un bel niente.*'

Teo pulled a bottle out of Renzo's pocket. She dabbed his forehead with a fingerful of the sticky Venetian Treacle. The wound disappeared.

'I thought the *magòghe* had killed you,' she whispered.

'I thought the same thing about you. I was in luck, the cats saved me. But how did *you* . . .?'

'*Those* cats? They don't look too friendly.'

'They can be helpful when they want to be. I think they did it for the Grey Lady.'

'Oh yes, they look like her, don't they? Oh my, they're *Syrian* cats, aren't they? They're gorgeous! Goodness, they've got *wings*!'

Renzo's arms were still around her. Teo stammered, 'I'm sorry . . . for what I said back there, outside the Games Pavilion. I didn't mean it. You're the bravest person I know. You're not . . .'

Renzo did not let go of her. 'You were upset. We were

both terrified out of our wits. Anyway, I've forgotten it already. You know, we should get up.'

'Yes, we should. You first.'

'No, you.'

'Come, the cats are watching.'

At that moment Teo and Renzo heard a sound that made them tremble.

Seven long groans from the High Water siren.

They scrambled to their feet. This was the signal from the mermaids that the battle was about to begin. It was too late to find Lussa and show her the spells tattooed on Teo's body. It was all very well that Teo had stopped Bajamonte Tiepolo from getting his hands on most of them, but unless the mermaids could make use of those that remained to give an advantage to the forces of good – then those spells were less than useless now.

46. Battle in the lagoon

late afternoon, dusk and night, June 14th, 1899

From the headland at Sant'Elena, Teo and Renzo watched helplessly as an extraordinary procession wove out of the *bacino* of San Marco. It looked so delicate, so exquisite, compared with the tribe of horrors that had burst out of the pavilion and was now making its way across the lagoon like a dark stain in the water.

The Key to the Secret City had squirmed like a cat about to give birth, finally delivering a pair of ornate opera glasses for Renzo and Teo.

'Look!' breathed Teo, pointing. The boats of *Il Traditore*'s grim fleet had sinister black cages swinging from their masts: all made in the crude outlines of men, mermaids and cats.

'For prisoners,' whispered Renzo in fury. 'And out of cowardice! Because if our troops are in those cages, our people cannot fire at the enemy boats.'

'I know it's war, but it's so beautiful,' breathed Teo, turning in the other direction to watch the mermaids' silk standard, embroidered in vivid colours, waving above each group of fighters. The standard showed a mortar-and-pestle, the symbol of the ordinary Venetian baker's wife who'd dared to destroy the hopes of Bajamonte Tiepolo.

The mermaids were leading the way. Some held flags out of the water to guide the forces. More of them were swimming underneath the gondolas and fishing boats, helping to speed them along. A grey cloud of pigeons followed in their wake, puffing out their breast-feathers with pride. Parrots, spotless white doves and Wild-but-Good Faeries swooped in and out among the sails, lighting on masts and rigging. Herons stalked through the shallows like important lawyers, with speckled pink squid pumping along in their slipstream and flying fish diving in and out of the water ahead. The fins of the bigger fish moved in disciplined formations. Swordfish and spotted rays glided just under the surface.

The noble ghosts, in their gorgeous velvet and silk costumes from each of six centuries, sat upright in the gondolas, with their hands on their antique jewelled weapons. The gondoliers' children rowed swiftly – the noble ghosts had no weight, even though they made a great deal of hot air, arguing with one another. Stacked in the boats were the children's only weapons – croquet mallets and lawn tennis racquets.

The gondolier children were whistling traditional Venetian boating songs. From the waves beneath them the mermaids added an encouraging harmony, though sometimes the words were not quite as refined as those of the original songs.

And just as Lussa had said, above everyone floated the Cherubim, the sweet, winged faces of children who had died of Bajamonte Tiepolo's Black Death. Like butterflies, they soared on the wind, keeping safely between the pigeons and the lions.

'And that looks like a . . .?' said Teo wonderingly.

The Rioba brothers' camel appeared, swimming lithely

through the water with all three of his masters seated grandly on his hump. And at the back, behind the Riobas, was a slight figure that Teo recognized. He wore velvet breeches and a tweedy waistcoat. Professor Marìn, the old bookseller, waved his paperknife and smiled.

Teo's mind worked furiously. The bookseller was a thoroughly good man, a member of the *Incogniti*, a friend of her parents: he could not be a ghost requiring redemption. Therefore he must be alive! He had not been murdered . . . he had somehow escaped *Il Traditore*. He must have gone, Teo realized, between-the-Linings, as she had done, for his own protection. That was why Lussa had been so mysterious about him!

'It will be wonderful to talk with him later,' Teo thought, 'about my parents! And about how he cheated Bajamonte Tiepolo out of another death . . . if he survives the battle. If Venice does.'

Through her opera-glasses Teo glimpsed the handsome Signor Alicamoussa on the shore, fearlessly fastening breast-plates and helmets to the winged lions.

All the boats, even the gondolas, had rigged up white sails with a single blue eye painted on them. Renzo explained, 'A sailors' superstition – that a ship must not be blind – it must be able to see the enemy.'

As they watched, the sky grew dark, and the battlefield was lit up with a curious white light. Now they saw legions of humble ghosts in-the-Cold, some of whom they recognized, walking through the water, each bearing a single, wavering candle, lighting up their tearstained faces. Street-cleaners, fishermen, water-carriers, lace-makers, bead-stringers, beggars – all their faces were illuminated with the same sad dignity.

'Pedro-the-Crimp!' exclaimed Teo, catching sight of the snaggle-toothed ghost. Pedro and his companions marched grimly through the water in their ragged clothes. Some, like Pedro, were leading horses, others dogs. Their only hope was to die a second time, but nobly, to redeem themselves. Whether they could save Venice at the same time – that was not up to them.

As the Venetians rounded the point of Sant'Elena and headed towards the Bone Orchard, they confronted head-on all the forces of evil that were now filling up the lagoon with a deafening roar. Those wicked creatures that could fly soared up into the air. The wingless scudded along in their black boats. Tongues of flame licked up the gaunt masts and sinister black sails that hung limply as dead bats from the rigging.

'The enemy boats are burning!' rejoiced Teo.

'No, I don't think so,' said Renzo. 'That's Saint Elmo's Fire, crackling sparks, not real fire. Sailors say that it is sent by Saint Elmo to warn of storms.'

'A storm? That's all we need now.'

'And remember what Lussa told us – insulting a mermaid will bring on a storm too. Listen to that filth!'

The sound of violent abuse floated over the waves to them. Bajamonte Tiepolo's forces were taunting the mermaids, 'Faint-hearted fishwives! Go make some lace, why don't ye? Leave the war to men and proper beasts, dribbling girlies that ye are . . .'

'They *want* to bring on the storm,' realized Teo.

But the mermaids were giving quite as good as they got, 'Ye don't have da brains of a jellyfish between ye, ye poxed cowardly swabs!' and 'Ye bilge-sucking blaggards!'

Faintly, over the waves, came the sound of Lussa remonstrating, 'Belay, Pretty Ladies! Let Us have an Elegant Warfare Here!'

'There's a *pantegana* in your fore-chains,' screamed one of the dwarves. And indeed, a scurry of rats could be seen climbing up the mast of one of the boats that the mermaids were pushing through the lagoon.

'Oh my!' worried Renzo. 'That's really the ultimate insult in old naval parlance. It means you run a dirty ship.'

'Yes,' shouted Teo, with a broad grin, 'but a rat! A rat is good! Rats only desert *sinking* ships. If the *pantegane* are coming back to Venice, it means they think that we can win.'

Renzo nodded, a little flash of hope lighting his face as he looked at her. 'I never thought I'd be so happy to see a *pantegana*! The forces look about equal in numbers, don't they? Don't they?'

Then a clash of arms out in the water drew both their eyes. A wave of grey washed overhead; the masked falcons of the Lombards fell on the little Venetian pigeons with a terrifying ferocity. Roaring, the winged lions swooped down for their first kills.

The battle had begun.

The fight raged into the dusk. The combatants ranged over the lagoon, around all sides of the Bone Orchard island. *Il Traditore*'s creatures fought dirty, ganging up three to one upon each Venetian fighter. Coming up from the rear, the werewolves threw themselves into the thick of the battle, biting, ripping and devouring every warm-blooded thing in their path. The Venetian forces were trapped between the werewolves and the pirates. Vampire Eels repeatedly wrapped their long white bodies around mermaids and dragged them underwater.

'No!' shouted Teo. 'Look at that!'

From the holds and over the decks of the enemy ships swarmed vast armies of *scolopendre*. They swam across the water and landed on the Venetians like a wriggling carpet.

The mermaids, ghosts and animals all writhed in the water, trying to claw the Mahogany Mice from their eyes and mouths, crying out as the insects stung them again and again.

From *Il Traditore* came the hoarse cry, 'Your masks, gentlemen!'

Back in their own boats, enemy soldiers immediately donned their masks. Teo recognized them at once: how many times had she seen them, heaped up on gondolas and in mask shops? – blank white masks each with a black mole, like their master's, by the side of the nose. In those masks, the *scolopendre* crawling over their faces did not bother them at all. And the masks gave them another advantage. Suddenly Bajamonte Tiepolo's shabby force appeared both efficient and enormous: instead of disparate clumps of ragged pirates, Serbs and dwarves, the Venetians now confronted a vast sea of uniform white faces, each with the same inhuman, heartless expression.

The masked enemy threw themselves into battle with renewed viciousness. But Bajamonte Tiepolo himself did not fight. He floated around the battlefield, shrouded in his furred white cloak, showing only his one restored hand. When he touched anyone – ghost or living being – with his green ring, they crumpled up in agony. Some went mad, others doubled over with searing belly pain. All his victims wilted down into the water, floating helplessly among the waves, face-upwards, with glassy eyes. Here and there, sharks lunged up and yanked them below the water.

And meanwhile the enemy's cages filled up with weeping mermaids and gondolier children and some of the gibbet cages contained spitting cats beating their wings.

Renzo cried out to the imprisoned gondolier children, 'Augusto! Sergio!'

'They can't hear you out there,' Teo reminded him gently.

'I should be with them,' whispered Renzo. A tear ran down his tense cheek.

The mermaids fought like Amazons, brandishing their tridents and lashing with their powerful tails. The ghost Stallions swam beside them, rearing up over the enemy and crushing the Lombards and Genoans with their powerful legs. The Wild-but-Good Faeries seized the beards of the Serbs and poked their eyes with their long pointed fingers.

The English Melusine each took on two enemy soldiers at once with their double tails. The London Sea-Monks and Sea-Bishops trailed their squid-tentacles around *Il Traditore*'s boats, dragging them below the waves. Gondolier children, armed with croquet mallets, swung at the dwarves and pirates and dislodged them from their boats for the spotted rays to sting with their barbs. The swordfish whirled around like clockwork creatures, decapitating low-flying *magòghe* and holing the sides of the black boats. The smaller lagoon fish bit the flailing ankles of the enemy, pretending to be piranhas, and doing quite a good job of it. The sharks took capsized dwarves and pirates too, not caring whose side they were on.

And the South Sea dolphins had arrived at last, not a minute too soon. Astride the great blue fish were beautiful blonde women armed with crystal spears. Teo cried, 'Nereids! Lussa said they would come.'

With their powerful beaks, the dolphins overturned more black boats and threw themselves in great hoops upon the ghouls and pirates. The Nereids showed unerring marksmanship with their spears.

But despite these reinforcements, the mermaids and the ghosts had now lost so many to the enemy that they were severely outnumbered and starting to fall out of formation. The water of the lagoon was dark with Venetian blood. The Vampire Eels thrashed happily among the corpses.

A flash of blue skimmed over the heads of the children and headed out to the lagoon.

'Kingfishers!' shouted Renzo, with a wobbling smile on his face. 'Like dolphins, a sign of good luck for sailors.'

Through the thickening fog, Renzo and Teo dimly made out the kingfishers routing the Ottomans by the simple strategy of unwinding the linen of their turbans and wrapping the fabric around their eyes. Whereupon the mist closed over the scene completely. Renzo and Teo grimaced with frustration. The next thing they heard was an urgent miaow.

'The Grey Lady!' was Teo's first, hopeful thought. 'She's come back!'

But the cats who flew out of the mist and surrounded them were not as large or as grand as the Grey Lady. And they had cat faces, not human ones like hers. They were the winged Syrian cats from the gardens, the ones who had saved Renzo from the *magòghe*.

'Ahoy! Good childrrren! We've come to carry you out to the battle. We need you to undo the fasteningsss of those cages on the gibbetsss!' mewed the largest cat.

If a cat could ever look humble, that cat did so just then. 'You see, we cannot do it with our pawsss. We need little human fingerrrs up in the futtock shrouds.'

'Futtock shrouds?' asked Teo.

'The lines joining the rigging of the lower and upper masts,' explained Renzo, resisting a strong temptation to give the cats a taste of their own silent treatment.

'But we're too heavy for you!' protested Teo.

In answer, the cats nudged open with their noses a pair of rolled Persian rugs that they must have foraged from some noble palace.

'Lie down on them!' the cats urged.

The cats took a corner each of the rugs and lifted the children easily into the air.

'Hold on! Grrrip with your clawsss!' mewed the cats, as they headed straight into the thickest part of the mist. Cold scraps of air brushed the children's faces and flattened their hair against their shivering scalps.

Just below her Teo glimpsed Doge Enrico Dandolo in mortal combat with an Ottoman commander. Shoulder-to-shoulder with Dandolo, Doge Marin Falier was getting the worst of an encounter with a Dalmatian pirate. The mist closed over them.

Within moments Teo made out the sinister silhouettes of the enemy boats. Mermaids, children and cats crouched wretchedly inside their cages. At the sight of the children on their carpets, they leapt up, cheering.

'Sssssssssh!' hissed the cats, pointing below, to where the enemy soldiers, oblivious, fought on. 'We don't want those villainsss climbing up to the crrrow's-nests now! The Dark Elves are verrry handy in the rrrigging.'

The cats wove between the futtock shrouds, dodging the occasional poisoned arrow that flew wide of the mark. The children grappled for breath in the pockets of deep mist that enveloped the masts.

'We can free the prisoners but we can't carry them on our rugs!' whispered Renzo to his cat-bearers.

The largest cat answered, 'Once you've brrroken all the locksss, we'll take you back to shore, and then rrreturn for the prisonersss, one by one.'

Renzo and Teo worked their fingers to the bone, worrying the massive black locks open. The cats flew them from mast to mast. Renzo levered chains apart with his *ferro* penknife. Once each cage was open, he paused to embrace the terrified children, to soothe them, and to give them hope, 'Sergio! You'll be safe now. Wait for the cats. Augusto! The battle's nearly won!'

Teo used *The Key to the Secret City* to smash down on the

318

stubbornest padlocks. Lussa's face on the cover grimaced slightly with each blow.

At her last cage, intent on splintering a lock, Teo did not notice a Dark Elf and a *Folletto* shimmying up the ratlines towards her. It was only when she felt a slimy grasp on her ankle that she looked down. The Elf had taken a grip of her, and the *Folletto* was crawling up over his colleague's back like the dragonfly he so much resembled. A sharp point at the tip of his spine hooked over like a stinger and his green insect eyes were fixed on Teo.

Teo kicked the Dark Elf loose and watched him drop like a stone down onto the deck below. But the *Folletto* took to the air, speeding up towards her face. Only at the last minute did the jaws of a flying cat close crisply over his wings.

'Back to shore! Now!' miaowed the cat, indistinctly, gnawing on the struggling *Folletto*. Teo threw herself onto the flying carpet gratefully and felt herself lifted high into the air.

The four cats purred all the way back to land. As they neared the shore of Sant'Elena, Teo glimpsed Signor Rioba and his brothers all spattered with black blood. Signor Rioba had made the werewolves his especial target. He slashed away with his sword, despatching them two at a time.

After ten breathless minutes Teo and Renzo were deposited, panting and dizzy, back at Sant'Elena. It was hard to believe that they had actually been out in the thick of the danger. Except that Renzo had an arrow hooked through his trouser leg, and Teo's curls were speckled with gunpowder and standing on end.

A thump and an encouraging mew; a small gondolier child appeared beside them, rolling off the carpet onto the soft grass. Then four pairs of cats' paws appeared, seized the carpet and flew off with it.

Prisoner after prisoner arrived out of the mist on the Persian carpets. Renzo and Teo busied themselves applying

Venetian Treacle to the wounds. The gondolier children hugged Renzo, and cried unashamedly with relief.

'You have done well,' he told them, and they glowed with pride.

'He's acting like a leader, not an outcast,' Teo realized. The children crowded around Renzo, who groaned, 'What a curse, this fog! I wish we could see what was happening.'

The Key to the Secret City rattled inside Teo's pinafore. When she opened it, the page brightened with a living map of the lagoon now hidden by mist and oncoming night. Closing in on the battlefield, the book laid out the scenes of fighting for them in miniature, with each protagonist no bigger than a mouse.

First the mermaids claimed an advantage, and then the pirates fought them back. Then the winged lions edged into the fray, only to be beaten back by packs of werewolves.

Suddenly clouds banked up like grey blancmange above the fight. Then the edges of the pages grew dark and a swirling blackness enveloped the scene with flashes of blinding white light that hurt Teo's eyes. The two sides were battling their way into the middle of a great storm of thunder and lightning.

With their bird's-eye view of the miniaturized lagoon, Teo and Renzo could see a new factor entering the fray. The tide in the lagoon was rising. Water cascaded down from the mountains, taking rocks and mud with it, and emptying into the estuary. The book led their eyes over the foaming estuary and the drowning islands. Towering dark waves swept in towards Venice from the ocean.

'Just like in 1866!' whispered Renzo. His tribe of gondolier children cried out with fear.

Bajamonte Tiepolo's first attempt to drown the city with a storm surge must have looked very much like this scene of pounding water. But *this* time, if the city flooded, it could fill up with a tide of poison generated by the Creature in the lagoon. And the water now was hotter than ever, heated up by the thrashing Creature. In places it was starting to boil.

The mermaids, the London Sea-Bishops and English Melusine cried out with pain as the hot water seared their delicate flesh. But they fought on bravely. The dolphins, however, grew limp and glassy-eyed as their skin changed from blue to a pale pink.

The book now showed an ornate cloud with a human face pursing its lips and blowing with all its might.

Renzo shivered. 'Do you feel that icy wind? That should *not* be happening in June. It's the *bora*, which normally blows in the winter. That will drive the water into Venice from the north-east . . .'

Teo interrupted, 'But I can feel a hot wind too.'

'Yes, that's the *scirocco*, from the Sahara, pushing the water from the Adriatic. Together, the *bora* and *scirocco* – that never happens! – but they will both fill the lagoon to bursting . . .'

'And then,' Teo suddenly remembered something her parents had told her, something they'd heard at the scientists' meeting, 'you would only have to drop a match in that dirty water . . .'

She kept swallowing and swallowing, to keep the tears inside her head.

Back in the cavern, the mermaids had explained to the children that the ghosts, whose miasmas were freezing cold, would move in and surround the Creature, and cause its temperature to drop so low that it would become dormant again.

Il Traditore must have guessed the plan, for his forces tried to cut the ghosts to pieces. In doing that, they just made millions of smaller ghosts, all pushing in the direction of the Creature whose shadowy form could be seen rising above the water near the island of San Lazzaro. Many ghosts were dragged under the water by the probing tentacles as they moved in to surround their quarry.

The English Melusine and the London Sea-Bishops created a diversion, launching a ferocious attack on Bajamonte Tiepolo's pirates, while the Sea-Monks cast fine golden nets over the clouds of *scolopendre*, dragging them down into the sea.

In the interval, a circle of ghosts and shreds of ghosts closed in on the Creature. There came a sound like a long, long sigh, but louder than any sigh could be, because it came from deep inside thousands of weary, desperate hearts.

And that sigh was the turning point.

The combined cold of that joint exhalation at one moment lulled the Creature into unconsciousness. The tentacles loosed their grasp on the gondolas, ghosts and mermaids they had seized, and sank limply under the waves.

Bajamonte Tiepolo's forces halted, regrouped and pulled back to positions of safety. Without the Creature to help them, they were outnumbered. The Vampire Eels, replete with blood, had grown sluggish and were floating out into the far reaches of the lagoon. True to form, the pirates had stopped fighting and were busy rifling the velvet cushions and gilded ornaments from the gondolas they had captured. The Dark Elves and *Folletti* were squabbling murderously among themselves over a stash of silver buttons. Discarded white masks floated over the sea.

At Sant'Elena a cheer suddenly rose from the rescued gondolier children.

'Look!' Renzo pointed.

The ghosts in-the-Cold had drawn together in a tight formation, all clutching each other and staring up into the sky with the same wild expression of hope on their faces. Then this great band of spirits, like a big white cloud, rose above the water.

At that moment, the Cherubim reappeared, their little faces alight with joy. They took their positions above the ghosts in-the-Cold and led them upwards and upwards into the palest tint of sky.

Meanwhile, mermaids, exhausted, swam to the shoreline of Sant'Elena, and lay on the rocks, panting and staring at the spectacle above them. Many of the mermaids were bleeding severely and there were far fewer of them than had set out for the battle. Lussa's eyes were crusted with salt. In the dim light, she simply could not see the pale lettering of the Spell Almanac tattooed on Teo's skin. Lussa nodded distractedly at the children, croaking, 'Lorenzo, Teodora, is the Spell Almanac safe?'

Teo said briefly, 'It is safe for now. And we have Venetian Treacle.'

Lussa's attention was dragged to twenty of the winged lions who now crashed down on the rocks. They started licking their wounds. The circus-master Signor Alicamoussa hurried up with bandages and liniments.

'Administer the Medicine,' Lussa ordered, over her shoulder. Renzo and Teo clambered down to the shore. Signor Alicamoussa, now spattered with lion blood, greeted them courteously, 'The Undrowned Child and Studious Son? How pleasureful!'

His eyes were the most vivid blue that Teo had ever seen.

'We've brought Venetian Treacle for the lions, Sir,' blurted Renzo, but Teo, remembering, cried sadly, 'Treacle doesn't help any of the cat family.'

It had not saved the Grey Lady.

''Tis true.' Signor Alicamoussa's voice was rich and musical. 'But worry not, my dears, I have the Milk of the Candelabra Cactus that shall furbish up the poor beasties most wondrously. Give your Treacle to our fellow *Incogniti*.'

He pointed to a small group of humans lying nearby. As

they hurried over, Teo recognized the doctor from the hospital. She looked eagerly for Professor Marìn, but there was no sign of him. The children busied themselves with the Treacle.

'Will ye look at that!' exclaimed a hoarse mermaid voice. 'Up there!'

Now all eyes were raised once more to the ghost cloud above them. Sweet, pleading singing floated down from the Cherubim leading the tight cluster of glowing spirits towards the heavens. The melodious cloud of Cherubim and ghosts rose higher. Teo craned her neck, hoping to see Pedro-the-Crimp. A ragged coat tail and some sorry breeches flickered into sight and then disappeared among the churning mass.

'Where are they taking the ghosts?' Renzo asked Lussa.

'They are going to their Peace, at last,' the mermaid explained, her eyes fixed on the horizon.

'Good luck, Pedro!' Teo whispered. 'There surely must be horses in Heaven!'

Suddenly there was a sweet, low sound, like a thousand children singing a lullaby very, very softly. The cloud of ghosts and Cherubim faded from sight even as the lullaby drew to a close. In their place appeared a shooting star. Then a beautiful perfume flooded the air.

Tears rolled out of Teo's eyes, and Renzo, his eyes moist, looked straight ahead, unable to speak. Lussa said, ''Tis Over & Done, this Part at least.'

Her voice seemed to come from a long way away. She was still staring into the distance, spent.

The clock of San Donato on Murano could be heard striking across the lagoon. It was not quite midnight. When the clock finished tolling it would be the anniversary of the fateful day of June 15th.

47. The Palazzo Tiepolo

a hot, misty dawn, June 15th, 1899

The children picked their way through the fog back to the hotel. The Hotel degli Assassini no longer looked like a one-star hotel; it was a dark, crumbling Byzantine palace. Fifty disgruntled guests sat on their suitcases outside. They had been squeezed out of their rooms because new – old – walls had grown in the middle of bathrooms and even between their twin beds. No one knew anything about the great battle in the lagoon. The impenetrable fog had distracted the whole city. And the scientists, including Teo's adoptive parents, were still huddled on the top floor of the palace in Cannaregio where they were conducting their increasingly frantic meetings.

A fleet of gondolas arrived. The former guests filed aboard, leaving the Campiello del Remer deserted. All over town, other hotels were evacuating too. Gondola after gondola wove through the mist, loaded with anxious tourists and their luggage. Even as the children watched, the traffic slowed to a trickle. Soon there was no one at all. Not a *vaporetto*. Not even a little *sandolo*. Just the occasional grey fin.

The opposite bank of the Grand Canal was bare. The

burnt-out shell of the Rialto Bridge arched over the water like the skeleton of a dinosaur. The market stalls, once so lively, were abandoned. And the tide was rising, slowly but surely, above the Istrian stone. Renzo said miserably, 'Even if Bajamonte Tiepolo lost the battle in the lagoon, he's killed the city, taken all the life out of her. And now he's drowning her.'

A wave of helpless sadness enveloped Teo. It was, she realized, how her adoptive parents must feel about her, thinking she was dead.

On the doorstep of the palace they found a pile of white masks, no doubt discarded by *Il Traditore* and his cowardly minions who had fled the battle. Renzo picked up two of them, handing one to Teo, 'Some kind of disguise is better than none. We don't want anyone seeing the writing on your face.'

He showed her how to tie the ribbons behind her head. Inside the mask it smelt sickeningly of old sweat, garlic and rum.

'Mine was a pirate,' guessed Teo, grimacing behind it. 'What's yours?'

'Euuch!' shouted Renzo, flinging his down. 'Ottoman! His turban must have caught fire . . . stinks of burnt hair.' He picked up another mask.

'And what's that one?'

A muffled voice replied, 'Better. I think it's from Genoa. I smell pesto sauce.'

The interior of the Palazzo Tiepolo was unrecognizable to Teo as the place where she had lived for the last two weeks. The carpets had rotted away to show stone floors. Lanterns smoked in long brick passageways festooned with garlands of dead flowers and tapestries rent with a thousand slits. Renzo said in an awed voice, 'This must be what happened when Doge Gradenigo's men stormed the palace in 1310.'

Teo felt suffocated by the weight of history and evil trapped between those dark walls. Instead of paintings, rapiers and crossbows hung from the damp-trickling walls. Beside each door lurked rusted suits of armour like great jointed insects. She shuddered at the sight of a vast Tiepolo crest carved out of wood. The swords of Doge Gradenigo's men had not spared that either: it was deeply slashed and scarred.

A strong scent of varnish raised goosepimples on Teo's arms. Sure enough, a pair of Brustolons reared up in front of them as they turned yet another corner.

'Brustolons!' whispered Teo, suddenly puzzled. 'What are they doing here in 1310? Aren't they from the sixteen hundreds? The doctor in the hospital told me . . .'

For once Renzo did not seem too pleased that Teo had absorbed some Venetian history. 'Ye-e-es,' he admitted. 'Brustolons are from just two centuries ago. But of course the figures they represent are much older.' He looked away.

'Why would Brustolons help Bajamonte Tiepolo destroy Venice, Renzo?'

There was a silence.

'Why?' Teo insisted. 'Every time I mention the Brustolons you go very quiet.'

Renzo sighed. 'I am afraid that the Brustolons represent the enemies of Venice who were . . . well, enslaved and traded here at market.'

'You mean there were *slave traders* in Venice?' asked Teo, genuinely shocked. 'That's perfectly disgusting!'

'It was a shameful period in our history, and not much talked about, but yes, Venice once had a profitable slave trade.'

'And profit meant more than those people's freedom? No wonder the Brustolons want revenge!'

They proceeded in silence, passing through a mediaeval-looking kitchen that reeked of something sickly sweet. The first shaft of dawn sun revealed long trestle-tables carrying trays of the green liquid that would become the Baja-Menta ice-cream. On the mantelpiece were two Murano glass goblets labelled 'The Mayor' and 'The Minister for Tourism and Decorum'.

'He plans to poison them too!' cried Teo.

'If he hasn't already. Just think how they have behaved these last few weeks, as if they were blind or drunk. They positively refused to see the danger, even when it was screaming at them. I think *Il Traditore* got to them before anyone else.'

The next room showed them how the Mayor and the Minister were to be rewarded for their complicity. A diagram pinned to the wall showed a terrible scene between the two columns of the Piazzetta. Renzo reminded Teo, 'Where traitors to Venice were traditionally executed.'

Two prisoners were standing on a wooden platform. Their top hats were nowhere to be seen, but twin moustaches showed that they were the Mayor and Minister, with expressions of terror on their faces. Bajamonte Tiepolo presided over the scene, with his hands raised high in triumph. Next to him a woman proffered the two poison goblets, her face alight with malice. Her cruel features were familiar.

'The nurse from the hospital!' cried Teo. 'She was working with Bajamonte Tiepolo all the time! Those poor children! Shaving their heads, making them sick!'

And displayed in San Marco, impaled and trapped in every kind of torture device, were Venetians: those, it seemed, who had tried to resist the return of Bajamonte Tiepolo. Each wore a white linen cravatte on which was scrawled, 'Ha! Ha! Ha!' apparently in their own blood. Here too, the children of Venice had not escaped. Rows of small corpses dangled from the lamp-posts.

Revolted, Renzo and Teo backed out of the room. Teo said quietly, 'I thought I hated the Mayor, because he sent me out of Venice and then he tried to pretend that nothing was happening. But I don't hate him any more . . . I am sorry for him. He'll be the first to die if *Il Traditore* succeeds.'

'Teo,' said Renzo slowly, taking off his mask. 'Don't you think it's a little strange that *Il Traditore*'s palace doesn't seem to be defended?'

Teo pulled off her mask too. 'If Bajamonte Tiepolo is hiding out here, *anyone* could get to him.'

It was only now that they had walked right into the heart of the building that the children realized that this might be just what *Il Traditore* wanted.

48. The trap

not the morning that was hoped for,
June 15th, 1899

Sure enough, a metal gate smashed down to the floor behind them, locking them in.

Teo wailed, 'He's lured us in here, Renzo. Now he can finish us off in the privacy of his own home.'

'And another thing, Teo – we didn't tell Lussa where we were going. If history repeats itself, which of course it will, our side shall soon be besieging this palace. They don't know we're in here. They'll try to finish off Bajamonte Tiepolo and raze his house to the ground again – but this time *with us inside*.'

Renzo had barely finished speaking when the attack started. The arrows of Enrico Dandolo's foot-soldiers pattered against the windows. An axe flew through an open window and embedded itself in a tapestry just inches from Teo's ear. The children fled away from the windows and deeper into the palace. In the distance, over the thudding of their own footsteps, they heard the sound of someone crying.

'Maria!' shouted Teo, running towards the noise.

At the threshold of the room that shook with sobs, Renzo grabbed Teo's shoulder. 'Don't rush in there. It could be another trap.'

330

Cautiously, they peered around the massive doorway.

Maria was standing in a room full of mirrors that was furnished with a vast array of frightful devices for torture. There was a stout chair carpeted with thousands of nails, with straps and weights to impale its victim for a slow death. The Iron Maiden was there – the wooden sarcophagus with long spikes in the lid. Hanging on the walls, like nightmarish sculptures, were helmets that would choke as they were fastened on. Thumbscrews were laid out in readiness on a table that was stained with what looked horribly like old blood. And in the fireplace, thrust into roaring flames, three branding irons were glowing white hot.

'One for me, one for Renzo and one for Maria,' counted Teo. 'And look! Brustolons too! At least a dozen of them. Stinking of varnish.'

'All the tools of his trade,' hissed Renzo. 'And with all these mirrors, he can have the pleasure of watching himself at work.'

'But Renzo, where did he get these atrocious things? Surely they were never used in Venice?'

Renzo hung his head, mumbling, 'The Inquisition . . . important state secrets.'

'To justify cruelty like this?' Teo was outraged. For the second time in a few minutes she was full of anger against Venice. The beautiful city had secretly traded in slaves and tortured her citizens.

Renzo seemed to understand her thoughts. 'Don't be a baby, Teo. Nothing in this world is perfect. Only a spoilt child expects it to be.'

But he squeezed her hand and said quietly, 'You're a Venetian now. You have to take the good with the bad. But there is more that could be perfect about Venice than there is about any other city. That is what I believe, and I hope you can believe it too.'

'Unless we can do something, you will have to rephrase that in the past tense,' Teo replied flatly. She did not think she would ever forget and possibly not ever forgive the things she had seen today.

Maria still had not noticed Renzo and Teo. She appeared unaware of the hideous tools that surrounded her. Instead, she was staring in disbelief at her reflection in one of the mirrors. She was now the very picture of a classic hunchback dwarf, stooped over and bursting out of her human clothes. There were actual carbuncles on her nose. Where the teardrop emerald once hung from her earring, an ugly black chain tethered her to a hideous basalt fireplace big as a cottage. A pewter bowl at her feet contained dry bread and greenish cheese.

Finally Maria tore her gaze away from her own image in the mirror.

'Teo! Renzo!' she screamed, rushing to embrace Teo. But the chain tugged at her ear and she winced, drawing back. 'You were right! Look what he's done to me! He acted so nice but he's horrible, and not young, like he pretended to be. I've seen his real face now. It's *awful*. But Teo, what are you doing, wearin' cosmetics? I thought you hated them? It don't suit you, you look appallin'. But who'm I to talk?'

She started crying again. While Maria talked, Renzo had been using his *ferro* penknife to work at the little padlock that had chained her to the fireplace. It snapped apart. Renzo wound the chain neatly around his wrist and then dropped the coil in Maria's pocket so that it would not drag on the floor. Renzo held out his hand. 'Come, Maria, let's get you out of here.'

Maria pushed him away. 'How can I let anyone see me like this?' she moaned.

'This isn't the time to be thinking about your precious looks!' shouted Teo.

Renzo said more gently, 'Ordinary people won't see the change in you.'

'Do not be too sure about that, Studious Son.' The words boomed out of a Tiepolo crest on the wall. Teo knew that voice, full of hatred, superiority and sarcasm.

Renzo whispered, 'That's . . . ?'

She nodded. Bajamonte Tiepolo's disembodied voice continued, 'Soon every living being in Venice shall see everything in the way that I tell them. And you, young man, delighted to make your acquaintance. I hope to know you better very soon, and indeed your most special secrets too. All with the help of my little black toys here.'

Renzo's and Teo's eyes were irresistibly drawn to the white-hot branding irons in the fire. Maria, noticing them for the first time, squealed.

Il Traditore continued, 'And you, Teodora Gasperin, piece of adder-spawn that you are, did you know that I had the acquaintance of your dear parents some years ago? Not so greatly to their advantage, I fear. And frankly, if I had known the trouble you would cause me, I'd have made sure of doing the deed properly. It was a foolish indulgence to leave your progenitors' little heiress alive to trouble me. Except, of course, by an irony, you have in fact acted as my own true and faithful servant, Teodora Gasperin, in bringing me my indispensable Spell Almanac not just once but *twice*!'

He laughed long and fruitily.

Teo flinched. It was true. She, who was supposed to be so clever, had foolishly wandered into a trap that would not have deceived a perfectly stupid child.

Bajamonte Tiepolo snarled, 'The second time you've crossed my path shall be the last time.'

'He's admitting that he drowned your mother and father and your grandparents and everyone!' whispered Renzo. 'The monster! He's actually gloating.'

'Your mother and father?' yelped Maria. 'Are they dead? Are mine . . .?'

'Fine!' hissed Teo. 'So long as he's gloating, he's not actually killing us. Or torturing us. Or taking the Spells off me. We could get away. There are no guards, are there?'

Her answer was a loud groaning and creaking of wood. The sinews and muscles of the Brustolon statues strained and trembled, the rich dark wood glowing in the lamplight. One by one, the statues lurched into life, burst off their carved chains and surrounded the children. Their leeches, jolted by the strenuous shaking of their wooden joints, sent copious streams of blood splashing out of their thick lips. Maria's mouth opened and closed again silently.

Teo whispered, 'Renzo! At Sant'Elena he printed a "Making Wood Alive" spell from my body! There are Brustolon figures in all the palaces and houses and hotels in Venice. If these ones can do it, they'll *all* be coming to life now!'

Renzo nodded wordlessly. Now no one in Venice was safe from the vengeful former slaves.

There was a scrabbling of claws against the window. The voice of Bajamonte Tiepolo was mercifully silenced for a moment. Teo and Renzo edged closer to the light and looked down to the banks of the Grand Canal below them. Gathered on the opposite bank, at the Naranzaria, they glimpsed the mermaids, the gondolier children, the lions, the English Melusine and the saints. Teo's heart yearned to be with them.

At the next window the face of a lion appeared, his wings beating behind it.

'The mermaids have sent him to negotiate with Bajamonte Tiepolo,' guessed Renzo. 'We've got to let them know that we are here.'

But the Brustolons moved to stand between the children and the window, blocking the sight of them. The lion fluttered at the window, attending to Bajamonte Tiepolo's disembodied voice with an expression of deep distaste written all over his noble muzzle.

Il Traditore announced, 'Tell your people I have a human girl, temporarily turned into a dwarf. It's all the same to me whether she stays a dwarf or goes back to being a dull little girl. But unless your people deliver what I ask, she won't be anything much anymore. Just a small, worthless heap of bones somewhere.'

Through the crest on the wall, Bajamonte Tiepolo's tone changed from mirth to an icy determination, 'I demand the word of the fishwives that I shall pass unhindered, and *that I shall have my own bones back.* My enemies were so rabbit-brained as to decently leave my corpse in one piece. And so, reunited with my bones, I shall become my old self, the one and only Bajamonte Tiepolo.'

The old conspirator mused, 'That's where I was mistaken before, in the splitting of our forces. Badoer going his way, and Querini the other . . . Damn them.'

Renzo whispered fiercely, 'No, it was because *you* were too greedy and insisted on looting before fighting. It was *your* fault the forces did not meet together.'

Il Traditore pondered on, unhearing, 'And what would have happened if the three of us had won our victory? It would have been another bloody war of succession then. This time there is only me and only one conclusion. When I marry the sea with my emerald ring, there shall be no more disputes about who is the ruler of Venice.'

'Marry the sea?' asked Teo. 'What does he mean?'

'It was something the Doge used to do every year, on Ascension Day: row out into the lagoon and drop a gold ring into the water. He would then say, "*Desponsamus te mare*," which means, "We marry you, Sea."'

'But isn't that good?' theorized Teo desperately. 'That Bajamonte Tiepolo wants to keep the old tradition going? He must not want to destroy Venice then.'

Il Traditore had been listening to them after all, for his voice boomed out now, 'My little fools, I plan a rather different manner of wedding. This wedding shall be of the style of 1866. That was a mere rehearsal of my great Nuptial Feast.

'Now, once again, I plan a wedding party to which all the waves in the sea are invited, one after another. Yes, the very tides shall do my bidding once I have my bones. And when my celebrations are over, Venetians shall have no more streets to walk upon. This time the waters shall not recede. Ah, Proud Venice shall eat mud! And choke on black water. One ton of mud for every Venetian.'

Renzo hissed, 'What about the people who live on the ground floors? The poor people, the people in hospitals, the people who haven't been able to get away?'

Il Traditore's voice rose joyfully, 'They shall no longer be living, on ground floors or anywhere. They shall be corpses floating out to sea, while Venice, *my* Venice, is shipwrecked in her own slime.'

Teo remembered the maps of Venice that were printed by the Ca' Dario Press. Bajamonte Tiepolo had always planned to hurt and humiliate Venice by half drowning her. The rest of the city, chastened by the dreadful punishment, decimated by the Plague, would be obedient to him ever after.

'Now I shall be ready in one hour, and I shall leave this palace in a gondola, for the lagoon. Such a lovely day for a wedding, do you not think? My bride, Venice, awaits me.'

Between the massive shoulders of the Brustolons, Teo glimpsed her comrades down by the Grand Canal. A collective shiver went through the mermaids and the gondolier children as they took in the faceless words of Bajamonte Tiepolo that boomed out through the air like the ranting of an angry and wicked god.

Il Traditore continued smoothly, 'In *thirty minutes* I desire to see my own bones waiting in the gondola below this palace. The girl Maria shall accompany me. Should my enemies make trouble, then my private retinue of sharks shall make a light supper of her. I presume there is *someone* here who'd prefer for that not to happen?'

Maria's parents? Teo thought of their cold faces. Maria, tears rolling down her cheeks, was clearly remembering the same thing.

'And in case you think the girl Maria a necessary sacrifice, I have other hostages too. My dear fishwives, when was the last time you laid your pretty green eyes upon your Undrowned Child, eh? Or your Studious Son? Yes, they too are currently enjoying my famous hospitality, and their lives will be the price you pay if you fail to cooperate.'

Teo heard a howl of 'Lackaday!' go up among the mermaids across the water.

'Yes indeed, your Teodora Gasperin, your *Lettrice-del-cuore*, your *Vedeparole*, came all the way here to my humble home to give me back my Almanac,' gloated the voice of Bajamonte Tiepolo. 'Sweet of her, no? There shall be time enough for me to print the contents of her body when I return in triumph from my wedding. I fear, good people, that her release may not be a part of the bargain. I have a fancy to disprove her title, "the Undrowned Child".'

He added, 'You may have your Studious Son back in the end, though I cannot be sure how gentle my Brustolons shall be with him. I'm delighted to offer them some sport, after so many years of suppression. And they do most comprehensively hate a good Venetian, that I understand he is.'

Renzo flinched. Teo reached for his hand. She felt a constriction in her chest and a wave of hateful sickness all over her body.

'What a coward!' she whispered fiercely, as if that might make her feel better. 'Always someone else to do his dirty work.'

The Brustolons surrounded them. Droplets of varnish fell down their black shoulders and their arms opened wide.

338

49. Don't worry

a moment of optimism, June 15th, 1899

'Don't worry,' whispered Renzo to Teo.

'*Don't worry*?! You're crazy. We're done for.'

'No!' said Renzo. 'If we can only get you out of here, I've come up with a way to dispose of Bajamonte Tiepolo for ever.'

'Simple then. Why didn't I think of that? Of *course* we have nothing to worry about.'

'I mean it . . . listen to me.'

'No, listen to *them*. The winged lions are roaring outside the window.'

The children held their breath and listened. The lions flew back and forth between the mermaids and Bajamonte Tiepolo. Graphic threats and insults were exchanged between the two sides. Thirty tense and silent minutes passed, and there was a shout below. The bones had appeared in a gondola moored right in front of the palace. They were still wrapped in chains.

'To save *our* lives, they're giving in to him,' moaned Teo.

Bajamonte Tiepolo himself strode into the torture chamber. Even after hearing his voice, it was a bodily shock

339

for Teo to see him again. He was wrapped in his white-furred cloak, for he still had no real skin, except for the hand. It was only an almost visible, almost touchable fury that held his bones together in that unformed mass. He pushed back the hood of his cloak and looked around. His tongue flickered like a lizard's. His blank white eyes were rimmed with fire. Renzo, who had not seen *Il Traditore*'s face before, took a step backwards, swallowing hard.

Their captor threw open a window, focusing an ornate telescope on the skeleton in the boat below. He bellowed, 'You are not above trickery, fishwives, though you pretend to be so honourable. Let us make certain that you have brought my rightful remains.'

Then he howled, 'Why do you present my bones in ignominious chains! And to show them to me in such a position, with the legs crossed like a woman!'

Bajamonte Tiepolo examined every inch of his bones with the telescope. He recognized all the scars of his murder back in 1310. Indignantly, he counted off each item of damage, the old splinter of a sword in his left leg, the little corner of his right elbow damaged by a stiletto dagger, and the broken bones in his neck where the state assassin had strangled him. A scream rose out of him, a scream of outrage and self-pity. 'Look! This is what Venice has done to me. I shall avenge every single way that Venetians hurt me!! Venice shall be made to feel my every abasement!'

Bajamonte Tiepolo threw down the telescope and turned away from the window. Maria whimpered, which was a mistake, for it drew *Il Traditore*'s attention to her. Terrified at his poisonous glance, she started to hobble away, but the chain fell out of her pocket and Bajamonte Tiepolo stamped his foot down on the trailing end. Tethered to the spot, Maria turned back to look at him and promptly fainted away. Two glaring Brustolons placed themselves between the unconscious girl and Renzo and Teo.

'Well, that makes it easier for me,' remarked *Il Traditore*, scooping Maria up. 'But first, a little Treasure Hunt, I think.'

With the limp Maria tucked under his arm, Bajamonte Tiepolo made a circuit of the room, pulling gold and jewels out of secret crevices in the wall. Trapdoors opened in what seemed like smooth mirrors. Secret hinges swung apart to reveal stashes of silver. At the sound of a low whistle, a suit of armour in the corner of the room creaked to life. It followed its master stiffly, holding open a decorated coffer into which Bajamonte Tiepolo threw the treasure. When the mirrored chamber was stripped, *Il Traditore* could be heard moving through nearby rooms. He shouted gleefully, 'Doge Gradenigo's men were not such skilful looters as my own!'

A few minutes later he returned, the suit of armour staggering under the weight of treasure. Bajamonte Tiepolo laughed, 'There's more gold to be found in the lower regions of the palace. Don't want it getting drowned.'

He raised his single hand to the Brustolon statues, and pointed to the children. Then he shook his head and pointed to the door, making the sign of a throat being cut. A dozen pairs of white eyeballs rolled fiercely under brows like hairy caterpillars. Bajamonte Tiepolo swept out of the room.

Renzo shouted at the top of his voice, 'Thank goodness for that!'

'Sssssh! Not that much to be grateful for, if you ask me,' Teo murmured, looking at the Brustolons.

Renzo cried, 'The statues are deaf! I suppose Brustolon never carved inside their ears. Didn't you notice? *Il Traditore* spoke to them with gestures. They can't hear us now.'

'But they are three times as big as us, Renzo. If we move, any of them could kill us both with one hand . . . They're great clumsy creatures, though,' she speculated.

Renzo pointed to her pockets, and his own. The children

were still carrying some bottles of Venetian Treacle.

'Oh! I see what you mean. Time for some of that famous Venetian charm?'

The children now stood smiling at the statues with as much cherubic innocence as they could paint onto their faces.

The Brustolons creaked their enormous heads to one side, bemused by these beams of girlish and boyish happiness. Meanwhile Teo and Renzo quietly emptied bottles onto the floor until the liquid spread in a pool on the polished marble. Those bottles were very small, yet infinite amounts of liquid kept coming out of them. The Brustolon statues, whose mystified eyes were fixed on the children's inexplicable smiles, noticed nothing.

'Are you ready?' asked Renzo.

'No, but I'll just have to pretend I am,' said Teo.

'Now! Jump!'

Teo and Renzo leapt over the puddle of liquid and sprinted for the doorway. They did not wait to look behind them but they could hear what was happening. The statues clattering after them had slipped in the sticky Treacle and were unable to get up. Again and again, they crashed heavily to the floor. There was the sound of wood cracking, and the smell of sawdust billowed through the air.

The children reached the corridor.

'Which way? We don't want to run straight into Bajamonte Tiep—'

Renzo did not finish because one statue had slid out into the hall on its belly and grabbed his leg in an iron grip.

'Go on!' shouted Renzo, as Teo turned back to help him. 'Don't be an idiot! It doesn't matter about me. We've got to get you out of here . . . Oh!' Even as Renzo spoke, the statue was dragging him right back into the room of mirrors and torture instruments. The torso of another statue appeared in the doorway, and a mighty wooden hand reached out for Renzo's other leg.

'I can't leave you!' Teo sobbed.

'I'll die anyway if you don't. We'll *all* die. Run!'

Teo ran blindly down the dark corridors of the Palazzo Tiepolo. She ran until she was out of breath. It seemed that she had been running for days, and yet still she had not seen a window or a door that looked familiar. She sprinted forwards, and then paused, choking on the stale air. She was sure she had heard someone cry out nearby.

Another scream. And this time, unmistakably Renzo's voice! Teo had run in a complete circle and was back near Bajamonte Tiepolo's torture chamber.

'The Brustolons are torturing him, the monsters!' Teo saw a red glare behind her eyelids and felt a fiery pain in her heart.

Teo was too angry to pause and think up a safe or clever plan. She charged straight into the room. She glimpsed the backs of all the Brustolons gathered around Renzo, trying to force down on his head a strange ass-eared helmet with a cruel lever for the tongue. Renzo's arms were pinioned. He was kicking and biting ferociously. His teeth made no impression on the Brustolons' wooden skin, but his violent wriggling stopped them from pushing the helmet down over his face.

That was all Teo had time to see. She had forgotten about the pool of sticky Venetian Treacle on the floor. First one leg jerked behind her and then she was hurtling flat on her stomach through the Treacle across the room towards the fireplace, straight at branding irons glowing white-hot in the fire.

The Brustolons, distracted by the squirming Renzo, had not noticed Teo's arrival and lightning progress across the wet floor. Renzo, however, saw her. Their eyes met for the briefest moment. He did not give her away. He just inclined his head violently towards the fireplace. Above his head she saw the words written in his unmistakable writing. '*Wood burns.*'

'Wood burns,' thought Teo, '*when you set fire to it.*'

Half a second later Teo reached the fireplace. She threw her hands in front of her to grip the stone surround and stop herself from landing straight in the flames. Her face blazed with the white heat of the three branding irons. She gripped one of the glowing handles and flung it at the nearest Brustolon. Pain seared her hand, and she felt the flesh open up where the handle burnt into her skin. The statue immediately exploded into flames.

Teo plunged her other hand into the fire and grabbed the second branding iron, throwing that across the room at another cluster of Brustolons. And the third followed immediately after. Five of the Brustolons were now aflame, filling the room with thick, black smoke. They lumbered around, crashing into their companions, and setting fire to them as well. The children were forgotten. Within seconds all the Brustolons were alight.

It was then that the agony of her burnt hands first came home to Teo. She held them up to her face. Blackened skin swelled over deep open cuts. But all she could think was, 'Did I burn Renzo too? Is he on fire?'

Renzo appeared at her side, the ass-eared helmet hanging off the side of his head. He took both of her hands and plunged them into the big puddle of Venetian Treacle. The relief was instantaneous. Renzo flung the helmet among the smouldering remains of the Brustolons.

Outside in the corridor, they leant against the wall, panting. Renzo's face was suffused with shame. 'Teo, it was horrible when they burned. They could not scream, but they writhed around in agony. I felt like a murderer.'

'They wanted to hurt *you*.'

'Teo, Venice misused them. You were right, what you said back there. They could only right their wrongs by violence. They can't talk, so they can't negotiate. Bajamonte Tiepolo only continued the tradition of exploiting them as if they were dumb beasts.'

'Could they have learnt to talk?' Teo mused. 'Could we have taught them?'

'Now is not the time . . . we have to get out of here.'

Halls, stairwells, vast chambers stretched off in all directions. They hesitated on the threshold of a vaulted dining room. Teo groaned, 'It's a maze! We could run straight into Bajamonte Tiepolo! Or end up back with the Brustolons!'

'Teo!' Renzo tugged her hand. 'Use your memory. Concentrate. Pretend each room is a page of a book! You can do it.'

Teo closed her eyes. For the first moment all she saw behind her eyelids was blackness. Then she forced her mind to walk calmly through Palazzo Tiepolo, corridor by corridor, retracing their steps from the moment they entered the building.

She opened her eyes. 'This way.'

The barred gate that had dropped down behind them was open now, as *Il Traditore* must have made his way past it on his happy treasure hunt. Pausing at every doorway, looking fearfully over her shoulder, Teo led Renzo past the murderous kitchen, the ripped tapestries, and out of the open door to the Campiello del Remer. They skirted around the edge of the palace and crept down to the waterside.

'There's nowhere to hide here!' observed Teo wretchedly.

'Yes, there is.' Renzo slipped into a crab basket tied to a boat at the edge of the water. He crouched down inside, pointing to another for Teo.

It smelt vilely of rotting fish inside the basket. The children were immersed in water to their laps. But at least they were invisible. From the baskets, they looked helplessly at all the gondolier children, the winged lions and the mermaids at the opposite side of the Grand Canal. All faces – angry, frightened and horrified – were raised up to the window where Bajamonte Tiepolo had appeared to them.

Some of the mermaids were busy pulling the chains and scraping the seaweed off the plain wooden poles that were bunched in threes with chains.

'The *bricole*,' explained Renzo. 'They mark the navigable canals.'

'Why are the mermaids doing that?' whispered Teo. 'It's as if they're grooming them.'

'I've no idea. The main thing is, how do we get *you* and the Almanac over to Lussa?' Renzo parted the slats of his basket and whispered across to Teo, 'We can't draw her attention to us, or *Il Traditore* will realize we've escaped. At least the Brustolons have stopped burning. There's only a bit of smoke coming out of the window now.'

'I can get to the mermaids,' said Teo. 'I can swim under water.'

'No one could hold their breath that long.'

'No one except me. I'm the Undrowned Child, remember. I did it when I was a baby. I can do it again.'

'I hate to mention it, but . . . the sharks . . .'

Teo blockaded a memory of the grey killers closing in on them at the Bone Orchard by demanding, 'Tell me the plan. That plan you were so confident about.'

Renzo did not look so confident now. Shyly, he whispered for a minute.

'That's it?' she asked. 'So simple?'

'So simple, it's the only thing that can work.'

Teo nodded. Through the slats of his crab basket, Renzo handed her his penknife and motioned her to cut a hole for herself. 'Below the surface. So they won't see you. I'll distract the sharks if they come.'

The knife slid easily through the straw sides of the basket. Teo slipped out into the water. At first, she tangled herself among the green weeds at the edge of the canal. Kicking off from the canal wall, she freed her legs and arms. She opened her eyes, saw barnacled hulls of boats and the tall poles that held up the palaces.

Almost immediately a dark shadow passed in front of her and circled back. It was joined by two others. Three pairs of ugly grey fins sliced through the water, making ripples around Teo. From their twitching noses, it was clear that the sharks had picked up her scent. They ignored Renzo's splashing from his crab basket.

She stopped swimming, hoping they would lose interest if there was no movement to detect. Her heart pounded and her lungs felt as if they would burst. The sharks foraged yards from her, tugging up an old fishbone from the bottom of the canal, and then squabbling over it. Teo waited. The seconds passed slowly as hours. Her cheeks puffed up like a chipmunk's. Her eyes were straining, her ears roaring.

'Water-baby,' she thought.

She had two choices, neither of them attractive. She could quietly drown down here, or she could swim up for air, drawing the sharks straight to her. She wouldn't even make it to the surface. Teo swayed under the water. Her head swirled. Starved of oxygen, she felt light-headed and vague. She was beginning not to care what happened to her.

50. History repeated

beneath the waves of the Grand Canal, June 15th, 1899

It was then that the first fish arrived: a young *branzino*, slender and graceful. He hovered in front of her bulging eyes, and nudged her tightly sealed lips. That was all she needed! Teo tried weakly to swat him away. But the fish persisted. Suddenly he lunged at her, opened her lips gently with his thorny little beak and tipped a mouthful of air down Teo's throat. Then he darted back to the surface for more air.

More fish came, each feeding Teo a mouthful of air. Each time she breathed it in, pushing the life-giving bubbles down through her lungs.

Lussa had once said, 'Fish are the kindest-hearted Things in the Sea.'

Teo's bursting head was flooded by a dreamy memory. She was a tiny baby, and it was the night of the shipwreck, when her real parents had died. In this dream-memory, little fish with bloated cheeks fluttered up to her baby mouth with their gifts of air. Others rushed off in the direction of the House of the Spirits, to tell the mermaids of the undrowned child under the sea.

'This is why I could never make myself eat fish,' Teo

realized. 'Part of my mind must have always remembered.'

And now, eleven years later, the fish were coming to her aid again – the fish of Venice, the delicate *branzini*, the sparrow-coloured *passere* and the little anchovies shooting through the water like silver bullets. They were careful not to scratch her with their fins: the trail of her blood would lead the sharks straight to where she hid.

Meanwhile, the fight over the fishbone had taken the sharks a few feet further away. One of the monsters had taken a bite out of its rival's fin. The water filled with cloudy shark blood. More long forms darted out of the shadows. The wounded shark was jostled onto its back, and its brothers began to lunge at it. The little *branzino* who first found Teo, now on his fifth trip portering bubbles, was caught up in the melée. One of the sharks snapped him in half. Teo's tears joined the water.

A cluster of fish hovered by her shoulder, pointing their round eyes and jabbing their fins towards the opposite shore. She took her chance, crawling on hands and knees in the mud at the bottom of the canal. Every two or three minutes another fish arrived with a delivery of air. She glimpsed the silvery tails of the mermaids, making little churning motions to keep their owners afloat.

Quietly she swam among them until she spotted Lussa's unmistakably jewel-like tail. She emerged. She knew she could count on Lussa's queenly composure.

'Teodora!' whispered Lussa. 'But How . . .?'

Between gasping for breaths, Teo whispered, 'Ssssh. He mustn't know I've escaped! Don't show surprise, in case he's watching with the telescope. Just listen.'

Lussa nodded tightly. She summoned a rank of mermaids to make a shield between Teo and the other side of the water. Then she ran a cool damp hand over Teo's flushed face. 'The Spell Almanac? *How?*'

349

'There isn't time to explain now,' Teo said urgently.

The colour drained out of Lussa's face. 'This means our Friend the Grey Lady is Dead?'

'Yes, it happened before the battle. Please, Lussa, I have to tell you . . .'

'Poor Creature. How Humanfolk can say that Felines are Faithless Beasts is quite beyond my Comprehension. There never was a more Staunch Animal than our Grey Lady. I regret that I never had the Honour of knowing Her personally.'

Teo said thickly, 'The thing is, Renzo has an idea. First, someone fast, who can dig, must go to the Bone Orchard and find the skeleton of a man drowned long ago. The bones must be the same size as *Il Traditore*'s. They must be brought here.'

Lussa nodded, realization dawning over her face. She motioned to the circus-master Signor Alicamoussa. He leant over the water so she could whisper in his ear. He bowed to his lions, who drew in, exhaling their hot, meaty breath over Teo's cold face. They looked curiously at the spells tattooed on her skin. One leant in close enough to tickle her with his whiskers. Signor Alicamoussa explained the plan to them in gestures and soft growls.

A small group of winged lions peeled away from the others, flexed their paws and flew off. Very quickly, they were back with dirty paws and carrying a second skeleton. The clean bleached bones were of identical size to those of *Il Traditore*. The mermaids deftly disentangled the chains from the bones of Bajamonte Tiepolo and wrapped them around the new ones, first snapping off the left hand, and breaking the neck. They laid the new skeleton in the gondola, in the same position, legs crossed, in which Bajamonte Tiepolo had inspected them with such fury from the palace window.

Lussa looked at Teo. 'Yar, tolerably convincing, methinks. What next?'

Teo pointed to the real skeleton of Bajamonte Tiepolo, laid out on the stones beside them. 'We must break up these bones and each *Stazio* of gondolier children must take a separate part of Bajamonte Tiepolo as far as they can, and as fast. We have twenty minutes left now. At the end of the twenty minutes, the children must find a piece of earth, and bury their part of the bones as deep as they can, leaving no trace on the surface. No member of any *stazio* must ever tell anyone from the other *stazioni* where their piece is buried. Ever.'

Lussa nodded respectfully. 'This could work. But the Children are scattered widely among our Troops. How are We to summon the Leaders of the *Stazioni*, without attracting the Attention of the Guards inside the Tiepolo Palace?'

Teo was silent. Then she unbuttoned one sleeve and raised it above her wrist. 'Can you use me to help, Lussa?'

'The Spell Almanac? Yar.' A smile started to flower on the mermaid's face.

Lussa took Teo's arm, and started to rub it with her finger, kneading the skin until the lettering of the spells stood out in sharp contrast. Teo could feel the letters growing fiery hot. The mermaid searched the spells with her fingers until she found one, near Teo's wrist, that made her exclaim out loud.

'This is a Telepathic Spell,' explained Lussa. 'It helps You put Notions into the Minds of Others. Teodora, my *Vedeparole*, You were Born to do This.'

Then Lussa placed her other hand on Teo's forehead, where the old bruise still throbbed faintly. 'Teodora, *think* what You desire for these Children to do. Think it *in Words*, as if It were a List of Written Instructions that They might read upon a Sheet of Paper. Think Slowly & Clearly. In Venetian, if possible.'

Lussa rubbed Teo's forehead in gentle circular motions. Teo struggled to marshal her thoughts like soldiers. She tried to recall every word that Renzo had whispered before her underwater swim. 'Please,' she begged, 'let me remember it all.'

She made her memory work photographically, the way it worked best. In her own head, she formed a picture of Renzo's words, as if they were visible in the air, the way words appeared to her. Then she read them aloud to herself.

Lussa pointed behind them to the gondolier children standing in the crowd of *Incogniti* and animals. Teo saw the faces of the children looking up, rapt, towards the palace of Bajamonte Tiepolo. And there were her thoughts, translated into perfect Venetian, written in her own handwriting on the wall of the palace . . . the one place where Bajamonte Tiepolo and the Brustolons inside could not see it! Teo had never seen her own words in writing before. It was a strange experience. Her thought-writing was not the tidiest, but it had a flowing style to it. Most importantly at this moment, it was fast as running water.

The gondolier children read. Their faces changed, as they realized the horror of what they had to do, and the urgency. If Bajamonte Tiepolo guessed what was happening, their lives would be worth nothing.

Finally, Teo thought to them, 'Do you swear, on the life of this city? That you shall never tell another soul where your part of the bones is buried?'

The children looked dubious. Teo felt fury rising within her. Would these children not help to save Venice? Did they not guess the consequences if they did not?'

'Don't you love your city?' she wrote furiously with her thoughts.

Suddenly, Teo saw the weak point in the plan. It was all very well for Renzo to envision it like a piece of history, like moving a chess piece. But how could she persuade these children to risk their lives, just for a faint hope of a sliver of an idea? They were only children after all, children like herself.

But then Teo realized why the gondolier children looked so mutinous. It was not that they lacked courage or didn't want to help. For them, the problem was in taking orders from a *Napoletana*, and an undersized one at that. Teo projected, 'You don't understand. I am really a Venetian! I am Your Lost Daughter! Your Undrowned Child! And this wonderful plan is your friend *Renzo's* idea, I'm just the messenger.'

She looked over at Renzo's crab basket on the other side of the canal. The back of his head was visible as he too read the writing on the wall. Right on cue, he turned around, stood up in the basket, and nodded vigorously back at her, and the children.

'Renzo's plan!' whooped the children. 'There he is! We shall carry out our Renzo's plan!'

The children held up their hands and solemnly swore.

A chef-mermaid used a jewelled meat-cleaver to segment the real skeleton of Bajamonte Tiepolo, into head and neck, torso, two arms and two legs. The crunch and splinter of bones echoed through the silent throngs waiting on the shore. One arm was of course missing its hand, for that was with the original owner. Teo shuddered to think what damage Bajamonte Tiepolo had effected with just that one hand – what would he do if he had his whole body back?

The bones were distributed in sacks. From their different sides of the canal, Teo and Renzo watched the gondolas streaking away, all the children grim-faced and leaning forward into their oars. A winged lion accompanied each boat, ready to dig the necessary holes.

51. A wedding with the waves

The young gondoliers were barely out of sight when the water gate of the palace burst open and Bajamonte Tiepolo strode out on to the jetty. He had changed his white bat-fur cape for one of emerald green silk, so shiny that when it caught the light, it sent off vicious sparks that hurt Teo's eyes. His hideous face, with a few sparse hairs growing from it now, was clearly visible. His nose had continued to grow, and now jutted out like the snout of one of his sharks.

The mermaids could be heard shouting, 'Figure of a rat!' and 'A disgrace to spaghetti!'

For once Lussa did not chide them. She murmured, 'Indeed, Time has been rather Spiteful to our Enemy.'

Under his arm, *Il Traditore* held a roll of richly-coloured cloth and a weeping Maria. Behind him creaked the suit of armour, struggling with the bulging treasure-chest. Bajamonte Tiepolo whistled. A school of grey fins appeared in the water beneath him. He dangled Maria over the edge, letting the sharks get the scent of her. He remarked, 'The trouble with a shark is that it does not make a clean kill. It will tear its supper to pieces, wasting much.'

Maria moaned with terror.

Then *Il Traditore*'s voice changed. 'Now, ladies and gentlemen, my gondola and my bones, if you please,' he hissed to the assembled company on the opposite bank. 'I desire to rouse up my little tame Creature again. With my body restored to me, that should be well within my powers. And then I shall be back to claim my Spell Almanac, and that shall be the end of all argument, and of Venice too, ha ha!'

Teo sank down to her neck in the water, keeping herself well hidden behind the ranks of mermaids bursting with unspoken insults. Lussa had her finger to her lips and a warning look in her eyes.

Her face stiff as a poker, Lussa now pushed the gondola with the bones the twenty yards across the canal. Bajamonte Tiepolo caught it expertly in the hand that slid out of his cloak. With an imperious wave, he stepped into the gondola. The suit of armour clanked in after him and took up the oar. Bajamonte Tiepolo unrolled the cloth under his arm. He threw the fine tapestry over the bones, and patted them tenderly under the fabric. He tied Maria to the prow of the boat, around which the sharks swam hopefully. The gondola moved away from the shore, passing by the boat where the crab baskets were tied. With her heart in her mouth, Teo watched Renzo duck down into the water inside his crab basket. Unfortunately, in the silence, his departure was marked by a soft but incriminating *plop*. All heads, on both sides of the canal, swung towards the ripples.

'Stop! Backwards!' Bajamonte Tiepolo ordered his suit of armour. As they approached the crab basket where Renzo crouched, *Il Traditore* reached out and cut it loose. He motioned to the armour to tie the basket to the stern of his gondola. The sharks immediately began to nudge it in a bullying way. Renzo's terrified face appeared above the water,

355

gasping for breath. Then he disappeared below the surface, pulling the basket's lid back down over his head.

'Onwards!' ordered Bajamonte Tiepolo. To the assembled crowd, he announced, 'Your Studious Son has joined the party. Hoorah!'

To his sharks, he snarled, 'Not yet, my friends! Keep your distance!'

The gondola made its way up the empty, silent Grand Canal towards the lagoon, followed – at a wary distance – by the escort of fins. Renzo's head reappeared above the basket. His eyes sought out Teo in the crowd, and never left hers as he was rowed further and further away. Teo moaned to Lussa, 'When Bajamonte Tiepolo realizes that those are not really his bones . . . Maria and Renzo . . .'

'If That happens, They shall only be the First to die,' Lussa stroked Teo's wet hair and pulled her close. 'Five Human Minutes gone,' she observed.

The minutes passed with agonizing slowness, ten . . . fifteen . . . seventeen. Everyone gazed at the gondola of Bajamonte Tiepolo speeding out to the lagoon to revive the Creature and marry the sea. Could Renzo's plan work? *Il Traditore*'s gondola ploughed smoothly through the water. Everyone held their breath.

In the midst of all the silence came a strange tearing sound that echoed up and down the Grand Canal. The water at the edges of the canal started to move in circular eddies.

'The tentacles of the Creature, the poles!' cried Teo, her heart jumping with fear. 'The Creature is already coming to life again! The Bubonic Plague . . .'

But the striped poles did not reappear. The movement came from the three-legged poles, the '*bricole*': the ones that the mermaids had been freeing from chains and seaweed. One by one, the *bricole* uprooted themselves and began to goosestep through the water in lumbering pursuit of

Bajamonte Tiepolo's gondola. Each one had a good *cocàl* seagull on top, gazing intently ahead, eyes shining in its little black head. It looked as if the birds were driving.

Lussa clapped her hands, 'At last! Our Ancient Treaty with the *Bricole* promised their Aid in the Ultimate Danger. They shall stop Bajamonte Tiepolo, by building a Wall of Themselves around Him.'

Teo's voice was frantic. 'But look how slow they are! They'll never catch up! And what about the bones and the gondoliers' children? How will we know if they have succeeded – or failed?'

Only the older children had gone with their fathers' boats. The younger ones still waited by a herd of gondolas. Teo grabbed an oar from one child and clambered unceremoniously into his gondola.

'I can't just watch,' she challenged. 'Are you coming? Are you coming to help me save Renzo and Maria?'

'You don't know how to use that, let me!' said the little boy. Teo recognized Sergio, one of the children Renzo had freed from a pirate gibbet during the battle.

Lussa and a dozen mermaids assembled around the stern of the boat and helped push it through the water towards the gondola of Bajamonte Tiepolo. By now his dark figure was barely visible in the mist, like a faint punctuation mark on a page.

Sergio wailed, 'The flood! It is coming now.'

On her left and right, Teo saw the water pouring into Venice. It had risen above the highest steps over every jetty, flooded every ground floor. Gouts of muddy water spurted out of the drains. Cataracts swept down the narrow alleys awash with chairs, clothes and food. Waves tore the paving stones from the streets, smashing windows. As they passed Santa Maria della Salute, Teo saw the yellow-flecked waves creeping up the steps of the church. To her left, the Piazzetta was a deep lake. A tide of books flowed out of the Marciana Library.

Sergio rowed on doggedly, his cheeks dripping with tears as he watched his city slowly drowning.

'One ton of mud for every Venetian,' Teo remembered. 'That's what Bajamonte Tiepolo promised.'

It was hard to chase after the very last person she wanted to see. Half of Teo silently urged the mermaids on as they shouldered the stern of the gondola. The other half silently begged them to go slower.

But in five minutes they had gained considerably on *Il Traditore*. He stared straight ahead, apparently lost in his dreams of victory and death. His sharks gamboled at a wary distance from their master's boat, in a happy mood at the thought of their forthcoming meal. Maria lay limp at the prow, not even struggling with the ropes that bound her.

'She's fainted again,' guessed Teo. 'That's good.'

It would be a mercy for Maria not to know what was happening to her now and what might happen next. Renzo's head appeared above the top of his crab basket every few minutes, as he gulped for air and retreated back into the safety of the cage. He too was staring straight ahead. He had not yet seen Teo and Sergio in the gondola.

They were half a mile behind *Il Traditore*, then a quarter of a mile, and then just a hundred yards away from him. Teo clutched the only weapon she had – *The Key to the Secret City*.

The passing seconds tolled audibly in her heart. At the twentieth minute the gondola suddenly stopped. A huge howl swelled up over the whole lagoon, like the worst rumble of thunder ever heard in the most violent tempest.

The silhouette of Bajamonte Tiepolo ripped the tapestry off the fake bones and stood up in his gondola, shaking with rage. The line of his sight fell on Maria, tied to the prow. He

358

lurched towards her, pulling a stiletto dagger from his robes.

Teo whispered, 'It's happened. The real bones are buried. And he knows. Oh no – *Maria!*'

Then she stared in disbelief. Behind Bajamonte Tiepolo's back, and just behind the suit of armour, Renzo was climbing right out of the crab basket and hauling himself up onto the stern of the gondola.

'Renzo! You don't have to die too!' she whispered, as if he could hear her.

A mermaid marvelled, 'Limber as a day-old goat!'

Teo would never forget what Renzo did next. To her amazement, he kicked the legs out from under the suit of armour. With one agile leap, he manoeuvred the suit straight into the water – where it plunged silently into the depths – and at the same time he took its place at the oar, so that the gondola continued to move forwards, fast and smoothly, without skipping a beat. *Il Traditore* was busily bent over Maria. He did not hear or see what was happening behind him.

'*Bravo,* Lorenzo!' exclaimed Lussa.

'Faster,' Teo pressed Sergio. 'Can't we catch them up?'

As their gondola sped through the water, Teo watched Renzo intent on Bajamonte Tiepolo's back. What was *Il Traditore* doing with that knife?

'Why doesn't Renzo do something now, while he has the advantage?' she moaned.

Sergio replied, 'An honourable Venetian would never strike an enemy from behind. We defend our history with dignity: that's what Renzo would say.'

'*For goodness' sake!*' expostulated Teo. 'That's just *vain* and *obtuse* and . . .'

At last Bajamonte Tiepolo rose and turned away from Maria. In one hand was the dagger. In the other was a long rope of Maria's beautiful hair.

As *Il Traditore* turned and saw Renzo, he shouted with anger. Renzo lifted his oar out of the water, turned it around till it was horizontal in his hands, and rushed at Bajamonte Tiepolo. His first blow struck *Il Traditore* in his side. Across the water came the sharp sound of ribs cracking.

For a moment. Bajamonte Tiepolo teetered on the edge of the gondola, dropping Maria's hair and the dagger in the water.

'Fall! Fall!' urged Teo and Sergio.

The sharks circled in closer, deeply interested in this new development. Maria's hair was snapped up by the fastest grey monster, which disappeared under the water in a fit of choking. Some of its companions followed it down, with not very kind intentions written on their ugly faces.

Their master still struggled to right himself. But at the last moment, just when it seemed he would topple into the water, Bajamonte Tiepolo lunged straight at Renzo. He grabbed the end of the oar and seized it, striking Renzo a ringing blow to the side of the head. Renzo stood swaying on the stern, holding his head with one hand. Blood pulsed out from between his fingers.

Teo and Sergio were now close enough to hear what *Il Traditore* had to say next. Behind Bajamonte Tiepolo's shoulder, Teo saw Renzo at last register the approach of their gondola with a brief, grateful smile.

'Heroics you want, boy?' *Il Traditore* snarled. 'Heroics you shall get!'

And he snapped the gondola oar in two, throwing one half to Renzo.

'Let's fight for your life!' he said sarcastically, as if offering an excellent bargain. 'That is to say, I might as well extract some pleasure from prolonging your death.'

'Lussa! Can't you do something?' breathed Teo.

'Not while They are aboard the Boat. If We tipped Them

360

in the Water, the Sharks are presently too Excited to be lulled by our Singing.'

Renzo grasped his length of oar gamely. Bajamonte Tiepolo laughed. 'For whom are you about to die, boy? For the girl Teodora Gasperin? Why bother? She'll be dead before nightfall. For the little shaveling down there?' He pointed to the unconscious Maria. 'She'll be the next to go.'

Teo breathed, 'Coward!'

Bajamonte Tiepolo continued, 'So, boy, are you throwing your life away for the pretty fishwives? They'll soon be poisoned by my Creature. Or do you wish to die for this doomed city that shall soon be mine?'

Renzo shouted, 'And what would *your* Venice be? A swamp with a few ruins half submerged and corpses floating around?'

'You paint such an attractive picture. But the point is, it would be *my* swamp. *My* ruins. I'd be the Supreme Ruler . . .'

'The Supreme Ruler of mud and death.'

'The Studious Son's up on his back legs!' commented a mermaid, admiringly.

Bajamonte Tiepolo quivered with rage as Renzo continued relentlessly, 'We all know you hate Venice. But what do you *love*, Bajamonte Tiepolo? You don't even love your own men and beasts. You left them to die when you fled the battlefield. You didn't care. You're *stupid*, Bajamonte Tiepolo. You only know how to hate. Which is much easier than knowing how to love. And you're a coward, through and through. You disgust me. I'm *sorry* for you.'

'Sorry for me?' sneered *Il Traditore*. 'You dare to be *sorry* for me?'

But Teo, leaning forward in her gondola, heard a catch in Bajamonte Tiepolo's voice. Renzo had said something that had penetrated all his pride and hatred.

Unfortunately for Renzo, while pity reduced mutilated

361

spirits in-the-Slaughterhouse to quivering hopelessness, it only made Bajamonte Tiepolo more murderous. He lashed out with his half of the oar, striking Renzo an ugly blow across the other side of the head. The skin broke and fresh blood poured out of the wound above his left cheekbone. Renzo sagged to one knee, dangerously close to the edge of the boat. Sergio gripped Teo's wrist painfully hard.

'It must be different for ghosts who are in-the-Meltings,' thought Teo, and was surprised to see that thought written out in the air a few yards away. Then she realized that Sergio was holding the same wrist on which Lussa had found the Telepathic Spell that projected her thoughts. The words hovered in the air behind *Il Traditore*'s back.

Renzo caught Teo's eye and quickly sketched the shape of an open book in the air with his left hand. Then he pointed to her head. She realized, 'He wants me to remember what Professor Marìn said about how to treat ghosts in-the-Meltings.'

Mentally, Teo rifled through *Ways with Wayward Ghosts*, skimming through the pages that explained their provenance and natures. At last, she slowed down, in the chapter on 'Dangerous and Conclusive Encounters'. She forced herself to read through entire paragraphs as they appeared in her mind's eye, desperately searching for something that would be relevant to a situation where her best friend was fighting single-handedly with one of the nastiest spirits that ever dwelled *in-the-Meltings*.

Renzo had risen back to his feet and was battling bravely. The clash of wood on wood rang out across the silent lagoon. The whole world seemed to be holding its breath: not a bird twittered, not a sigh of wind stirred.

Il Traditore's weak points were his legs and feet. They did not hold him up as solidly as Renzo's. This fact had not escaped Renzo and he was parrying expertly now, wielding the oar first one side and then the other, trying to topple Bajamonte Tiepolo from the boat.

At last Teo's memory lit on the right page. She read, 'When fighting one-to-one with a Ghost who is *in-the-Meltings*, always . . .'

Her concentration broke, for Bajamonte Tiepolo had struck Renzo another sharp blow, this time to the shoulder. A rip in his shirt showed a jagged wound bristling with splinters of wood. Teo felt the pain in her own shoulder. Renzo righted himself again and used his other arm to push his end of the oar under *Il Traditore*'s knee, tripping him up.

But Bajamonte Tiepolo leapt to his feet again instantly, jeering, 'This has been slightly more amusing than I thought it would be. But enough is enough.'

'Renzo!' sobbed Sergio. 'He's going to be killed.'

'Just keep holding my wrist. Just there. Hard as you like,' Teo said fiercely. She covered her eyes and tried to bring her mind to focus on *Ways with Wayward Ghosts*.

She found the page again. 'I can't believe it,' she whispered, shaking her head. 'It cannot be that simple.'

52. How to destroy a spirit in-the-Meltings

midday, June 15th, 1899

Professor Marìn had written, 'When you need to destroy a spirit in-the-Meltings, the thing to do is to drown him in ink. *Be* the weapon. Curse him to death.'

'Press my wrist harder!' Teo whispered to Sergio. Renzo stole a moment from combat to read Professor Marìn's last sentence hanging in the air. He looked at Teo despairingly. She could see what he was thinking: exactly the same thing that she was thinking. What did *she* know about cursing? She knew only two really bad swear words. It was Signor Rioba who could curse the bladder out of a weasel. Had he even survived the battle? The light went out of Renzo's eyes and he took another savage blow from Bajamonte Tiepolo, this time across the knees.

Teo's heart lifted. Her thoughts appeared in the air: 'I am the weapon. I am the Spell Almanac. I am written all over with spells and curses and baddened magic. We just have to turn them on Bajamonte Tiepolo.'

She whispered, 'Sergio, Lussa – I'm afraid that I'm going to say some absolutely terrible things now. Cover your ears.'

Teo closed her eyes and tried to think through her skin. At first, nothing came to her; just an unpleasant tingling in her fingers and toes. Then the tingles grew into sharp stripes of pain, as if she was being peeled in strips or cut by a whip. The agony spread all over her body. Suddenly, it was too strong to hold in. Teo started to speak in a voice that sounded nothing like her own: it was hoarse, old, and full of hatred.

'Bajamonte Tiepolo!' the voice called.

For the first time he turned to face her.

'Teodora Gasperin!' he shouted. 'What are you doing . . .?'

He did not finish his sentence because words had begun to pour out of Teo like a fountain of black ink. As she spoke them, they hung in the air, hovering over the head of Bajamonte Tiepolo.

'I curse you,' said the dark voice that came out of Teo's mouth. 'By the Lagoon, by this City, by the Good Dead Beneath it, by the Unresting Spirits you Roused to Evil, by the Moon and by the Stars, I curse you unto death, Bajamonte Tiepolo.'

Il Traditore sagged under these words as if he'd been struck by an iron bar.

One of the mermaids whispered hopefully, 'Aye, his rigging's slack. His ratt-lin's are fray'd.'

A new voice came from between Teo's lips now – a light, menacing young man's voice from another age, centuries before, 'Bajamonte Tiepolo, I anathematize thee, Malefactor. May the Heavens and the Earth, and all the Good Creatures remaining thereon, curse Thee, Dregs of the World. Be Thou cursed wherever Thou be, most Heinous of Villains. Be Thou cursed in living, in dying, in breathing, in drowning, in weeping, in speaking, in screaming . . .'

'Why these different voices?' Teo asked herself. And then she remembered. The Spell Almanac was a kind of anthology of baddened magic conceived by thousands of witches and magicians from hundreds of years past.

The words flowed out of her. She was barely aware of what she was saying. Some of it was in Latin, some in Venetian. She knew only that it was deadly. Such curses as these, which were supposed to be used one at a time, she was now flinging at Bajamonte Tiepolo all together in one lethal string.

Bajamonte Tiepolo groaned and toppled backwards. He lay palpitating on the floor of the gondola. Yet another voice issued from Teo's lips – this time that of an old woman, low, sibilant and with a heavy foreign accent, 'May you be cursed in all the faculties of your body. May you be cursed inwardly and outwardly. May you be cursed in each hair of your corrupt head. May you be cursed in your vile brain. May you be cursed in your evil forehead, in your damned ears, in your dark eyebrows, in your hollow cheeks, in your jaw bones, in your nostrils, in your teeth, in your lips, in your throat, in your fingers, in your breast, in the interior parts of your rotten stomach, in your veins, in your groin, in your thighs, in your knees, in your feet, in your joints, and in your nails. May you be cursed in all from the top of the head to the sole of the foot, and most particularly, and forever, in your heart. So be it.'

There was one more curse left to say. Teo saw it written on the air above her head, but she could not bring herself to open her mouth and let it come forth. To utter it would be a cold-blooded act of murder. She felt Sergio fanning her with his hat, Lussa reaching over the prow to hold her hand. But Teo's eyes had filled up with red fire, her head drummed unbearably.

'Please let him be dead now,' she begged. 'I cannot bear to say any more. Please let Renzo and Maria be alive.'

Her first wish was not granted. For the next thing she heard was the voice of Bajamonte Tiepolo. It was weaker, and it was halting, but it was still there. It howled 'Teodora

Gasperin, I have not finished with yo-o-o-o-o-o-u . . .'

She opened her eyes. Bajamonte Tiepolo's gondola was starting to turn around in a circle. The turn gathered momentum. Soon it was creating a dark whirlpool around itself. The sharks disappeared like spiders down a plughole. Bajamonte Tiepolo, still howling, reached to clamp his hands around Renzo's neck just as a cloud of winged lions with dirty paws came flying back from their mission to bury his bones. Roaring hungrily, they swooped down towards *Il Traditore*'s gondola. Renzo slipped backwards into the crab basket and crouched down low.

'Renzo!' yelled Teo. 'Maria!'

'Don't look!' cried Sergio, and he put his hand over Teo's eyes.

Then he lifted them off. 'Look!' he shouted, pointing.

The winged lions dipped down into the frothing waves. One of them hovered over the crab basket and picked up Renzo by the scruff of his jacket. Another ripped the cords off Maria's body and lifted her into the air. Maria's legs dangled lifelessly from the lion's huge jaws.

One of the mermaids cried out hoarsely, 'Gorblimey, *she's* a goner, for sure.'

Another observed, 'Nay! 'Tis just the vapours.'

Renzo's lion flew over to Teo's gondola and gently dropped him onto the velvet cushions at the prow. Renzo rolled over on his side and smiled through hair matted with blood and seawater. The lion spat hugely into the water, and wiped his whiskers repeatedly to get the taste of boy blood out of his mouth. The breeze from his beating wings blew the gondola further away from the whirlpool.

Teo leant over Renzo, and gently brushed his hair from his face.

'Hello, *Napoletana*!' he croaked. 'Having a nice holiday in Venice?'

Teo only realized that there were tears streaming down her cheeks when Sergio handed her a sodden, salty handkerchief. He murmured, 'I can see why Renzo likes you so very much, Miss Teodora.'

Teo's fears surfaced above a brief warm moment of happiness. 'Bajamonte Tiepolo could still escape. He lived under the water for so long – he might be able to swim away from the whirlpool.'

A heavy thudding, like the footsteps of giants, shook the floor of the lagoon.

'It's the *Bricole!*' cried Lussa, pointing to the three-legged poles that were now, at last, approaching the whirlpool. They gathered in a circle around it until a solid wall of wood stood sentinel over the dark pit of water. The howls of Bajamonte Tiepolo could still be heard over the barricade.

Tears and pleading were the last things heard from *Il Traditore*. That dark masterful voice was reduced to a pathetic splutter. He whimpered. He cajoled. He promised kingdoms and riches to any rescuer.

Then came words that took Teo's breath away. 'Undrowned Child! I know that you are there. I feel you watching.'

Teo flinched to hear her name again from that dark voice, even though this time it had a wheedling tone to it.

'Teodora Gasperin, I wouldn't hurt you a hair's breadth. I spared you when you were but a babe. You are the Undrowned Child because of my mercy. Take pity on me now.'

Renzo growled, 'Teo, you are *an orphan* because of his so-called mercy!'

Teo leant forward in the boat. The whirlpool had sucked the gondola and its occupant below the level of the waves. Only *Il Traditore*'s white head was visible above the water. His black mouth opened in a bellow of despair. 'Come, *Lettrice-*

del-cuore, read my heart. You shall find nothing written upon it but pure remorse! Say the word, Undrowned Child, and I shall live! Do not have my death on your conscience.'

The words hung in the sky. A heavy, sweetish perfume flowed through the air, making her feel drowsy. She whispered, 'I never killed anyone . . .'

Her hand twitched. Could she touch Bajamonte Tiepolo's heart and save him? She could swim across to the wall of the *bricole* in a moment. Her feelings teetered on a knife-edge. *Il Traditore* had been treated badly by Venice, like the Brustolons. He'd been spat on, hounded out of town. His home had been razed. His remains had been mutilated. He had made mistakes, certainly, but then so had she. Chissa was dead because of Teo, but Teo had been forgiven. When had Bajamonte Tiepolo ever been given a chance . . .?

Lussa's bell-like voice rang out from the stern of the gondola, 'Teodora, He uses Baddened Magic & Perfumed Potions to hypnotize You! This is a Despicable Blackmail & a Base Ploy. To touch his Heart would be Instant Death for You – Just think, Teodora, What You would feel? A Bolt of Hatred deadly as Lightning. Moreover, 'Tis not in your Power to bestow Life on *Il Traditore*. Or Death. All Venice, which He wished to kill, has decided upon This Course.'

A tear-strangled moan came from the water. 'It's so cold . . .'

Bajamonte Tiepolo was dying a second time, in just the same way as he had lived – as a coward.

Renzo protested, 'He's taking the skin of Marcantonio Bragadin down with him!'

'That will not do!' Lussa lifted a conch to her lips. A winged lion swooped down. Deftly, it seized the fragile skin in its muzzle, pulling it off Bajamonte Tiepolo's body without tearing it. Then it flew off in the direction of the Church of Santi Giovanni e Paolo.

Finally, only the skeletal hand, fingers open in a begging

gesture, remained above the water. The hand spoke with *Il Traditore*'s voice. It rasped, 'Spare me.'

Then it too disappeared below the water, taking the emerald ring down with it to the depths.

Excited mermaids shouted, 'He has handed in his tally!' 'He has gone to Davy Jones's locker!' 'Aha, he has the Davies On!' and 'Yes, he'll be eating his Seaweed Salad by the root from now on!' until Lussa clucked over them, 'Belay, pretty ladies, that will be *quite enough.*'

Sergio shouted, 'Hurrah!' He pointed back at the Salute Church and the Piazzetta. The waves that had engulfed them were draining away, dragged towards the black mouth of the whirlpool. Down it swirled, rivers and showers and storms of water that Bajamonte Tiepolo had summoned for his murderous wedding with the sea.

Then Renzo cried, 'There's Maria!'

She was standing on one of the three-legged poles out in the lagoon, with little *cocai* seagulls twittering around her head and a solitary small shark leaping up to snap at her ankles. Lussa motioned for two mermaids to bring her to the gondola.

'That reminds me,' exclaimed one of the mermaids. 'Anything here by way of eating? I could murder a Piri-Piri Pea Pie and a little Curried Butter on top wouldn't do me no harm neither.'

'Me too! I'm fixin' to croak of hunger!' the other mermaids chorused.

A clump of seaweed floated loose from the *bricole* and wrapped itself around the prow of the gondola. The first mermaid scooped it up and sniffed. 'Makings of Hot-and-Sour Stew, don't ye think? See if I can't wrastle somethin' up . . .'

53. Loose ends and story-ends

the rest of the day, June 15th, 1899

Then everything happened very fast. Teo used the last drops of Venetian Treacle to wash away Renzo's wounds. While she was doing so, a school of mermaids swam in from the lagoon to report that the Creature had been sung back to a sleep from which it would never again wake up.

''Twas "Bobby Shaftoe" that finally bedded it down but good,' one mermaid mentioned, somewhat throatily. 'We got da notion to change the words a bit . . .'

The Vampire Eels had been gathered, dragged to shore and burnt in a pyre on the old Plague Island of the Lazzaretto Vecchio. The *magòghe* had repented and pleaded for mercy. They were now helping to round up the last of the *scolopendre*, a particularly fine redemption as the brown insects tasted exceedingly nasty and were very wrigglesome to swallow down.

'Seein' as it takes 'em some time to put their socks on in the morning,' one mermaid observed sagely.

The dolphins, who had scoured the furthest-flung outposts of the city, came leaping in to shore with the glad news that the pirates, the dwarves, the Ottomans, the Genoans, the Serbs

– had fled far beyond the lagoon, and not a trace of them remained except a few stinking tunics floating in the water.

'And Doge Falier? Doge Dandolo?' asked Teo.

Lussa said soberly, 'They are no longer in-the Slaughterhouse. They are Redeemed & Whole, and their Spirits are at Rest.'

Renzo asked quietly, 'You mean that they died in the battle?'

'They died for Venice. They shall be Honoured once more.'

'And Signor Rioba?' asked Teo anxiously.

A stream of curses answered her. 'Do ye think that I'd be such an *anchovy* as to get myself killed to death by a rabble of baboon-faced ghouls?'

Signor Rioba stomped into view, dragging a brace of dead werewolves.

'What're ye staring at? There's creatures worse off than me!'

He pointed at the rescued Maria, who lay wrapped in blankets in Sergio's gondola. So many wrongdoers had redeemed themselves and gone to their reward, but Maria was still a hunchback dwarf, and now her beautiful hair had gone. What was left stuck out of her head in short clumps, as if a rat had gnawed it off. She lay limp and silent, breathing fast and shallowly.

'All the Venetian Treacle is gone!' wailed Teo.

'Let's take her to the apothecary shop,' suggested Renzo.

A crowd of gondolier children volunteered to row them to the Ghetto and helped them carry Maria to the Two Tousled Mermaids.

'We need to be alone now,' Teo told them.

'*Brava*, Teodora. *Bravo*, Renzo,' cried Sergio. After a short round of applause and some back-slapping, the little group disappeared.

The children laid Maria carefully on the dispensing counter. Renzo climbed up to fetch down a majolica jar of Treacle while Teo gently unbuttoned all Maria's muddy crested clothing. Then Renzo turned his back while she spread handfuls of Treacle over Maria's distorted shoulders, face and legs. The sweet smell of the drug filled the room. Maria moaned and cried out in her sleep.

'It's not helping?' Renzo asked anxiously.

'Yes it is.' It was painful for Teo to watch Maria writhing in agony. 'It's just her bones stretching back to their proper dimensions, poor thing.'

'That will have to hurt,' said Renzo sympathetically.

Fortunately Maria had regrown her human shape before she completely awoke. Teo barely had time to wipe the worst of the lagoon mud off Maria's clothes and rebutton them.

'Where am . . .?' She looked up at Teo's and Renzo's smiling faces, down which tears of relief were finally falling.

'Why are you crying? Am I dead?' Maria demanded. Automatically, her hand flew to adjust her hair, which had grown back to its former glossy glory.

'No!' Teo hugged her close. This time there was no pain on contact with Maria's chest. She felt nothing but warmth when her skin touched Maria's.

Maria raised herself from the dispensing counter and slid weakly to the ground. She looked at her reflection in the plate glass window of the shop in silence. Then she shook herself, as if casting off an old skin, and turned to Renzo and Teo.

'I have been a complete idiot. I'm so ashamed.'

Her old drawl was gone. Nor was her face painted with the false sweetness of that day in the cavern, when she had pretended to go along with Teo's plan.

Maria continued to apologize until Renzo and Teo shouted 'Stop!'

'Why are you dressed up like that?' Maria asked Teo. 'It's

so hot! You've got all those clothes on! You don't need that make-up, Teo. You're pretty just as you are.'

Silently, Renzo and Teo exchanged looks.

'I just felt cold, everything's been so frightening,' said Teo quickly.

'I know what you mean. I could really do with a warm bath myself.'

'Why not go back to the hotel? Your parents are so anxious. They'll be thrilled to see you are safe.'

Maria answered sadly, 'We both know that's not true. But thank you for being sweet enough to say it.' She turned to leave, paused to wave and smile at them, and mouthed 'thank you' again.

'Maria . . .' Teo started.

'Teo, this time you know I will not say *one word*. The story is safe with me, truly. I'll tell my parents that I lied about seeing you. I don't care how much they punish me. But I hope you will come back to us properly soon, Teo?'

She put her hand on her heart, and smiled.

'I'll do everything I can to make that happen,' promised Teo. Shyly, she leant over and kissed Maria's cheek. Maria kissed her back, a quick little kiss like a feather landing on Teo's face. Both girls flushed scarlet, and Maria walked away quickly. Renzo had a sudden attack of loud, tuneful whistling.

'She is not such a bad sort, really,' he remarked in a choked voice, as Maria disappeared around a corner. 'Perhaps her parents *will* be pleased to see her?'

'I am afraid they won't even notice the change in her.'

'Will they punish her for going missing?'

'They'll think of something horrible, no doubt. Now, I'm dying of heat.'

'Considering all the other things you've nearly died of this week, Teodora Gasperin, that seems a very boring way to go.'

'Before that happens, we have to find a safe place for the spells.'

The smell of cooking was the first thing that struck Teo and Renzo as they climbed down the stairs to the mermaids' cavern. Teo sniffed: spices, rich, sticky sauces, squares of chocolate melting . . .

Next it was the quietness that struck them. The Seldom Seen Press lay motionless on its table. There was no more bad news to spread, no more warnings to deliver in Signor Rioba's gruff voice. In fact, the only sound was the gurgling of their own empty stomachs. The children looked around eagerly for the butler-mermaids and their customary enthusiastic offers of food and drink.

But Lussa was alone in the cavern, writing on a long scroll draped over a floating lectern in front of her. The sounds of rolling pins, saucepans and bubbling butter were sadly distant.

Lussa looked closely at Teo's uncomfortable clothes and blotched face-paint. 'Forgive Me! We have been indulging in Strenuous Preparations for our Celebrations. Meanwhile, I am writing an Account of the Battle for our Seldom Seen Archives. I had forgotten that our Business is not yet Finished,' Lussa sighed. 'Or perhaps I wished to forget the Necessary Final Outcome. We must free You from the Almanac, Teodora.'

Lussa's face was a study of regret, nobility and fear.

Renzo looked at her anxiously, 'What is it, Lussa? Why are you so sad? Will it be hard to do?'

Teo asked bluntly, 'Do you know how to do it?'

'The Very Answer shall be written upon You, Teodora.'

Lussa asked Teo to take off the jackets, shirts and stockings that hung from her in rags. To Teo's

375

embarrassment, Lussa insisted that she undressed right down to her last and flimsiest petticoat. Renzo turned his back ostentatiously, but he did not leave the cave. When she took off her pinafore, Teo handed him *The Keys to the Secret City* over his shoulder. He clutched it lovingly.

Lussa pointed to a trestle table. 'Lie there, Teodora,' she commanded, applying a coral wand with a caged firefly at its tip to the wicks of the candles of a vast candelabra. Soon it was blazing like a tree on fire. The light illuminated Lussa's sad face, showing the groove of a frown and the glitter of a tear in her eyes.

In all the battle preparations, in the worst moment when Chissa had died, the children had never seen such fragility, such sorrow in Lussa.

'What is it, Lussa?' Teo asked. 'Why are you so sad?'

'Hush, Child.' Lussa ran her hands over Teo's wrists, her ankles, her knees. Finally, just above Teo's left elbow, the mermaid exclaimed, 'Aye, here 'Tis.'

'What happens now?' Renzo asked anxiously, his back still turned.

Lussa started to chant words that were foreign, words with an ancient ring to them, and many syllables, all repeated in a sweeping cycle. Teo grew drowsy. Like a child hearing a lullaby, she felt dreams tugging her away. As her eyes fluttered shut, a thought crossed Teo's mind. 'Lussa, can you tell me what happened to me between June 1st and June 3rd? When I disappeared from the hospital?'

'Do not ask Me that, Child. Please believe Me, Teodora, there will soon be a Time when You will be grateful not to know the Answer to that Question.'

The mermaid resumed her hypnotic chanting. Teo's eyelids sagged and her body slackened, as if porridge and not blood was running around her veins.

Her eyes shot open. 'Lussa, Renzo, I must tell . . . I did not quite finish cursing *Il Traditore*. There was one curse that was too dreadful to say. I was a coward . . .'

'Your Work is Done, Child,' soothed Lussa. Her voice seemed to come from a long way away, but there was a dim edge of worry to it. The last thing Teo was aware of was Renzo's voice in the background. It sounded shaky, as if he was biting back tears. 'Will she be all right?'

Lussa replied gravely, and with a little sob catching in her throat. 'Yes, *Teodora* shall be Unscathed. I, however . . .'

Teo's ears roared and then she heard nothing at all.

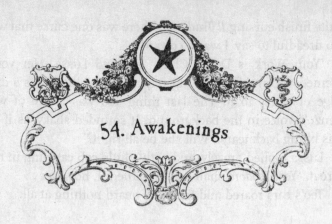

54. Awakenings

dawn, June 16th, 1899

Someone was combing her hair, very gently.

She could feel the slats of a comb making sense of the wild tangle of her curls. The comb never snagged on a knot; it rolled softly through her hair, soothingly . . .

. . . someone was holding her hand, pressing it softly . . .

. . . there was a definite kiss on her lips, a little light thing that did not linger . . .

When Teo woke up, the first thing she did, even without opening her eyes, was to feel her arms. The Braille-like writing had gone – they were smooth again. She was lying beneath something soft and silky that smelt slightly of fish.

'It's paper, Teo, from the Seldom Seen Press. They don't really go in for blankets down here.' It was Renzo's voice. 'Don't worry! You can open your eyes now. It's all worked perfectly.'

The candelabra had burnt down to a few short stubs. Renzo was sitting beside the table where she lay, hastily pushing something into his sleeve. He handed her *The Key to the Secret City*, a trifle reluctantly, as ever. An exquisite comb made of a jewelled codfish skeleton dropped out of his sleeve onto the floor, and he blushed like a fire engine. To spare him, Teo asked, 'But where's the Spell Almanac gone?'

'Lussa took it on herself.'

'But her lovely skin?' This explained Lussa's sadness before she performed the spell. She had known that her beautiful face would ever after be disfigured with the Spell Almanac of Bajamonte Tiepolo.

Lussa's own voice came floating through the chamber: 'Venice cannot afford a Vain Defender.'

She swam into view, surrounded by her subjects. Her body was now covered in glistening blue scales up to the neck. Teo could make out tiny raised letters on the scales. On Lussa's face, the spells were picked out in delicate gold.

'Teodora! You are well? Yar?'

'Oh yes, but your face . . .!'

'You must be Hungry as a Lamprey,' said Lussa. 'Lorenzo too. Nothing would induce Him to go adrift from You while You lay sleeping, even though I distinctly heard his Belly growl like a Barracuda. Now join Us for our Celebratory Feast! You must try the Fenugreeked Fiddlehead Ferns & Madras Egg Rosti.'

Butler-mermaids appeared with steaming trays of food.

'But where,' asked Lussa, 'are the Potatoes with Two Sauces – Hot & Extra Hot? That was always Chissa's Favourite . . .'

The hubbub stilled for a moment then, as someone called out, 'A minute's silence for Chissa and our fallen sisters.'

A sad stillness fell. Then Lussa lifted a chalice of Seaweed Frappé and a heaped plate of Turmeric Mash, saying 'Chissa would wish Us to remember Her like This.'

A trumpet sounded. Chef-mermaids arrived bearing poles on which gold plates spun round and round. On each plate was a different kind of chocolate cake, each flavour indicated by a marzipan fruit on the top of the ten layers of sponge and cream. Teo counted chocolate-and-orange, chocolate-and-strawberry, chocolate-and-nectarine, chocolate-and-black fig, chocolate-and-watermelon . . .

The last spinning plate bore a cake of chocolate-and-chilli-pepper.

'But first,' called one of the mermaids, 'a performin' of the Hopscotch, if ye please! By The Studious Son and the Undrowned Child!'

Nineteen games of Hopscotch certainly gave them an appetite. After a stupendously greedy meal, Renzo and Teo walked up the stairs very slowly indeed. Their bellies were positively sagging with food. The afterburn of chilli-chocolate lingered pleasantly on their tongues. The garden of the House of the Spirits seemed almost lonely without the ghosts, all of whom had redeemed themselves in the battle. The saints had gone back to their reliquaries in the churches, the stallions to the Cavallerizza, the lions to their walls and pedestals, though unmistakable traces of the animals' presence could be seen all over the once immaculate lawn.

Teo and Renzo stood in the empty garden, not yet ready to leave. Renzo asked, 'Now you will go back to your parents? I mean your adoptive parents?'

Teo sighed. 'At last. I hope I can make it up to them for the agony I put them through.'

'It wasn't something you did deliberately. You couldn't help it. And it was for the sake of Venice, and theirs too.'

'But I can never explain that to them.'

'Would they not believe you?'

'Renzo, I can't expect them to understand. They're scientists. Their whole lives are founded on rational facts. Ghosts? Mermaids? Werewolves? No, it's kinder not to upset them. Remember, you're the one who told me that it's not a perfect world and that I have to accept it.'

'You sound as if you are older than them! Why not give them a try? Perhaps they can learn to . . .'

Teo shook her head. 'I love them the way they are. I don't want to change them.'

'Perhaps *The Key to the Secret City* could show you a way . . .'

'Renzo, I know you adore that book! But I just don't think my parents would believe in it. They'd want to study it scientifically and pick it apart to see what it's made of. They'd probably assume it was some curiosity of nature that could be explained away with expert knowledge.'

She'd seen her parents 'explain' crabs and sea creatures in their laboratory. All that was left of the animals were their broken shells.

Renzo hinted, 'Well, if the book's not safe with you . . .'

Teo changed the subject. 'Of course I'd invite you to visit me in Naples – if I thought you wouldn't die of disgust in five minutes there.'

Renzo smiled. 'I would love to see Naples, Teo. I'm convinced that it's a perfectly splendid city. It's even got some history, I understand.'

'History only tells half the story sometimes, I guess.'

Renzo smiled. 'You can only learn so much by reading.'

55. A new discovery for the scientists

a splendid morning, June 16th, 1899

While the rest of the city had evacuated, the scientists had remained at their meeting place in a palace in Cannaregio. When the battle had raged in the lagoon, and the city had been wrapped in blinding fog, the scientists had continued with their work, desperately trying to come up with possible solutions. Unable to search for Teo in the mist, her parents had been working harder than anyone. After all, anything that would help Venice now might also save their missing daughter.

Teo created quite a storm, arriving in the middle of proceedings and marching straight up to the stage where her parents were giving a paper on marine predators.

'There have been numerous unexplained disappearances of people in Venice since the water temperature has risen. The sharks have demonstrated an ability to . . .' Teo's father was saying with a tremor in his voice, while her mother pointed to a diagram of a shark's teeth. Meanwhile, a fearsomely accurate drawing of a Vampire Eel was placed on the podium by an assistant.

Standing by the curtain, it tore Teo's heart to see her

parents dressed in deepest mourning. How pale their cheeks were! How dark the circles under their eyes!

She stepped out to centre-stage, reaching out her hand towards them.

Before coming to the conference, Teo had tidied herself thoroughly, and herded her curls back into plaits. So now she strongly resembled the **LOST GIRL** posters.

At first, intent on their notes, neither Leonora nor Alberto Stampara saw her approach. They were mystified when the other delegates suddenly rose to their feet, erupting into roars of delight and thunderous applause. They looked back in confusion at the drawing of the Vampire Eel, which seemed to have created such joyous excitement. Cries of horror and fear would have been much more appropriate.

'No!' shouted the scientists. 'Look behind you!'

First Teo's father and then her mother turned to see what exactly was causing such a sensation. Their faces drained to white.

Teo ran into their arms and stayed there a long time, until after the clapping and shouting had stopped, and everyone had dried their eyes, and said that surely the reappearance of Teodora Stampara must be a good omen for the saving of Venice.

Teodora *Gasperin* did not correct them.

A good omen? That was not scientist-talk, was it? In the emotion of the hour, even those scientists were human beings first.

'Teodora, darling, tell us what happened to you!'

Finally, Teo understood why Lussa had refused to explain how she got from her hospital bed to that grave in the park and what happened to her between the night of June 1st and the early morning of June 3rd. Now Teo was sincerely grateful for her loss of memory, and even more so for Lussa's tactful failure to give an explanation, because it meant that she could look into her parents' eyes as she declared, 'Mamma, Papà, I have no idea what happened to me at the hospital. Or afterwards.'

Teo was interrupted before she had to grapple with more difficult explanations.

A young scientist burst into the hall, waving a vial of water in his hand and a broad smile painted all over his face.

'Tremendously good news!' he shouted, and Teo was thankful to see that all eyes turned from herself to him.

The gathering of scientists was of the collective opinion that the tempest in the lagoon had reversed the dangerous decline of the city. The new measurements were showing quite unbelievably improved results now: Venice's lagoon was cool and clean, more so than the untouched waters around a Pacific island. Salt levels were returning to normal. And the water was dropping down to its normal height with astonishing rapidity.

The city was filthy, cruelly damaged by the water, but officially saved.

The news spread fast to the mainland, where thousands of Venetians were waiting to hear if their city had survived the storm. Within hours a huge re-migration had taken place. The streets were flooded, not with water, but with grateful Venetians, all looking at their mud-bathed city with loving eyes. On every corner, you could see people holding each other and weeping for joy. An army of Venetians with buckets and mops sloshed through the mud to clean up their streets.

The printing presses of the *Gazzettino* and the *Nuova* were silent, clogged up with a rich soup of machine oil and mud. So everyone seized on Signor Rioba's bulletin, the only news in town. The Seldom Seen Press obliged one last time.

'As you shovel your stinking silt, Venetians, remember who let this happen to ye. Who told ye there was nothing to worry about? Yes! Your great steaming heap of a Mayor. Wrapped that one up tight, didn't he just? Didn't know shucks about nuffink, did he? Ye'll have your chance with him yet, Venetians. Election Day is coming . . .'

By the time the Venetians returned to their city, the Hotel degli Assassini was back to its modern-day dimensions, but with a new coat of paint on all the walls. The winged lions all had their benign expressions back. Some were a little chipped from the battle, but their paws rested on open books, for Venice was no longer at war. The stone wells stopped gushing hot water. Everyone was relieved, for once, to see a sparkling High Water flood into San Marco, the lowest point in the city, at the natural phase of the moon. Not so many people were happy to see the rats coming home.

An impromptu *Carnevale* broke out all over town. Everyone was celebrating the saving of Venice – both the ordinary human beings and the mythical creatures. In their party clothes and masks, the Nereids and Wild-but-Good Faeries could mix unnoticed with the human beings. There were processions down the Grand Canal and balls in San Marco. The Mayor returned to Venice to take credit for the city's salvation, not that anyone believed him. Standing on a ribboned podium, he announced that the Campanile would be rebuilt exactly where it was and how it was. No one was listening.

Excited children stripped to their underwear and dived into the Grand Canal. There were no more sharks in the cold, clear water.

'Oh my, what inelegance!' remarked Teo, watching the excited boys and girls leaping in and out of the water in their cami-knickers and vests. Then she laughed out loud at herself. 'How awful. I sound just like Renzo. What a snob!'

There was only one more magical happening that needed to be accounted for by the Mayor and the Minister for Tourism and Decorum.

A week after the storm, the column of infamy, with its inscription about Bajamonte Tiepolo's crimes, mysteriously turned up in the Campiello del Remer. The reappearance of the column after six centuries inspired the newly working newspaper presses to print the story of the Tiepolo conspiracy again, reminding the Venetians of their narrow escape from disaster. The Minister for Tourism and Decorum, in an interview, actually compared the defeat of *Il Traditore* in 1310 with the city's recent deliverance from a watery peril.

Reading the slightly muddy *Gazzettino* at the hotel breakfast table, Teo grinned from ear to ear. If only the pompous old fool knew how very accurate his metaphor really was!

The Minister mused on and on about the column of infamy and its inexplicable provenance. 'Vandals do the strangest things.' 'However, all our tourists shall love the new attraction. People who've been before – why, it's an excuse to come back!'

Renzo, reading the *Gazzettino* at his favourite bar, scoffed to himself, 'Just what we need, more foreigners.' Then he stopped himself. 'That's not quite fair. *Teo* was a sort of foreigner . . .'

When Teo opened *The Key to the Secret City* in bed that night, just out of habit, a single word wrote itself on the first page: *Grazie*.

When she closed the book Lussa's smiling face, now lightly gilded with the inscriptions of the Spell Almanac, winked at her one last time, and whispered, 'Fair Winds, Teodora. Steady as You go!'

56. A reunion

a beautiful afternoon, June 17th, 1899

There was one more thing that Teo wanted to do. She could not leave Venice without saying thank you to someone that she had not even met, or at least whom she could not remember at all. Renzo agreed to come with her when she told him, 'I don't know if I can do this on my own.'

At the House of the Spirits, Teo asked permission to visit the old nuns. She had bought a bouquet of flowers and dressed as carefully as she knew how. The caretaker smiled and waved her in.

Teo and Renzo wandered through the gardens, so different during the day – so delightfully lush and peaceful. The ghosts, of course, had gone to their reward. The old nuns sat quietly on benches in the sun, knitting and embroidering handkerchiefs. As Teo passed by they gave her such sweet smiles that they could almost have been nutritious.

It was the oldest nun of all who first recognized Teo. She was almost transparent with age; her face whiter than sugar, her skin creased like old silk. But such beauty shone out of her that Renzo bowed as if she was a great lady.

'Teodora,' said the nun in a soft, crackling voice. 'It does us a wonder of good to see you again. Come sit with me a moment.'

She drew Teo down to a bench and stroked her forehead with a papery hand.

'Did you know me when I was a baby?' Teo asked simply.

'Yes, I did, Teodora, I did. You were put into my arms first of all when you arrived. You were cold and limp, and we thought you might be dead. But I warmed you with my own skin and cuddled you until you came back to life.'

Both Teo and the nun were now weeping unashamedly, and Renzo was trying very hard not to kick the nearest bush with embarrassment. If he didn't do something, he might start crying himself.

'Thank you, Sister,' wobbled Teo, pushing the flowers into the nun's hands.

'It was not just myself, child. All the nuns wanted to hold you. We passed you round and round like a precious parcel. Whenever it was my turn, it was so very hard to give you up.'

Shyly, Teo took the old nun's delicate hand in hers and squeezed it. The gentlest pressure answered her back.

'And we prayed for your parents and your family, too.'

'Did I go to their funeral?'

'Yes, I carried you myself.'

'Did I . . .' Teo made a huge gulp. 'Did I cry?'

'No, you seemed to be greatly occupied with some deep thoughts. You stared intently at the priest who gave the service.'

'She was probably seeing his words.' Renzo's voice was not quite steady.

'Yes, I have heard that you have that talent, little Teodora, as your parents did. And that it has served you well.'

'And served Venice well,' sobbed Renzo, abandoning any pretence of not crying.

'And who is your sentimental young friend?' the nun asked Teo.

'He is Renzo, the Studious Son of the old prophecy, and I could never have done anything for Venice without him.'

'Something in my eye,' muttered Renzo.

Teo smiled at the nun. 'Did I stay long with you here at the House of the Spirits?'

'A few months. You were already talking when you left, though not walking. You were rather precocious that way. We had a suspicion that you were teaching yourself to read when we weren't looking.'

The nun looked deeply into Teo's eyes. 'There is something I always asked myself. Did we do the right thing, to give you up and send you away from Venice? It hurt us so badly, and yet it must have been for the best, because you are still alive.'

Teo asked, 'Would you mind . . . could I possibly touch your heart?'

'You are also a *Lettrice-del-cuore*, dear child? Of course you may.' The nun placed Teo's hand on her snowy habit.

'Ahh,' gasped Teo, for the feeling in her fingers was like the most exquisite perfume flooding through the veins of her hand. 'You followed your heart,' she told the nun, 'when you sent me away, and your heart is completely pure. Yes, yes, yes – you did the right thing.'

'Now,' said the nun. 'There is someone else here who has been longing to talk to you. He was forced to counterfeit his own death before the forces of evil made it a reality. Another of our number, the circus-master, Sargano Alicamoussa, provided some animal blood to make the death seem more real. Then we hid Professor Marìn here. And now he has become our archivist and librarian. We *Incogniti* must keep our identities secret even from one another, so we could not tell you that he was safe – until now.'

She waved to an open doorway.

Professor Marìn, the old bookseller from Miracoli, walked out of the House of the Spirits, smiling broadly and holding out his arms to Teo.

'Come, dear child,' he said. 'I have many things to tell the daughter of Marta and Daniele Gasperin.'

57. And some farewells

an amicable breakfast, June 18th, 1899

'Shall you be sorry to leave Venice, pet?' Teo's father asked. Her adoptive parents were sipping their last coffees on the terrace of the Hotel degli Assassini, from which the Tiepolo-coloured curtains had now vanished. Fresh white muslin and the Venetian flag fluttered in the breeze instead. Everyone was gathered there for a final breakfast before their return to Naples.

Teo wanted to say, 'Unbearably sad, because it is where I come from. Where my friends Professor Marìn and the nuns live. Where my real family is buried . . . .'

But she had promised herself not to tell her Naples parents what she now knew. Legally speaking, anyway, she would still be in their care for another seven years. In seven years she would be able to decide what to do with her own life, and where to live. Then she would come back to Venice, go to Ca' Foscari University and study the history and language of the city, until she knew just as much as Renzo. Well, almost as much as Renzo. Even with her photographic memory, she would probably never catch him up.

Seven years! It seemed impossible, but she had already lived eleven years away from Venice.

Teo was concerned to see Maria looking miserable. Maria's parents had thrown away all the jewels and scarves. There would be no more glittering gifts from Bajamonte Tiepolo. Teo complimented Maria on her simple cotton dimity dress. Maria looked like a pretty girl, not a girl masquerading as a fully grown coquette. In the past days Maria had also given up her affected lisp. The fashionable crowd at school would not recognize their former little princess.

'They'll jeer and talk about her behind their hands if they see her like this,' worried Teo.

Nor did Maria try to flirt with Renzo when he came to say goodbye, and to be introduced to all the parents. He joined them at the breakfast table, looking a little awkward in his white shirt and a pair of not-very-new flannel trousers.

Teo jabbed him in the ribs. 'You look rather *casual*, Renzo!'

He blushed fiercely, muttering, 'There are more things in life than looking perfect all the time.'

Teo's father joked, 'So you're the young chap who's swept our daughter off her feet.'

'Papà!' agonized Teo. But Renzo picked up Teo's hand and bent over it for a moment, not quite kissing it. He executed this gesture without embarrassment and with a touching amount of dignity. His hand felt warm and light, holding hers.

The hotel manager, who was passing by, commented, '*Ecco* – a lesson for everyone. A true Venetian always has a lord's manners, *Signori*. This is how a Venetian gentleman greets a respected lady of his acquaintance.'

'A respected lady,' whispered Maria with awe. 'So elegant!'

She looked Renzo straight in the eyes without fluttering her eyelashes and held out her hand to shake his. It was as if to say, 'I know I don't deserve for you to kiss my hand, like Teo.'

'Thank you, you saved my life,' she said simply and quietly. Renzo shook her hand and smiled.

Maria's mother scoffed, 'Typical Maria. Always melodramatic and attention-seeking. Boarding school will sort that out.'

'*Boarding school!*' thought Teo. 'They're going to send her away? Poor Maria.'

Teo's parents exchanged sad glances. Maria's father said, 'As it turns out, there's a really tough convent school here in Venice that takes hussies like this young miss and turns 'em into decent little girls. Been to see the headmistress already. What a battleaxe!' Signor Naccaro added with admiration. 'Face like a charging bull!'

Teo saw Renzo squeeze Maria's hand under the table and smile at her encouragingly. He whispered, 'Don't worry about your parents. You'll be in Venice! Their loss is our gain.'

Teo felt a little shock of something disagreeable. Maria in Venice with Renzo, and Teo herself back in Naples – that was not easy to swallow. But it passed in a moment. She was more glad than sorry that Renzo was at last being genuinely friendly to Maria. And now, she thought protectively, Maria wouldn't be left to the tender mercies of the fashionable crowd back in Naples.

'We can come and visit Maria, can't we?' she asked her parents.

Teo's mother's look clearly said, 'I never thought I'd hear you ask *that!*'

'You want to come back, Teodora? After your frightening experience here?' asked Teo's father.

Teo reflected privately, 'You haven't the least idea how frightening, Papà!'

She tried not to meet Renzo's eyes across the table. If she

did, they would both explode into uncontrollable laughter, and in her case, perhaps even tears.

'Mind you,' said Teo's mother, blushing, 'we have come to be rather fond of Venice. I never thought we would be, but its charm has grown on us. When we were looking for you, we spent so many days walking the streets . . . even though we were miserable, the beauty of the city helped raise our spirits. Then we started thinking . . .'

'We began to see what *you* see in the place, Teodora,' admitted her father. 'We began to see that Venice has a magic of its own. We could not hate this town. It brought you back to us.'

Charm. Beauty. Magic??? These were not words that usually came from the mouths of Teo's highly rational and scientific parents.

Teo had no time to answer because the manager came bustling up with a fat manila envelope in his hand. It was addressed in purple ink to 'the Honourable Alberto and Leonora Stampara', their names underlined with flourishes.

'This was delivered personally by the Mayor,' he announced reverently. 'I had no idea that we were hosting such important guests in our humble establishment.'

He bowed low and backed away. 'I leave you to your highly confidential correspondence.'

Teo had a strong feeling that he had not been able to resist reading the letter before he delivered it. Her father opened the envelope, scanned the contents and handed it to her mother, saying, 'I don't believe it.'

He slumped in his chair, grinning broadly. Teo's mother turned pale as dust as she read the brief letter. Her hands seemed to be suddenly without bones, and the letter dropped onto the table. But a smile played about her lips.

'What is it?' Teo could not wait any longer. She picked up the letter.

'*Honoured Professors,*' she read aloud, '*your excellent work on the marine wildlife of Venice has come to my attention, courtesy of our famous Venetian naturalist, Professor Marìn, author of many celebrated volumes. Here at the Town Hall we have quite fixed our ambitions upon the founding of a living museum in the lagoon, a way to study and preserve our dear native creatures. Think of how many new visitors such an attraction would bring to Venice! We feel that you would be the ideal candidates for the positions of Director and Chief Scientific Officer. We hope that you will consider our offer. You shall find our terms more than generous, and naturally living accommodation in Venice will be provided, and schooling for your precious daughter Teodora, who has been so felicitously returned to you . . .*'

The Mayor signed himself off with many extravagant compliments and assurances of his undying esteem.

Teo glanced over to Renzo, whose face was lit up with joy.

Then she took one of each of her parents' trembling hands. 'You don't have to decide this minute, you know,' she told them. More than ever, it was as if *she* was the adult and they were the children, who could not make up their minds and were fearful of doing the wrong thing.

'Our jobs in Naples . . . our home . . . your school,' stuttered her mother.

Teo said calmly in her new grown-up voice, 'But Mama, Papà, is this not a vast promotion for you both? Your very own museum to run?'

Teo's and Renzo's eyes met across the table for a long look, and each simultaneously winked. Meanwhile, under the table, Teo passed Renzo a parcel wrapped in flowered lining-paper that she'd removed from the drawer in her hotel room. There was a note inside, which she had written earlier in her best Venetian dialect. He would find it when he got home.

Dear Renzo, I think there was one more reason why you were chosen for this adventure. It's your job as a historian to write the story of what happened these last weeks in Venice, and to put it inside this book.

Anyway, I could never take The Key to the Secret City away from here. The book belongs to you and Venice. Thank you for sharing them both with me for a while.

I love the book, but I don't need it any more. Conoso Venessia come e me scarsee, *I know Venice like I know my own pockets. After all, I've been* between-the-Linings. *And back.*

Teodora Gasperin, Venice, June 18th, 1899.

Places and things in
THE UNDROWNED CHILD
that you can still see in Venice

Just behind the clock tower in San Marco is the **Sottoportico del Cappello Nero**. If you look up and left you can see a relief of an old woman with the mortar-and-pestle that felled the standard-bearer of Bajamonte Tiepolo.

Piazza San Marco, the square of San Marco is where Bajamonte Tiepolo lost the battle with Doge Gradenigo's loyal forces, and where, in this story, his torture instruments appeared hanging from the lamp-posts and where the Baja-Menta ice-cream seller pitched his trolley.

The Campanile in San Marco *did* fall down in 1902, three years after the date of this story. The spectacular collapse was foreseen by engineers. So the only casualty was the caretaker's cat. It was rebuilt 'as it was and where it was' by 1912. The Venetians call it '*el paron de casa*', the owner of the house, being the highest building in the city.

In the Piazzetta are the two columns between which Bajamonte Tiepolo's fellow-conspirator Badoero and also the Butcher Biasio were executed.

Ca' Dario is the 'haunted' house where Bajamonte Tiepolo made his fake Brustolons. It's not open to the public, but you can see it from the Grand Canal and Campiello Barbaro behind. Since it was built for Giovanni Dario in the late fifteenth century, there have been an unusual number of mysterious and bloody deaths there.

The Campo dei Mori is the home of the statue of Signor Rioba and his brothers Sandi and Afani, who were spice merchants, possibly from Morea in Southern Greece. And there's a relief of a camel on the Palazzo Mastelli, not far away, near the Church of Madonna dell'Orto. It is sometimes called Palazzo Cammello. A small note: it was unlikely that Signor Rioba wore underwear beneath his tunic. Modern underwear was unknown in the twelfth century, when he probably lived. Perhaps he had a *'camicia'*, or undershirt. He acquired his iron nose in the nineteenth century.

The Church of Santi Giovanni e Paolo contains the tomb of Marcantonio Bragadin with the hero's skin inside. Bragadin did indeed suffer the terrible fate described in this story. Just outside the church is the place where the children met the headless Doge Marin Falier and persuaded him to join them. Next door to the church is the hospital.

The children found the ghost of the blind Doge Enrico Dandolo at **Barbaria delle Tole**. He was, in fact, buried in Istanbul. He died a year after his great massacre of the civilian population there.

The Doges' Palace, in the *Sala Maggiore*, still displays the frame in which Doge Marin Falier's portrait is blacked out. His palace is thought to be at Santi Apostoli, and is now a hotel. There's another Palazzo Falier on the Grand Canal, near Santo Stefano.

The Correr Museum, established in 1830, moved to the square of San Marco in 1922. Among its holdings are relics of the Bajamonte Tiepolo conspiracy, including the flag that the old lady was authorized to hang from her window after quashing the rebellion with her mortar-and-pestle.

The Rialto Bridge is now built out of stone. The earlier wooden version was burned down by Bajamonte Tiepolo in 1310, and another collapsed when too many people crowded on it to watch a noble wedding procession.

Campiello del Remer: there are several little squares of this name in Venice. The one where the original Tiepolo palace was built (and destroyed) is in Sant'Agostin, but there's another on the Grand Canal opposite the Rialto market, and this is the site used for the Palazzo Tiepolo in this novel.

The Naranzaria is on the Rialto market side of the Grand Canal. In this story, it is the place where the mermaids and their troops waited for Bajamonte Tiepolo to emerge from his palace on the opposite bank.

The stone lions – with their paws on open books – are everywhere in Venice. Recently scholars have cast doubt on the old story that the lions sculpted in time of war were always shown with closed books, but this idea has been popular for centuries.

The House of the Spirits is not open to the public but you can look into the garden from the bridge at the opening to the Sacca della Misericordia. You can see the place where Renzo and Teo climbed across boats to get to the water-gate of the garden. The Palazzo Contarini del Zaffo, which one sees from the street, is today known as *La Piccola Casa della Divina Providenza 'Cottolengo'*. The Cottolengo nuns devote their lives to helping the sick and disadvantaged.

The House of the Spirits at the end of the garden is the home of a group of elderly nuns of this order, who help to look after old people in the rest-home. There's a neo-classical chapel in the garden, and a beautiful free-standing fireplace in a courtyard. There was once an orchard there. There is an atmosphere of kindness and humour about the place. The nuns say that when a certain wind blows there is indeed a special howling or whistling noise that reverberates around the house. At the time when this novel was set, the house was still in private ownership.

The Gardens of Sant'Elena are where the winged Syrian cats saved Renzo. Near it is the sports stadium – the Games Pavilion of the book.

There is a small second-hand bookshop in the **square of Santa Maria Nova, behind Miracoli**.

The Bone Orchard is more usually known as the San Michele cemetery. From the Sacca della Misericordia you can look across the water where Teo and Renzo swam with the mermaids and where they were attacked by the sharks. You can reach the cemetery by *vaporetto*.

For an idea of how an old Venetian apothecary used to look, you can go to a shop at **Santa Fosca**, and look at the old majolica jars through the window. Its original name was *Farmacia Santa Fosca all'Ercole d'Oro,* which means Golden Hercules. Other beautiful Venetian apothecaries can still be seen at Campo San Polo and on the island of San Servolo. *Alle due Sirene scapigliate,* the Two Tousled Mermaids, is still open, and situated near the ghetto. It is now known simply as the Two Mermaids. The owner says it lost the '*scapigliate*' of its title some time in the twentieth century. There is also an apothecary called *Il Lupo Coronato*, the Wolf-in-a-crown, at Santi Filippi e Giacomo.

Along the Grand Canal, you can still see **the striped poles** that were the tentacles of the Creature in this book. In the lagoon you can see the *bricole*, the three-legged wooden poles that strode out into the lagoon to surround Bajamonte Tiepolo at the end of the story. Also the *stazioni* – the command posts for the various groups of gondoliers and also the tower-shaped lamps where Renzo left instructions for the gondolier children.

La Riva di Biasio, named after the Butcher, who lived nearby, is on the Grand Canal, near the station.

Calle del Angelo lies behind San Marco. There is still a relief of an angel on the palace wall to cover the hole made by the devil in the shape of a monkey, after he was exposed by a priest and forced to make a hasty escape. (*The Key to the Secret City* takes Teo there in Chapter 12).

The large crab baskets, where Teo and Renzo hid from Bajamonte Tiepolo, used to be made out of straw, but now tend to be hexagonal wooden structures which can still be seen in the Venice lagoon. They are called *vieri* – an abbreviation of '*viveri*' from the word '*vivere*' (to live) as live crabs and fish were kept inside them.

Saint Lucy still lies in a glass casket, wearing her mask, in **the Church of San Geremia (or Santa Lucia)**. You can see her bare feet and fingers. Santa Lucia is the patron saint of eyesight: her martyrdom was to pluck out her own beautiful eyes, but God restored them. A traveller to Venice a century ago recorded that near her body the offertory boxes were overflowing with notes begging, 'Santa Lucia, please save my eyes!' It seems that these prayers could be effective, because there were also spectacles in the box with notes saying 'Thank you for restoring my sight!'. Venice has relics of more than seventy saints. The little leg of the child-saint Tryphon can be seen at Sant'Apollonia. Santa Maria del Giglio also has quite a few reliquaries.

A former convent near the Frari has housed the **Venetian state archives** since 1814. Before that, different archives were stored all over the city.

The elegant **Hotel Danieli**, on the Riva degli Schiavoni, is where the pirates attacked the tourists in this story. It is close to the Bridge of Sighs.

Visitors to Venice will see and hear the *magòghe* (singular *magòga*) or *gabbiani reali*, the huge fierce seagulls, and the smaller black-headed gulls the Venetians call *cocai* (singular *cocàl*). They may even see a rat, known in Venice as a *pantegana* (plural *pantegane*). The other birds mentioned are all natives of the Venetian lagoon. Sharks and swordfish can also be seen – sold in slices on tables at the Rialto fish-market. Vampire Eels are an invention of the author.

What is true,
and
what's made up?

Bajamonte Tiepolo

Renzo's account of Bajamonte Tiepolo is accurate historically, though a little drawn out. After all, it's Renzo who is telling it.

The Tiepolo's family palace at that time was in the Campiello del Remer at Sant'Agostin. But in this story Bajamonte's palace is at another Campiello del Remer, on the Grand Canal, where there is today a hotel called Palazzo Lion Morosini.

Lussa's account of the Column of Infamy is also true. One of Bajamonte's henchmen knocked it down soon after it was put up. That accomplice paid for his vandalism dearly – he wasn't as noble as his patron, so his punishment was to have a hand cut off and his eyes put out and then also perpetual banishment from Venice. The damaged column was re-erected by the church of Sant' Agostino, sold to a nobleman in 1785, and finally ended up in the garden of an antiquarian's villa in the garden of a villa by Lake Como on the mainland. The column now belongs to the Fondazione Musei Civici di Venezia and is stored in their depository.

The Column of Infamy was inscribed with the words:

'Di Baiamonte fo questo tereno
E mo per lo so iniquo tradimento
S'e posto in chomun per l'altrui spavento
E per mostrare e tutto sempre seno.'
This land belonged to Bajamonte
And now, for his iniquitous betrayal

This has been placed to frighten others
And to show these words to everyone for ever.'

Although the column is no longer to be seen at Sant'Agostin, there's a stone to mark where it must have stood. The palace when Bajamonte Tieopolo's palace once stood is now called Calle Bajamonte Tiepolo.

Bajamonte Tiepolo died in exile. Or so it is said.

The Butcher Biasio

In the early 1500s, a sausage-maker called Biasio Cargnio had a shop in the Santa Croce *sestiere* of Venice. He was famous for a kind of stew known as *sguazeto*, which was very popular with the local people.

Then children from that part of the town began to disappear. And one morning a workman found in his bowl of *sguazeto* the top part of a small human finger, complete with fingernail. He took it to the authorities.

Biasio, or Biagio as he is also known, confessed to having kidnapped and slaughtered children to make his stews. He was beaten with a horse-tail from the prison to his shop, where he had both his hands cut off, and was tortured with pincers all the way back, to be finally decapitated between the two columns of San Marco, and cut into quarters that were hung at various crossroads of the city. His house and shop were razed to the ground, and the *riva* where he had lived was from that moment onwards known as Riva di Biasio.

The Bubonic Plague

The Black Death ravaged Venice several times, killing vast numbers of the population. The city was particularly vulnerable because its people lived at close quarters, and because merchant ships arrived daily from plague areas around the Mediterranean. Plague never completely disappeared. At the time this story is set there was a terrible outbreak of the disease in Asia, and it had only just been discovered that the bites of rat-fleas were the means of transmission of the plague bacillus to humans.

In fact, Venetian Treacle was not very efficacious against the plague.

Venetian Treacle and Venetian Apothecaries

Theriaca, otherwise known as Venetian Treacle, was held in high esteem by the apothecaries of Europe for centuries. Venice was famous for its Treacle. It was exported as far away as Arabia and India. Its manufacture was closely regulated to the point that the making of it became a kind of performance art, with the apothecaries in their robes mixing some sixty-four ingredients in front of health magistrates and a fascinated public. The ingredients included ground-up vipers and apothecaries kept their own tanks of snakes. According to the Oxford English Dictionary of 1693, 'The chief use of vipers is for the making of treacle'.

Venetian Treacle was said to be good for every ailment, including sea-sickness, although originally it was intended as an antidote to poison. Treacle-manufacture flourished wherever poisoning was rife. Another thing that would have made Teo unhappy: the state of Venice was once famous for using poison to despatch its enemies.

The Venetian apothecaries began as spice-shops and so were originally called *spezier*. These fragrant establishments often had very picturesque names, such as Golden Head at Rialto, The Ostrich at Ponte de Baretteri, Adam and Eve in the Frezzaria, the Salamander at San

Pantaleone, and The Column and a Half at San Polo.

Some, like The Madonna at Campo San Bartolomeo, are still in business but under modern names: in this case the Morelli Pharmacy.

It is said that the grooves one can see in the pavement outside some of the old apothecaries in Venice are from the Treacle cauldrons used for the public displays of concocting the drug.

A cheaper form of Treacle, without vipers, was made in England at one time, and went by various names, such as Poor Man's Treacle, the Countryman's Treacle, London Treacle and the Churl's Treacle. It was supposed to be rather full of garlic.

The Brustolons

Andrea Brustolon (1662–1732) was indeed a famous sculptor in Venice. His rather terrifying statues can be seen in Ca' Rezzonico and other noble homes. Sadly, it is also true that there was at one time a thriving slave trade in Venice, and equally true that this fact is not much mentioned by the historians.

The Language of Moles

Fake facial moles were used as make-up during the glory days of Venice. You can still see some streets by the name of '*Mosche*' or 'Flies', which were made of velvet and backed by a sticky gum. And it was true that there was a secret language of moles, though like any secret language, it was never quite fixed in certainty. Many people used to think that you could learn much about a person's character or destiny from the position of their natural facial moles. Such information was to be found in books like: *Every lady's own fortune-teller, or an infallible guide to the hidden decrees of fate, being a new & regular system for foretelling future events, published in London, 1791*. This book warned, for example, that people with a mole at the corner of either eye would be liable to a violent death, whereas a mole on the nose meant good luck. But a mole on the belly meant that the person was addicted to sloth and gluttony. Of course, there is no scientific basis to any claim that a mole beside the nose indicates a murderer. The author has one there herself.

Mermaid Language, Curry and Parrots

Many sailor slang words had their origin in India and were spread from there throughout the British Empire by British sailors, as was the taste for spicy exotic foods. The Rialto Market in Venice was famous for its spices from the East.

Sailors often used their long voyages to train parrots to speak. They did so by hiding behind a mirror and talking to the bird, which would then think another parrot was conversing with them and be encouraged to mimic in reply.

Mahogany Mice

This is an old sailors' term for very large brown cockroaches. The *scolopendre* of this story are really to be found in Venice, unfortunately, as they love the damp. They are not true cockroaches, though they resemble them, but torpedo-shaped millipedes that move very fast indeed. They can bite, if handled. *Scolopendre* feed on insects smaller than themselves, using poisonous jaws to kill their prey.

Boats, Trains and Horses

The railways arrived in Venice in 1846. Steam ferries (*vaporetti*) began to transport passengers from 1881. Gas lamps were first introduced in San Marco in 1843. The first road-bridge to Venice, now known as the Ponte della Libertà, was not built until the 1930s, running parallel to the old railway bridge. Given the topography of Venice, horses have never lived in great numbers in the city, though a few rich noblemen did keep them at the *Cavallerizza* by the Mendicanti church. And it is said that the stairway of the Campanile was made wide enough for a horse to walk to the top.

The most famous horses in Venice are the four bronze ones from the façade of the Basilica of San Marco. They have lived an adventurous life. They were plundered from Constantinople in the fourth crusade by the blind warrior Doge Enrico Dandolo. Then they were stolen by Napoleon after he conquered Venice in 1797, and taken to Paris. When Napoleon fell from power, the horses returned to the city. Now excellent replicas look over the square, but the real horses may be visited inside the church.

Venice in 1899 and 1310

The population of Venice was more than twice what it is today – 130,000 in the 1880s. It is now 60,000 and shrinking. Yet the annual tourist population is twenty-one million, and rising. Modern Venetians do make their way '*per le fodere*', through the linings, to avoid the tourist crowds. A tranquil parallel universe is secreted in Venice, often just yards away from the thronged tourist haunts.

In many ways the Venice of 1899 would be recognizable to modern eyes. All the famous palaces, even the *vaporetti*, were part of the Venetian landscape in Renzo and Teo's time. However the Venice of 1310 would have been very different. Many of the buildings, including the Rialto Bridge, were made of wood in those days. The great Gothic palaces were not built until the fifteenth century, and the vast Renaissance palaces a hundred years after that. Gondolas would have been painted in many colours – it was not until several hundred years later in 1562 that a law decreed they must all be black.

In Chapter 16, Renzo mentions Venice Beach, California. In fact, the famous American resort was not established until 1905. But it had an arcade of 'Venetian' architecture and even gondolas.

Strange Art in Venice

The art Biennale started in 1895, and its artists have often produced weird displays around the town. In 2005 huge red penguins were lined up on various balconies on the Grand Canal. 2007 saw twenty-foot-long purple crocodiles climbing buildings at Rialto.

Venetian 'Bone Orchards'

'Bone Orchard' is an old sailors' term for cemetery. Until Napoleon came to Venice at the end of the eighteenth century, Venetians used to be buried in the historic centre. Many churches had a '*campo dei morti*' – a field of the dead. Napoleon closed these local cemeteries and insisted that all further burials would be on the island of San Cristoforo in the lagoon. The island, despite expansion to join up with its neighbour San Michele in 1837, has not proved big enough for all the Venetian dead, so after a dozen or so years their bones are usually dug up and taken away to another island, making room for new corpses.

The Big Flood

Venice suffered a disastrous flood on November 3rd 1966. It was very like the 1866 one described in this story. A tidal barrage called MOSE is currently under construction, to try to deal with a similar set of circumstances should they ever occur. Many conservationists are against MOSE, believing it will harm the lagoon's wildlife.

The Spell Almanac

Some of the spell fragments are borrowed from the classics:

ulcus acre
A nasty sore. (Martial, *Epigrams* XI.98)
nunc morere
Now die! (Virgil, *Aeneid* II)

The curses laid on Bajamonte Tiepolo at the end of the book are based on a Papal malediction recorded by James Grant, in his book *The Mysteries of All Nations, the Rise and Progress of Superstition, Laws Against and Trials of Witches, Ancient and Modern Delusions Together With Strange Customs, Fables, and Tales*, 1880. Teo might have found this volume in her school library.

Italian witches were thought to use seashells to send out their spells. They would inscribe the shells with words and then leave them on the shore to be taken away by the tide.

The *Incogniti*

There was a group of intellectuals in Venice in the seventeenth century who called themselves *L'Accademia degli Incogniti*, The Academy of the Unknowns. It was founded by Giovan Francesco Loredan. The academy fostered publishing, lectures and debates. Friendship was at the core of the Academicians' philosophy.

Syrian Cats

Renzo's account of their origins is true. There used to be a great number of wild cats in Venice but in the last few decades a charity called DINGO has taken them off the streets and to a sanctuary, once on the island of San Clemente, and now on the Lido. Sadly, it is rare to see a wild cat on the streets in Venice these days. But a few shops have their resident cats, and the author knows where they are, if anyone wishes to ask.

Acknowledgements

A profound thank you to Sister Fiorangela Teruzzi at the House of the Spirits (otherwise known as the *Piccola Casa della Divina Providenza* 'Cottolengo') for permitting me to write the scenes set there *in situ*, and for explaining about the ghostly echo. And a deep thank-you to Dottore Camillo Tonini of the Fondazione Musei Civici di Venezia for his generous help in hunting down the column of infamy of Bajamonte Tiepolo.

This is my first book for younger readers, and I welcomed the help especially of Emily Pentreath, my very first reader, and Jake Peri, Sarah Zachs-Adam (thank *you*, Sarah, twice over!), Elliot Tassano, Malcolm Drenttel, Marcelia Benson, Alice Appleton, Helena Moore and Holly Bookbinder. And I'm grateful to all their parents, for lending me their children (with apologies for the shark nightmares).

This book would never have come to life without the enthusiasm and kindness of Sybille Siegmund-Stiefenhofer. Patricia Guy, Jeff Cotton and Jill Foulston offered perceptive advice on early manuscripts. Rose La Touche put to rights the characteristics of The Grey Lady. Paola de Carolis and Ornella Tarantola helped with the Italian, Bruno Palmarin and Tiziano Scarpa with the Venetian. Bill Helfand, as ever, injected my pharmaceutical history with a dose of realism. Vladimir Lovric advised on medical matters. Any inaccuracies or exaggerations in this book are mine alone.

I've been most fortunate in the generosity of my children's

book agent Sarah Molloy, and also in the scrupulous copy-editing of Michelle Misra and Kristina Blaggojevitch. My editor, Jon Appleton, has been deft, droll and fathomless in his encouragement.

No one writer could ever sufficiently thank the dedicated staff at the London Library and the Wellcome Library, but I think we should all try. The excellent books of Alberto Toso Fei were of enormous help, as was the indispensible *Curiosità Veneziane* by Giuseppe Tassini.

Finally, deepest thanks, as ever, to all the Clink Street writers, who welcomed *The Undrowned Child* from the start.